THE
MEMORY
PALACE

Christie Dickason

HarperCollins*Publishers*

HarperCollins*Publishers*
77–85 Fulham Palace Road,
Hammersmith, London W6 8JB

www.harpercollins.co.uk

This paperback edition 2004
1 3 5 7 9 8 6 4 2

First published in Great Britain by
HarperCollins*Publishers* 2003

ISBN 0 00 710128 7

Set in Meridien

Printed and bound in Great Britain by
Clays Ltd, St Ives plc

For Tess, my sister,
first playmate and fellow palace builder

My warm thanks to the many friends, family and colleagues whose knowledge and experience helped to patch the gaps in my own:

John, my theatre consultant, mechanical artificer, and amazer.

John Fox, Sue Gill and Welfare State International, for introducing me to the power of theatre in every day life.

Ruth Waterman, international violinist, for her creative help with Doctor Bowler's fiddling.

Composer Cecilia McDowall, who interrupted her own intense work schedule to help me research barrel organs.

Stephen Wyatt, writer, friend, colleague and recipient of my 999 calls, for patient listening and inspired suggestions.

Jeremy Preston, of East Sheen Library, for research support and reassuring me that books matter.

The staff and volunteers of many National Trust properties: Chasleton House, Parham House, The Vyne and, above all, Hardwick Hall, where the curator's generous gift of information inspired the 'bones-in-the-plaster' show-down in *The Memory Palace*.

Harry Dumler for ornithological advice.

And to those without whom . . .

Nick Sayers, my editor, sword and shield.
And Rachel Hore, of the unerring eye for placing red flags.
And Joy Chamberlain, who guided in the landing.

Andrew Hewson, agent, friend, and fisherman.

My son Tom for IT support.

And Sadie, for reminding me to look at the ground.

'What House more stately hath there bin. Or can be than is Man?'   George Herbert

The only principles which our intellect draws purely from its own resources are those of mathematics and logic. And so the extension of space must be measured along Mathematic parameters.
                                                    – Descartes

Poiesis – the making of something out of nothing

PREFACE

Letter from John Nightingale, at Southampton, to Zeal Beester of Hawkridge Estate, near Bedgebury, Hampshire. October 1639.

Sweetest Zeal – My messenger stands with outstretched hand. My ship is spreading its wings. I would tear out my heart and send it if I could. In its place must come mere dogged, struggling words. I want no mistaking. I meant what I said. I will stay true to you. If you now, or ever, regret your own vow to me, I beg you to tell me at once.

Exile is kinder than the block, for leaving can be undone while death cannot. So, farewell forever, England. But our finite parting, though scarcely bearable, must be bridged by passionate hope.

To pay my passage so suddenly, and with my lands and modest fortune now forfeit to the Crown, (I still swear that I am no traitor!) I was forced to sell myself as indentured labour to a M. Etienne Baulk, tobacco farmer on the island of Nevis for the usual term of seven years. Seven years. These are not beyond us to survive – a sea captain and his wife, or a soldier's family, often endure as much. On release from servitude, I am promised ten pounds – a fair beginning for the fortune I mean to make for us in the West Indies. When I can be sure of a life safe for a woman, I will send for you. I beg you, write to me often. To know that you are there, and love me, will give me strength to do whatever I must to ensure that we can be together again.

Oh, my beloved girl, my other self – though writ in a somewhat smaller hand – keep safe. And keep faith in me, who by

1

the Grace of God, will be your husband — John.

   Post scriptum Think of me whenever you see that cursed cat which still has leave to occupy your bed, and remember who gave him to you. I kiss your eyes, and must stop there with my pen but not in my thoughts.

1639

1

Philip Wentworth stepped, unsuspecting, out of the tack room into the quiet grey autumn dawn of the day that would change the rest of his life. A pleasing smell of polished leather and horse clung to his frayed, old-fashioned clothes after his night on a straw mattress among the harnesses and saddles. The world still slept. He stood for a moment listening to the hush. He might have been the only man alive and he liked it that way.

Then a drowsy blackbird sang a single muted note. Another replied. A thrush interrupted. Sparrows disagreed. Suddenly, voices in every tree, every bush, every tall tussock of grass joined the clamour until the air vibrated with their exuberant racket.

He watched the quick flicks of movement. His ear picked out a late chiff-chaff calling its own name, the repeated song of the thrush, the mellow, heart-breaking fluting of a blackbird. Then the churr of a white-throat, and the warbles of robins.

It was a trick he had learned, of paying close attention to every small detail of life. If he gripped hard enough onto the observations and sensations of each moment, he could haul himself hand over hand through the day without having to remember.

He set off across the corner of the stable yard with a sack slung over his shoulder, carrying a fishing pole stout enough to hold a twelve-pound tench. As on every other day, he meant to fish.

At the shadowed dung heap behind the horse barn, he

5

leaned his pole against the dung cart, took up a fork left leaning against the brick wall of the barn and began to turn over the steamy clods. From time to time, his stocky figure leaned forwards to pick out the pale squirming maggots which had been generated (so his reading of Pliny assured him) by the heat in the crumbling clumps of horse shit and straw. He dropped the maggots into a jar half-filled with damp grass cuttings. He straightened to draw in a deep breath.

The silence of the stable yard was thick with the warm smells of animals, fresh hay, dung, the damp iron of the pump by the watering trough, and a sharp yeasty punch to the back of his nose which seeped from the brew house.

But the smell of the iron threatened to stir memories.

Too much like the smell of blood.

He forced his attention onto the feel of the polished wooden handle of the fork, the heft of the dung.

Why, he asked himself as a distraction, are horses so superior to both cattle and pigs in the quality of their excreta? Even though horses eat much the same diet as cows?

A good try. Will it work?

He put three more maggots into the jar. Made himself notice their velvety wriggle between his fingertips.

On the other hand, horses were undeniably superior to cattle in both nature and intelligence. Could there be a positive correlation between elevation of nature and quality of base elimination?

An interesting question, though not one that he could debate with just anyone. There were so many questions to be answered when a man at last began to ask them. Questions also filled the moment. As did books, if approached with care.

He put both hands in the small of his back and stretched impatiently.

Not many men of your years can still sleep well on a tack room floor, he reassured himself.

Liar! You slept badly and your joints ache.

I'm not taking to age with good grace . . .

Grace. There's an interesting thought.

Suddenly, without warning, he had arrived at another dangerous moment.

Inside the barn, aroused by his presence, the horses began to stamp and blow loose, flapping sighs.

Listen. Just listen.

In the loft of the hay barn behind him, a groom sneezed. Then he heard the murmur of sleepy voices. From the cow barn came a pained lowing and the first rattle of buckets. A rat scuttled for cover, its claws tapping the cobbles like a quick tiny shower of rain.

Moving swiftly now, he put the jar of maggots into the sack and collected his fishing pole. Beyond the cow barn, an explosion of cackles announced the arrival of breakfast for the hens. He walked fast to escape before anyone who still had not learned better could try to snare him in cheerful conversation. To be certain, he scowled ferociously.

However, he paused outside the gate from the kitchen garden onto the rough turf of the slope between the house and the fishponds. A radiant sliver of hot light glowed above the beech hanger to the east of the house. On the crest of the hanger, sparks of light flashed through the dark, stirring mass of the beeches. As he watched, the rising sun began to lay a flush across the water meadows upstream. Then all the trees on every side suddenly turned unnaturally vivid shades of green, punched with holes of black shadow and touched by red, orange and gold where the chilly nights had begun to bite.

A gift I don't deserve, he thought. The more poignant because I can't know how many more such gifts I may get, deserved or not.

He set off again towards the river, frowning and shaking his square, short-cropped head. If a man had to think, he should limit himself to mathematics or fish. The future was no safer than the past. For Philip Wentworth, it was a road down which death advanced at a steady pace. Even the present alarmed him just now.

Lodging here at Hawkridge, where the Scottish war and the wrangling in London between the king and his detractors seemed as distant as Caribbean thunder squalls, he had tried, with mixed success, to become as thoughtless as the frogs on the banks of the fish ponds or the silly, empty-headed hens.

Wouldn't mind being an old tomcat either, he thought now. Like you, you cocky devil. He watched the sinuous, purposeful explorations of a ginger tom.

Come from sleeping on her bed, have you? Our young mistress Zeal should know better than to woo you away from your proper profession of barn cat.

He imagined lying stretched out on a wall in the sun, filled only with heat and comfort, twitching once in a while in a dream of the hunt. As for the rest of a tom's business, well. Never mind. But, once. Oh, yes.

Silver-haired, and barrel-chested under his frayed, old-fashioned black coat, he looked a bit like an ancient greying tom. He even had the slightly stiff-legged walk as he followed the track from the house to the river.

This track led first to the lowest of the three fish ponds made two generations earlier by diverting water from the Shir. A plank footbridge crossed the sluice that spilled water from the lowest pond back into the natural flow of the river. Around the banks of the ponds stood an incongruous coven of marble sea nymphs conceived for some great Italian garden. Now they tilted and yearned on their ornate marble plinths on the muddy country banks where they found themselves instead.

The old man laid his hand on the cool bare buttock of the nearest nymph. Psamanthe. Or perhaps Galatea. A pretty thing, either way, cradling her conch shell half-raised to her lips, as if to sip from it, or play it like a horn. Sir Harry, who until recently had owned Hawkridge Estate, may, in his aspirations, have confused this Hampshire backwater with a grand villa in Rome but at least he recognized a pretty woman.

All too well, as it turns out, but that's none of your affair, you old frog.

He patted the buttock and turned left up the line of ponds to continue the careful, habitual construction of his day.

As he did every morning, he first examined the carp in the top pond. They were grazing on snails among the pots of grass sunk into the clear green water. The largest of the polished golden brown shapes, four of them, each weighing as much as a medium-sized piglet, were being saved for Christmas.

Retracing his steps back downstream, he next eyed the brassy-flanked chub and black-striped perch in the middle pond, where they swam with the senseless placidity of creatures whose every need is met. Until the net and cooking pan.

'As for you, my friends . . .'

In the deep water of the third, lowest pond, the long still shadows of pike hung poised in the shadows of lily pads. Fresh water wolves, forced to wait for a careless duckling or reckless frog. Their natural prey in the middle pond taunted them from behind the safety of one sluice gate. Another gate below locked their cage.

He stared down into the water. The pike seemed to him to radiate a silent, waiting rage.

He turned away to head down river. These creatures were the fish man's affair. He never fished for the captives in any of the ponds.

The burnt ruins of the central hall and west wing of Hawkridge House now lay on his right. The low brick sheds of the basse-court – the dairy, the wash house and the still room – had survived the recent fire, as had the chapel and the east wing to which it was attached.

Thinking selfishly, the damage could have been worse – and he tried to spare himself the discomfort of thinking any other way. He could sleep again in his usual chamber behind the chapel, which he occupied for forty pounds a year, as soon as the inner wall of the east wing was braced against collapse. His books and small number of other possessions were safe, although smoked like hams. The tiny globe of his present world had not been much shaken.

Someone was on the very edge of the chapel roof.

He already knew that his world had just been given a violent shove. Nevertheless, he tried to resist.

He crossed the bridge over the bottom sluice, headed for the track that followed the river downstream to the mill. Then he looked back again at the chapel.

Never look back, he told himself fiercely. Remember where it got Orpheus and Lot, all of them, heathen and otherwise.

Bright hair caught the early morning sun, as vivid as an autumn leaf.

In a flash, he abandoned ground won painfully over nineteen years. He threw down his sack and pole. Turned back. With his black coat jouncing like a loose animal pelt, he began to run.

2

The top of Hawk Ridge began to glow as if the seam that stitched it to the sky had parted to let fire leak through. By then, Zeal had already broken her promise to herself. She had vowed that by dawn she would find the courage to jump off the roof.

As she feared only two things, losing control and ignorance, she found jumping doubly hard. First would come the helpless fall. And no one could ever teach you how the end would feel.

Perhaps my heart will stop before I hit, she thought. The more she imagined falling, the more likely that seemed.

She had spent the night on the chapel roof, arms wrapped around her knees while her thoughts scrabbled and squeaked in panic. Reason, when she could catch hold of it, always hauled her back to the same terrible place. There was no other way.

All I have to do is tilt forwards. Fold my wings and stoop like a hawk into darkness and safety.

But those intolerable seconds of falling had to come first.

She leaned out over the edge of the chapel roof, steadying herself with one hand on the crenellated parapet. Now that she could begin to see them in the growing light, the brick walls and paved walks of the herb garden below her looked far harder than she had imagined during the night. The welcoming pillow of darkness had turned into a hungry mouth full of sharp-cornered teeth.

She observed a quiver of terror, beginning just behind her ears, then shooting down through her throat, chest and belly to crimp the skin on the tops of her knees.

One of my . . . of this body's . . . last sensations, she thought.

She swallowed and felt the pressure of her tongue against the back of her lower teeth, the slight roughness of the teeth and the smooth slippery wall of her lower lip. In a few more moments, all this feeling would end. She could not think where it would go instead. Along with all the other stored-up sensations of her seventeen years. As precious as they were to her, such sensations seemed far too petty for Heaven. About which she was not certain, in any case.

If only it weren't going to be such a beautiful morning.

I can't bear to miss it! she thought.

The sun had grown too bright to look at directly. Its light now reached the bottom of the river valley where the house stood. She had seen the Shir rise after a heavy rain until it spread across the water meadows in leaden sheets. Now, it glinted between edgings of willow like a line of dropped coins.

She looked down at what was left of her house.

The fire burned again against her eyelids. During the night and following day while it had been alive, the fire was an overwhelming presence, like God or royalty, hungry, terrifying and beautiful at the same time. They had all seemed so puny and presumptuous in fighting it. Except John, on the roof, possessed, taking chances she could not bear to watch, but did. She had breathed all her strength into him, held him safe with her will. If he had fallen and died, her emptied shell would have crumbled into ash.

'But I knew you wouldn't let me fall,' he told her, when she later reproached him for taking such risks, touching his face, his hair and hands.

Now she tested the texture and resilience of her own cheek, as of storing up memories of herself to take into the darkness. Her fingers explored her lips, testing how they might feel to another hand. Even now, their softness still startled her. Until recently, she had never thought of herself as being fashioned to give delight.

His delight had astonished her so much that once she had even, with curious disbelief, and the door barred, examined her quim in a hand-glass.

It had been hard to look straight at it. She could hardly believe that the little ginger beast, that hairy sea shell, had anything to do with love. She believed even less that the sight of it could give such pleasure.

She stroked the peach fuzz on her upper lip.

Only three weeks ago, she had stood on this same roof, with Hawkridge Estate spread out below her, watching for his return from his own estate at Richmond, near London. Even waiting had been delicious. She had spread her arms to the late afternoon sun, closed her eyes and imagined herself lifting, like thistledown caught in an updraught, so alert and alive in every fibre that she had shivered with delight at the tug of a faint breeze on the hair at her temple.

She shuffled her buttocks a little farther over the edge. Breathed in, to fill herself with the void in advance, so to speak. To join it by degrees, as if such a thing were possible.

Don't look down. Just do it.

Please, God, don't let me scream.

As she leaned forwards, a sharp corner of his letter in her bodice prodded her breast.

I'll read it just once more before I jump.

She unfolded the paper, still warm from her skin.

Sweetest Zeal, . . . I would tear out my heart and send it if I could . . .

She rocked in misery. She had shouted at him when he told her, had blamed him for pig-headedness that had brought about this horror. Even without other cause, she deserved to die for that cruelty.

. . . I meant what I said. I will stay true . . .

And so will I!

I regret only that I did not make you take me with you,

regardless of the dangers. I should have followed secretly and stowed away! I would have worked in the fields beside you.

She held his letter against her face, breathed in the smell of damp paper and the wax seal, imagined that she could also smell a trace of him.

I will be true to my vow, she thought. Faithful until death.

She saw the fine, lean lines of his hand and how the tendons shifted under his skin as he moved the pen. Her fingers searched like a dowser's wand for the exact places he had touched.

She could not wait seven years. She could not wait even seven months.

She wondered if he would feel the shock in his own sinews, lift his head as if at an unexplained noise.

3

'It won't work!' At the foot of the ladder, Philip Wentworth stood panting and clinging to a rung as if holding himself upright. 'Did you hear me? It won't work! Not high enough!'

She closed her eyes. 'Go away!'

'I'm coming up.' Without waiting for her answer, he began to climb the ladder.

Jump now! she warned herself. Or you'll have to endure another night like last night, all over again. But if she did jump, he would now feel responsible.

She sighed and leaned back. It was beyond belief that the old estate hermit should choose now, of all times, to turn sociable. She heard him stop on the way up to puff and wheeze. Then his head appeared above the parapet. She looked away, pinched with desperate fury. He heaved himself onto the roof and settled beside her on the edge. After a moment, his breathing eased and he gave a little cough.

They sat in silence. The intense greens and yellows of the beech hanger began to bleach in the growing brightness of the sun.

'So?' she asked at last. She still could not look at him.

Silently, he tossed a fragment of moss out into the air and watched it fall into the garden below. 'You're waiting for argument?'

'I'm not a fool.'

'But I understand the pull of the edge. If you're secretly hoping to be dissuaded, I'm not your man.'

'Then why did you climb up?'

'If you wish it, I will, of course, be glad to argue that you're young, beautiful and much needed on this estate. I will even, if you like, add that the world is precious, that despair is a sin and that taking your own life is a worse one.' Another clump of moss arched through the air. 'I've always wondered what fool decreed that suicide was a crime to be punished by death.'

She finally turned to look at him. 'Why come up?'

'To advise you the best way to do it.'

'You've come to help me kill myself?'

'You sound outraged.'

She shrugged, then shook her head.

'Don't mistake me. Nothing would please me more than to talk you out of dying.'

'Hah!' she said with grim triumph.

'Is there no other way? At seventeen you haven't begun.'

'I knew you were lying.'

'I need to be certain,' he said quickly. 'And don't be a fool! This roof is not high enough for a clean death.'

She leaned. Closed her eyes.

'Oh, go to the devil, then!' he said sharply. 'But I tell you, you will survive! Most likely crippled and helpless as a babe, depending on others to eat, to dress . . . even to change your soiled clout. I know, I've seen it.'

She opened her eyes and looked down. 'What else do you suggest, then? Must I drown myself in one of the fish ponds? Or impale myself on a hook?'

'There are other ways.'

'Believe me, I've considered them all.'

'I very much doubt that.'

'What can you know, living here . . .? Forgive me, I'm too desperate to be civil.'

'I'm not in the least offended.' He stared at his hands while he opened and closed them five times. 'I understand, madam, that this is difficult for you. But it is not altogether easy for me.'

'All it will cost you is words of advice.'

'But my advice involves confession, you see.' He fell silent and stared moodily across the valley to the slopes of Hawk Ridge.

She studied him sideways with a surge of curiosity. He had come with the estate, like its fields and trees. A rent-paying, gentleman sojourner, already in residence when she had arrived as a fourteen-year-old bride.

'I can't,' he said suddenly, with decision. 'Forgive me. But I had sworn never to reveal myself to anyone here.' He prepared to rise.

'Even when it concerns her life?'

'Even then.'

'But if I am dead, I will have to keep your secret. Your confession will cost you nothing while it will oblige me.'

He sighed and looked at her at last. She saw a profound uneasiness in his eyes. 'Very well. You prevail.' He levered himself to his feet.

'Where are you going?' she asked.

'With your permission, I would like to continue this discussion at a lower altitude.'

'If you are toying with me, I shall jump right now.'

Giving her a cool look that made her heart jump against her ribs, he slapped at the back of his long black coat. 'Don't threaten me, mistress. I said I'd tell and so I shall.'

He held out a hand to help her rise. 'I'll hold the ladder for you to go down. And I'd be grateful if you'll do the same for me. Will you come fishing?'

Zeal followed Wentworth to retrieve his pole and sack from where he had dropped them by the lowest pond. In silence, they crossed the sluice bridge, then followed the muddy track downstream towards the mill.

How did I come to be here? she thought.

'You don't want my advice,' he said at last. 'You want the advice of my former self.'

She looked sideways at his strong nose and pugnacious

17

chin. Though he was not as tall as John, and was a little stiffened by age, she had to walk fast to keep up with his
purposeful strides.

'And what was that?' she asked.

'An adventurer, you might say.'

'I thought you were going to say you had been an executioner, or a footpad, or a murderer.'

'Who told you that an adventurer is not all those things?'

'Do you have a gun?'

He gave her an amused look. 'Can't shake you loose from
the main point, can I? Yes, I have a gun. Most likely rusted
solid among my nightshirts and stockings. I also have a dagger,
a Spanish rapier, a dented buckler, an old-fashioned broad
sword, and a poison ring bought in Italy. You can take your
pick of 'em.'

He plunged off the track down a narrow, nettle-lined path
along the very edge of the bank. They passed a hectic narrow
rush where the river first stretched over hidden rocks like
pulled sugar candy, then crashed into turmoil.

He is toying with me, she thought as she slipped on the
mud and yanked her skirts free of the bushes.

Around a smooth elbow of a bend, the Shir widened into
a polished pool rimmed with rushes and weed.

She stopped to untangle her hair from an overhanging
branch. 'What is a dangerous adventurer doing here at
Hawkridge pretending to be a fisherman?'

'I take exception to your saying that I pretend to be a fisherman . . . here we are.' He stopped and peered down into the
water.

Though he lived in her house, as many solitary people
lodged in houses not their own, she had never before had
opportunity to observe him. When not out fishing, he kept
to his own two small rooms. He ate alone and refused all
invitations to join the house family in the hall. He never came
to prayers in the chapel. From time to time, he had shared
a pipe in the gardens after supper with John and Doctor

Bowler, the estate parson. Infrequently, he visited their neighbour Sir Richard Balhatchet at High House, where Zeal and
some of her house family had been lodging since the fire. But
Zeal had never met him there. She had had to feed her
curiosity with distant glimpses of his still figure by the edge
of one piece of water or another.

He was at least sixty years old. Still a large man. Thick
through the chest, but the shins beneath his stockings were
pared down to sinew and bone. The rest of him between neck
and knee was hidden under his bulky old-fashioned coat. The
coat itself was tailored from fine wool and silk but had worn
as smooth and green as a horsefly's tail on the collars and
cuffs.

A dangerous old man, she thought with interest. He must
not think that I trust him or his promises. He won't outwit
me, whatever he might intend. I can't let him.

She rubbed at the welts of nettle stings that had sprung
up on the backs of her hands. 'How must I die, then?'

Wentworth leaned his pole against a waterside oak and
studied the undulating scales of light on the greenish surface.
He gave a small grunt of satisfaction. Then he threw a handful
of maggots into the water and returned to sit on the exposed
roots of the oak. 'We must wait till they recover from our
arrival and start to feed again. Please sit down. You'll frighten
the fish.'

She continued to stand. 'Were you also a hangman? And
a highway man?'

'I was a plain soldier,' he said, with an edge of irritation
in his voice. 'Will that satisfy you? And my first concern is
pain . . .' He held up a warning hand and jerked his chin
towards the water. 'Expostulate if you must, but *sotto voce* . . .
Those bent on dying imagine only the end of suffering but
ignore the anguish of the road to oblivion. Believe me, the
soul clings on by its fingernails. I've seen men live for days
after a battle when you could barely recognize them as
human.'

'Master Wentworth, don't imagine you can frighten me. I think you're trying to change my mind after all!'

'As a friend, how could I not? Quiet, I beg you!' he hissed.

'You gave me your word!'

After a moment, he replaced the jar in his sack and stood to face her. 'Well then. The truth. I admit that it pains me to see a lovely young creature determined to throw her life away. Nevertheless, I accept your decision.' He collected his pole again. 'Therefore, we must find you the kindliest way. Shall we go back? I'm no longer of a mind to fish.'

Zeal's heart began to race. She felt suddenly more terrified even than on the roof. Then, she had at least known what she meant to do.

They walked in silence until they regained the sluice at the bottom of the fish ponds and had scrambled up the shallow bank to the edge of the lowest pond. For a moment, they gazed up the length of the three ponds and their fringe of sea nymphs.

'They do look absurd here, but I love them,' said Zeal.

The statues stood mostly upright, though some of the plinths had begun to tilt in the mud of the banks. At the top of the highest pond, Nereus, the father of the nymphs, leaned forward as if trying to show his dolphin something in the water.

'I thought Harry was mad when all those carts arrived from London, but they've settled in like the rustics they originally were.' Zeal stroked the marble thigh of the nymph Panope, then smiled when she spied a hen's nest between the marble feet. 'I imagine they're happy to be back where they belong. I would be.'

She turned her head to see Wentworth watching her. With the morning sun behind him, the grey stubble on his chin glistened. Dried oak bark and pieces of leaf had stuck to his ancient coat.

'You're not ready to die,' he said. 'You overflow with life. You can't deceive me.'

'Please,' she whispered. 'I have reasoned it through, again and again. You won't change my mind. Don't make it even harder for me.'

'Why are you so set?'

'That's not your concern. But it's my only reasonable choice.'

'I'm offering a dreadful service. You owe me the truth.' He bent to pick a large grub from the grass at his feet and tossed it onto the pond.

In silence, she watched the spreading circles, then the violent spasm on the surface as a pike struck.

He cursed under his breath. 'You will love again, you know! Even if John Nightingale is never able to return.'

'Don't presume!'

'Grant my age some small advantage! Please believe me – love comes and goes without apparent reason. You think you will never love again. Then it strikes . . .'

'You're wrong to think . . .'

'Your heart was a desert and then it bloomed. And now you fear the rain will never fall again. Is that why you despair?'

'How dare you!'

'Forgive me,' he said at once. 'But I do not understand your rush to self-destruction. Nightingale may come back . . . in spite of what I said . . . Men have been pardoned before, exiles have returned home. They have even survived sea voyages, as I myself can testify. The man's ship has scarcely cleared Southampton. Why not defer despair for a year or two?'

Zeal backed away from this unexpected outburst of passion. She hugged herself tightly. 'I can't afford to wait.'

'You're pregnant.'

'How do you know? Is it so clear to see?'

'You just told me.' He threw another grub into the pond. 'Is it Harry's or John's?'

'John's.'

'Does he know?'

'When he left, I wasn't sure.'

Wentworth studied the water for some time. 'Could it not possibly be husband Harry's?'

'Never! By my own testimony!'

He raised his eyebrows.

'I didn't see the danger then.' She laid both hands on her belly. 'Like a fool, I swore falsely, as Harry asked me. I lied under oath and swore that I was still a virgin, that the marriage was never consummated. And Harry was judged never to have been my true husband.'

'Ah,' Wentworth said. 'I see. I wondered at the ease of the annulment.'

'So, whoever is deemed to be its father, the babe is still a bastard. It can never inherit this estate nor anything else. What sort of life could it have? A beggar! And it's my fault, for lying! I should never have agreed!'

Wentworth raised a hand to try to calm her.

'As for me . . . a criminal either way.' She shivered. 'Either perjurer or fornicator, no escape. And our parish minister is violent against all odious depravity . . . unlike our own forgiving Doctor Bowler. Doctor Gifford will want to see me naked at the back of a cart.'

'I don't think . . .'

'But I have thought! Again and again. Carefully, reasonably. Can you see a sworn virgin turned unwed mother trying to act as the mistress of an estate? Always assuming that the estate is not made forfeit! But I can't kill John's child secretly and still live myself. I can't have the child and survive the consequences. Death is the only reasonable way!'

'I have a kindlier way.'

She waited, eyes closed, as if he had offered to deliver the fatal blow himself.

'Marry me.'

4

'There you are!' Rachel, a ripe twenty-four, had acquired Zeal as her mistress while the latter was still a Hackney schoolgirl and did not intend to change her manner just because the girl now owned an estate in some godforsaken corner of Hampshire. 'I left your tray on your bed back at High House. Did you want me to do something with this?'

'Not yet!' Zeal snatched back the letter she had left to be sent to John after her death.

'Your skirt hem is covered in mud.' Rachel did not quite dare to ask where she had been so early. However, Zeal felt curious eyes on her back as they trudged up the track that led to High House.

'We both have wet feet now,' observed Rachel.

'Don't be ridiculous,' Zeal had said.

Wentworth flinched. 'Is it my age?'

She shook her head.

'The only ridicule I fear is yours,' he said. 'I meant the form of marriage only. Please don't fear that there's any need for love. Warm friendship, perhaps, in time.'

'No.'

'Is it my modest circumstances, then?'

'At least you can offer me a set of fine fishing rods. All I would bring you in jointure are a bastard, ridicule, a burned-out house and a few sheep. It's a fine gesture, but I can't accept.'

'Don't mistake me, Zeal. I'm not a man for fine gestures. I'm old and lonely. You would do me a great favour.'

23

She stepped back and collided with the nymph. 'You know very well which way the favour lies. To marry a woman with a bastard in her belly, abandoned by both husband and lover . . . you won't survive the laughter.'

'Laughter has never concerned me so long as I get what I want.'

Their glances collided for the length of a heartbeat.

'Master Wentworth, only three weeks ago, I vowed to stay true to John Nightingale.'

'A vow won't help him if you're dead.'

She did not reply.

'I hate to think that death is preferable to a few years of my company,' he said.

'You don't want to marry any more than I want to die. I've never seen a man so content with his own company.'

'I want the child.'

She caught her breath.

'I've no children who are alive to me,' he said. 'I'd be proud to claim Nightingale's pup as my own. Until he wants it back, of course.' He shouldered his rod. 'In the name of the man you love, consider my proposal. Save his child. Life need not change much. Take time to reflect. I won't retract my offer. You will find me at Pot Pool, below the mill.'

Zeal had not meant to go back to High House, but now that Rachel had intercepted her, she could not think what else to do. She had used up all her will on the chapel roof during the night. The two women paused for breath on the brow of the grassy ridge that separated the two estates.

'Winter's coming.' Rachel gazed back across the ruined house at the bright slaps of colour on Hawk Ridge.

'I need to sit down,' said Zeal.

'Madam! Think of your skirts,' cried Rachel, too late.

After breakfast, Zeal rode her mare back to Hawkridge. While she waited in the office for her estate steward, Tuddenham, to finish in the stables, she picked up a stack of sooty papers, then set it down again. The old lethargy sucked at her again.

Wentworth offers a way out. Take it.

But I vowed to stay true to John. I believe that excludes marriage to someone else.

But this would be merely the form of marriage. An arrangement.

A rush of nausea sent her outside where she was sick onto the forecourt gravel.

'Madam! Are you ill?' Anyone who met Tuddenham on a dark road at night, would hand over his purse without waiting to be asked. Even when concerned, the steward glared.

She stared at him blankly. 'No,' she said at last. Then she remembered that illness was preferable to the truth.

She could not accept. The answer lay in her bones. Reason could not touch it.

'I made a schedule for the salvage and clearing the house site,' said Tuddenham. 'Sir Richard has spared us five men to help. We might be done by Christmas. Begin rebuilding after Twelfth Night, weather permitting.'

She almost said, 'I won't be here by Christmas.' The day was catching her unprepared. Expecting to be dead, she had let go of the strings that tied one day to the next. 'Will you send a boy to High House to make my excuses at dinner?'

Tuddenham glared even more ferociously and agreed at once.

Zeal took a straw hat from the office, crossed the sluice bridge and began to climb the hill beyond the river and ponds. She did not look at the river as she crossed it, lest she see Wentworth.

I can't marry anyone but John, she told herself again. But that can't be, because if I don't marry Wentworth, I must die.

Arrangement or not, marriage would give him rights and power over her. She had learned the dangers of marriage in any form.

How do I know I can trust him?

She could not think straight because she had not expected to be alive to make such a decision. She had used up the deciding part of herself last night on the roof.

Still queasy, she crossed a low grassy curve on the shoulder of Hawk Ridge itself and picked up the straight track, peppered with sheep droppings, which led towards the old Roman garrison town of Silchester. She grew tired far too soon, perhaps because of the child. She wished she could ask advice of the older married women, but dared not risk even reading about pregnancy and childbirth in her books.

She turned back, then found that she had to rest.

He was clever to have used the child.

The faint clanging of the bake house bell woke her. She had fallen asleep in the grass with her back against a rocky outcrop where she had often sat with John, seeming to talk of estate affairs or gazing into the valley in shared silence, but with all her being concentrated in the small part of her arm that touched his. A flock of her own Wiltshire Horns, rangy goat-like creatures, was grazing past her. She set off back down hill with damp skirts and the metallic taste of dread and indecision still in her mouth.

5

She took her place at the middle of the long, scrubbed elm table in the Hawkridge bake house kitchen where the small house family most often ate supper following the fire. Even this outbuilding smelled like the inside of the smokehouse, but with a colder, seeping edge. A light dusting of ash from the fire seemed always still to salt the food. She looked at the familiar faces around the table with a stranger's eye. She might as well have been a Mede or Ethiop dropped by magic carpet.

Since the recent fire, the estate residents had split their lives between Hawkridge House and assorted temporary lodgings. Her nearest neighbour, Sir Richard Balhatchet, had given rooms at High House to Zeal and Mistress Margaret, who was the unmarried aunt of Harry and John. Their two serving women, and Agatha, the chief house maid, and Doctor Bowler the estate parson also slept at High House. Others of the house family, including three house grooms, two kitchen grooms, and John's former manservant, Arthur, slept where they could in the outbuildings and barns. The large mid-day dinner was served at High House to those not in the fields. Apart from the house family, the rest took supper wherever they found themselves.

Thank the Lord, Master Wentworth never comes to the table, Zeal thought. I could not bear to see him just now.

According to Mistress Margaret, he had never eaten in company since he first took up residence on the estate long before Zeal arrived.

Now, as they sat on borrowed stools along either side of

the long table, their voices and laughter, the sound of their chewing, the scrape of stool legs on the stone floor, a dropped knife, all made her flinch.

As Mistress Margaret supervised the passing of rabbit stew, she hummed with grim glee at news that a neighbour (not Sir Richard) had been fined five hundred crowns for ploughing across the boundary of an adjoining estate. 'He always takes the largest portion at table, too!' she said. 'And the last sweetmeat.'

Doctor Bowler paused for a polite beat of silence then ventured, 'But surely, that is exactly what the king did to John! Boundaries, I mean, not sweetmeats.'

The king meant to cut across John's land – the very same estate so recently awarded to him for service to the Crown. A great wall was to be built right between John's new horse barn and his paddock, to enclose a royal hunting park at Richmond, taken from common grazing land and other men's farms.

'But the king is the king,' protested Mistress Margaret. 'Our dear neighbour is not even a knight.'

'Do you mean to say that the right to trespass is defined by rank?' asked Doctor Bowler with a degree of heat uncommon in him. 'Do you say that John did not have good reason to protest to the king? Did the king have the right to call such reasonable protest "treason"? I expected more support for your nephew's cause!' Doctor Bowler turned to Zeal. 'Are you not proud of him, my lady? He did not creep away with his tail between his legs like so many others who were equally wronged.'

Zeal stared blankly at their animated faces, then realized that they were expecting her to speak.

Mistress Margaret and Zeal's serving woman, Rachel, exchanged looks.

'Zeal,' begged Mistress Margaret, her face mottled pink with emotion. 'He puts words into my mouth! Why don't you help me? Our parson has me at an unfair advantage with all his education. We women are never taught the tricks of debate.'

'Why gild the lily?' murmured Doctor Bowler. He peered closely at Zeal across the table and changed tack. 'Isn't it excellent news, my dear, that Sir Richard plans to give us that wagon load of oak beams from his old barn to help us rebuild the hall and west wing?'

'Indeed,' cried Mistress Margaret, diverted into this new turning. 'We could never afford to buy them! It's all very well to say that the Lord will provide, but kind neighbours are more certain.'

Doctor Bowler pounced with delight. 'And who do you think prompted this Christian charity in Sir Richard?'

I must act, one way or another, thought Zeal. And if I can't decide for myself what to do, I must leave it to chance. Or ask Doctor Bowler's advice.

'My lady . . . ?' The little parson always requested attention as if certain that you had far more important things to do than talk to him.

Zeal forced herself to smile at his anxious face, with its slightly too-close eyes. She sometimes thought of him as an earnest moth. A man of infinite good will and equal fragility, Doctor Bowler should never have taken on the moral burdens of a clergyman.

While Sir George Beester was still alive, Bowler, an Oxford man, had been tutor to the baronet's two nephews, Harry Beester (who had married Zeal and brought her to Hawkridge) and John Nightingale, the son of Beester's only sister. His sweet temperament, urgent curiosity and good Latin and Greek made him an excellent tutor for a willing pupil like John but a poor task-master for the likes of Harry. He had survived on an allowance from Sir George, and on small tithes, eggs and milk from estate tenants whom he christened, confirmed, married and buried. When John took over running the estate, which Harry inherited after their uncle's death, Bowler bent his classical education to the estate accounts.

When on the annulment of their marriage Harry deeded the estate to her, Zeal saw no reason for change.

'When you have a moment,' Bowler said now, 'if such a time should ever arrive, I would be grateful for your thoughts about the Fifth of November.'

'The Fifth of November?' She gazed at him blankly.

A flush slowly rose all the way to the top of his shiny bald head. 'The bonfire. Bonfire and Treason Night. It seems a little . . . After what happened. In any case, I've heard some . . .'

'Of course. We'll speak whenever you like.' She could never consult Bowler. His own helplessness would cause him too much pain.

'Troublemakers!' said Mistress Margaret briskly. 'It's the young men.'

'Some older heads agree with them,' protested Doctor Bowler. 'Doctor Gifford for one. Then we also have to consider the bells.'

Zeal looked at them both as if they were speaking an alien tongue.

With revulsion, she eyed the rabbit stew in front of her, smooth white flesh to which adhered a blob of shiny, mucilaginous pork fat. She swallowed against her rising gorge and smiled brightly in the direction of Doctor Bowler's voice.

'Does anyone have a coin I could borrow?' she asked.

When supper finally ended, she put on her wool cloak and took Doctor Bowler's farthing to the solitude of the orchard. The quincunx of trees shifted before her eyes, one moment apparent disorder, the next a harmony of straight lines.

'Good evening, to you, madam.' An estate worker intercepted her cheerfully. 'Can I have a word about moving the piglets?'

In the dusky shadows under the trees, she was free at last of all those eyes.

She felt out of control, as if bits of her might fly off without warning. It was a new experience. The world had given way, in the past, more than once. It was the nature of the world to give way. But she herself had always survived, clamped down like a limpet to the best piece of rock she could find at the given time.

She threw the farthing in the air, caught it, covered it with her other hand. Then she put it back into her hanging pouch without looking.

She sat in the grass and leaned back against a tree, trying one last time to think straight. She felt as if she were already a ghost, out of place in the living world. Her hands moved in her lap like small restless animals.

She had already been Harry's wife when she first met John. If John should find her married again, neither of them would survive it, she was certain.

But Wentworth was an old man. Anything might happen in seven years.

She stopped, appalled at her own wickedness. If she did accept him, she must not ever let herself wish for his death. He was a good man, to make such an offer.

Even though he did trick me down from the roof.

He was also taciturn, solitary, obsessed with fishing, spent most of his days on the water and his evenings alone in his chamber. He disappeared during feast days and celebrations, when work eased enough for people to take fresh note of each other in their unfamiliar clothes and exchange glances of startled rediscovery as they passed each other in a dance. He ate and walked alone. He was less present in her life, in fact, than the cat.

His offer was all the more surprising because she felt that he avoided her even more than he did the others. It was perfectly reasonable for a man of his age to find an inexperienced chit like her to be of little interest. Her guardian, of much the same age as Wentworth, had no more than tolerated her, and he had had the use of her fortune.

Wentworth's generosity deserved better than she could ever give him in return.

She began to pace the diagonal aisles between the trees. Fallen pears squelched under her shoes, releasing little gusts of fermentation.

He offers a solution just as reasonable as death. And kinder to everyone.

But marry him? Marry anyone but John?

No, she thought. She tried to imagine Wentworth in a nightshirt, in her chamber, without his flapping black coat, but her thoughts started to slither like a pig on ice.

She made another turn of the orchard. Plucked a leaf from overhead, shredded and dropped it.

Try once more to reason it through.

Have the child and expose herself as either blaspheming perjurer or fornicator? Impossible.

The parish minister was a fierce Scot named Praise-God Gifford, who brought the unforgiving spirit of Calvin with him to England when he had trotted south with his clergyman father in 1604, after Elizabeth died, at the heels of the Scottish king who had come to rule England. As he grew older Gifford added a moral ferocity all his own.

She feared that she could not trust her standing as a landowner to protect her from him, even if she somehow escaped the civil law. He would want to make an example of her all the more, she who stood above her people like the sun and should lead them into light, educating through her own peerless example. She had seen one poor girl – not from Hawkridge, thank the Lord – stripped naked in front of all the parish council and have her hands tied to the tail of a cart. Then she was whipped all the way from the Bedgebury market square to the May Common. As the lash laid bloody lines across the girl's skin, Zeal had seen the eager faces of some of the watching men. The girl had later drowned both herself and her babe.

The brilliant light of the day had now softened into a lavender haze that promised a warm night. In the distance, a few cows complained that they had not yet been milked.

The orchard smelled richly damp and sweet, with a prickling of rot.

If I died, I would so miss this place, she thought. She began a circuit of the high brick walls, noting the ripeness of espaliered apricots and cherries. She picked and ate a sweet black cherry and spat out the stone.

Try to hide the child?

Others had succeeded in that deceit, she knew. Fine ladies who put on loose-bodied gowns and paid a married woman to unlace her stomacher and pad her petticoats, then produce the babe as her own.

Not here on this estate. Rachel already knew the truth from washing Zeal's linen. Though she would never tell, others might guess as she had done. Secrets here were as safe as pond ice in May, and now that they lived hugger-mugger on top of each other since the fire, any such sleight of hand stood even less chance of success.

'If your mind's not set that way,' Rachel had said, 'you know as well as I that not all babies that get planted need to be born.'

When Zeal did not reply, Rachel had folded the petticoat and pressed it flat with both hands.

'Could you do it?' Zeal finally asked.

'Perhaps I have.' Rachel met Zeal's eyes defiantly. 'Better than a public flogging, I daresay you'll agree. But you won't have to fear that, madam. You're a lady.'

'Would you take that risk, with Doctor Gifford?'

If I kill John's child, I might as well kill myself at the same time.

She reached the far wall of the orchard and turned to look back at the chapel roof.

But life had carried her on past that point, with a push from Philip Wentworth. Not knowing quite how it came about, she had fallen out of love with that flight into darkness.

People really do wring their hands, she thought, suddenly

noticing that her own were turning and twisting together against her apron.

You are feeble, she told herself. Take a grip!

She climbed up into the nearest apple tree. No one can see me now, she thought, as the shadowy leaves closed around her. At the centre, near the trunk was like a secret house. An abandoned nest sat close above her head.

How lucky the birds are, she thought. She and John had first looked at each other properly, soon after she arrived, when he had caught her up an apple tree in her bare feet and mistaken her for one of the estate girls.

She smiled, shut her eyes, and remembered the warmth of his hand closing around her bare ankle, and the shock of their unguarded recognition. She had slipped and showered down leaves in catching herself, while he stood looking up at her with an expression both startled and benign.

'I'm sorry,' she said when safely on the ground, clutching stolen blossom, aware that she wore only her petticoats.

'They're your trees,' he said. 'Harry's, anyway.' After a moment, he added, 'Trees ask to be climbed.'

For the next two years, they tried to pretend that look had never happened.

She pressed her forehead against the bark of a branch and felt his hand encircling her ankle again. Then it came to her how she could decide. She would not trust her life or death to the pettiness of a farthing, but Chance could take more noble forms than a plucked daisy or a tossed coin.

She climbed down and went to the estate office. In the thick dusk, she felt along the top of the mantle piece until her fingers found what they wanted. John's glove, dusted with ash, like everything else.

I will accept the answer, she vowed. Life, or death. Either way.

She went to sit beside Nereus on the bank of the upper pond, to wait until she was alone. She found the old sea god's company comforting. Like her, he could never have expected to end up at Hawkridge, and she was sure that he was equally content to be here. A white dove sat on the head of the nearest nymph, who also wore a wilted daisy chain around her neck. Her sister just beyond still had a fishing line tied to her wrist.

'I don't suppose any of you knows what I should do,' she said. 'Never mind. I mean to ask elsewhere.'

The estate workers and house family usually collapsed soon after supper, worn out by the battle to keep up with daily chores, while also salvaging whatever they could from the house, restoring what they could recover and remaking or rebuilding the rest. Meanwhile the advance of autumn brought its own burdens of digging, cutting, picking, binding, threshing, butchering, salting and preserving.

When she passed the bake house on the way to the ponds, Rachel and Agatha had nearly finished clearing supper, with the help of the kitchen grooms. The two women stood side by side in the last of the dusk, sleeves rolled to the elbow, scrubbing the last of the spoons and cups with fistfuls of green horsetail pulled in the water meadows.

The two kitchen grooms came out to the ponds with the dry ends of bread and hard-baked dough trenchers they all had to use until the cooper could make more wooden plates. These, in their turn had replaced the pewter plates Sir Harry had taken when he left Hawkridge for London. The grooms threw the bread onto the middle pond and disappeared downstream towards the mill where they were nested.

While she waited impatiently for all the others to go to bed, Zeal stared up into the sky. A faint glow in the haze showed where the moon was trying to press through the clouds.

Six ducks splashed down and jostled each other aside to get at the bread. With obscure pleasure, Zeal watched a female snatch a crust from under the jabbing beaks of two battling drakes. The mêlée reminded her of a gang of drakes she had once seen pile onto a single duck and drown her in their eagerness to tread her.

A carp slapped the water with its tail. Sheep bleated raggedly in unending querulous complaint. Frogs had begun to sort themselves into soprano, alto and bass. In the still air, the voice of a house groom carried clearly from the stable yard, headed at last for bed in the loft of the hay barn. She heard Rachel and Agatha set off with Mistress Margaret and her maid on the long walk to High House.

The moon pressed harder against the restraining clouds. In the final luminous glow as dusk slid into true night, straight lines wavered and the black humps of bushes breathed. The nymphs around the ponds stirred and reached out their hands to her. She felt their concern, and a pull, as if they invited her into sisterhood.

If only I could turn to stone and stay here with you, she told them.

In the remains of the house, Doctor Bowler began to play his fiddle in the dark, in the chapel antechamber. His tune was fierce, incautiously pagan, and totally suited to her present purpose.

6

When Zeal unlocked the gate into the kitchen garden, next to the orchard, Ranter, the night mastiff on patrol, pushed his huge head into the front of her skirt and swung his rope-like tail.

She heard Arthur's laugh. A door slammed. Somewhere, closer in the darkness, a hen muttered to itself. With Ranter bumping and huffing at her heels, Zeal walked slowly between the rectangles of the raised vegetable beds.

Moonlight, triumphant at last, began to pick out the fruit trees espaliered to low internal walls. Late pumpkins and gourds, which should already have been harvested, gleamed like huge jewels against the dark earth of the beds. The blade of a forgotten weeding knife sparked in the grass. Absently, she picked it up.

Until John had unlocked her heart, she had imagined no love greater than that she felt for this place – house, gardens, fields and hills, its people, its sheep, even the ducks.

She looked back. Had the whole house been standing, she could have been seen from one of the upper windows. Even so, she stepped into the deep shadow of the garden wall. Doctor Bowler might smile forgivingly on sinners, but Doctor Gifford had a keen nose for sulphur and a personal mission to save souls. Unlike Bowler, he would not turn a blind eye. Gifford would never doubt that she meant to practise witch-craft.

Ranter gave her a final friendly shove and settled under a gooseberry bush.

She unfolded the pale ghost of a linen handkerchief onto

37

the ground. With the point of her own knife, which always hung at her belt, she pricked the end of her left thumb. She had not pried, exactly, but her curiosity had always set off in hot pursuit after rumour. From all that she had been able to overhear and otherwise learn from her books and the talk of the women, she should have marked her charm with her monthly flow. She made a dark smudge on the linen with her thumb.

She sat back on her heels in the heap of her skirts. The moon looked cold and dead, like a bleached bone. At least it was waxing. Always sow your seeds in a waxing moon. Don't try to conjure hope under a dying one.

She turned her head sharply at a falling leaf. The air in the garden was so still that she heard snail tongues rasping at the leaves of the cabbages and late beans. Even the distant sheep and ducks were temporarily silent. Then Ranter, who had also raised his head, gave a gusty sigh and flopped his dewlaps down onto his forepaws again.

Reassured by his indifference, she spat on the napkin. Then she lifted her pleated linen collar to dig under her armpit with the handkerchief. With a glance at Ranter's tranquil shadow, she reached up under her skirts and wiped the napkin between her legs.

She took John's glove from her bodice and held it to her face. She inhaled his scent beneath the salty tang of the leather. Felt his body heat and hard smooth muscles. Almost saw him. Then the details wavered and blurred.

I should have fed my eyes in our last moments together, she thought. Committed him to memory, inch by inch and hair by hair, instead of shouting at him in rage for abandoning me. I dared to be angry with him when he was going off to be little more than a slave.

The harder she tried to see him, the more he eluded her.

She put her hand into the void left by his and bent her fingers to fit the curves and bumps that he had shaped. Then she laid her hand in his glove against her right breast.

She looked down at the dark leather against the pale wool of her bodice. As a very young girl, she had imagined that such a touch would feel wicked. Instead, when it finally came, she had felt a deep peacefulness, as if a tightly-wound spring had loosened inside her. She had been waiting without knowing it, for his hand to arrive exactly there.

She put the napkin to her nose and inhaled her own musky smell. Suddenly, as clearly as if he had been there, she smelled the rich warm brew that rose up between their naked bodies after love.

She wiped her eyes with the napkin.

Ranter raised his head.

'Good dog,' she whispered.

The great rope of his tail thumped on the damp grass.

She kissed the glove formally, as if it were a bishop's ring or a sword before battle, and folded the handkerchief around it. With her knife, she cut a long strand of hair from her nape and tied it around the bundle.

The mastiff rumbled like an earthquake and hoisted himself to his feet. Zeal froze. He lumbered to the back wall of the garden, growled again. A violent scuffling announced that whoever had begun to scale the wall had decided urgently against it. The sounds of retreat faded into the night.

She listened for a long time at the back gate. As mistress of Hawkridge Estate, she had the right to walk where she liked, at any time, however odd. The tenant farmers and her own house family, the gardeners, stockmen and grooms should all be clutching at sleep while another day of work rushed at them all too fast. But no one was in his or her right place just now. And boys slipped out to poach fish from the ponds. Unmarried couples, like Rachel and Arthur, sought darkness and solitude under the trees. The bundle she now carried could hang her.

Ranter gave a low reproachful bark when she finally closed the door behind her. 'Stay, sir!' she whispered through the wooden grille. 'Guard my back.'

As she climbed the flank of Hawk Ridge, her feet slipped on the damp, crumbly beech mast and silvery patches of damp moss. Just below the spine of the ridge, in the darkness under the leafy roof, panting from her climb, she reached out to touch one of the dark columns.

He sat under this tree, and I leaned against him, rocked gently on the rise and fall of his breath.

As she began the last steep scramble, the chill of total solitude engulfed her. Here all human fires were quenched. A thick roof of branches shrouded the night sky and blotted out the moon. The air felt thick, as if a great weight pressed down on it. Though the night was almost windless, the trees around her rustled and sighed as if alive.

You enter the Lady's realm, they murmured.

Nearly blind now, she hauled herself up the last sheer yards, slipping and clutching at branches, into the cavern of darkness cast by the Lady of Hawk Ridge. Hands outstretched, she felt her way towards the ancient beech that had chosen human form. Her hands met damp, cool bark. Found a familiar wide taut hollow, and recognized a curve.

The Lady sprang upwards into the sky, feet first, from a short trunk twenty feet around. Her head and her raised arms remained imprisoned in the trunk, while her sappy fingers twisted into roots deep in the earth under Zeal's feet. Her body, that of a giant female, was the lowest branch of the old beech, which spread close to the ground, the result of coppicing one hundred years before.

Zeal felt outwards along the damp bark from the hollow of the Lady's throat until she reached the two large boles of her breasts with their broken stumps of nipples. Though lost now in the darkness, the Lady's waist, hips and crossed legs curved upwards until her ankles sprouted, ninety feet above the ground, into an angular network of springy twigs. The Lady of Hawk Ridge rose naked and unashamed from the earth with such force and purpose that she seemed to hold its centre in her buried hands.

Zeal had overheard the muttered gossip. The Lady, not Gifford, was Doctor Bowler's chief rival for souls on the estate. Zeal had admired the little parson for his pragmatic discretion on the subject of the estate oracle. Now she too, like so many others, would let the Lady decide her fate.

As she felt along the giant rib cage, she gave a little 'hah!' of terror and snatched back her hand. She had touched something cold, limp and damp.

She stared at the darkness until she thought her eyes would burst. After a time she began to make out a shape against the beech bark. It swam in the darkness but did not move away. Zeal clenched her teeth and forced herself to touch it again.

Wet feathers. Crumpled, wiry claws. A dead bird. Then her fingers found the noose of twine from which it hung and she smelled the whiff of putrefaction. She turned to flee, then reminded herself that she had plucked too many scalded chickens to run from a dead crow or thrush.

She crouched among the Lady's roots and, with a sharpened yew stick she had carried in her belt, began to dig. Her fingers felt a sharp edge. A folded parchment.

Another desperate petitioner, she thought. Perhaps the one who left the bird. She covered over someone else's private hope or grief and dug again. She buried her bundle. Then she stood, stretched up her right hand and found the triangle where the Lady's legs divided. The damp bark under her fingers felt as rough and complicated as her own red-gold bush, though much colder.

'Lady,' she whispered. 'If you can do what they believe . . . do it for me. I beg you, tell me. What should I do?'

Will I understand if she does answer?

The tree inhaled and exhaled. Zeal heard it clearly.

He is truly gone. Will never touch you again. You will never hear his voice.

'No!' Zeal cried aloud. 'That can't be!'

I imagined, she told herself. Heard my own fears speaking. The wind.

'I shall ask three times,' she told the tree. So as to be sure of what I hear.

Be careful what you ask and how you ask it, she told herself. Remember the stories. Beware of the literal and murderous precision of magical wish-granting!

Her mind leapt from danger to danger.

'Will I ever see him . . .' she asked carefully '. . . alive and not dead? . . . Don't answer me yet! I must think.' She pressed her free hand to her face. Her skin felt hot in spite of the chill under the tree.

'With all his limbs and senses?' Though I would love him without.

What other danger have I forgotten?

'Will he still love me?'

With her hand still on the cleft of the Lady's legs, she pressed her forehead against the dark, cold bark beside the dead bird.

No reply. What should I make of that?

She was no longer certain what she had heard the first time.

When her pulse had quietened a little, she tried a third and last time.

'Speak to me now,' she begged the Lady. I'm ready to listen.

The grove around her was absolutely still. The night held its breath. The tree did not speak.

'Please, give me a sign, Lady! Shall I marry Wentworth and try to endure for seven years?'

Don't even think about what might happen then.

'Or should I kill myself?'

Why should I trust it? she suddenly thought. Why does everyone assume it's friendly? If so, why does it want dead offerings?

The night still held its breath. Still the tree kept silent. Not a twig or leaf stirred.

Zeal sat, closed her eyes. Fortunate Daphne, she thought. Transformed to a laurel tree. All grief ended . . . she presumed that trees do not feel grief.

She dug her fingers into the leaf mould, imagined the chill of the ground rising slowly towards her heart, reaching it, slowing its beat until her thoughts darkened and faded into a long dream of leaf fall, rain, nesting birds and slow rot.

She sat upright with a jolt of terror and tried to remember where she was. Who she was. Not a tree. Almost, but not yet. She scrambled up, tripped on petticoats, half-fell when a numbed foot gave way. The darkness and chill pressed on her like water. She could not breathe. This was not mere fancy. She felt the silent presence in the grove, which had refused to help.

I am such a fool, she thought.

In a growing rage at the Lady, at herself, she slid and stumbled back down the slope away from the tree. Back in the clear moonlight of the kitchen garden, Ranter still waited just inside the gate.

'Nature does not trouble itself with our petty human affairs!' she told him, with ferocity. 'And why should it care? Why should I expect anything, even Chance, to relieve me of my decision? I shall have to make up my own mind, after all!'

She could not bear to go back to High House, to be among all those breathing bodies, the snores, the night time farts and cries, to be attacked by the miasma of other people's dreams. She stalked down river to the mill, where she climbed out on the narrow platform that led to the great wooden wheel. She glared down briefly into the water while moss dripped near her head and pale leaves slid into the current of the race and dived beneath her feet.

Ask nothing of anyone. I've always known that.

She had to keep moving lest she start to take root again.

Upstream, where the suck of the race did not disturb it, the surface of the millpond looked cold and as hard as metal.

Though the tree had stayed silent the night now seemed filled with advice. As she crossed the sluice bridge at the bottom of the ponds, the leaping water burbled, 'Build a little, build, build, build.'

'Dieeee!' cried a sheep.

'Build, build a little,' insisted the water below the sluice.

'Yes,' whispered the trees on the riverbanks.

'Wait, wait, wait!' instructed a pair of antiphonal frogs.

Her blood pounded in her head. She could tolerate indecision no longer, felt ablaze with furious purpose, though she could not yet say what it was. She wanted to tear through the milky membranes of the night, sweep away the clouds. Propelled by a horror of that quiescent stillness in the beech grove, not knowing what she would say, and without thought for the hour, she headed for the tack room to find Philip Wentworth.

7

'One moment!' The heavy door muffled his voice. There was the thud of a chest lid. Zeal imagined she felt the remains of the east wing tremble. The door opened so suddenly that he nearly caught her with her ear against it.

He was still arranging his coat. His shirt collar was caught up on one side, the ties still undone. His eyes widened when he saw her.

'I think I've come to say, yes.'

He cleared his throat. 'Think?' He smoothed his silver hair with his hand.

'May I come in?'

He stepped back and left the door standing open behind her.

'You shouldn't be here,' she said. 'I looked for you in the tack room. If you won't stay at High House, you should sleep in the tack room until that wall is braced. The back staircase shook under my feet just now.'

'I didn't expect you so soon.' He finished tying up his shirt.

'You won. Aren't you pleased?' Her eyes darted around his little room. A chilly breeze blew from the corridor onto her back. 'Or didn't you expect me to accept? Do you want to retract your offer, after all?'

He took her elbow and sat her on a back stool in front of the low fire. 'Stop talking for a moment.' He took a glass from his cabinet, blew into it, then poured wine from a jug which stood on the table behind her.

She turned in her chair. He had been working. Papers lay higgledy-piggledy. A pewter mug, a dirty wineglass and a pair of spectacles sat among the papers. A sempster's candle stand, fitted with a lens set vertically, focussed the light of the flame.

'Tell me again,' he said.

'I said, yes.'

He gave her the glass of wine. He had rolled back his cuffs from strong broad hands flecked with age spots. Then he refilled his own glass. He pulled out a second back stool from the wall and sat on the other side of the fire. He raised his glass. 'To friendly union, then.' The greying bristle of his chin glistened in the firelight.

Now that she had agreed to marry him, she had difficulty in looking straight at him. From quick uneasy glances, she saw he had a scar on the edge of his slightly box-like jaw, and deep lines from nostril to mouth. And a strong nose with a square tip, where two paler points sat just under the skin. Grey hairs curled from the open neck of his shirt. His wool stockings were wrinkled, his feet shoved into soft, scuffed leather house slippers. She smelled worm-wood against moths and a faint alcoholic mist when he exhaled.

The firelight coiled at the bottom of her glass. She did not know whether or not she had responded to his toast.

For forty pounds a year, Wentworth occupied this small parlour and an equally small sleeping chamber beyond. He lived frugally, without a manservant. Through the far door, she saw the dark shape of a narrow bed, with curtains on plain square-sectioned posts. She had seen these rooms only once before, with his permission, when she first took stock of her new realm. Wentworth had otherwise forbidden all entrance to his rooms, except twice a year to clean.

His floor now seemed to slant. The corners of the room were not quite true. Thirty feet beyond his door, the corridor leading from the back stairs to what had been the front of the house dived suddenly downwards and opened onto the night.

'What if the rest of the corridor gives way?'

'I'm not going to retract my offer,' he said.

She nodded mutely.

'Drink a little,' he said. 'It's no small thing we propose to do. But not so great as I suspect it feels to you just now. Drink a little. Steady yourself.' He drank. 'It helps me to sleep.'

Her chin jerked up. 'Before I lose my courage altogether, I must speak honestly . . .' In spite of herself, she looked at the bed. 'You might yet want to withdraw.'

He smiled and waited.

'You said this morning that you hoped only for friendship. But you might have said that just to win me round. So that we have no misunderstanding, I must make it clear that I cannot love you.'

'How many marriages insist on love?' He poured himself more wine. 'I might, in time, aspire to your affection. Does that terrify you? As for the rest . . .' He nodded over his shoulder at the bed. 'I've put all that behind me.'

Their eyes met briefly. She sighed.

'I want you to be certain,' he said.

'I do have one other condition.'

Wentworth looked at her sharply, then raised his eyebrows in good-humoured question.

'I know I have no right to impose any conditions at all . . .'

'It has never been your unassuming meekness for which I admired you.'

She blinked at the idea that he had admired her at all, then plunged onwards. 'I must know who you are.'

The good humour vanished. His face set into thin, tight lines. 'I said I used to be a soldier. Is that not enough?'

'No. I need to know if Philip Wentworth is your true name. Will I truly be Mistress Wentworth, or should my name be something else? What sort of adventurer were you? Why did you bury yourself here?'

He shook his head.

'I beg the truth from you as a wedding gift.'

'I can't give it.'

'I swear that nothing you tell me will change my mind about the marriage, but you must see that I need to know more of the man I will be living with.'

'Live with the man I am now. That other one has nothing to do with you.'

'It was only the promise of making his acquaintance that got me down from the roof.'

Wentworth closed his eyes and rubbed his forehead.

'Can't you see that the more you refuse, the more necessary it becomes for you to tell me?' She stood up and handed him her empty glass. 'Otherwise I retract my acceptance. How can I pledge myself, even in friendship, to a man so vile that he can't confess what he has done even to his own wife? If you can't tell me more, then you should never have confessed anything at all!'

Philip Wentworth shook his head again, but this time with wry humour. 'Caught in my own snare.' He crossed the room to set their glasses on his worktable, where he stood for several moments with his back to her. 'Is your condition absolute?' he asked without turning around. 'Will you really retract if I don't agree? Think what that means and take your time in answering.' He leaned his weight onto his clenched fists and waited.

'Would you still help me to die, as you first promised?'

'Yes.'

She shut her eyes. After a long while, she said, 'It is absolute.' Watery knees tipped her back into her chair.

'I was merely a soldier, as I said. Nothing more. But it's not a world a man wants to share with women.'

'Master Wentworth,' she begged, 'please understand! All my life, the things I did not know and could not expect have always brought me the greatest grief.'

'You have nothing to fear from me.'

'That may be, but I have learned to fear ignorance more

than I fear death. I can't bear knowing that I don't know and waiting for something to happen that I can't see coming. I can't bear what I imagine. And that's the truth.' She blew out a deep breath. 'Reasonable or not.'

He turned and studied her with a slightly chilly expression. She saw no trace in either his eyes or bearing of the genial old hermit who had proposed marriage.

How far we have already moved, she thought, even from where we were on the riverbank.

'I can't go on living on any other terms.' She looked at him pleadingly.

'What if I said that I was lying, up there on the roof? That I had nothing to confess? No other life than the one you see?'

'I would know that you are lying now.'

This answer seemed to please rather than anger him. He eyed her a moment longer. '*Concedo*,' he said at last. He held his arms out to the side like a defeated swordsman exposing his front to his foe. 'I accept your terms. You shall have your gift of truth, on our wedding night.'

Scalding relief told her how much she had wanted him to agree.

'But in return I have one condition of my own.' He crossed back to the fire. 'Stand up again so I can see your face in the firelight.' He took her hand to help her rise. 'I, for my part, cannot live with uncertainty. You must lay down the sword you have just threatened me with and swear that so long as I live and you are married to me, you will never again threaten to take your own life.' He held both hands now. 'Look at me and swear.'

She nodded. 'Why would I want to?'

'Swear,' he repeated.

'I swear.'

'So we're agreed at last?'

Zeal could now only nod wordlessly. The relative simplicity of the choice between life and death was reshaping itself into something more subtle and infinitely more complex.

I should tell him about the seven years, she thought. And that John will be sending for me.

But those complications were beyond her at this moment.

'I shall speak to Doctor Bowler tomorrow,' Wentworth said. 'And seek Sir Richard's advice on how best to obtain a special licence. I see no need to delay by posting banns if we can avoid it, do you? The sooner we can wed, the better for the babe.'

Rather than make the long walk back to High House at that hour, she made herself a nest among the ledgers and piles of salvage in the Hawkridge Estate office. Then she curled up under a smoky quilt on a feather bed that smelt of wet hen, still trying to comprehend what had just happened.

She did not have to kill herself, after all. She was to be married again. The Hawkridge Hermit had agreed to open himself to her like a gift. For the first time since his proposal that morning, it occurred to her that the balance of power between them might not tilt entirely in his favour. That thought made her like him even better. Nothing he might tell her would make her dislike him now.

She turned onto her side and wrapped her arms tenderly around her belly. John sat at his table in the office – the table she now used – his face serious and intent, acorn-coloured hair falling over one dark, fierce eyebrow. One foot was tucked back under the stool. The other was stretched under the table, showing the long elegant line of his thigh. She lay fondly watching his ghost. For such a gentle, schooled man, he looked deceptively like a pirate. He glanced up and smiled, then bent his head again.

Our child can live, after all, she told him. I no longer have to pretend it isn't there.

She no longer needed to keep the door of her heart locked against it.

When she looked at the table again, John had gone. But she still felt him in the air around her. In the child.

We shall manage somehow.

She drifted, saw herself waking on a summer morning in bed with John, their babe kicking its feet, as warm and fragrant as a kitten between them. Though of course the child would be older by then. In her dream, Philip Wentworth was the child's grandfather.

She woke the next morning with a sense of startled well-being. It was all still true. She did not have to die. She was to marry Master Wentworth instead. Soon she could carry John's child openly and rejoice in its birth. She would rebuild Hawkridge House to help fill the time.

She turned her cheek against the smoky pillow. Only seven years to be survived. With the child, and work, she could bear it now.

The ginger tom that John had given her as a kitten had found her in the night. It now rearranged itself against her feet with a thump of protest at being disturbed. She placated it by wiggling her toes while she tested the steadiness of her new humour. She threw back the covers. The paralysing spell of the last weeks had indeed lifted. Today, she would regain her grip and take command once more.

In her chemise and wrapped in a blanket, she sat at once at the office table and began to write.

Zeal's Work Book – October 1639

Salvage what we can from ruins, to rebuild with and clear the site

Borrow feather beds and blankets for winter sleeping

Set all maids to weave new blankets

Dry feathers in ovens to make new beds . . .

She raised her head while she thought what to write next.

If John had been there, he would have helped her with the list of tasks for the gardens.

He had left an old coat, hanging on a peg behind the door. Apart from his glove, the quill pen, and a few books and curiosities kept here in the office, all his other belongings had burned in the fire. She got up and put on the coat.

It was made of rough wool from their sheep, dyed brownish black with walnut skins. The sleeves hung down over her hands and the bottom of its skirts fell almost to her ankles. She raised her arm to her nose to sniff the sleeve and caught her breath sharply, then inhaled again. Through the smokiness, she thought she could smell the warm salty sweetness of his body. She ducked her head to sniff inside the coat. A miasma of his being inhabited it with her. She pulled it tightly around her and his child, rolled back the cuffs and began to write again.

Set hedges

Plant spinach, kale, purslain and poppies . . .

She imagined that he whispered in her ear.

. . . Set artichokes, strawberries and garlic cloves

Transplant leeks

Salve sheep against the scab . . .

Wait, she told him. I've just remembered something else.

Buy needles for sewing new clothes

Buy 20 ells of fine linen to make Christmas shirts for the women . . .

She set down the pen. She needed a morning to write it all. But it was a start.

Without Rachel's help, she did not try to put on the corset she had thrown last night onto the office table. In any case, it was filthy with soot. Still wearing John's coat, she set off for High House, to reassure Rachel that she had not disappeared for a second time, and to put on her working clothes. Then she would assess the possibilities for salvage.

8

She left her mare grazing nearby. Then she picked up her skirts and stepped through the charred brick doorway into what was left of Hawkridge House. The remains of the oak door looked like a crust of burnt toast.

The cat had refused to follow her and now sat outside on a piece of broken masonry in the pose of a heraldic beast, watching her with courteous disbelief.

Tuddenham had warned her that there might still, even three weeks later, be pockets of hot coals in the rubble. Crunching over the lumpy black landscape that had been the hall, she imagined that the soles of her shoes were growing hot, that her petticoats flared into flames and transformed her into a burning flower.

Her foot crushed what might once have been a stool leg. She stared down at the glistening black fragments, then at a puddle of dark oily water. Then at the jagged rim of a charred wall.

Here I once lovingly rubbed honey-scented beeswax onto the wooden panelling, she thought. Only three weeks ago.

In spite of her revived spirits, the blackened wreckage made her feel light-headed and queasy. She was not alone. Everyone on the estate still walked a little uncertainly, as if drunk or ill. They forgot simple things, would break off whatever they were doing and go to stand and stare at what was left of the house. They told each other the same stories again and again. How Master John had stamped out embers on the precipitous bake house roof. How fish had been carried up from the ponds in the fire-fighters' pails and fried by accident. How the children had brought rain by singing hymns, though not in time to save the great hall or long gallery. They compared how many inches of hair and beard had been singed off. They debated how the fire had started – which chimney might have held a bird's nest, which fire might have bred lethal sparks as so often happened, or whether malice, even, might have played a part. They wept suddenly without warning over trivial losses.

Near her right foot, a carved oak rosette fallen from the great staircase gleamed with buried fires like a crow's back. It looked solid, perfectly intact, but she knew that at the lightest touch, it would crumble to dust. For a moment, she froze, afraid to move. She felt that her whole life lay lost under this black, unfamiliar ruin. The shapes of the last three years, of her marriage to Harry, were fragile shells of ash.

The stairs and the dog-gate had burned. The upper landing hung like a black flap from the slanted floor of the upper hall. Her charred marriage bed had crashed through the floor into the back parlour, where it seemed to struggle to rise to its feet like a cow, hindquarters first. The massive headboard tilted. Black ribbons of the costly hangings that had so grati-fied Harry fluttered gently in the open air.

She could see past it right through the back wall of the house to the nymphs around the ponds. The cat now crouched in the grass studying the charred remains of a fish.

She looked back at the bed. Heard the hollow chomping of her mare, children shouting, cooing from the dovecote, the thump and slosh of a churn. A woman laughed loudly in the bake house. A creamy dove landed on the shoulder of one of the nymphs.

My life is not in ruins at all, she thought suddenly. Only my life with Harry has burned. All I have lost, in the end, is this house. Harry's house. The rest remains. So long as I am patient and steadfast. The child. John, who loves me. My people. My estate. Even the tribe of magnificent water spirits who so kindly look after three very ordinary fish ponds for me.

She took three crunching steps. Then she jumped and landed hard with both feet. Crunch, crunch. She walked to the bed and kicked it. A half-burned foot-post shivered into a shower of black chunks. She kicked again. Shattered the footboard. Stamped the fragments into dust. Burying Harry and his lies and his disdain for all her efforts to please him. She yanked down the shreds of the hangings in one succulent, gratifying rip.

So much for his ruinous extravagance!

She would abandon this ashy nothing entirely. Clear it all away and build a new house. Her own house, not Harry's.

Then she spied a gleam, pulled a diamond of unbroken glass from under a dusty black skeletal bench. She spat on it and rubbed with her thumb. When she held it up to the sky, a hot coin of sunlight fell on her cheek.

I will have such light in my new house, she thought. My house, which I shall build. Not Harry's. With great windows so that even on the darkest days we will be able to see clearly. Mistress Margaret will not need her spectacles except to sew.

With black hands and smuts on her face, she imagined the God-like act of creation. *Ex nihilo*. She would abandon this ashy nothing entirely, knock down everything but the chapel and fashion her own place on earth exactly as she wanted it, where she wanted it. A prodigy house, shaped by her own imagining, as some men built houses in the shape of their initials, or of a cross as witness to their faith.

She gazed at Hawk Ridge, rising beyond the fishponds and the Shir. All would be fit and in just proportion, echoing the vaster proportions of God's universe. Glass, brick, stone, timber, both seasoned and green. Tall, wide-eyed windows to let in the sun and scour away shadows. Generous fireplaces to heat every room, moulded fire-backs, drainpipes like young trees, friezes as rich in incident as ballads on subjects of her choosing. Lintels, columns, door panels, handles, the iron butterflies of hinges, nails. She was as ignorant as a pig about all of these, but she would learn. After all, the fourteen-year-old schoolgirl had learned to run an estate. Unexpectedly she had arrived on the safe, joyful solid ground of intense purpose.

Then it occurred to her to wonder what part Master Wentworth might want to play.

He won't want to do all that talking, she decided. To all those joiners and masons and painters and glaziers. He'll most likely be content to carry on fishing and leave it to me. She could almost love him just for keeping her alive to arrive in this moment.

The cat was back on its plinth, now curled as if asleep but green eyes watched her above the curve of its tail as she carried the glass windowpane across the rubble and laid it carefully on the grass. A watery shape rippled in its depths as her hand moved over it, like an oracle in a well.

When three boys raced towards her down the curve of the drive, Zeal raised her head without premonition or alarm.

9

'Horses coming, mistress!' Tuddenham's son, Will, spoke for the three of them. 'And ox carts.' All three boys pointed back up the drive towards the high road.

John has returned! Zeal thought, against reason, with a surge of suffocating joy. He never sailed! Doctor Bowler's prayers have been answered. The Lady Tree exerted her influence after all.

How will I tell Wentworth?

'Four carts . . .' 'No, three!' 'Four!'

Why would John have carts?

'Empty ones,' said one of the boys. 'And lots of men.'

'Are they soldiers?' she asked in alarm. 'Wearing insignia?'

The boys stared at each other in excited disagreement. Soldiers? Yes, no. But one of the gentlemen on horseback could have been an officer.

Best prepare for soldiers with requisition orders. And it won't matter which sort they are, they'll take, either way. Mustering and provisioning on the way north to fight the Scots, or come back without pay, hungry and filled with rage.

Rachel, her maid, appeared at the forecourt gate, which led to the bake house and stable block. 'Madam, did you know . . . ?'

Dogs began to bark.

'We must hide the food,' said Zeal.

She sent the two house grooms, Geoffrey and Peter, both just old enough for mustering, off to hide in the woods. They reeled away under the weight of six flitches of bacon each. Rachel and the dairywoman began to pack eggs and cheeses into baskets. Tuddenham sent half a dozen children to try to catch and hide the best laying hens. The horses had already been turned out into the Far. The beer would have to look after itself.

She sniffed her sleeve, which smelled of smoke like everything else. Her hands, and most likely face, were black with soot.

The first ox cart creaked out of the tunnel of beeches that lined the drive, followed by three more. All were ominously empty except for a half dozen small bundles, some tools, and what seemed to be long poles wrapped in canvas. Seven men, including the drivers. All strangers. Two muskets between them, but no pikes or swords that she could see. Nor armour, nor regimental badges.

Bailiffs, come to enforce the king's levies? They'll not find much worth taking.

Last out of the trees rode two horsemen, a richly dressed gentleman and his manservant. The gentleman kicked his mount forward and passed the first cart as it entered the forecourt.

Zeal knew this man far too well.

'He's back, madam,' Tuddenham announced glumly, as he arrived at her side. From his tone, he would have preferred soldiers.

The horseman peered down from his saddle with a near-comical mix of defiance and unease. His blue eyes slid away from hers.

Who else, in these circumstances, would leave his hat on and forget to dismount? 'Harry!' she said, sick with desolation.

'Madam.'

Sir Harry Beester, John's cousin and the former master of Hawkridge Estate. Zeal's former husband, or rather, husband who had never been.

So much for throwing off the past.

* * *

At fourteen, an orphaned heiress still sequestered at boarding school and with no experience of men, she had found Harry Beester's cheerful self-satisfaction to be charming. She had even imagined that some of his self-esteem might infect her and make up her lack of it. With a free heart she gave in to his ardent wooing. She chose his puppy-like youth and sunny good looks over the rather alarming, paunchy maturity of the two suitors urged on her by her guardian. Her formidable will, as much as Harry's inheriting and reconfirming of his uncle's title of baronet, along with a London house and two small country estates, had induced her guardian to overlook the young man's lack of both cash and mercantile connections. It was not Harry's fault that, in her inexperience, she had imagined that his stupidity would make him biddable.

How ignorant and wilful I was, she thought, looking up at him now, watching undisguised thought cross his handsome pink and white face. First, that she should have called him 'Sir Harry'. Then, that it probably wasn't worth making the point. Might, in fact, be dangerous.

To your dignity, my dear Harry, if to nothing else.

Tuddenham stared at his former master's costume in open disbelief.

To journey from London on horseback, Sir Harry had worn a deeply slashed crimson silk-velvet doublet over a fine linen shirt. In spite of the October chill, his boot hose were of silk, not wool, and topped with pale waves of Brussels lace (matching that on his soft falling-collar) which foamed around the hems of peach silk leg-of-mutton breeches. A black fur-lined cloak swung nonchalantly over one shoulder. More lace edged his gloves. A single pearl hung from his left ear and two long crimson foxtail plumes bounced behind his wide-brimmed felt hat. Though cape, trousers and lace were all spattered with mud, and though the plumes had begun to clump damply, Zeal read the intended message clearly. In spite of herself, she wished she had had time at least to wash.

'Is this just a friendly greeting in passing?' Zeal asked, 'or should we send to Sir Richard to set another plate?'

At last Sir Harry swung down from his horse and handed the reins to his new manservant. He glanced sideways at the ruined house, then averted his eyes. 'I have food and lodgings back at Ufton Wharf. Don't mean to stay long.'

'I didn't imagine that you were yearning for the rustic wilderness again.'

I chose this man of my own free will, she thought with amazement.

'I won't pretend,' he said. 'London suits me best.'

'And Lady Alice?' She had not meant to ask.

Sir Harry beamed. 'Splendid. Splendid woman. Thank you.' Then he caught himself and blushed.

'I'm sure she deserves you,' said Zeal.

Harry cleared his throat and looked around him. 'Tuddenham still serving you well?'

Zeal detected the hope that Tuddenham might not be. 'He's a splendid fellow!' She resisted the temptation to turn and catch the steward's eye.

'Good, good.' Sir Harry glanced around him once more.

'Harry,' said Zeal. 'Why have you come?' She might consider him a fool, and he might be just the least bit frightened of her, but he had already proved that he could be dangerous.

Mistress Margaret came from the bake house with a mug of beer, crossing the forecourt with the painfully stiffened gait that made her roll like a sailor. 'I suppose you'll want to rinse the dust from your mouth. Nothing fine, not like London. Take it or leave it, this is all we've got.'

Harry took the beer but eyed his aunt around the glass.

Curious faces began to fill the arch that led from the stable yard. 'Morning, sir,' called two or three voices.

'Can we walk apart?' he muttered to Zeal. 'I'd have thought they all need to be hard at work somewhere.'

'Anywhere in particular you'd care to go?' she asked. 'For old times' sake?'

He shook his head impatiently.

She led him through the trampled ruins of John's knot garden and around the chapel at the east end of the house. They walked in silence except for the sound of his boots crunching on the cinders still covering the ground until they reached the grassy slope above the fish ponds.

'I've come for the statues,' said Harry abruptly.

'No!'

'They're movables, you should know. My movables. Neptune and all his daughters.'

'You mean Nereus! And you can't take them. Not now!'

'I'm afraid I can.'

'But you deeded this estate to me. As the price of my warbling to your tune so you could go stalk your precious Lady Alice. You've had all my money. The estate is now mine.'

'You're welcome to the land and the house – or what's left of it. And the barns, sties and so on. The carts and ploughs . . . hardly need those in London. I even let you keep the animals, though I could have sold them all if my mood had been less kind.'

Or less frantic for your freedom to chase another, richer wife, she thought.

'But the movables were mine. And I count the statues as movables! In any case, you don't need them. What use do you have down here . . .' His sweeping hand brushed away the fields, the beech hanger, the ponds, the ruined house. '. . . for art?'

'As much as any Londoner.'

He sniffed in derision. 'Debate is pointless. I bought those figures and I'm taking them back. A wedding gift for Lady Alice, as a matter of fact.'

They reached the edge of the middle pond.

'Ha!' Harry pointed. 'Case proved! Finest Italian marble, bought from a friend of the king's own agent, and you use them as nesting boxes or to anchor fishing lines!'

Indeed, the line was still tied to Amphritite's wrist, while a duck now squatted on the nest Zeal had seen the day before between the feet of another nymph.

'Perhaps they find it peaceful here,' said Zeal. A shivery rage in her chest had begun to make it hard to breathe. 'Perhaps these ponds are more like their original home than a London courtyard surrounded by stench and noise.'

Arrived at the top pond, Harry stood with his head on one side and hands on hips beneath his open silk coat. 'You misunderstand. They're intended for Lady Alice's Bedfordshire estate. They'll have a garden worthy of them there.'

The old sea god, Nereus, seemed to list even farther forward than yesterday; his dolphin peered even more closely into the depths.

'My men will start at once, should finish tomorrow. Then I'll not trouble you again.'

Zeal lowered her voice to avoid being heard by the boy who passed them on his way to the dovecote in the paddock. 'This estate is all I have left. You've taken enough.'

'On the contrary, I believe I've been most generous. I rescued you from that Hackney hencoop, didn't I? Turned you from a dowdy little smock of a schoolgirl into a fashionable lady.' He pursed his lips in triumph at this wounding shot.

I've only myself to blame, she thought. Killing him now won't change that fact, however much satisfaction it would give me.

She turned away and walked along the bank.

'I spent nothing that wasn't legally mine,' Harry called after her. 'Mine in good faith, as your husband. At the time.'

She shook her head and kept walking away. He followed.

'You were happy enough to collude!' His voice quivered with emotion. 'I know how things stood between you and my cousin!'

'Never!' She turned on him. 'Never while it still suited you to admit to being my husband! And you know it!'

'I know nothing of the sort.'

They stood poised in murderous silence.

Harry recovered first. 'I don't mind anyway,' he said loftily. 'Couldn't care less. We're nothing to each other now, any more than we ever were. Let's let sleeping dogs lie, shall we?' He swung away from her towards the front of the house. 'Fox! Pickford! Here!'

To Zeal, he added, 'You perjured yourself just as I did. If you try to cause me trouble, I vow you'll come off the worse.'

Two of the carters arrived through an arch in the yew hedge at the west end of the house, near the top pond. Behind this hedge, John had planted a maze the previous summer. Both hedge and infant maze, though badly scorched, promised survival with a pale green frosting of the past summer's growth.

'Take Neptune first,' Harry told the men.

'I forbid it,' said Zeal.

The men exchanged startled glances. Then one looked into the distance, while the other studied his stockings.

A shilling-sized spot of red flared on each of Harry's cheeks. 'Carry on,' he said. He took Zeal by the arm and led her aside. 'Go read the deeds, if you've forgotten what they say.'

'I know what they say,' she said loudly. She yanked her arm free. 'And if you touch me again, I will kill you.' He was right. In law, she could not stop him. If only he had taken them at once and not left them to become part of her life.

Arms crossed, she perched on the corner of Amphritite's plinth and summoned up her most chilling basilisk eye, though she felt more like weeping.

With wary glances at Zeal, the two carters circled the statue of Nereus. They tested the mud at the base of the plinth with the heels of their boots. They sucked their teeth, shook their heads.

Zeal felt a twinge of hope. Nereus was eight feet tall and made of solid marble. He might choose to stay.

'Seven of you should be able to manage,' Harry said impatiently.

The one who turned out to be Fox went to fetch rein-
forcements.

Zeal followed him through the arch in the hedge. 'Don't
trample the maze!' she called sharply.

He soon returned, with thick coiled rope and a heavy
wooden pulley block, stepping carefully across the low maze
walls. Behind him came a youth with a younger version of
the same face, carrying a second rope and block. The youthful
Fox chose to follow the paths of the maze. He approached,
then suddenly veered away. He circled, turned again and at
last emerged with a triumphant grin, released back into the
unmeasured world. Behind him, three more men staggered
under the weight of the long canvas-wrapped poles. After a
brief conference, they elected, like the elder Fox, to play
colossus and bestride the complexities in their path. One of
them lost his balance and trod on a young box.

'Take care!' cried Zeal.

The men's burden proved to be three stout wooden poles,
each as long as a May Pole, wrapped in a canvas sling large
enough to lift a horse.

Several children and dogs followed the carters from the
forecourt. Some ran the path of the maze, others, like the
dogs, leapt over the walls. A dairymaid came up the track
from the mill, where she had no doubt gone to hide a basket
of cheeses.

With one eye on their audience and a touch of swagger,
the carters threaded one of the ropes through the pulleys and
tested that it ran freely. Then they linked the three poles
together at one end, and hoisted the linked end into the air.
Their audience gave a gratifying 'ahhhh,' as a great spindly
tripod rose above the head of Nereus and settled its feet in
the mud.

The carters next spread the canvas sling on the ground
beside the statue. Then they tied the pulley rope to Nereus's
thick bearded neck. They secured the second rope like a belt
around his dolphin's belly. Fox set four men on the taut ropes.

'Now.'

His son thrust a large jemmy under the plinth and dropped his weight onto the iron bar. The crowbar slipped in the soft mud of the bank. Young Fox grunted, fell against the dolphin's nose and swore.

'Take care not to chip him!' cried Sir Harry.

The old sea king did not budge.

'Perhaps he's not a movable after all!' called Zeal.

'He will yield to our machines, madam,' said the elder Fox. 'You can raise siege cannon with these sheer legs. A statue such as this is nothing.'

'What are they doing?' called Doctor Bowler in alarm, from the far side of the middle pond, book under his arm and a leaf in his fringe of hair.

'Giving us a lesson in how to raise cannon,' Zeal replied across the water.

The audience continued to gather. Four women of the house family, their hands busy with knitting needles or the quick rise-and-fall of drop spindles. More children. A tenant farmer and his son leaned over the hedge of the Roman Field. Ducks, never known to be sensitive to the moment, gathered on the water below the struggle and quacked to be fed. Even the cat watched from a neat hunch on the edge of the still house roof.

Young Fox sucked his bleeding knuckles.

'Bring on a grown man!' shouted one of the onlookers. The young carter gave him an evil look.

Under his breath Harry asked Zeal, 'Can't you find useful employ for these idlers elsewhere?'

'What could be more useful than a chance to observe and learn from London men at work?' Zeal replied sweetly.

Pickford took the crowbar. Young Fox was set on the end of the restraining rope. But after several more attempts, Nereus still stood unmoved.

'Fetch a shovel,' said Pickford.

'If to labour is indeed to pray,' observed Doctor Bowler,

now crossed over the sluice bridge to join the crowd, 'these must be the most devout men in England.'

Suddenly, Wentworth's voice asked quietly in Zeal's ear, 'Can Harry do this?'

'He has the right.' She made a helpless gesture. 'But I'm happy to say that whether he can still seems to be in question.' She looked over her shoulder at Wentworth. 'You left your fishing for this?'

'You might need me.'

She did not look at him again but felt him still standing at her back. His words made her feel odd and needed thinking about at some other time.

After a short break for dinner, which they took from their bundles on the carts, the carters dug away the mud from under the forecourt side of the plinth. Five men pushed. At last, Nereus consented to give way, as reluctantly as a deep-rooted tooth. Slowed by the two ropes, he tilted ponderously onto his side in the centre of the sling, with his head hanging over one long edge and his feet over the other.

'Don't break the dolphin's nose!' shouted Harry.

'He looks just like a sausage pasty,' said one of the boys. The rest of the on-lookers, fewer in number than before dinner, seemed torn between groans and a natural instinct to cheer.

'Now fill the hole you've made in the bank,' said Zeal. 'I recall no mention anywhere of a legal right to dig holes.'

Harry ignored her, but Pickford gave the shovel to young Fox.

'Now back one of the carts down here to the pond,' ordered Harry.

'How?' Zeal stood up from the corner of Amphritite's plinth, where she had stayed on guard during the dinner break.

From the arch in the hedge, Fox and Harry contemplated the maze. Then Fox set off towards the forecourt, traversing the maze with exaggerated care. A few moments later he reappeared with a measuring rod, which he held against the opening in the hedge.

'We can't get a cart down to the pond in any case, sir. It's too wide to pass through this arch.'

'Then cut down the hedge.'

'That right is not given in the deed,' said Zeal.

Harry turned to the estate manager. 'Tuddenham, bring us that bill you had earlier, and three others, and an axe. The hedge is already ruined. And no one has mazes any longer, in any case.'

'Tuddenham, please do nothing of the sort.' To Harry, she added, 'I have a maze.'

The watchers shifted in anticipation of new drama.

With an oath, Harry seized the nearest boy by the arm. 'Come, my lad. You show us where the things are kept!' He dragged the boy towards the stable yard, with carters hopping over the maze walls behind him.

Wentworth cleared his throat.

Zeal called a second boy and sent him to fetch her neighbour Sir Richard Balhatchet. 'Beg him to make the greatest possible haste. For our part, we must hold them off until he arrives.'

Wentworth touched her arm. 'Do you recall what you asked me yesterday morning?'

She and he arrived back on the pond bank just as Harry's men returned with four billhooks and an axe. When Harry gave the order to attack the hedge, Zeal produced Wentworth's pistol from the folds of her skirts.

'Shit!' said Pickford under his breath.

Harry was the only one to laugh. 'She won't shoot,' he told his men. 'Carry on.'

There was a long uneasy silence. Zeal leaned against Amphritite and braced her arm, which had begun to tremble under the weight of the gun. She aimed first at Fox. Then at his son. Then at Pickford.

Pickford scratched his neck and sat down. The others looked from her to Harry and back again. They laid down their billhooks.

Zeal watched Harry eye the tools as if considering even the gross impropriety of taking up one himself.

'The law is on my side, madam,' said Harry. 'I shall call for a constable if you don't let us proceed.'

'Better than that, I've already sent for a magistrate.'

After examining the deed, which Zeal kept in a casket in the estate office, Sir Richard was forced to agree that Sir Harry did indeed have the right to remove the statues. But, on the other hand, Sir Richard also had to agree with Zeal that Harry could not cut down either hedge or maze.

'That's absurd!' Sir Harry reached over Sir Richard's shoulder to take the deed for a closer look. 'What am I supposed to do?' He threw his arms to the Heavens in protest.

'Mind the candlestick on the mantle,' Zeal said quietly.

'This is a madhouse!'

'Let me see that deed again.' Sir Richard frowned at the document as if it would yield something it had failed to say before. Zeal wondered if the old knight had simply forgotten what it said. His once-keen mind had seemed to lose its edge quite suddenly, early that past summer, and his memory had begun to misplace things.

'Most definitely can't cut the hedge,' said Sir Richard.

'Then how am I to take possession of what is lawfully mine?' demanded Harry. 'Perhaps Doctor Bowler would care to pray for a miracle . . . should be easier to move hedges than mountains.'

They trooped out of the estate office back into the forecourt, where the carters, Wentworth, Bowler, Mistress Margaret and the others waited with faces ranging from expectant to glum.

'Legal niceties!' said Sir Harry bitterly. 'All law and no justice!' To Fox, he said, 'You're going to have to figure out how to get the statues without going through there.'

Sir Richard lowered his massive head and glared at Harry through his eyebrows. The carters examined the entrance to the paddock to the west of the maze garden.

'Can't get a wagon through over here, either.'

Beyond the paddock, stretching up to the high road, lay the hedge of the Roman field, reinforced with stones and willow hurdles set to try to stem the constant leaking of sheep. The stable yard and walled garden blocked access around the eastern end of the house.

'I'm taking those statues, and I don't care how!' said Harry. 'I'll stay until someone works it out.'

'An ox without a cart could reach the ponds through the paddock.'

Heads turned towards this unexpected voice. Harry looked startled, as if he had not known the man could speak at all. Indeed, given Wentworth's absence from table during Harry's short time on the estate, perhaps he had never before heard the older man utter. 'You can't drag a statue across the ground like a plough.' Nevertheless, Harry eyed Wentworth with hope.

'The Indians of the New World shift blocks of stone twenty times greater than that statue, without even horses, let alone oxen or carts.'

'Pray, enlighten us,' said Harry.

Though she was curious to hear Wentworth's solution, Zeal went to see Sir Richard off on his horse.

'A word in your ear, young mistress,' the old knight murmured as he prepared to mount. 'Keep an eye on that Fox man. Wanted me to have you arrested for threatening him with a gun. I told him not to be a fool, that you wouldn't hurt a fly. What a business!'

When Zeal returned, the carters were prising planks from sides of two of the carts.

'I've no doubt, sir, that you'll pay me to replace the sides of my carts,' Fox said to Sir Harry.

'I'll pay you if you ever manage to do the job you're contracted to do.'

'Four will be enough,' Wentworth told the men. The reclusive fisherman had assumed authority with apparent ease.

The carters obeyed him without question.

'Imagine him knowing about things like New World Indians,' said one of the knitters. 'Or talking so much,' said another.

As he gave orders, Zeal observed her future husband with increasing interest and surmise. *I must ask him more about those Indians.* She was looking forward to his wedding gift of truth even if she avoided thinking about any of the rest of it.

On Wentworth's instruction, the carters led one of the draught oxen through the paddock. Then they laid the four cart planks on the ground, end to end in pairs, beside the recumbent statue.

'You haul him up . . .' Fox pointed at the two men on the pulley rope. '. . . then you lot over there swing him over the planks, crosswise, mind. Then you . . .' he pointed at the first pair again '. . . let him down again, nice and easy. Ready?'

The men settled their feet and drew deep breaths.

'Heave!' cried Fox.

Nereus did not wish to be heaved. Instead, his weight drove the feet of the poles down into the mud. The harder the men tried to lift, the deeper they drove the poles into the ground.

'I did say,' said Pickford. 'Straight off. Soon as I saw all this mud.'

'God's Teeth and Toenails!' cried Sir Harry.

'I've never had such trouble, ever before!' exclaimed Fox. His scowl included Zeal in the trouble. 'The thing acts as if it's been cursed!'

Doctor Bowler began to sing quietly as if to himself.

The sun was sinking, orange as a pumpkin beyond the water meadows.

'"To labour is the lot of Man below,"' sang Doctor Bowler. '"When God gave us life, he gave us woe."'

'Put something flat under the feet,' said Fox. 'Is there anything about that we can use?' He looked around for Wentworth, who had seemed to be the only sensible authority, but Wentworth had gone.

'Leave the wretched thing till tomorrow!' Harry wiped his face and jammed his tasselled handkerchief back into a slash in his sleeve. 'We soon won't be able to see the road back to Ufton Wharf.' He glared at Zeal. 'If anything is taken or harmed, I shall have you indicted for theft and wilful damage. In spite of your tame magistrate.'

If I were a man, I could call him out, thought Zeal as she watched Harry ride away up the drive, leaving Nereus abandoned on his sling. Now there's a grand thought! Rapiers, not guns. Snick, snick, snick. Cut off his buttons. Whisht! Whisht! There go the bows from his shoes! Whisht! And a tassel from his handkerchief! And he'd never touch me. Not even close! With enough people watching such humiliation, I wouldn't even need to draw blood.

After a quick supper at the long table in the bake house, Zeal slept in the estate office again, to be on the spot in the morning in case Harry arrived early. With John's coat beside her, she yanked the smoky coverlet up to her chin and imagined setting her grooms on him with clubs. She would borrow Sir Richard Balhatchet's old falconet, which he had recently had cleaned and made fit to fire.

Then she heard again the danger in Harry's voice when he warned her against opposing him. He might be a fool, but he was a fool with powerful friends and infinite self-esteem.

Why do I care so much? she asked herself. They're only stone!

Her feet were now cold. She crawled to the end of the makeshift bed and tucked the coverlet in again, then banged her head ferociously back into the pillow. She still did not know how to deal with the hole where a piece of her life had been excised and then declared officially never to have existed.

'We must find a way out!' Harry had said one night on one of his rare and brief returns from London. He wore a grim but shifty look that told her he had already decided how to get his way.

'From our marriage?' She dared not hope that he meant to set her free. 'But you need an Act of Parliament to be granted a divorce!'

'Don't be a fool! Do you confuse me with old King Harry? I don't have that much influence yet.'

'But given another wife, with grander connections, you mean to get it?' she taunted him. 'Lady Alice, whose fortune you have not yet spent.'

But, oh, how she had snapped at his bait!

The fleck of decency in Harry's soul, which Zeal had once mistaken for a far larger portion, was the cause, ironically, of her fall into the crime of perjury. Harry had a mutually advantageous plan. If she would collude to dissolve their marriage, he would give her Hawkridge Estate.

She rolled onto her side, then onto her back again. The ash still in the coverlet made her sneeze.

Their bargain gave him the freedom to trade Hawkridge for Covent Garden and to pursue London heiresses with larger fortunes than Zeal had ever had. It left her free to love Harry's cousin, John Nightingale.

She turned her head to look at John's stool and table. Then she reached out to touch the smooth polished dent at the base of one of the stool legs where he had always rested the heel of his right foot.

She would have sworn to anything.

She had sworn under oath that she had been younger than the legal age of fourteen when she and Harry were betrothed, which could well have been true. She also lied and swore that the marriage had never been consummated – for, who but Harry and she could ever prove otherwise? Particularly as the lack of issue was commonly taken as sufficient proof in such cases. Zeal's guardian, who, by her marriage, lost all interest in either her or her fortune (now squandered by Harry, in any case), had been happy to testify that she had married against his wishes, as indeed she had. In the end, there had been almost excessive grounds for voiding the marriage and rewriting two years of her life.

As always, her head began to throb at this point. Now came the part she could consider only sideways.

Annulment meant that the marriage had never been. Therefore, if, as it had been ruled, Harry had never been her legal husband, then he had never had the right to spend her fortune. He had, nevertheless, gone through it all (and, of course, he really had been her husband all along).

Almost worse, she had never been Lady Beester, no matter what she had believed at the time. She had not had the legal right to fall in love with Hawkridge, nor to delight in its gardens or the charming irregularity of its outline or the ornate chimneys, the unexpected hens' nests, the dusty cupboards full of other people's lives. She had had no right to feel full and warm, as she moved about the house, her house now, aflame with domestic purpose.

Orphaned at six, she lived thereafter with relatives, with guardians or at boarding school. At Harry's Hawkridge, she thought she had finally found her proper place on earth. She still felt as if she had missed a step in the stairs and wasn't at all where she had thought she was, and was sick with the shock and unexpected pain.

Outside the little office window, birds were beginning to shout out their territorial claims. The sky had just begun to lighten. Not much night left. She put one of her pillows over her head to muffle the birds and tried to think how to set about building a new house.

10

Sir Harry and the carriers returned an hour after what would have been sun-up if the sky had not been a chilly grey. The weather, as well as erosion of novelty, led to a thinner audience than the day before. Also, the smokehouse needed tending and there was the autumn ploughing, bread to bake, the butchering of a ewe that had crippled itself, and arranging warm lodgings to see them all through the winter.

The carters brought flat stones to place under the feet of the tripod to keep them from sinking into the mud. But when the ox began to drag Nereus along the track of planks, the dolphin's nose dug into the ground and acted as a brake.

Once she had grasped the principle of Wentworth's method, Zeal left the men grunting and puffing in their effort to roll the old god onto his other side. Back in the office, she began to list all the different building parts she had envisioned with such delight the morning before, and the stuffs needed to make them. This morning, however, she found the work tedious.

She had imagined a house built of brick.

Therefore, I know I will need bricks. But will it be less costly to buy them or to hire men from Southampton to enlarge our own kiln? Need . . . dear Lord . . . how many thousand? How do I work it out?

I'm not sure I can do this alone, after all, she thought. Do you suppose Master Wentworth knows about houses, as well as about New World Indians?

The carters reached the forecourt. Unable to keep her mind on her great purpose, she went out to watch the final lifting of the old sea god onto the cart. On the firm footing of the forecourt the sheer legs and pulleys worked perfectly. The surrender was easily achieved by only three men.

Amphritite was next. Her fishing line had vanished during the night. As she stood on relatively dry ground, the traitorous nymph, unlike her father, yielded easily to her abductors.

'We'll be done by evening, after all.' Fox sounded greatly cheered.

Zeal returned to the office. Then she had to confer with Mistress Margaret in the bake house kitchen about collecting more urine for soap making. She could not help walking back to the ponds. Unlike her sister, Panope resisted until just before dinner. After dinner, although the carters had begun to get the measure of both subjects and terrain, they shifted only Galatea, Psamanthe and the last three nymphs on the near side of the ponds. Eight more waited on the opposite banks. Harry left in a vile temper for a second night at Ufton Wharf, where the barges were moored, at his expense.

Unhappily, Zeal examined the muddy track that the ox's hoofs had churned up across the grass of the paddock.

By the third morning, the battle had lost all novelty for the estate residents. Also, a slow, depressing drizzle had begun to seep down from the sky. Wherever she was, however, Zeal could still hear Sir Harry shouting from his shelter under the rear portico, and the curses of his workmen out in the rain. She felt paralysed by his presence. Life on the estate was frozen so long as he was still here. More than anything, she now wanted him gone for good.

The rain stopped in mid-afternoon. A warm clammy wind blew down the river valley and tugged dying leaves from the trees.

'Only two more to go,' said Sir Harry as they left for yet another night at Ufton.

Fox said something under his breath.

*   *   *

Mid-morning the next day, shouts and splashing sent her running out to the ponds.

Only one nymph remained – Thetis, mother of heroes and nest guardian. The muddy berm where she stood, at the far end of the pike pond just above the weir, was too narrow to give the feet of the sheer legs a firm base. When the statue finally toppled, the leather loop holding the sling to the lifting rig snapped. She now lay on her back with an arm raised in mute protest, her right hand snapped off at the wrist.

Young Fox was searching among the lily pads, ducking his head under the surface, then lifting it to gasp and splutter.

'Mind the pike!' a boy warned. 'They'll bite your fingers off! They nearly ate my baby brother's whole foot!'

'Farewell at last?' Zeal asked, in the early afternoon. 'Or will you be back when you suddenly remember something else you want to give your new bride?'

'Your manners have not improved with time.' Harry swung up into his saddle, then leaned back down to her. 'I have influence in London now, mistress, so don't challenge me.' He turned and kicked his horse so savagely that she had to jump back out of the way of its swinging rump. 'And when you get around to draining the pond, I want that hand!'

Zeal resolved to have the fish man rescue it as soon as Harry had gone.

As his cart passed her, Fox made a sign against the evil eye.

When the last cart had gone, she went to the ponds and scuffed her foot on one of the bare mud patches on the banks. Hawkridge felt deserted. There was too much raw empty air around the ponds.

She watched the fish man groping in the mud of the pike pond.

The duck's nest lay smashed on the side of the bank.

The day had chilled. The sky was turning a purplish-black.

There's a storm coming, Zeal thought as she turned back towards the office, carrrying Thetis' wet marble hand. If

Nature weeps for the sorrows of men, the present sky must reflect my desire to give Harry a black eye. Nature was not usually so sympathetic nor obliging, no matter what the philosophers might say.

In her ignorance of what was to come, she found the thought entertaining.

The news reached Hawkridge long after dark. A short time later, Sir Richard came out of the night, looking both irascible and miserable. Zeal went to meet him.

'Trust him to wreck a man's sleep!' he said as he handed over his horse. 'Well, my dear. What a business! Best get it over and done with.'

Mistress Margaret had long ago gone to bed in Sir Richard's house. The group which gathered solemnly in the bake house included Zeal, Rachel, Sir Richard, Tuddenham, a man named Herne, who was the current parish constable, another named Comer, who was a parish councilman, and Doctor Gifford, the parish minister. Fox and Pickford stood uneasily to one side, looking at the floor, while Zeal studied them in perplexed astonishment.

Sir Richard had just cleared his throat to begin when Wentworth, with his odd new taste for appearing, entered and set his rod beside the door.

'What is this I hear?'

'The self-satisfied pup has gone and got himself killed,' said Sir Richard.

'Harry's dead,' said Zeal. 'And these two here say I did it.'

11

'Smashed his head like it was a ripe melon,' said Fox. 'On a rock.'

'Speak when I ask you.' Sir Richard flipped his coattail over a stool and sat down at the bake house table. 'You stand there.' He waved Fox forward. 'Now, then.'

Given the late hour, he had decided to hold his preliminary inquiry in the Hawkridge bake house rather than shift the entire company back to his little courtroom at High House. Zeal found a half dozen precious beeswax candles to lend dignity to the background of dough bowls and ovens. The air was warm from the banked fires and fragrant with the scent of the day's baking. Pale cloth-covered loaves sat in orderly rows on shelves behind Sir Richard's head.

'I'm sure we're all grateful to be brought the news in such unparalleled haste,' said Sir Richard. 'But I'm still not certain why you feel the matter is so urgent it can't wait till morning.'

'Murder seemed urgent to us, sir,' said Fox. 'And Sir Harry was murdered.'

'By his horse?' asked Sir Richard. 'I was told you arrived saying Sir Harry's horse had thrown him. You're not under oath yet, but take care.'

'It threw him because she charmed it.' With averted eyes, Fox tilted his head at Zeal, who had perched on a stool at the far end of the table.

Sir Richard glanced to his left at Doctor Gifford, fierce-eyed and eager to sit in judgement, even at this hour. He glanced to his right at Geoffrey Comer, who had the misfortune to be the nearest parish councillor, and sighed. 'When I was dragged from my bed, I expected an urgent legal matter. If this case has any substance at all, the issue is witchcraft, and it should go to the church courts. Or else the whole thing might be a load of buffle.' He regarded Fox through his eyebrows as he had studied Harry earlier. 'I hope for your sake that you're not wasting my time.' He raised a hand to quell an urgent movement from Doctor Gifford, the minister. 'You'll get your turn, sir.' Sir Richard turned back to Fox. 'Are you formally accusing our young mistress here of causing Sir Harry's death by witchcraft?'

Fox hesitated.

Herne, the constable, began to stare at Zeal with an open mouth.

'Or by any other means?' asked Sir Richard.

'More like raising the possibility, sir. We thought you might . . .'

'Oh, just the "possibility" . . .' Sir Richard rocked back meditatively on his stool then slammed the front legs down again. 'Why?'

'Sir?'

'Why rouse a magistrate, a minister and a parish councillor in order to "raise a possibility"?'

'Justice, your honour. And also, we've already been away from London much longer than we contracted for. So, if we are to be witnesses at the inquest on Sir Harry . . .'

'Don't think for a moment you will be,' said Sir Richard.

Pickford had been breathing audibly. Now he stepped forward. 'Please, your honour. That woman threatened to kill Sir Harry. "I'll kill you," she said. Everyone heard her. And all the time we were here, she showed herself to be a wild and dangerous woman . . .'

'Dear me.' Sir Richard turned his head to gaze at Zeal. 'Did you know you were dangerous, my dear?'

She shook her head dumbly. These men and their accusation were absurd. On the other hand, if you were angry enough, perhaps your rage might shape itself into an independent being, a spirit, like a ghost, and act on your behalf without your permission.

I was very angry with Harry. Is it possible that I did somehow will his death?

'You may laugh, sir,' said Pickford. 'But we know she set the evil eye on us when all we did was obey Sir Harry's orders to remove the statues. Call the others and ask them. We all felt it.'

Zeal rubbed her hand across her mouth. She had no idea that her glares had been so effective.

'And no one can deny she threatened to shoot us, just for trying to do our job. And us with only a shovel to defend ourselves.'

'You forget that I was present . . . Just one moment, Doctor Gifford, I beg you!'

'She killed him in revenge for him taking the statues back.' Pickford looked defiant. 'It's too much coincidence. Evil eye. She threatened him and then he died. Think about it.'

'Thank you. I hadn't planned to.' Sir Richard scratched his earlobe and studied Zeal's accusers in silence, until she began to fear that he was having one of his lapses.

Surely these comical men could not make real trouble for her.

'I'm not clear on one or two points.' Comer seized the opening, just before Gifford, who was leaning back on his stool, shaking his head in impatient dismay. 'Was Mistress Zeal present when Sir Harry died?'

'No, sir.'

'Was she anywhere nearby?'

'No, sir.'

'Did she at any time approach his horse while it was at Hawkridge in order to tamper with it?'

'Not so far as I know.'

'But she killed him nevertheless, at a distance, by subverting his horse?' Sir Richard stepped in again, back in full flow.

'Such things happen,' said Fox defiantly. 'Ask the minister there.'

'You all are missing the true wickedness,' said Gifford. 'If you will but allow me . . .'

Sir Richard snorted. 'There was a storm tonight? Yes? While you were on the road?'

'An uncanny one, sir,' agreed Fox. 'Blue sky one minute, lightning and hail the next. Lightning filled the sky like noon. Even our own beasts gave a start and offered to bolt. Not usual lightning. It was yellowish, like sulphur. Not your usual lightning at all. If you follow me.'

'I detect the Lord's hand,' said Doctor Gifford. 'Sir Harry was struck down like the Canaanites who worshipped heathen idols.'

'But these fellows don't seem to be raising the pos-si-bi-li-ty . . .' Sir Richard seemed to examine each syllable in turn. '. . . that He had anything to do with it. More like the other one, if anything.' He turned to Zeal. 'My dear, how do you plead? Care to throw yourself on the mercy of the court?'

'I did not have anything to do with Harry's death,' Zeal said quietly. 'We all speak more fiercely than we could ever act. I am sorry that he died . . . I don't quite believe it yet, if you must know. And I never meant to shoot anyone. Only to keep Harry and these men from taking the law into their own hands before Sir Richard could arrive and sort things out.'

'Hnmph!' Sir Richard nodded with satisfaction.

Comer leaned forward again. 'But you did threaten to shoot unarmed men? That is an offence in itself.'

'The gun is rusted solid,' said Wentworth suddenly from the wall where he had been leaning with crossed arms. 'I gave it to her. It hasn't been fired for twenty-three years.'

'Did she know this?' asked Comer, who struck Zeal as a reasonable man and surprisingly good-natured, given that he, like Sir Richard had been called from his bed.

'Of course. I dare say she wouldn't have touched it otherwise,' said Wentworth.

Comer and Sir Richard laughed. Zeal bristled but saw the wisdom of keeping quiet.

'Well, gentlemen.' Once again Sir Richard looked at his two colleagues. 'These two don't want to make a formal accusation. I see no need to clog up the courts with "possibility". Where are the rest of your number, by the way? They less keen to see justice done?'

'Went on with the statues to London, sir,' said Fox. 'To deliver as ordered. And Sir Harry. But, if you want him back, we can always . . .'

Sir Richard cut across him. 'I shall, of course, report this meeting to the inquest, wherever it's held, but the coroner will undoubtedly conclude what seems clear to me – that Sir Harry died by misadventure – horse startled by lightning and so on. Or maybe, as Doctor Gifford says, he got a clout on the ear from God. If anything changes, I shall let you know. Good night to you all. I'm off back to my bed.' He levered himself to his feet. 'As for you two, if I hear of you still in the parish tomorrow morning, I'll clap you up as vagrants.'

'There is also the question of our wages,' said Fox.

'At last we come to the nub,' said Sir Richard. He leaned on the table with exaggerated patience. 'Speak.'

'We did our part as contracted. Sir Harry hadn't paid us when he died. The statues came from Hawkridge estate. And then my carts . . . That gentleman over there ordered them wrecked . . .'

'Get out!' bellowed Sir Richard. 'Herne! Tuddenham! See them off the estate.'

The two men gave Zeal wide berth as they fled.

'Londoners!' exclaimed Sir Richard before the door had quite closed.

'I must have my turn to speak!'

The trumpet of Gifford's voice arrested the general surge of rising, adjusting clothes and preparing to leave. Zeal pulled back her hand from pinching out one of the candle flames.

The minister gathered them up with a penetrating gaze as

he did his congregation before commencing a sermon, his fierce presence far greater than warranted by his small size. 'No one has yet named the true wickedness in this case!' He pointed a knobbed forefinger at Zeal while his eyes probed her soul. 'Mistress, you may not have murdered Sir Harry, but you still must be chastised for your true crime.'

Zeal inhaled sharply and sat down on her stool again. He has sniffed out the fornication, she thought. Those eyes of his can see that I'm pregnant.

She knew without doubt that her guilt was both infinite and written clearly on her face.

'She already knows what I will say!' cried Gifford in triumph. 'Look at the knowledge in her face!'

'Knowledge of what?' she managed to ask.

Gifford shook his head as if in pain at her mendacity. 'I do not doubt that your former husband was struck down by a righteous God for his prime part in it, but you too must share the blame!'

He knows about the perjury! She felt she might faint.

He knows that the annulment was a fraud. He knows everything.

She gripped the sides of her stool and braced herself upright.

'When, like Moses, madam, you see that your people worship idols, you must do as he did and take those abominations and burn them in the fire, and grind them into powder and strew that upon the water and make the people drink of it.'

Zeal stared, trying to make sense of his words. Idols? Was I spied at the Lady Tree? Does he want me to chop down the tree?

'You know what I speak of, madam. Don't pretend.' The pointing finger stabbed at her across the width of the table. 'You have tolerated abomination! As for your parson, I am dismayed that he did not counsel you like a Christian. I hold him, too, responsible.'

'Doctor Bowler is guilty as well?' Zeal managed to ask at last.

'The statues, madam! Graven images! Lewd, naked, heathen idols, standing there for all to see. Sir Harry may have set them up, but I expected you to tear them down as soon as he took his authority away with him.'

'The statues?' Zeal swallowed and took a deep breath to hold down a belch of hysterical laughter. 'This is all about Nereus and the nymphs?' In spite of her effort at self-control, she hiccuped.

'"And the smoke of their torment ascendeth up forever and ever and they have no rest day nor night who worship the beast and his image." Are heathen idols not wickedness enough for my concern?'

'I did not think of them as idols, Doctor Gifford. Nor, I'm sure, did Sir Harry. They are works of art. Representations of abstract beauty and the wholesome ideas of nature, as given form by the Classical authorities . . .'

'"Woe unto them who call evil good, and good evil."'

Zeal sighed with frustration and looked about for assistance. Sir Richard was studying the ceiling.

'The only authority you must study is God's Holy Word,' added Gifford.

'Doctor Bowler says that Man creates beauty only to glorify God. He will quote you scripture to prove that God delights in . . .'

'Bowler!' Gifford said in a surge of fury. 'That false man of God who pollutes your worship with *music*! And flowers! And all the other vain deceptions of the world! He is not a man of God, merely an obscene . . . fiddler!'

'"Make a joyful noise unto the Lord,"' replied Zeal.

'I hold Bowler responsible for this young woman's sins,' Gifford told Sir Richard and Comer. 'She is still young and ignorant while he is . . .'

'I'll be responsible for my own sins,' Zeal interrupted.

'Madam.' Gifford collected himself. 'A masterless woman

is always at risk in this wicked world. Under no man's rod, who knows how she may err? Your own words prove my case. I must keep you under my eye from now on. I shall impose no penance this time, but you and all your people must henceforward attend my church at Bedgebury.'

'We worship very well here.'

'I think not. I shall expect you for all services. And all the estate workers.'

'But that's impossible! We're over-busy here, with winter coming, and the house . . . Your church is half an hour's walk away. We will do nothing else but traipse back and . . .'

'All of you, at all services, including morning prayers.' Gifford began to button his coat. 'I won't let you continue to risk your eternal soul, nor the souls of those who look to you for example. You have no husband or father to guide you. I must therefore take their place.'

'That's most decent of you.' Wentworth spoke for a second time. He sounded entirely sincere. His dusty black coat rustled as he stepped away from the wall. 'Perhaps a compromise might be found, which would allow for the pressure of work.'

Zeal thought that perhaps the surprise and interest that had greeted his earlier demonstrations of speech were now touched by irritation that the man was putting himself forward out of turn.

'Have we met?' Gifford asked coldly. 'I don't believe I've ever seen you in church.'

'Don't be an ass,' said Sir Richard, who had listened to Gifford with open mouth and raised brows. 'That's Master Philip Wentworth, the Hawkridge sojourner. Been in the parish twice as long as you. Full of ingenious ideas. You can thank him for getting rid of those heathen idols we didn't know enough to grind up into powder.'

'What is your compromise, Master Wentworth?' Gifford's tone softened by a degree.

'If you abate the schedule of attendance, I will undertake to be this woman's guide.' Wentworth crossed to stand behind

Zeal's stool and laid his large square hands on her shoulders. 'I can vouchsafe for her future behaviour. The ship no longer lacks a rudder. She is to be my wife.'

Zeal sat frozen with the weight of his hands on her shoulders and the heat of his belly against her back.

Sir Richard broke the silence with a violent coughing fit. When Comer had thumped him on the back and offered a handkerchief to mop his eyes, words began to emerge between the splutters. '. . . old dog. Lucky old bastard!' He straightened. 'My congratulations!' He blew his nose. 'Suppose I'll have to arrange a bridal chamber at High House then. Can't have your wedding night in a barn!'

Graciously, if tentatively, Gifford offered his own congratulations. 'I shall marry you in Bedgebury, it goes without saying.'

Wentworth gave Zeal a warning look. She kept silent while Wentworth and Gifford at last agreed that the Hawkridge attendance at his services in Bedgebury could be limited to one Sunday a month.

'I would have touched the gun!' Zeal said tightly to Wentworth when Gifford, Comer and Sir Richard had gone. 'I would have fired it if I could!'

'Of course.' He gave her a conspiratorial smile. 'But never confess anything in the presence of a judge.'

12

'Tell me the old sot was raving in his cups!'

Zeal was alone in the bake house the next morning blearily eating a slice of cheese with her morning ale when Mistress Margaret arrived breathless and alone, on foot from High House. The sun was barely up. The ovens were still banked.

Mistress Margaret lowered herself onto a stool and wiped her red face with her apron. 'Tell me you are not going to marry that old man!'

'You heard this before dawn?' Zeal picked up a knife. 'Bread?'

She had not slept.

'Not dawn. In the middle of the night! Sir Richard was roaring around as drunk as an owl till he keeled over at cock-crow . . . Give that old loaf to the hens. I'm about to bake more . . . I haven't slept since I heard about Harry, and then that other nonsense Sir Richard was spouting.' Mistress Margaret had loved her nephew John fiercely.

Zeal kept her head down as she began to cube the stale bread. 'It's all true.'

Mistress Margaret squeaked like a small rusty hinge. She got up and took the yeast sponge from the oven where it had been rising overnight along with a bowl of water. Still silent, she beat down the puffy yeast mix with a wooden spoon, measured flour by the hand full, mixed all together. Her amethyst ear drops trembled.

Zeal swept the bread cubes and crumbs into the hens' basket, then stooped to feed the sleeping fire under the first bread oven.

'I don't understand,' said Mistress Margaret at last. 'If you love my nephew as you claim, how can you bolt to the altar before his ship has scarce cleared the horizon?' She turned the dough out onto the floured tabletop and attacked it with both fists. She pinched her small mouth, then sniffed angrily. 'I expected better of you, my girl.'

'I'm sorry.'

Mistress Margaret turned the dough and slapped it, though not as hard as she might have done before the knuckles of her hands had grown swollen and red. She worked for several minutes with her head down. 'I'm not sure I can live here if Wentworth becomes master. Even if he deigns to permit me. But where can I go? How can you do this to me, at my age?'

Can't she see what's before her eyes? Zeal wondered. Even if she's never carried a child herself? Rachel guessed.

She ached to tell the older woman, but Mistress Margaret had kept a secret just once in her life, and then only when her nephew's life had depended on it. 'I won't let him turn you out, aunt. In any case, our lives won't change that much. He has no ambitions beyond his fishing. We shall carry on just as before.'

Fiercely, the older woman pressed down on the dough, folded and turned it then pressed down again. The smell of raw yeast began to fill the air. 'I had thought – at the worst, if it came to it – that you might have to make a business-like marriage to bring in some money to help run and repair the estate. And pay our Crown levies. But all Master Wentworth can settle on you is a bucket of trout! And not even his own trout, at that! Most likely *your* trout! The old wrinkle-shanks!' She thumped the dough again and raised her voice. 'And I don't care if he hears me!'

She paused as one of the dairymaids staggered in from the cow barn with two full pails. Together the three women lifted the heavy pails to pour the milk into a shallow lead sink rescued from the dairy house, so that the cream could rise to the top for skimming.

'The churn Mistress Wilde lent us from Far Beeches needs to be scoured and set to dry in the sun,' Zeal told the maid.

'Waste!' muttered Mistress Margaret, pummelling her dough again.

Zeal began to pump the bellows.

'I like the man well enough, don't mistake me,' said Mistress Margaret.

Slap, thump.

'. . . As far as I've had a chance to know, that is. It's not that . . . can you find me the seeds?'

Slap, thump.

'. . . but he's old. And odd.'

Thump!

'. . . keeping to himself, forbidding anyone to clean his chamber. He might be a murderer for all we know. Have chests full of severed heads.' She sliced the dough into six smaller lumps.

Zeal took a lump and began to shape a cob loaf. 'I like him well enough too.'

'"Like!" La, la!' Mistress Margaret stood staring down at her loaf. Then she burst into tears and hobbled out of the bake house.

Before Zeal had shaped her second loaf, Rachel came into the kitchen. Without speaking, she went straight to the second oven and began to work the bellows.

After several minutes, Zeal said into the silence, 'Yes, it's all true.'

'God be praised!' Rachel's elbows flapped as if she were a duck trying to lift off a pond. 'I can save my tears then.'

When Zeal passed him in the forecourt mid-morning, Doctor Bowler wore the expression of a kicked dog and avoided her eyes.

'Terrible, terrible about Harry,' he said. Though he did not mention the proposed marriage, she knew by his odd manner that Wentworth had spoken to him as promised.

By the end of morning milking, the rest of Hawkridge estate seemed to have heard the news of both death and marriage, and split into those for the match and those against. John Nightingale had been popular during the fourteen years he had run the estate, first for his uncle and then for his cousin. Wentworth shunned friendship and had often given offence by repulsing well-meant overtures. Few were in favour.

'They'll work it out soon enough,' Rachel told her, having caught Zeal near tears in the still room. 'But we must get you into a safe berth first.'

Zeal pinched her lips and drew a deep breath. 'And what do you hear about Sir Harry's death?'

Rachel peered into a tiered muslin sieve, which was dripping a greenish juice into a crock. 'Everyone on the estate knows the truth of what happened. Any rumours will soon die.'

Zeal had never before felt out of favour here, even when first proving herself to them as Harry's new, fourteen-year-old wife. Now the averted eyes and pursed lips hurt her. She hated the way talk stopped whenever she entered a room. She was frightened by the occasional assessing eye that measured her waist. Wentworth was right. They must marry as soon as possible.

That morning, Wentworth abandoned his rod and the river to spend several hours with Sir Richard. Then, he borrowed a horse from Zeal and set off for Winchester.

She watched her betrothed settle into the saddle and gather up the reins. *At least I now know that he can ride.*

The beech avenue swallowed him.

Perhaps he has gone for good. His proposal was a cruel jest. And he has taken my horse. How can I know differently?

She had planned to write that morning to tell John of her proposed marriage. Now she decided to wait until she knew for certain that Wentworth was coming back. It was best not to tempt fate.

*   *   *

Wentworth returned three days later with an ordinary ecclesiastical licence issued by the diocese, which allowed them to be wed at once, without calling the banns. Though the growing child was the reason for this saving of three weeks, Zeal was grateful that news of the marriage need not be published throughout the parish. The disapproval and curiosity on Hawkridge Estate alone were as much as she could bear. She did not ask how Wentworth had managed to acquire the licence. Nor did she know that both Sir Richard and Master Wilde of Far Beeches had each stood surety for a large sum of money, to guarantee, accurately or not, that Wentworth's written allegation presented to the archdeacon contained no falsehoods concerning her state of legal spinsterhood.

After one night back, on Michaelmas Day, Wentworth borrowed the horse again, this time to ride to Basingstoke.

'Surely I must settle a jointure on you, not the other way round,' Zeal told him unhappily. 'Do we need a lawyer to ensure your right to my pile of ashes?'

On marriage all her property became his, as it had become Harry's. She had much less now than then, but nevertheless, if Philip had had a male heir, that heir, not she, would have the right to whatever remained after Philip's death. Or a creditor of his might attach the estate, or the king might declare it forfeit if Wentworth committed a crime.

From the little he had told her so far, an unknown crime did not seem beyond possibility. These risks were the price of her child's life.

The lawyer Wentworth brought from Basingstoke was eating toasted bread and cheese at the bake house table while a kitchen groom held another slice on a knifepoint over the fire. The man's papers and pens waited on Zeal's table in the estate office.

Wentworth nodded curtly at yet another of the house family who had found an excuse to visit the bake house kitchen. 'Am I a specimen in a menagerie, that all these people must come peer at me?'

The second dairymaid's face disappeared from the kitchen door.

'You're not often seen. And, by day, this is always a busy place.'

'Small wonder I prefer the riverbanks!' He led her to one of the little windows and stooped as if to look out. 'I will almost certainly die before you,' he said quietly. 'I want no one to find anything irregular in our union. For the child's sake.' He glared at the kitchen groom, who fled. 'Also, I want to make secure your absolute title to Hawkridge again after I am gone, not just dower rights or a widow's annuity.'

She nodded. It was kind of him to think of such things, although she would be leaving Hawkridge in any case, when John sent in seven years for her to go to the West Indies. None of which Wentworth knew. 'Arrange things as you wish,' she said, avoiding his eyes.

He scratched the bristle on his chin and smiled. '"On my obedient wife, Zeal Wentworth, I settle, herewith, two fishing rods of willow with copper rings, four Brown Queens, two Peacocks and a dozen hooks of the finest Spanish steel."'

Zeal laughed.

Wentworth looked at first startled and then pleased that he seemed to have amused her.

'You might find use for my rods, if you'll allow me to teach you to fish. Then you can leave them to the child . . . the thought pleases me. I might even leave the cub my books direct.' He peered through the window again. 'And here comes Sir Richard at last, to be our witness. I swear he's making his horse trot on tiptoe to spare his head.'

That image of her neighbour, short, round and undoubtedly sore-headed from his night of drinking, made Zeal laugh again.

Wentworth again looked both startled and pleased.

He's grown used to amusing only himself, she thought. At

the least, I can give him my laughter. I think he really does mean me well.

The lawyer finished the last of his bread and brushed the crumbs from his long white collar as Sir Richard opened the bake house door.

The old knight took off his hat and fanned himself. 'Oho! The happy couple.' He mopped his bald head and replaced his hat. His reddened eyes sat in their puffy sockets like specks of grit in two oysters. 'Don't know how you'll take to this news, but Doctor Gifford sent me word that he can make time to marry you Saturday next, if I have no objections as magistrate.'

'That's only eight days!' cried Mistress Margaret, returning with ale for Sir Richard in time to hear. 'How can we prepare in eight days?'

'But surely our own Doctor Bowler must marry us!' Zeal protested. 'If he's willing.'

Sir Richard and Wentworth exchanged glances.

'Doctor Gifford is the parish incumbent and a strong voice in the parish council,' said Sir Richard. 'Doctor Bowler merely your estate parson.'

'All the more reason for him to bless an estate union.' Zeal folded her arms. 'I don't like Gifford. He will be a weight dragging us down. Doesn't the man know that God resides above? He should lift spirits, not always be tugging them down towards damnation.'

'I can't stomach the man,' said Sir Richard. 'But it would not be politic to offend either him or the parish vestry.'

'Why not?' she demanded.

Sir Richard and Wentworth exchanged another of those maddening male looks.

'We must give no one any excuse to question the marriage,' said Wentworth.

Zeal pursed her lips and wound a sleeve ribbon around her finger until the tip looked like a ripe cherry. She tried not to think of the darkness that Gifford would cast over the wedding. The whole venture was already as fragile as a bubble. 'He must agree at least to marry us here at Hawkridge in our own chapel. I shall tell him so.'

'Best leave that to me,' said Sir Richard hastily. 'I've an examination to make in Bedgebury tomorrow in any case.'

The lawyer cleared his throat politely to indicate that he was now ready.

The next Sunday, as negotiated on the night of the inquiry into Sir Harry's death, Zeal took herself and her household to their monthly service in Bedgebury parish church. Sir Richard, of course, had not been part of the deal and waved them off with too much gusto for Zeal's liking. Wentworth had never attended prayers and apparently did not mean to begin now.

He's the blasted rudder after all, Zeal thought crossly as the little procession set off along the track downstream along the river to Bedgebury. But I don't suppose Gifford is worried about *his* soul.

Doctor Bowler, however, trudged glumly at her side, still avoiding her eyes. 'All that sermonizing,' he said. 'I won't be comfortable. And with no hymns or Prayer Book! I shall feel as if I'm talking to a stranger, not my own God.'

'I wish you were marrying us, not Doctor Gifford,' said Zeal.

They both huffed and waved their hands to disperse a cloud of late gnats, which hovered in a sunny patch.

'Will you want wedding music?' Bowler enquired carefully as the shady tunnel closed round them again.

'Oh, yes! But I feared to ask.'

'Because Gifford will disapprove.' He nodded in understanding of her difficulty.

'Gifford can't be allowed to order everything in the parish!' She glanced at his long, hound's face. He suffered so when he found himself at odds with anyone. 'No, I didn't ask because I know you don't approve of the match.'

They crossed a little hunting bridge in silence. Then, as they joined the larger track that led from Far Beeches to Bedgebury, Doctor Bowler said, 'I had thought I might compose an epithalamium.'

Zeal beamed. 'Dear Doctor Bowler!'

'But what of Doctor Gifford?'

'Master Wentworth seems to know how to deal with him. I'm sure that if I say I want your epithalamium, we shall have it.'

They smiled at each other with the delicious relief of truce.

'Would you also deck the chapel?' she asked. 'If Master Wentworth and I are to be united by that dispiriting Scot we can at least cheer ourselves with the sight of ivy and green boughs.'

'And sheaves of ripe corn,' said Bowler. 'And pumpkins. All the bounty that autumnal Nature provides.'

'Apples.'

'Grapes and peaches.' Bowler flushed with excitement. 'It will give me great pleasure both to decorate and to compose a celebratory piece for you.' He gazed up into the trees. 'Seth must re-string his viol so we can march on the firm ground of his continuo.' He hummed a few notes in an exploratory way. '. . . great pleasure.' He seemed as relieved as she was at his relenting.

She had heard it said that Bowler failed as a clergyman because he always understood both sides of any question with equal conviction. He could not find it in himself ever to condemn. Anyone who wanted to know exactly where he or she stood in relationship to Heaven and Hell or whether to play shove ha'penny on Sunday, had to attend church in Bedgebury, where Doctor Gifford delighted in firm pronouncements, invited or otherwise.

She smiled sideways at her parson as they trudged onwards towards Bedgebury. He continued to frown and hum, waving his hands from time to time, even voicing a few notes.

How dare Doctor Gifford dismiss him as a clergyman?

Though perhaps an over-forgiving shepherd for wayward sheep, Doctor Bowler gives us rich gifts of the spirit in return for his milk and eggs.

She glanced over her shoulder at the straggling procession behind them.

From among those walkers Bowler had formed a chapel choir of an excellence surprising in such a rural backwater. For this choir, he composed psalms and hymns exactly suited to their voices. From among those same estate residents, he also mustered and tutored a consort of instruments, which included his own fiddle, a double bass viol, a *viola da gamba*, several pipes, a tabor and the smith's great drum. He and this crew played for church festivals and for dancing on secular feast days with equal fervour and delight. But Bowler's unique gift was his voice.

It was high, but not falsetto, nor was it a simulacrum of a woman's soprano, like the voice of an Italian *castrato*. Its piercing purity of tone suggested some other instrument than a human voice, an instrument not known on earth, the vibrating of a silver reed blown only in Heaven.

Bowler loved to sing as much as he disliked making judgements. For feverish children, who saw wolves and demons among the bed curtains, he stood diffidently in the sick chamber and sang light into the shadows and smiling faces onto the foot of the bed. He sang a small green grass snake into his pocket and a robin onto the corner of the pillow.

For the dying, he sang stars of light into dusty folds of hangings. He sang the smell of fresh pine and the sweetness of witch hazel blooms. He sang long-vanished faces around the bed. He sang clear still water. He sang rest.

For the others, he sang rising barn walls, candles, leaping flames, magic cups that were always full. Sweet meats and diamonds. Golden arrows for the hunter's bow. God. He could sing warmth around the heart, lightness beneath the ribs, fizzing in the belly. He could lift the hair on your neck with the sound of hope.

For Zeal, Doctor Bowler's music would bless her strange, uncomfortable marriage with a joy she saw nowhere else. She did not see that she had just declared war against an unreasoning enemy, with her little parson as both ally and cause.

13

Gifford nodded with gratification when he saw their party arrive in the Bedgebury parish church. Heads turned in the congregation. Some bent together to whisper. Elbows nudged ribs.

Zeal missed the pleasure of singing hymns and had difficulty suppressing yawns during Gifford's long sermon on the spiritual perils of revolt. She found the undecorated stone walls of the parish church astonishingly plain for a house of God. Otherwise all seemed well enough, until they left.

Doctor Gifford stood in the porch bidding farewell to his sheep. As Zeal and Bowler stepped out into the sunlight, he gave the parson a letter.

'But I am certain, madam, that you will wish to note the contents.'

Zeal knew instantly that she would not wish any such thing but, mindful of the caution voiced by Wentworth and Sir Richard, she bade the minister a civil farewell.

Bowler clearly shared her premonition about the letter. He fanned himself with it, unopened. He shoved it into his pocket, then took it out again. He studied the outside as if for a hint of what lay within. He sighed.

'We both know we won't like whatever's in it,' she said. 'Let's get it over with.'

Bowler nodded and broke Gifford's seal. 'Oh, dear,' he said after a moment. All colour drained from his cheeks. He held the letter out to her. 'What are we to do now?'

Doctor Gifford wrote:

. . . I am gratified to inform you that at the last vestry meeting

it was agreed to ban the decadent Roman practice of playing music in church services of any sort, throughout the parish from this date forward. All Psalms are henceforth to be read, not sung. All prayers must be spoken. Any making of music during holy worship (full list of occasions given below for avoidance of confusion) will be deemed a return to the outlawed practices of the Church of Rome. All violations will be punished with fines or other more severe penalties, at the discretion of the vestry council. May God's hand guide you always, Yours most sincerely, in Christian brotherhood . . .

'We ignore it,' said Zeal. 'If I don't have your music to buoy up my spirits, I don't think I can go through with the wedding at all.'

'Oh.' Bowler looked both pleased and alarmed. 'My dear. Goodness.' He blushed but bit his lower lip at the same time. Then he looked at her with concern.

'I'll pay the fines,' she said, pretending to misunderstand his real question. 'I'll say I ordered the music. Don't fear. What with summer plague and a war in Scotland, and no parliament and all the new taxes, people have more important matters to worry about than whether I have music at my confounded wedding.' She folded the letter and stuffed it into her sleeve. 'Don't tell anyone else about this yet.'

They turned back onto their own track along the river and walked a silent, thoughtful furlong. Then Bowler began to hum. '"Praise Him with timbrel and dance,"' he sang quietly. '"Praise ye the Lord."'

'And so we shall!' She felt lighter for having at last hinted to someone how she really felt about the marriage, in spite of all those approving nods from Reason.

Having been given licence by Zeal, Bowler went to work with fervour. She sometimes wondered whether it was wise to defy Gifford. Then she heard Bowler's plangent countertenor leading the estate children in rehearsal among the trees beyond the ponds. From time to time, the heavy clanging rhythms from the forge gave way to the boom of the smith's drum. Twice she caught groups of girls practising a dance with garlands.

Mind you, she reassured herself, Gifford's letter did not forbid dance. She knew that she should warn Sir Richard of all they planned. He must have had a letter too. But what if he said that she must obey it?

Apart from the music, Zeal tried to keep the celebration a modest one. But anticipation wrote its own rules. A rest day for any reason was to be made the most of. The wedding gathered its own momentum in spite of the bride's half-heartedness. There was much urgent cooking, laundering, and stitching. There were secrets behind closed doors.

Mistress Margaret relented far enough to confer with Sir Richard's steward about the details of the wedding feast, which was to be held at High House.

'The weather should still be fine enough for us to dance outdoors,' she reported. 'Sir Richard will let us move back into his great hall if it rains.' The old knight himself began to trap and shoot anything with wings or fur that might be eaten at the feast.

While she had agreed with Wentworth about the special licence, Zeal would have been content merely to exchange promises before witnesses, which was enough to make a legal marriage. However, Wentworth had insisted, for the child's sake, that they have a church blessing. 'And more witnesses than any man could ever be accused of bending,' he said.

Zeal feared that preparations would interfere with the autumn work, already behind schedule. Five pigs remained to be butchered and preserved. The brewing was at a critical stage. They had to make enough soap to replace their entire stock, which had melted in the fire. Sheep waited to move to winter pastures where shelters still needed repair. Cows had to come in for the winter. Their quarters must be prepared and dried bracken laid on the ground. There was hay to cut and get into the barns. Winter lodgings to find for the house family who now camped in the outbuildings. And, of course, the salvage of building stuffs from the old house.

On the other hand, she saw that the wedding was bringing an unforeseen benefit. In spite of any reservations they might have about the match, Bowler, Mistress Margaret and all the others had grown animated again and brimmed with purpose as they had not done since before the fire. Zeal clamped tightly to her rock and let the sea wash over her.

She nearly washed off and drowned the night she saw John leaning against the doorpost of her chamber at High House, smiling at her. Even as she sat bolt upright and opened her mouth to cry out his name, he shook his head and faded.

He's dead! she thought. His ghost came to tell me that his ship sank. He has drowned like my parents.

The next morning she took up a quill pen to write to him. If she acted as if he still lived, then he did.

She remembered his hand holding a pen. A hand browned by the sun, with a scar wrapped around the base of his thumb. A strong making and building hand. Standing in this same office, she had watched him trim the end of a split quill, locked with him in a shared silence like the breath between two musical notes.

He had felt her gaze, looked up and pinned her like one of his moths. She let herself be studied, wings, antennae and all. Then he smiled ruefully and she had smiled back. Their silent complicity felt like the embrace they had not yet shared and did not imagine would ever be possible.

My dearest love, she now wrote.

She leaned back. Now what? *My dearest love, I miss you so painfully that I am to marry someone else in three days' time.'*

She bent her head over the paper again. *I . . .* Again she stopped.

How can I write that I bear his child but that it, like me,

will soon belong to another man? She could think of no words strong enough to survive that burden. The truth would melt and reform into dreadful smoking lumps like the disasters of an apprentice smith. In any case, she did not yet know exactly where to send a letter.

I will wait until he writes again, from Nevis, she decided. So long as I write before rumour can reach him. I shall use the time thinking what to say.

She pulled a pile of accounts over the letter.

The day before the wedding, she peeped into the chapel and felt an easing at the base of her throat. The colours – the bright leathery red of the oak branches, the golden firework sprays of oats, the deep musty greens of fern and ivy, the polished, sweet-scented russet and gold of apples heaped in baskets – were a soothing draught for her senses.

Things may turn out all right, after all, she thought. So long as I try not to think. Just look and listen and work and care for John's child. I'll get through those seven years. John will write again and let me know that he is alive. I will write back in such a way that he will understand and forgive me.

Somehow, she did not ever get around to discussing Gifford's letter with either Wentworth or Sir Richard. Sir Richard would have mentioned it, if he thought it important, she told herself.

And Gifford won't dare make a scene in front of Sir Richard. Not once we have all begun.

A harsh observer might have said that, in spite of reason, she wanted to prevent the wedding. She had most certainly misjudged the minister.

14

In the chapel gallery, Bowler's musical consort struck up a sedate march. Zeal and Wentworth entered under the swag of ivy above the chapel door, with Gifford close behind them. Mistress Margaret, Sir Richard, Rachel, Arthur and other house family followed the minister.

'No!' Gifford stopped so suddenly that Mistress Margaret bumped her nose on his back. The minister's cry held such horror that there was a general pressing forward by those still outside to see what calamity lay within. The music broke off.

Zeal's precarious calm wobbled. I should have gone ahead and jumped! I've always known it. Here comes the confirmation!

Gifford's eyes widened. '"What is this that thou hast done?"' His face flushed purple. 'I will not solemnize any union amongst these pagan trappings!' With the clenched brow of a man struck by an excruciating megrim, he surveyed the ropes of ivy around the pillars, the swags of red oak leaves, the jugs of wheat sheaves and golden oats. His eyes fell on a pair of stuffed cloth figures, each a foot high, propped side by side on the altar among heaped baskets of apples and pears. Zeal and Philip Wentworth, recognizable by his silver hair, black coat and fishing rod, by her red-gold hair. Both dolls wore crowns of plaited wheat, and they were tied together by a golden thread.

'Idols!' Gifford whispered in an exhalation aimed at the back pews. His terrier body vibrated with emotion. 'The props of witchcraft! I am struck dumb with horror!'

'Not so you'd notice,' someone said at the back of the

crowd, just loudly enough to be heard by all.

The minister's head swung around, rusty hair bristling. Bland faces looked back at him from the chapel porch. Then Gifford spied the choir of children, dressed in green, standing beyond Bowler near the altar.

'How dare you?' he demanded of Bowler. 'You were warned yet you disobey! Oh, rebellious soul! And you!' He pointed a shaking finger at the children. 'You wait to do the devil's work here! Quake in terror of God's wrath, for you are lost. You are fallen!'

Two of the younger children burst into tears.

Zeal heard a rustling from the gallery behind them as the string players ducked out of sight.

Ignoring Zeal, Gifford gripped Wentworth's arm. 'You will come to Bedgebury to be wed. This place was always a temple of Rome. It should have been destroyed with the others!' His eyes razed the acrobat, fish and monkey pew finials, smashed the tiled pomegranates in the floor and torched the carved Rood screen to which Doctor Bowler seemed to be clinging.

Wentworth detached his arm from the minister's grip.

Gifford's glance fell next onto Zeal's cat, which was pretending to be asleep on a pew. He looked away quickly. 'How dare you permit such desecration?' he demanded again of Doctor Bowler, gesturing at the decorations. 'What do you think you are doing?'

'Letting all Nature reflect the general joy,' the parson replied. He tightened his grip on the wooden arch post.

Wentworth stepped just a little too close to Gifford. 'I think my betrothed wishes to be blessed here on her own land, among her own people.' Though Wentworth's voice was quiet and his bearing restrained, Gifford retreated. Wentworth towered over him by a head, and the older man's square jaw had set like a pike's.

'Too far to walk from your place to High House,' said Sir Richard, who had been rocking on his feet, watching calmly.

'Some of our guests are too young. Or too old. Wouldn't care to do it myself.'

The cat woke and sensibly slipped away.

Gifford circled around Wentworth. He swept the dolls to the floor then upended a basket of apples, which rolled and bounced across the stone floor. 'There can be no marriage until you clear away these abominations.'

'But the marriage will take place here?'

Gifford tilted his head toward Zeal and narrowed his eyes as if drilling into her soul. He looked again at Wentworth, then at Sir Richard. 'Your actions must now reflect the Lord's admonition to be plain and pure in both thought and deed. Most of all when you are about to enter into the sanctity of marriage. Strip away these vanities. I shall return after dinner. Then I shall decide.'

The crowd parted to let the minister through to the door. With the keen sense of timing that made his sermons so popular with a like-minded congregation, he paused at the threshold. 'Doctor Bowler, pray come with me. I want a private word.'

'You may speak with Doctor Bowler when he has finished stripping away these abominations,' said Zeal hotly. 'Not before!'

Wentworth set a warning hand under her elbow. 'Perhaps after the wedding,' he suggested. '. . . if we are to be ready by early afternoon, as you ask.'

Sir Richard clapped a genial hand on the minister's shoulder and pushed him out the door. As he went, however, he cast a stern questioning look over his shoulder at Zeal.

Mistress Margaret and Rachel began collecting up the fallen apples into their lace-trimmed aprons.

'I'm so sorry, Doctor Bowler.' Zeal tried to smile at the dismayed faces. 'And all who helped you. It looks exactly as a wedding should. And I shall tell Doctor Gifford that it was I who insisted on music.'

Doctor Bowler waved a hand abstractedly. 'Never mind. Should have seen it coming. The man's never been a Solomon with eyes for the virtues of ivory, apes and peacocks. As for music, well . . . we did know.'

Zeal imagined a glint in the parson's close-set eyes which agreed with her own furious disappointment. 'I don't intend to apologize for wanting to hear your epithalamium.' She retrieved an apple from behind a pew.

'It's all right, my lady. We might manage it yet. And leave the clearing away to us. Which we'd best start at once.' The parson beckoned to his unhappy choir and retrieved his fiddle from behind the altar. He stared up at the hammer beams of the roof, then down at the tiled floor. 'Would you know, sir,' he asked Wentworth for no apparent reason, '. . . does Sir Richard keep a boat on his lake?'

Zeal felt a little as she did when she came down from the chapel roof. Having got to the point of jumping, she feared she could not bring herself to it a second time. After Bowler shooed all but his workers out of the chapel, she stood on a brick path in John's herb garden, trying to think what to do next. She looked down at her lace-trimmed apron and yellow silk skirt. The cheeses needed turning. But there was not time to change to workaday clothes and then change back again. Sir Richard's household allowed no interference with their preparations for the wedding feast. Even so, Mistress Margaret had gone back to High House to hover while they awaited Gifford's return. Rachel and Arthur had stayed in the chapel to help Bowler. Sir Richard had said he would go shooting. Zeal had to do something or she would find herself fleeing over Hawk Ridge and not stopping till she reached York.

'Come fishing with me,' said Wentworth.

She suppressed a rush of irritation. Gifford had told Wentworth that the wedding must move to his church in Bedgebury, as if she, the mistress of the estate, had not been standing three feet away.

He is not the master yet. I have a few more hours as my own woman, not a wife.

'We need not speak,' he said. 'Indeed, best if we don't.'

Who is this old man? she asked herself. Can I truly be about to marry him?

Perhaps Gifford's refusal was a sign.

Wentworth stood with his hands on his hips. For the first time, she saw that he was wearing a new black coat. 'The next few hours are time that does not exist. You may do anything with them. Why not fish?'

Raised, urgent voices came from the chapel. Three boys ran out of the door like animated bushes, arms full of boughs, with only their legs exposed.

'The tranquillity of the riverbank might ease your mind. Come hide with me from all the consternation.'

I dare say, other women have been even unhappier on their wedding days, and lived.

She tugged at her cloak, on which she was sitting, to protect her skirt hem from the damp earth under the willow.

Wentworth stood motionless, some way downstream, planted like the stump of an ancient tree. Every once in a while, his hands moved, making some fine adjustment to the placement of his line.

Why am I so angry with him? she wondered. He didn't put a foot wrong during all that dreadful scene with Gifford. Indeed, Gifford was afraid of him. Maybe he does keep chests full of severed heads as Mistress Margaret said.

She considered the still, solid figure on the bank. A finger of breeze stirred a strand of his silver hair. Otherwise, he seemed not even to breathe.

What a lather he was in to get away from the chapel, she thought. I suppose I should be flattered that he finds my company tolerable. So long as we don't speak.

Please, God, let it all be over soon.

When the bake house bell rang at dinnertime, she did not move. Wentworth merely shifted farther down stream.

She shut her eyes. Otherwise, she might see John poised

naked on the bank, preparing to dive into the water. Or coming through the trees on fire with urgency to show her the fringed miracle of a double buttercup.

The pealing of the chapel bells woke her. The sun was slanting low through the trees.

'They're ready for us.' Wentworth gripped his wriggling chubb and dislocated its head with a quick jerk. He put the fish into his sack, then helped her to her feet. 'Back to the fray.' He shouldered his rod and set off up the riverbank with Zeal trudging behind, her hands upraised like a supplicant so as not to be married while covered in nettle welts.

What am I doing? Philip Wentworth asked himself. How did I let myself get so tangled in other lives after all those careful years?

The most absurd fact was that he wanted to go through with this *commedia*. He was wilfully, in full knowledge of his risks, putting himself in danger again.

15

To judge by his open relief at the denuded chapel, Gifford had clearly expected more resistance. The reassembled company were fewer in number and subdued. None of the children had returned, and who could blame them? Nor was Doctor Bowler there.

Zeal imagined him seated alone somewhere, gathering the courage to be chastised by the man who had wounded him.

She could not look at Gifford as he married her. A smirk of satisfaction had followed his relief. Now his pale eyes shot forth spears of will to pin her in place while he prescribed marriage as God's remedy against sin.

If only he knew the worst of it!

She could smell scented sheep's grease on his hands. When he spoke, his lips stretched and curled like two bristly caterpillars. And how she loathed that mellifluous voice, which belonged by rights to a larger man! Such authoritative cadences, such swelling diapasons and profound rumblings could not possibly emerge from that scrawny body.

He's a rusty-furred terrier, she decided. Not a large hunting sort but one of the smaller quivering breeds designed to go down rat and rabbit holes. Given to leaping up and yapping at the slightest sound.

Yes, she thought. He has a terrier's large head and short, slightly bowed legs. And its tenacity.

Dwelling on her rage at Gifford made the ceremony itself seem less real.

Watching his eloquent eyebrows distracted her from the vows she made. And those made by Philip Wentworth.

Then she found herself signing the marriage book. 'Mistress Zeal Wentworth.' She wore a ring on her hand. She stretched her mouth in a smile. Nodded. Accepted a kiss from Mistress Margaret. Stretched her mouth again at someone else.

When Wentworth, Sir Richard, and Gifford had also signed the marriage book, the minister led the small glum procession from the chapel towards the track to High House for the wedding feast.

I miss the children, thought Zeal as she walked. I would have liked to hear their voices. They would have cheered me. Beside her, Wentworth – now implausibly her husband – was frowning at the ground. Even the two escorting dogs trotted with heads down and tails tucked tightly into their hindquarters.

The next hours, she thought. I can't. The false determined jollity. Everyone else stretching his mouth too. All getting drunk and flinging themselves about dancing as if motion and noise could simulate joy.

She glared at Gifford's back. Unless he tries to forbid all dancing and drinking as well as music, even though it's not Sunday. Nor in church.

Then, as they passed the forge, a sound like a gunshot cracked the afternoon air.

Gifford ducked. Mistress Margaret and several of the other women gave little shrieks of alarm.

'Someone just fired the anvil,' said Wentworth with interest. The sulphurous smell of burnt black powder reached them.

'A poor jest in troubled times,' said Gifford.

Wentworth gazed around. 'And we seem to have lost Sir Richard.'

Zeal looked back at the procession in time to see meaningful glances and smothered smiles. A little farther on, she spotted an apple, set on the dirt at the side of the track like a copper coin. Gifford pretended not to see it. Zeal picked it up and sniffed its sweet fragrance with a first stirring of anticipation.

'What is that?' Gifford suddenly set like a hound, his head cocked, listening.

From beyond the trees ahead of them, where the track led into the drawn breath of the first of Sir Richard's meadows, against all reason, came the faint sound of a string consort playing a Psalm. Gifford lowered his head and set off again like a man charging into enemy fire

More apples marked their way, some gold, some like drops of blood. Around the next bend, they came upon an arch made of willow branches twined with the seed heads of Old Man's Beard. A small pale-haired boy and silvery girl waited on either side of the arch, a pair of nature spirits holding crowns of ivy. Zeal stooped down and bent her head to the girl.

Wentworth stared at the boy for so long that Zeal thought he would refuse the crown. Then he, too, bent his head. He took Zeal's hand. To the accompaniment of the unlikely music, both wearing their green crowns, he led her under the arch into the open meadow. Gifford walked around one side of the arch and followed unsteadily.

Two farmers and the estate carpenter sat on stools on a rocky outcrop in the grass, dressed in their finest clothes, playing a fiddle, a *viola da gamba* and a double bass viol. Silhouetted against the last light of the low autumn sun, they looked both incongruous and wonderfully dreamlike. In the vast open space of the meadow, the voices of their instruments were small, yet clear and hard-edged like the cries of birds.

Gifford rubbed his mouth. 'Where's Bowler?' His breathing was so tight he could hardly speak.

'We're in Sir Richard's domain now,' said Wentworth firmly. 'You must speak to his chaplain, not Bowler.'

But Sir Richard was not to be seen either, nor was his chaplain. Gifford's eyes skated over the musicians and slid away. 'I am humbled by my failure so far here amongst you. But you will learn that I am resolute.' His eyes grew watery. 'I shall return to Bedgebury and pray for guidance. In the

Lord's war I will not be vanquished. I will never abandon so many souls to damnation.' He turned and trudged back into the trees.

As she listened to the Psalm, Zeal felt delight and astonishment blossoming under her breastbone. Her little parson had routed Gifford, after all. He had given her the music she needed to lift her spirits. The singing strings, the warmth of the setting sun, the soft damp earth under her best slippers must be signs. Heed them, not Gifford, she told herself. These things are the truth.

When the consort had finished their piece and accepted the applause, Rachel waved a large handkerchief. 'Now, madam, I must cover your eyes.'

Zeal gave herself to whatever the game might be. Her last sight was of Wentworth, grinning, his wreath askew.

'Come with me.' Rachel took Zeal's hand. Giggles and laughter followed behind.

Her feet told her that they had left the track and were walking through long grass. At first she feared she might stumble and fall, but Rachel's hand was steady and her directions clear. Very soon, Zeal's feet became two small animals, sniffing out their own path without help from her thoughts. She floated through the darkness, tethered to the earth by Rachel's warm, firm hand.

When Rachel removed the blindfold, they stood in a far corner of the field at the bottom of a slope near the tree line, beside a tiny pool of water overhung with grass. A slow constant drip of water oozed from the ground. The nearby bushes were swagged with garlands from the chapel.

Rachel put a silver pin into Zeal's hand. 'You must make a wedding wish, madam. Don't tell us, mind.'

Zeal held the pin until it grew warm in her palm.

I can't wish for what I truly want, not today.

She closed her eyes. I can't use his name today.

In time, let me love and be loved. She knew what she meant.

She opened her eyes and threw her offering into the tiny pool of the spring. Hard as she tried, she could not stop the flash of memory.

John surfaced from his dive, sleek as an otter and dripping water like a sea god, laughing up at her, his skin brown to the waist from the sun.

She kept her eyes on the spreading rings on the water as they bounced back and cut across themselves. She knew that Wentworth was watching her with a wry smile.

Far more cheerfully than it had left the chapel, the wedding procession crossed the ridge and headed down the far slope towards Sir Richard's fishing lake. Then Zeal saw the missing children.

They stood near the lake in two long lines, linked to each other by garlands. The two lines formed a corridor leading away from the track to the edge of the lake. When the procession drew near, they opened their mouths like nestlings and, at a nod from one of their number, began to sing:

> *'Mistress and Master, so newly bound,*
> *Here await transport to realms*
> *Where bliss and joy are found!'*

In unison they gestured towards the lake.

The hair stood up on Zeal's arms.

In the early twilight, a white veiled figure carrying a lighted torch glided towards them, across the surface of Sir Richard's lake. The apparition moved smoothly, with long reaching strides, splashing a little but supported by the water.

> *'Bid Hymen welcome,'* (carolled the children)
> *'As he welcomes you.'*

Mistress Margaret gasped and clutched her heart.

'The Second Coming,' muttered Zeal's new husband into her ear.

The god of marriage lurched, seemed to fight for balance, then stopped some way out from the shore, still miraculously afloat, and gestured with his torch towards the left end of the lake. There, the musicians, panting, had regrouped on

114

the bank, joined by the smith and his drum. At the signal from Hymen, they began to play again. The notes of their introduction fell on the air like clear water drops.

'Weep not, O solitary heart . . .'

When Hymen began to sing, Zeal recognized Doctor Bowler's high unearthly voice.

'The heavens have found thee thy other part.

Thy other part, thy other part,' (echoed the children)

'Thou hast already skill to achieve thy wish,' (sang Hymen)

'O, Piscator,

O, noble Petrus of our time,

Go thou and fish.'

Hymen gestured again, this time to the right. As Zeal watched, a punt pushed off from Sir Richard's little wooden dock, poled by Tuddenham's son, Will. In it sat a stocky figure holding a fishing rod and wearing a dusty black coat that could only have been Wentworth's. A hat masked the face but Sir Richard's red cheeks and white whiskers could be easily identified. He seemed to be suffering from severe stage fright for the tip of the rod shook. On the prow of the skiff sat the Wentworth doll, from the chapel altar.

'Weep not, O solitary heart . . .'

Hymen and the children together repeated the verse. Then, while the consort on the left bank furiously sawed out a long dramatic tremolo, the fisherman in the boat hauled up the tip of his rod. The smith suddenly thumped his drum. A strike! The hook had been taken. Over another tremolo, the fisherman pulled in his line. A hush gripped the watchers. From the water, dripping like a mermaid, slowly rose a small figure with red-gold hair.

'O, Piscator, blessed soul, alone no more.

This golden fish is thine forevermore.'

The fisherman held up his catch, to cheers from Hymen and the choir.

'How was that?' demanded Sir Richard's voice from under the fisherman's hat, exuberant with relief.

There was a splash as Hymen, retreating to the far shore, fell off the unseen support into the water up to the waist.

Zeal wiped her eyes, both laughing and weeping. Wentworth laid his hand on her shoulder.

'I would have made a more subtle and ingenious rhyme,' explained Doctor Bowler, as he stood dripping in the hall of High House, accepting claps on the back and shouted congratulations. 'If I had only had more time. And Jamie should have sung the part, of course, as he has the voice. But given the short time . . .'

Zeal kissed him. 'Nothing so fine has ever been seen in a Whitehall masque!'

'Masters Davenant and Jones must fall on their swords in envious despair,' said Sir Richard.

In the end, when Sir Richard complained that his arse had been soaked, she and Wentworth had walked around the lake to the house rather than be ferried across in the punt. Any risk of otherwise dampening the celebration was long past.

The original epithalamium was finally performed in Sir Richard's great hall, to further cheers, with Jamie, the pale-haired boy, singing a descant which soared high above the rest, like a hawk hanging on the clouds.

When the string consort had taken off their coats, downed a pint or two, and settled in for their real evening's work, Zeal danced first with her new husband, who (she noted) displayed the tutored nimbleness of a gentleman. Then she danced with Sir Richard, who was amazingly light on his feet and filled with wonder at his part in the afternoon. Zeal smiled at him but still felt Wentworth's hands on her waist.

Doctor Bowler had more drink pressed on him that evening than ever before in his life and fiddled himself into an ecstasy. Meanwhile the young men clamoured for their fleeting right to dance with the bride and to claim a kiss.

'Should you be dancing, madam?' Rachel whispered once in her ear.

'I must, or they'll suspect,' she replied. In truth, she wanted to dance.

At last, they sat down to the wedding dinner, now a wedding supper thanks to Doctor Gifford. Only then did Zeal realize that no one had asked Wentworth to kiss his bride.

As servants began to bring in platters of roast meats and moulded jellies, Sir Richard launched into the first toast. Glasses rose into the air.

Zeal glanced at her new husband. Perspiration stood on his forehead. One hand gripped the edge of the table. The other sat clenched in his lap. His eyes were fixed on the platter that someone had just set before him. His breath came in quick gasps that made the strings of his collar quiver.

At the chorus of shouted good wishes, he nodded without looking up. He leaned to Zeal and muttered, 'You must excuse me.' He rose and left the room.

A hush followed him. Then Sir Richard shouted after him in triumph. 'Ten years older, Wentworth! And I still outlasted you! And I danced two dances more!' He winked at the company. 'He wants to save his strength.' He lifted his glass again to Zeal. 'And who can blame him?'

Mistress Margaret caught Zeal's eye. Zeal ignored the heavy meaning in the older woman's glance and stretched her mouth gratefully at Sir Richard while the company laughed, drank some more and pretended to forget the groom's odd behaviour. The earlier joy deserted her. Apprehension began to settle like a November fog.

Wentworth still had not re-appeared when Zeal, no longer able to make herself keep smiling and counterfeiting an appetite, at last pleaded tiredness. As she was carried up the great dogleg staircase in a chair of crossed arms, clinging for her life to the heads of a stable groom and one of her tenant farmers, she reflected that, whatever else he might be, Wentworth was no fool. He had contrived to escape this rowdy bedtime send-off that was the fate of most newly-weds. She could not decide whether or not his sudden departure had left her looking the fool instead.

Rachel closed the door on the boisterous drunken faces on the landing. Caterwauling and a banging of pots began outside beneath the windows.

Now I learn whether or not I still have a bridegroom, Zeal thought. Perhaps he has gone fishing as usual. He had said that life need not change much. A flicker of relief lightened her apprehension.

Nevertheless, she was puzzled by his absence from the bridal chamber. He had been so firm for all the other legalities and show of marriage.

16

While Rachel readied her young mistress for bed, the maid's nose twitched as it always did when she was trying not to speak her mind. She clamped the bone pins between her teeth and stroked the silky red hair.

'I'll never sleep so grandly again,' said Zeal, to avoid saying anything else.

Sir Richard had lent the newly-weds his best upper chamber. The bed was a squat sturdy galleon of oak from the days of King Harry, with sails of heavy red brocade and enough yards of gold braid and twisted fringing and tassels to rig a navy. Turkish carpets covered every horizontal surface in the room except the floor. All four of Sir Richard's grandparents tilted forward avidly in heavy six-foot gold frames. You could have stabled a horse in the fireplace.

Rachel sniffed the armpits of Zeal's yellow silk dress and draped it over a chair to take away and clean. 'That's fine, then,' she said enigmatically.

Wentworth had not gone fishing after all. He lifted aside the Mortlake tapestry that protected the closed door from draughts. He wore a night shirt, and a long sleeveless robe, and carried a leather pouch and his ivy crown.

'You may go, Rachel,' he said.

Zeal folded her arms tightly. When Rachel had left, she said, 'Sir, I am accustomed to directing my own maid.'

Wentworth looked amused. 'Forgive me, I'm out of practice at being husband and lord. And young women have changed.'

Zeal watched him set down the pouch. He then put on the

ivy crown and leaned against the side of the great four-posted bed. He did not offer to explain his sudden flight from supper.

'Well, here we are,' he said, fingering a honey-suckle garland which had found its way to the bridal chamber and wrapped itself around a bedpost. 'Against all odds and the counsel of just about everyone.' He grinned suddenly and looked many years younger. 'Spiting wiser heads has never before brought me so much pleasure nor such a rich reward.'

'And just what is that?' she asked warily.

He sat and held out his hands to her. 'At the very least, marriage makes for warmer sleep. Unless you have cold feet . . . have you?'

'No, sir.' She put her hands behind her back in alarm. She had thought that without his black coat he would shrink, but sitting here on the bed in his night shirt and gown, he seemed larger even than when he was dancing, more fleshy, noisier. More solid and male.

'Zeal, trust me.' He took off the crown and set it on the floor. 'I'm safer than most men I know, including your former husband. Come over here, by me. Or do I repulse you suddenly.'

She crossed and took his outstretched hands. They felt dry and very warm.

'That's better.' He lifted one of her hands and kissed it. She could smell the wine on his breath. 'We must keep up appearances. For the child's sake, I beg lodging for the night. Apart from that, my manly pride won't have everyone on two estates whispering that I slept alone on my wedding night.' He stood. 'Which side do you sleep? Or is it the middle?'

Zeal pulled her hands free, walked around to the far side of the bed and climbed up under the linen-covered quilt. He removed his loose robe and climbed into bed on his side.

'Sweet Lord, it feels good to lie down!' He extended his left arm towards her. 'Come, lean your head against my shoulder. We must practise appearances. And friendship.'

After a moment, Zeal slid across the mattress. She had

never touched him without several thick layers of clothing between them. Now there were just two thin films of linen. She looked sideways at the grey hairs which curled from the open neck of his night shirt.

He sighed. 'I had never thought to feel the warmth again of another human creature against my flank. Are you comfortable?'

She nodded.

'But are you at ease?'

'Not entirely.'

'Do you want to wander off again across that vast cold expanse of mattress?'

She took a deep breath. 'Are you at ease, sir?'

'I am perfectly content.'

'Then I shall stay where I am.'

They both stared straight ahead.

'Bowler is an astonishing man,' said Wentworth.

She nodded.

'Don't forget the gift of truth you promised me,' she said after a moment of silence.

'Ah, you remind me, I have something else for you first.' He extracted his arm, threw back the coverlet and fetched the leather pouch.

'I had these from a young friend I want you to meet. Just back from Italy and ablaze with fervour for the Italian architecture. I meant to give them to you earlier as a wedding gift but forgot in all that to-do over pagan abominations.' He unrolled a drawing in sepia ink. 'Inspiration for rebuilding Hawkridge House. What do you think of this for the new south front?' He flattened against the coverlet a finely drawn fantasy of stone corbels, architraves, pediments, niches and tapering steps. 'Or is it a little rich for Hampshire?'

'It's beautiful, but I could never afford to build such a thing.' She touched the drawing with a tentative finger and sighed. 'And I wouldn't know where to begin. There's so much to learn.'

'You've had a long and tiring day. I should have waited until morning.' He picked up the drawing again. 'You must sleep now. I forgot your condition.'

'That's rich – considering that my condition is why we're both here!'

'Hurrah! You can jest about it!' He rolled the drawing. 'On reflection, it's a touch pompous for Hawkridge Estate.'

'I like that frieze of garlands. Do you think our own Jonas Stubbs could guide his chisel into such intricacies? What a shame that we can't afford to import Dutch stone masons.' She looked up and caught him watching her with satisfaction. 'Please, sir, do tell your friend that the drawing is very fine.'

A young friend with an interest in Italian architecture. Another crumb of information.

Wentworth put the pouch on the floor , snuffed the candle on the ledge of the bed, and settled to sleep. To Zeal's relief, he did not offer his arm again. On the other hand, he seemed to think his evasion had worked. If she were to survive their bargain, he must not assume that he could always play her as he wished.

'Your promise!' she reminded him.

'No, my dear. Not tonight. My speech is grown as rusty as my gun. And I talked more today than in all the last ten years. Tomorrow night, I swear.'

Zeal felt the silent tussle between them. 'Marriage should not begin with a broken vow,' she said at last.

'Not seven hours wed and hen-pecked already.' Though still good-humoured, his voice held an edge of irritation.

Zeal clamped onto her rock and waited.

Wentworth sighed and sat up in the dark. 'I shall give you an opening chorus, no more. Then I need to sleep even if you don't. I'm an old man and not used to dancing.' He shuffled his buttocks up the bed to lean against the bolsters.

'Close your eyes. Now imagine a ship. *The Golden Seal*, bound for Hispaniola. Unfurling its white sails with the sound like a thousand wings battering the air. Shouts . . . men crawl like ants along the spars. The wind catches. The first swell hits her so that she lies over and drops into the trough, already yearning towards her demon lover, the seabed. Or so it seemed to the young man I once was.'

'Were you already a soldier then?'

'Yes.'

'How did you come to be one?'

'If you want me to relate every tedious detail of birth, rearing, names of dogs and horses and so on, I won't live long enough to reach the end of my story.' He shifted under the coverlet. 'Jump four weeks. A ship set for the West Indies must call first at the Canaries, to take on fresh water and the last fresh food until landfall in the West Indies. After Madeira, it begins a long ride on the currents which sweep round in a great curve, first eastwards towards Africa, then turning south west again to pour themselves into the Caribbean Sea . . . have I lulled you to sleep yet? . . . Pity! . . .'

He seemed to debate with himself for a moment, then continued. Like water trapped behind a dam, his story forced itself through the narrow sluice of his throat and teeth.

'Whatever he thought of himself, that young man was an innocent, crammed full of images from books and travellers' tales but with no experience farther afield than the grey skies of England and a few skirmishes in the Low Countries . . .'

Aha! she thought. Finally let slip a fact about himself instead of all that navigation.

'As they sailed south,' said Wentworth, 'the sun felt like a fire seeking him out to temper and burnish. It was a crucible in which all men were transmuted by its power into something new and strange in their own eyes . . .'

'John sailed for the West Indies,' said Zeal.

'Yes.' The bedclothes rustled as he re-crossed his feet. 'Yes, he did.'

After a long silence, she said, 'I didn't mean to break the thread.' When he did not respond, she pressed him. 'Why were you sailing to Hispaniola?'

'Ambition.' He cleared his throat. 'Greed . . . you see how truthful I am being.'

'You wouldn't want to buy my life with counterfeit coins.'

He made a sound she could not interpret. 'This ambitious young man,' he said. '. . . this former self, who had rattled with arrogance when he boarded, now found himself trying to stay out of the way of running sailors and uncoiling ropes, like a cur in a busy kitchen. He hunted down a quiet place, above the hen coop, as it happened, where he could perch and stare out at the sea, hour after hour, unable to stop staring.

'The earth had disappeared forever. He was a speck in infinity. He felt no advance through space, just an endless rolling up and down in the same place. They were all trapped, immobile, under the vast cupping heavens. He wanted to think of himself as a brave man but his guts were crimped with an unexplained terror that had nothing to do with an understandable distaste for drowning.'

She saw John at the rail, squinting at the water, already changing from the man whom she had loved at Hawkridge.

Wentworth again fell silent.

'Is that the end?'

'Yes. For now.' A moment later, however, he added, 'I shall give you a short epilogue.'

'One night, this young man lay on his back on the poop deck, where the captain had graciously permitted him access, looking up at the stars. Suddenly, he found that he had given himself over to the constant rising and falling and was taking pleasure in riding those arcs through space. Then a bright star fixed him with its beam. No longer trapped, he climbed the shaft of light, higher and higher, until he began to feel he might be sucked through a hole in the sky and vanish into whatever lay on the other side. He gripped onto the light beam for safety but his hands closed on nothing.

'He sat bolt upright, heart pounding. Pressed his palms flat on the deck, felt the sun's heat lingering in the planks, was grateful for their relative solidity. And for the scents of tar, resin, damp wool, and wet feathers from the hen coop. His senses clung to an everyday world on which his spirit had almost lost its grip. He laid his hands on his belly, then on his face, to remember later how they had felt at this exact moment. He knew he was already changed from the man who came aboard. He feared that the man who returned from this voyage would barely recognize the one who had sailed. He also felt an intense thrill.'

And if I ever see John again, I won't know him. That's what Wentworth is trying to tell me. His story is not really about himself at all.

'Enough confession for one night,' said Wentworth. However, he continued to sit against the bolsters, staring into the shadows of the bed.

Zeal curled onto her side with her back to him. Could any woman's love rival that thrill of adventure? She tucked her elbows into her sides, missing the comforting warmth of the cat, which had stayed to guard its territory at Hawkridge.

She must have slept at last, for she woke with a start, then tried to scream. Someone was in her bed. The candle was alight again. His bulk seemed to fill the enclosed space.

'Hush,' said Wentworth. 'I didn't mean to wake you.' He held a knife.

She could not speak. The thing she had not known was to destroy her after all.

'To avoid all question,' he said. With the knife, he cut his finger. 'We must not forget that you are a virgin.' He wiped his finger on the bed sheet. 'Go back to sleep. I'm sorry to have disturbed you.'

17

The day after the wedding, Zeal sat down with resolve at the estate office table, where she and John had worked. Though the wing in which the office lay had escaped the worst of the fire, everything smelled of smoke, including John's quill pen – the last he had cut – and his coat.

She took the coat from its peg and put it on again. Held the front away from her body and bent her head to catch his odour, to conjure him.

There they were. At the table, two ghosts, reaching for papers, bending their heads together to read the same bill or list.

'We must . . .' They spoke at the same moment.

'Cows?' she asked.

'Barns.'

They looked at each other. 'Dried bracken,' they said in unison. They laughed. She had been absurdly amused by this small, mundane coincidence.

She now sat at the table, on the same stool as her ghost, and picked up his quill pen. She drew the edge of the plume across her cheek. The occasional accidental brush of his hand against her own had stirred in her a contradictory mix of agitation and peacefulness. She had not known, then, how to interpret it. As she was still married to Harry, it did not, could not, occur to her that she might be falling in love with someone else.

She smoothed the barbels of the feather between thumb and forefinger, then kissed the pen.

My dearest Love . . . she wrote.

She leaned back. This task grew no easier with time.

If only he sat beside her now, and she had only to speak.

My dearest Love, Your child and I now belong to another man . . . though of course, you do not yet know about the child . . .

She bent her head over the paper again. '*I* . . .' Again she stopped. The words closed between them like steel shutters. The stool at her side was empty.

She did some calculations on the paper, then dropped her head into her hands.

Seven years made two thousand five hundred and forty-something days to be survived.

The child. The new house. Keeping everyone alive and fed. Learning who Wentworth was. More than enough to keep her occupied.

She pulled a pile of accounts over the letter and began to make notes in her work book.

18

Zeal's Work Book – November 1639

Choose new house site

Go with forester and carpenter to Pig Woods and Coombe Hay to choose timber for cutting and planking. To season till next year. (How does one judge a tree? she asked herself. And how many are needed?)

Dig Quarry pit for small dressing stones for windows and doors as may be. Ask Jonas Stubbs how many more apprentices, masons and labourers needed

Least cost of carriage of stone from Ufton Wharf, is 5 shillings the load. (But how many loads will I need? How will I know?)

Make place for burning and slaking lime. Buy sand to cover it until next year. How many mortarmen? Unskilled wages are 8d the day

Dig up brick clay and spread on field for frost to work

Timber hovel for Sam to work, as present forge is too small. When work permits, send Sam to London to choose iron for:
> *Clamps for stonework*
> *Glazing bars*
> *Fire-backs*
> *Hinges*
> *Nails*
> *Costs?*

Nota bene: By Grace of God and good will, Master Wentworth has secured gift of an old barn, all timbers and slates, from acquaintance near Midgeham. Carriage gratis by Thames to Ufton. Thereafter to me.

Consult with those who have built a house

To meet costs:
  Sell some pasture with way to river to Master Wilde?
  Sell eggs?
  Salvage all lead from Hawkridge House as cost of new lead is very great
  Master Wentworth suggests approaching Lord S. for monastic lead granted to him
  Dismiss some house servants until again needful, thereby saving expense of their food and clothing

(How will I pay the king's new levies, on top of the other taxes?)

19

'Samuel,' announced Gifford. 'Chapter thirty-two, verse thir-teen. "I know the pride and naughtiness of your heart."'

His congregation stirred in universal guilt. Zeal and Wentworth exchanged glances. To her surprise, he had chosen to accompany her.

After long thought and much prayer for guidance, Doctor Bowler too had decided to accompany the Hawkridge party on their next required attendance at Bedgebury church.

'As a gesture of peace and goodwill,' Bowler explained, to himself as much as to anyone.

But even before Gifford announced the day's Scripture, Zeal knew that Bowler's gesture had been misjudged. As soon as their little party arrived, the minister began to vibrate with buoyant tension, like a young girl approaching her first flir-tation. He knew he held power. He knew his target. He meant to test his power.

'We live . . .' Gifford skewered individuals with hot, rusty-lashed eyes, '. . . in the land of darkness and the shadow of death. In a land where light is as darkness and darkness is seen as light.' He looked straight at Zeal.

'Job, Chapter ten, verse twenty-two, more-or-less,' murmured Doctor Bowler on Zeal's right.

A large-breasted woman in the opposite pew, whom Zeal knew to be Gifford's wife, turned to glare.

'In our ignorance, we believe that we are safe in the hands of the Lord,' continued Gifford. 'But we, poor fools, ignore our danger. Even as we toil at honest labour, even as our innocent children take their places beside us, we are all in mortal danger. And let me tell you why this is.'

He leaned forward over his pulpit and lowered his voice as if he feared being overheard.

'There are deceivers among us.' He glared about, seeking these demonic spies. 'Wolves dressed as sheep. They are among us, even here, even now as I speak. Today, in this house of God.'

Backs straightened. A sharp intake of breath flared a number of nostrils. Most of the congregation kept their eyes forward, but a few could not help speculative glances at their personal candidates for wolf-in-disguise.

Gifford had the edgy need to make his mark that sometimes affects small men in a warrior society. As a student, he had seemed to soften his Scottish Calvinism. He held his tongue on the subject of Anglican bishops and celebration of Anglican mass. He made much of the shared Anglican and Protestant hatred for the Great Whore of Rome. At the same time he cemented his connections with the growing number of English Puritans who opposed what they saw as the recidivist Catholic tendencies of the king and of Bishop Laud. Once he had a congregation, his political and religious views hardened.

'When a king abandons his people to Satan, then a man's conscience must be his king,' he often said, if rebuked for speaking against the Crown. 'Would you entrust any English soul to a half-Danish monarch, married to a French Catholic who now declares himself ready, given certain conditions to once again declare Catholicism to be a true religion? Though his own father banned the Roman church from English shores!'

Gifford, like many others, recognized the beginning of a foreign conspiracy to bring Catholicism back to England. The burnings would begin again. New Protestant martyrs would be made. Like a plague detector, he sniffed out the faintest symptoms of infection in his parish. Only constant vigilance could forestall the enemy, who might be anyone – your landlord, your neighbour, your manservant, even your son.

With a glance at the Hawkridge party, Gifford shifted back to declamatory mode:

'England is become a battlefield for the souls of men. We are not torn between King and Parliament, as many would have it, nor even between Englishman and Scot, though these armies are at war even now. No, our choice is between the Lord Our Father and the Great Harlot of Babylon! And, my friends, beware! The battle is come to us, here among these peaceful fields and clear-running waters. Even here in our own parish, the soldiers of the Antichrist are at work. They corrupt. They seduce with music and sweet perfumes . . .'

Doctor Bowler flushed until his scalp glowed like a beacon. He trapped his hands between his knees and sucked his lips in between his teeth.

'They dare even to profane the calling of clergymen. They profess to speak for God, yet lead their sheep ever farther from the light of His Grace. These ravening wolves of Satan disguise themselves as shepherds in order to lead their flock into the slavering jaws of Hell!'

Zeal sat up as if her spine were a spear stuck quivering into the pew. To stay was intolerable, but to leave would be as good as hanging Doctor Bowler up in the stocks with a label pinned to his coat.

'The Lord would have the wicked cease from troubling. You must not by your idleness sanction the work of the Antichrist.'

There was a murmur from the back pews.

Doctor Bowler had turned chalky white. His mouth pulled and jumped at the corners, seeking an acceptable expression in which to rest.

'You must sharpen your eyes to the vision of angels, listen with the ears of the pure. You must be the sword of God. You must be the purifying fire!'

'Yes!' shouted a man's voice, at once multiplied by other voices.

'He means to stir up a hanging mob right here in church,' said Wentworth between his teeth. 'And I had to leave my sword . . .!'

'This battle,' cried Gifford. 'Yes, this bloody battle is come to us. "We must swallow up the ground in fierceness and say among the trumpets, 'hah, hah!' and smell the battle! Oh, the thunder of the captains, the shouting . . ."'

Bowler sat motionless, making himself very small.

Zeal gave a small moan and fell sideways in a faint. She kept her eyes closed during the ensuing confusion. Felt Wentworth lift her and carry her out of the church, staggering only once.

'You can put me down now,' she murmured when they had cleared the churchyard. 'Unless Gifford is hot on our scent.'

'He's still holding his hounds on a leash of words.'

'Is she ill?' Bowler's urgent voice had caught up with Wentworth.

'Not in the least,' said Zeal as Wentworth set her back on her feet.

Gifford's tragedy was that he wanted to love but doubted his own talent for it, as both minister and man. His neighbour called forth no tenderness from his heart. On the contrary, Gifford's quick mind found most people tedious. His fellows, whom he knew he should love with a pure, selfless generosity roused in him chiefly impatient thoughts and twitches of irritation. And he knew that each such thought, each twitch, pushed him towards damnation. After years of attempted charity, he had begun to suspect himself of a deep, destroying coldness. He was not certain that he loved even his brisk, melon-breasted wife, whom he serviced nevertheless with a mixture of carnality and guilt, and not as often as the imp of Satan between his legs would have liked.

With fervour and relief, therefore, he embraced the simpler, crystalline passion of holy rage. If he could not love, he would cleanse and save. Such good work might, perhaps, hold him steady in God's Grace.

He saved souls the way other men hide coins in old socks, to be ready as a form of ransom, as if God might in the end be willing to make a deal. The more valuable he secretly felt a soul to be (though he knew he should hold them all to be equal in God's eyes), the greater his rage when he failed to rescue it. And because he possessed considerable intellect and perception, the souls at Hawkridge, young Mistress Wentworth in particular, both stirred and challenged him more than the usual tedious run of Bedgebury sinners. She would be a precious gem to offer to the Lord.

'The purifying fire!' Gifford shouted again, to quell the hubbub amongst his congregation and pull their attention away from the door.

That young woman had a way of going at life full tilt that almost guaranteed she would fall off the tightrope of virtue. How she had got from Lady Beester to Mistress Wentworth had, in itself, fuelled many of his prayers. She was young and fresh, with the time (given the right guidance) to put her soul in order and hope for Divine Grace. The fire that had consumed her house should have been enough warning, but not even that little Arminian parson of hers had read the sign.

Gifford had hoped that that new husband might rein her in, but the old pantaloon had shown nothing but indifference and ill breeding in the matter of the wedding chapel. To educate the body, you must begin with the head. Which, in this case, was not the putative master, but the young red-haired hussy who (yet another transgression) tried to run the estate as if she were the man.

The word 'fire' reminded him of a recurring dream from which he had wakened in a sweat again the night before, of her naked young body suffering eternal torment, her hair turned to bright tongues of flame.

That night, Zeal woke to see Wentworth dressing by the light of a candle.

'Go back to sleep,' he said.

'Fishing at this hour?' she asked.

He hesitated. 'Wish I were.' He opened a chest and took out the pistol, which he had spent a day dismantling and cleaning shortly after Harry died.

Zeal sat up. 'What is it?' she asked in alarm.

'Visitors down at Hawkridge.'

She got out of bed and reached for her over-gown. 'Who?'

'Tuddenham says that Sam brought word back from Bedgebury . . . some damn fool hotheads took Gifford at his word and think they're meant to be flaming swords raised against the Antichrist.'

'Bowler?'

'So I fear. If I'd been a lout looking for an excuse for a brawl, that sermon would have served me nicely too.'

Zeal bent and felt for her shoes on the shadowy floor.

'You're staying here,' said Wentworth. He tugged a heavy leather jerkin into place on his shoulders.

'No, coming.' She forced one foot into her shoe. Her feet had begun to swell after she missed her second monthly flow, and the shoe pinched. 'Poor Doctor Bowler. He must not be hurt!'

'You stay.' She had not heard Wentworth use this tone before. 'It may come to nothing. But if there is a ruckus, you mustn't risk a blow or a fall.'

She put on her other shoe.

'Zeal, I am not yet too old to represent you in this. You will stay.' He buckled on his sword belt.

She stared back at him. Life was not entirely unchanged after all.

Was I ever so meek before? she asked herself, as the door

closed on him. All the same, now that she was dressed, she saw no harm in merely going to observe what happened. She would stay well clear of any fighting.

She knew the track so well by now that she did not need a lantern. As on her wedding day, her feet found the way. She stopped on a hump on the Hawkridge side of the final slope, where she would be able at least to hear what was happening.

Below her, lights moved through the stable yard. One climbed the drive and vanished into the dark mass of the beech avenue. Still others skirted the ponds and probed the shadows along the river. She heard voices, but in urgent exchange rather than argument. A cluster of lights gathered by the chapel, near Doctor Bowler's chambers.

A chill began to creep through her cloak and gown. Her shoes grew wet and cold with autumn dew. She walked a little farther down the slope.

A burst of distant voices exploded from down river near the mill. But these were quick verbal shots fired in succession, not the sustained roar of a mob. Wentworth's voice cut through the shouts. Then his voice dropped so that she could not hear what he said. Several lights moved quickly in the direction of the trouble, though she counted five left on guard by the chapel.

She strained to hear what might be happening. Three lights came back up from the river. The others began to disperse.

'. . . back another time,' she suddenly heard Wentworth say out of the darkness, headed her way up the slope. If Wentworth and Arthur had not been talking, they would have caught her on the hillside.

Am I under that man's rod after all? she asked herself, as she fled back to High House, intent on being found in bed, demure and desperate for information she already knew.

Too late, she remembered her wet shoes, on the floor beneath the window. She tried to distract Wentworth with eager questions but could not tell if he were deceived or not.

'They were cowards,' was all he said. 'Quick to run at the sight of a sword.'

'Will you teach me to fight?' she asked, partly to distract him from the shoes, partly in earnest.

To her surprise, he did not laugh. 'After the child is born, if you still wish it. There's never harm in knowing how to defend yourself. I'm not what I was on the battle field but I could most likely manage the part of tutor.' His eyes rested on her shoes.

'You still owe me your gift of truth,' she said quickly. 'You have only just begun to keep your promise.'

Now he laughed. 'Not tonight. I am quite certain that you need to sleep now, for the child's sake!'

20

Zeal knew at once that she had interrupted Wentworth and Sir Richard in some masculine matter. They both looked alarmed at her entrance. Wentworth made as if to hide the letter he was holding, then changed his mind. The two men exchanged glances.

'Is it Doctor Gifford again?' she asked.

Neither of them replied.

'Or shall I simply disappear again?' She stepped back towards the door.

'I think she should know,' said Wentworth.

Sir Richard pulled his side-whiskers. 'Not so certain . . .'

'Master Wentworth is right,' she said. 'He already knows me that well.'

'She will know how we rate it.' Wentworth held the paper out to her.

Dear Sir Richard, Conscience will not let me stay silent. I have intelligence that an old man of your parish has been bewitched into marriage by a young woman whose history, investigated by me, fills me with alarm. I fear that she means to serve him as she has served others, that is to say, that his life is in danger. As the Holy Bible enjoins us 'Do not suffer a witch to live.' I leave this in your hands as magistrate. – A Christian Well-wisher, who would see God's natural order preserved.

Written in heavy slashing strokes, the letters awkwardly formed, as if the writer had disguised his or her hand.

'Don't trouble yourself, my dear,' said Sir Richard. 'There's always a mischief-maker in any parish squinting and peering after other people's sins.'

Zeal returned the letter to Wentworth, who re-read it, then stood with it gripped in his large square hands as if waiting for it to speak the author's name.

'From Doctor Gifford?' she asked stiffly.

'Could be.' Sir Richard glared at the ceiling in thought. 'Could be anyone. But that ". . . I have intelligence . . ." And the rest. Don't sound to me like the words of the man who did the marrying.'

'At first, I suspected the carters,' said Wentworth. 'But as you dismissed them so fiercely, they would write to some other magistrate. Or even the bishop . . .'

'How old are you, in fact?' asked Sir Richard.

'Sixty-two,' said Wentworth.

'Hah! I got it right at the wedding feast.'

Wentworth smiled slightly and continued to study the letter. 'The hand smacks of an unsteady temper. Look how fiercely the pen was pressed into the paper.'

Sir Richard held out his hand. 'I'll set it against all those sad, bile-soaked letters I am continually sent. It may match the hand of another. Such creatures sometimes persevere until I'm forced to catch them at it.'

'It's only words,' Wentworth said to her. 'You heard Sir Richard. An over-zealous addle-brain.'

Zeal nodded as if convinced, but she still felt as if a stranger had suddenly stepped out from a crowd without warning and struck her.

That night, lying alone in bed, Zeal decided that, in spite of the anonymous letter, and the sense it gave her that an unknown intruder had invaded Hawkridge, she had never-theless made a fair beginning to the project of surviving the next seven years.

Since their wedding night, Wentworth had left her alone and gone to sleep wherever he now chose to sleep. Or else, like tonight, he camped on the river, fishing. Although his absence from their bed meant that he had not yet continued his promised revelations, he had at least begun. She would work out how to deal with him in his night shirt, and he would learn that she, too, could fish patiently, in her own fashion.

Meanwhile, he had more to say than she had expected on the subject of the new house. That afternoon, he had walked with her to look at the burnt ruins. Together, they had climbed Hawk Ridge itself, and gazed back down into the valley. A little below them, the ridge flattened into a strip of meadow. At the edge of the meadow rose the rocky outcrop where she and John used to sit at the end of the day, flank to flank, not talking, content just to feel the other's warmth and to know that their eyes watched the same flaring sunset or swooping bats.

There! she thought.

'I think I might build just there,' she said, pointing down, expecting a short reply.

'A fine fair-standing,' said Wentworth. 'Needs only a little work to level it and dig cellars.' He gazed down a moment longer. 'Yes. A fine place to build. The house looking south, with Hawk Ridge at its back. Protected from north winds. Above the miasmas and damp airs of the valley that plagued the old house.'

She looked away from his surprising enthusiasm lest he read her true reason for choosing this spot.

Each time I look from my window, I will know that what I see is also recorded in John's memory. The glinting Shir, line of fishponds, beech avenue climbing the far slope to the high road, and dirty beige sheep grazing in the Roman Field. No matter what else may happen, a small part of our thoughts will always be exactly the same.

But I must write to tell John that the statues are gone, so he can adjust that part of his memory.

Wentworth turned to face west, looking upstream past the water meadows. 'I'm certain you could divert water from the river upstream, there, above the upper weir, and bring it almost to the house. Let it lift itself the last few feet with a small wheel. I've seen such things working. Water brought straight to the house in wooden pipes.'

'Worth more in everyday life than the finest gold plates.' She turned back to the south again. 'I can just see the chimneys of High House from here,' she said happily. 'Hawkridge Estate rises in the world.'

When he did not reply, she glanced at him. He stood with his feet planted squarely, hands on his hips so that his old coat flared out like the tail of a bird, gazing into the distance, far beyond the chimneys of High House.

'Sir?'

He did not hear.

Where has he gone? She studied him curiously. When he sighed and shook himself back to the present, she resolved to insist that he take her with him, in her imagination at least.

'Sir,' she repeated. 'I hope you are not still sleeping in your old chamber. The entire wing may collapse at any time. I don't wish to be made a widow so soon.'

Now he looked at her. 'How long would you like me to wait?'

Guilt made her flush. 'You know that's not what I meant!'

He smiled. 'Don't trouble yourself on the matter. I don't.' He set off down the slope.

She scrambled after him. 'I meant only to say, that you should sleep comfortably and safe. And to say that you are welcome to return to our bed.'

And story telling. Now, at least, her scarlet face might have a more friendly explanation.

He grinned widely and cocked one eyebrow. 'Thank you for that kind invitation. When not otherwise occupied or on the river, I will accept.' He turned away and began to pace out the distance along the brow of the site. She watched him grow smaller.

'One hundred and five paces,' he called back. 'You can build a palace here, if you like.'

'I like!' she called back. 'I lack only the means!' When he had come closer again, she added, 'And also the least idea of how to set about it.'

'The latter, at least, I can help you with,' he said. 'I'm neither a master builder nor surveyor, but if you tell me how you want it to look, I can help you draw a rough plan. As for means, we can begin by begging and might consider stealing.' They both laughed.

'Have you read Bacon's essay "Of Building"?' he asked. 'I shall lend it to you.'

So now she had an unexpected ally in her great project, and a sense that building a house might after all be within her power. All that troubled her now was the need to write to John as he had begged her to do.

My darling, she said silently into the darkness of the bed. If only I could send my thoughts instead of a letter. Then you would have heard from me every day and night.

I shall definitely write tomorrow, she told herself.

She fell asleep making a list of what she needed to do the next day. Her last thought was that she still had not spoken to Doctor Bowler as he had asked, about his sermon for Bonfire and Treason Day.

Tomorrow. Letter to John, and Bowler, tomorrow.

21

Doctor Bowler had good reason for concern over his sermon for the Bonfire and Treason service. Everyone, however unschooled or indifferent, knew the reason for the country's chief holiday – the foiling in 1605 of a treasonous Catholic plot against both King James (father of the present king, Charles) and Parliament. The last minute discovery and the terrible vengeance taken on the traitors were worthy of the most exciting stage play.

When the king declared an official holiday on the anniversary of his escape, Parliament (Protestants, Puritans, and Laudians alike) established by statute that all people must rest from work on that day, in order to reflect on God's protection of his anointed representative on earth. They must also thank both Providence and the king's generosity for giving them freedom to drink, bowl, ride (if they could afford a horse), fight cocks, bait dogs and bears, dance, make love, or just sit and stare idly into space. They must also, by law, attend a special church service. And here Doctor Bowler's difficulties began.

Although, as a good Anglican, he accepted the authority of the bishops, he was not an extreme Arminian, whatever Gifford might say. He did not, like Archbishop Laud, embrace everything Catholic except the pope and the authority of Rome – incense, rich robes, bells, services sung in Latin, and saints. But he needed music as a fish needs water.

Doctor Gifford, on the other hand, was more extreme than even the severely reformed Puritan Anglicans, who accepted the authority of bishops but were otherwise almost identical to the pared down plainness and personal witness of Presbyterians. He was not merely a Presbyterian, rejecting bishops in favour of the forum of the presbytery. He was an extreme Calvinist Presbyterian, preaching the bleak doctrine of election and predestination in a formerly Anglican parish church. A spiritual brother to the men who were tearing out church organs, pulling down bells and plastering over religious pictures on church walls, he confused many of his older parishioners by banning Saints' Days and refusing to celebrate any festival that ended in 'mass', including Christmas. He wore only plain black wool.

'We are ordered by Doctor Gifford to burn the pope.' Doctor Bowler held a letter between the tips of his fingers, as if it were the very end of a lighted candle. 'And I must read out a prayer he has written, at our service on Gunpowder and Treason Day. I have prayed for guidance before troubling you, but find that I cannot judge the broader . . .' His voice trailed off.

'Let me see it.' As she took Gifford's letter, Zeal noted that his writing did not resemble that of the anonymous letter.

'There seems to me . . .' said Bowler, '. . . well, a smell of . . . at least, I would feel uneasy speaking such words . . .'

'You are right to resist,' exclaimed Zeal. 'This is treason! An open attack on the queen for adhering to the Church of Rome! And here, here, he prays to protect Parliament from all rebellion against the good of the people, even if the rebels should be royal. As if the king could rebel against his own people!'

In neither religion nor political belief did Bedgebury parish, any more than the rest of England, fall neatly into opposing halves like a sawn log. The fault lines more nearly resembled the crazed cracking of smashed ice or shattered window glass. There might have seemed to be a rough correlation between religion and politics. The majority of Puritans were Londoners, most often merchants, tradesmen and apprentices. A majority of courtiers were Anglicans. Yet there were Puritan noblemen and Arminian cobblers, just as there were Parliamentarian earls and farmers who were loyal king's men.

In Bonfire and Treason Day, James, that most pragmatic of kings, had given his subjects what they needed – a secular and somewhat ambiguous holiday. As both king and Parliament had been spared, Royalists and parliamentarians, Anglicans and Puritans could all celebrate with a clear conscience. Gifford, like many others, exploited this ambiguity to his own ends. In this case, he cited the church wardens and parish vestry as his authority.

'I am on the rack,' said Bowler. 'Also received from Winchester a new prayer written by the Archbishop Laud . . . makes a special point of the sin of rebellion against the Crown . . . D'you think he had got wind of Gifford's message?'

'May I see the archbishop's prayer?'

While Bowler went to fetch it, Zeal studied Gifford's hand-writing again. The minister's small tight script marched in precise straight lines across the page, interrupted by occasional florid capitals. She tried to judge whether this same hand could possibly have made those mad, slashing characters of the anonymous letter.

'I see that Parliament sits safely in both prayers,' she said when she had read the archbishop's text. 'His reverence would have us rejoice that it was preserved along with the king.' She thought for a moment. 'I won't be dragged into other men's quarrels. Read neither. Merely offer the usual thanks – the king's life preserved, etcetera.'

Bowler looked deeply unhappy. 'I would not wish to provoke any further . . . in the circumstances . . .'

'Don't fear,' she said. 'I doubt that the archbishop will trouble himself to send spies. As for Doctor Gifford, he's in the wrong this time. I can't think how he dares to write such dangerous poison. In any case, we've already routed his would-be Myrmidons once. And furthermore,' Zeal added, 'Sir Richard, with his usual generosity is paying again this year for both the pealing in our chapel and your sermon. He will join us. Even Gifford can't force you to preach treason in front of a magistrate who is also a minister of parliament.'

Bowler nodded without conviction. 'Do we dare have hymns?'

'Most certainly! I never feel reverent until I've heard you and Jamie send up your voices to delight the ear of God.'

Bowler gave a shaky sigh, but speculation already misted his eyes. 'And should I prepare music for dancing at the fire? You know Gifford's views . . .'

'That man doesn't speak for England and he most certainly does not speak for me. Let him try to prevent two parishes from taking their traditional exercise and delight! In any case, Bonfire and Treason Night is not a church festival. We are ordered by statute to celebrate. It would be high treason not to dance!'

She read both prayers again and sighed. 'As for burning the pope . . . I believe that our neighbours, the Wildes, were formerly Catholics. Peace and good fellowship will not be served by such naming of the enemy.' She held up the two prayers. 'With these weighty stones grinding on each other, we must try to stay from between them.'

Zeal's queasiness suddenly stopped troubling her. As she had determined, she wrote at last to John, a cheerful evasive letter, brimming with detail of their daily life and plans for rebuilding, but short on substance. The only truth she trusted to survive the long journey to reach him was how she missed him and feared for his safety. A little lightened, though still uneasy in conscience, she waited for his reply.

With renewed fervour, she now threw herself into the preparations for the Bonfire and Treason festival. It came at a good time, when the weather was often still very fine, before the darkness and cold of winter. And because it was a secular holiday, it escaped the restrictions on drinking and dancing which dampened the festivals of the church calendar.

The bonfire itself offered a good way to get rid of the last of the rubbish from the old house. Men and youths from Bedgebury and all outlying estates constructed it on the May Common, where the May pole had stood before Gifford ordered it taken down six years earlier. Half-burnt furniture, charred curtains, the surviving corners of blackened carpets, and the old front door all joined the heap, along with hedge trimmings saved and dried for the night, old fence palings, musty straw, and enough good logs to make a firm foundation for the rest. Many other households threw on their own combustibles. Groups of people could often be seen admiring the swelling pile and discussing how it might improve it.

Zeal set Mistress Margaret to making soothing unguents for burns, as every year some young fool singed his breeches trying to leap the fire, or a firework shot off in the wrong direction, or hot fat from the roasting pit spat into the face of a cook.

Doctor Bowler walked about deaf and unseeing, humming fragments of tunes. He practised dance tunes to be sure of remembering every note and re-strung his bow to ready it for hours of vigorous play.

Half-grown children taught the smallest ones, too young to have attended the last year's bonfire, to do the Shepherd's Hey and Strip the Willow. In the bake house kitchen, Aunt Margaret and Agatha oversaw the making of pickles and kept salted meat back from the autumn preserving. Hawkridge would also contribute two hogs heads of ale, and two sheep, which grazed under appraising eyes, in ignorance of their starring role to come.

*   *   *

The Archbishop of London might not send spies to Hampshire, but Zeal noticed three Bedgebury faces in the Hawkridge chapel on the morning of 5 November.

Wentworth noted them as well. She saw him lower his chin and stare at the intruders briefly. Through most of the service, he sat with his lower lip slightly stuck out and his brows pulled together. He was tardy in his responses and mumbled almost as an afterthought. Twice Zeal had to point out their place in the prayer book.

As they sat behind her, Zeal could not see whether or not the visitors joined in singing the hymns. They made no disturbance during Bowler's service, however. Nor did they seem to object to the anthem sung by Bowler's choir, with Jamie's sublime descant floating above them all. After the service, they left quietly, but Zeal felt uneasy nevertheless as she watched them go.

That afternoon, she went to the office to rest for a few moments, as she had more and more often begun to feel the need. She touched John's coat, then lay on her smoky pallet and looked for the cat, which should have been hunched asleep in the window. Her growing need to sit down, or even recline, had delighted the cat as much as it irritated her, as if she did it solely to oblige the creature with a lap.

I intend to dance tonight, she told herself. By Christmas, the child will show and no one will allow me. She suddenly remembered the firm warmth of Wentworth's hands on her waist when they had danced together at the wedding.

Who would have thought he would be so nimble? I wonder what other skills he is hiding. Even though I'm so tired every night, I must make him continue his tale. He entertained me well enough on our wedding night but told me almost nothing of what I want to know. And now he uses the child as an excuse to put me off.

When she woke, the cat had still not come to sit on her feet. She looked briefly in the gardens at its favourite perches, and the spot by the upper pond.

It must have gone to the barns for a mouse, or to the paddock for a young dove. There was no time to look further as she had to ride to High House to dress for the evening.

Zeal sat happily on a barrel on May Common and fanned her scarlet face. Sweat, beer and smoke perfumed the night air, which was otherwise clear and cool enough to make people happy to stand by the fire. She was startled by her own unexpected sense of well-being.

A perfect evening, she thought. God is smiling on us. He agrees with the king that men must have time for joy as well as work. I'm sure that John would agree too.

She was a tiny bit drunk, and ecstatic from dancing. Content now just to watch. Everyone so transported, sweating, happy. Arthur swung past, grinning like a benign demon with Rachel in his arms. Bowler on fiddle, Sam on his drum, a pipe. An unfamiliar taborer from Far Beeches. All those neat feet, one minute spinning in tiny compact self-contained worlds, then, at signal from the music, launching into a joyous charge across the earth. They cantered, jounced. The dancers became a single creature with one mind. Like birds in flight they wheeled, interlocking paths, miraculously always missing. Never colliding. Always arriving, again and again, at fresh beginnings.

'Country pleasures!' called Sir Richard as he passed her again clutching Mistress Wilde.

Zeal saw hope in the dance. You lose your partner, she thought. Go seeking, experience the miracle of finding him again. Move on and with every new partner, play out the same miracle of racing geometry. Shatter. Regroup, order, laughing panic and once more, the blissful resolution into order – your first partner, a double line, an arch of arms, a circle of red, fire-lit faces, beaming, frowning in concentration. They were together, fitting, teetering together through the universe trusting their safe place in the shape of the dance. Their faces gleamed in the firelight.

'Madam, you'd best not dance any more!' Rachel was carried away again.

Zeal loved them all. The feel of their hard-working hands, toughened like her own. The smell of their sweat, their excitement. John's people. Her people. Her creatures. Her family.

How lucky I am, after all.

Only a few weeks before, she had determined to kill herself. Now she rested her hands on her tight rounded belly and blessed Philip Wentworth, even though he had disappeared soon after they arrived at May Common and she had not danced with him after all.

A few people watched the dancing with pinched lips and whispers. Some had voiced disappointment that no effigy was to be burnt.

'A small tithe for our parson! Drink for the new bell ropes!' Sam, the smith, now stood at the ale barrels, shouting like a fair ground hawker, having lent his drum to someone else. Tuddenham, with red nose and eyes like an eager squirrel served the beer and collected the pennies.

Suddenly Bowler's fiddle squawked discordantly. His bow hand dropped to his side. The music stopped.

Zeal stood up, frowning. The dance crumbled back into single beings, a little dazed by their transformation.

'Lechery and idleness!' Gifford cut through the crowd like Moses come down from the mountain. A tight group of his male parishioners followed close behind. 'You overheat your loins and stir up obscenity!'

'And I thought we were enjoying ourselves!' cried a man's voice.

Gifford spied his target. 'Doctor Bowler! Playing a fiddle to encourage wantonness!'

'Don't he do it well?' shouted a woman.

Bowler lowered his instrument and stood at bay.

'Oh, my fallen children!' Gifford sounded close to tears. 'I grieve for you all!' Then he saw Zeal. 'And you, Mistress

Wentworth, what example do you set with your lewd cavorting?'

'I obey the king by celebrating, Doctor. I, for one, am not turned rebel against the Crown.'

'Do you imagine that a temporal injunction is your line of scarlet thread which shall preserve you from the Lord's vengeance?'

'God can not possibly hate joy as much as you would have it seem!' cried Zeal. 'Where is the sin in simple pleasures?'

'You are wilfully blind, madam! Or already lost beyond all hope. How can you encourage those under your authority to give themselves to such vain, frivolous wasting of their precious souls? Cavorting like beasts, stirring lasciviousness.'

He turned next on Tuddenham and the smith. 'As for you, remember how Christ served the moneychangers in the Temple! How dare you claim to serve your Lord with drunkenness and venality?'

'"Shall mortal man be more just than God?"' asked Bowler, tremulous but defiant.

'Give me that devil's instrument! Onto the fire with it, where it belongs!' Gifford reached for the fiddle.

Bowler bared his teeth and kicked at Gifford's shins while holding his fiddle at arm's length. Gifford seized the instrument in both hands. Doctor Bowler sank his teeth into the minister's wrist.

Gifford yelped and staggered back.

'Doctor Gifford!' Zeal shouted across the growing hubbub. 'You are welcome to join us but you may not stay to spoil another festival for me!'

'I'm bleeding!' exclaimed Gifford. 'He's a mad dog!'

'Which will it be?' asked Zeal.

'Madam, unspeakable torment awaits you unless you let me guide you to the light.'

'I have light enough, sir. This fire will do me nicely.'

'Yes!' Gifford pounced as if she had suddenly spoken his cue. 'Your pagan fire. I see that you do not burn a figure of the pope as I ordered. Are you dainty on that point? Does your Doctor Bowler perhaps nurse a secret reverence for Babylon?'

'I ordered that there should be no pope on our fire. I see nothing godly in miming death and baying with frustration that we can't burn the real man.'

'I smell rebellion,' said Gifford. 'And rebellion is as the sin of witchcraft . . .'

'You are the rebel, sir, not I! With your treasonous prayer! In your place, I would guard my tongue and hope to keep my head in place.'

Gifford took this defiance with a smile. 'You threaten me with puny temporal power, but I wield the sword of Eternity. I will have this fire be as the fire of the Lord and burn away all sin, as it will destroy all enemies of England, even the mightiest . . . as it will consume all followers of the Antichrist!'

He waved his followers forwards.

Four of them carried a straw and wicker effigy of a man dressed in a loose robe of tattered silk. A paper mitre dangled by one edge from his head. As his bearers advanced, he quivered in their hands and gave out a faint scrabbling sound.

'Throw the Antichrist into the flames.'

There were scattered cheers as the straw and wicker figure was pitched onto the top of the pyre. Some faces looked at Zeal with dismay. But all eyes turned back to the fire as crackling flames seized the tips of the straw and turned them to glowing orange wires. The silk robe caught. The figure stood in an envelope of fire.

It gave an unearthly shriek. The wicker head jerked. A shadow writhed inside it.

Several women in the crowd screamed. The crowd gaped. A few applauded the verisimilitude.

The figure shrieked again, a high-pitched desperate yowl,

unidentifiable as man, demon or beast. The figure twitched and fell onto its face in the centre of the flames.

'There's something alive in there!' shouted Zeal.

Another wail of terror and pain pinched her heart and lungs in a cold vice.

Then two or three voices shouted, 'Death to England's enemies!'

'What have you done?' screamed Zeal. The heat was as solid and impassable as a wall.

The wail stopped abruptly. The flames snapped and roared around the silence where the scream had been.

Zeal saw Gifford watching her with a twist of satisfaction on his lips. She was trembling.

'Do you object to the execution of our enemies, madam?'

'What creature did you put into the effigy?' Now she smelled burning fur.

'Your creature, madam. A beast that is grown familiar enough, I hear, to share your bed. A witch's familiar. I fear that Satan is made all too welcome at Hawkridge.'

Three men tried to pull her off him.

'God hates you!' she yelled at him as she beat at his head with her fists. She would kill him. 'You are the evil in our parish! Wicked man! Wicked, wicked, cruel man!'

'Fetch Master Wentworth!' someone shouted over the growing mêlée. 'Where's Wentworth?'

The repulsed Bedgebury myrmidons had returned to the attack and found eager opponents.

'Mistress! Leave him!' Arthur hauled at her shoulders.

The minister's eyes gleamed with satisfaction and fear. 'That creature would have seduced you!' he cried. 'Even if you did not yet know it as a familiar, it would have seduced you! It perished for the good of your soul.'

Beating at the source where the words poured out, she cut her knuckle against his teeth.

Gifford raised his forearm against her blows. 'I will not let you be damned, mistress!'

'Zeal! Let him go!' Wentworth's urgent voice reached her at last. Zeal saw that she had fastened one hand in Gifford's rusty hair and the other on his collar, with which she was trying to choke him.

'I can't strike a woman!' croaked Gifford. 'Someone, help me please!'

As Wentworth pulled her off the minister, she saw that the battle had spread. Gifford's men had found clubs. Arthur narrowly missed her with the fiery end of a log he had pulled from the edge of the blaze.

'Go back to High House!' Wentworth shouted at her. 'Run! Find your horse.'

When she ran at Gifford again, Wentworth grabbed her arm. 'We don't know what other violence they mean to do. I won't have you harmed, do you hear?' He gave her arm a little shake.

'Where were you?' she asked. 'You must help me!' She turned to the fire.

'Your cat is long dead. You can do nothing for it. Now, I order you to put yourself out of harm's way!' He looked away, assessing the battle. She saw that he wanted to join it, that she was holding him back.

'Come, madam,' said Rachel. 'This is no place for either of us now.'

'I go! I go!' She pulled her arm from Wentworth's grip. Saw him exchange glances with her maid as if she were a stubborn brat.

'As soon as the child is born, I swear I will learn to fight like a man! Then you won't be able to dismiss me so easily!'

'You landed a few blows all the same,' Rachel said as she led her away. 'I vow you split his lip.'

Zeal stomped across the field, crushing Gifford's face beneath every step. She sucked her bleeding knuckle. The God who prompted such vicious cruelty could never be her God.

'Gifford is the deceiver in our midst!' she cried. 'It's he who sees darkness as light!'

Behind her a scream cut across the ugly shouting around the fire.

She turned in sudden terror. 'Was that Master Wentworth's voice? I must go back . . .'

Rachel seized her sleeve. 'Master Wentworth can look after himself better than most, madam. All I fear is facing him if I don't get you back to High House. Our horses are just over there.'

Zeal paced their chamber, reliving her attack on Gifford, hearing the shrieks of the burning cat and seeing the frantic shadow trying to break out of its wicker coffin.

My poor little beast! She wanted to weep but was dried up by the heat of her rage.

How could anyone wittingly cause such terror and pain to another living creature?

'For the good of my soul!' he said.

My soul is not worth it. Any soul bought at the price of such meanness and cruelty is tarnished beyond redemption.

She pushed open the window to listen, but May Common was too distant for the sounds of battle to carry. A faint smell of smoke, however, had already drifted up Sir Richard's valley.

I will never attend another of his services, she thought. No matter what fines or sanctions he imposes. I can't listen to that man pretend to speak for God. Even to be seen sitting in his church would make me the worst sort of hypocrite.

'What news?' she demanded of Rachel when her maid came into the chamber with a soothing posset, which Zeal had not ordered.

'A rout! A rout!'

Zeal rushed to the window an hour later to see the returning warriors marching noisily up the valley towards High House. She ran down to meet them at Sir Richard's front door.

'Refreshment for the troops!' shouted Wentworth. Sir Richard's chief house groom rushed away to oblige.

'Your poor beast is avenged,' Wentworth told Zeal.

'You should have seen them run!' Arthur agreed. 'But then we had us a real general.' He nodded towards Wentworth, who was now congratulating the men. 'Master John left us all in good hands, eh?'

Having seen that her husband was uninjured, Zeal slipped back up to their chamber, relieved but unable to share the general high spirits. She also felt that she should perhaps have reproved Arthur for over-familiarity but she did not have the heart to dampen his jubilation at the Hawkridge victory.

'That settled them! They seem to have misplaced their flaming swords.' Philip had entered without knocking and still blazed with the heat of battle. His square jaw ploughed great furrows in the air, his feet thumped the floor. He took off his sword belt and slung it on its hook, then sat on the bed and began to pull off his boots. When she did not reply, he looked up.

He has decided to sleep here, she thought. For the first time since our wedding night.

'My poor darling! I'm sorry about your cat.' He stood and embraced her. 'I was once even jealous of the unfortunate beast. At least we saw them off and did some serious chastising of our own. I hope we might have quenched a little of that man's lethal fervour.'

She felt the delight still in him. 'You were a soldier again.'

His chest bucked against her cheek as he gave a snort of laughter. 'More like a common brawler, but my fists still knew what to do.' He released her in order to pace the room to use up unexpended force. 'May I lie here tonight?' The question was mere formality.

He will talk freely tonight, she thought suddenly. He will want to relate other battles.

He climbed into bed in his shirt and under-drawers.

But when they sat side by side in Sir Richard's great bed, he said, 'Other memories also stir, I'm afraid.'

She looked away from the hummock that had risen under his shirt.

Wentworth did not pull the coverlet over his erection but contemplated it with his head to one side and his lower lip stuck out.

'Will you touch him? No more than a touch . . . just once more in my life . . . for tonight.'

Reluctantly, she reached out her hand. His penis felt warm and solid through the thin fabric. He is my husband. There's no sin in it, she told herself. Though it feels like one. She shut her eyes lest she see John there in the room with them.

Wentworth sighed. 'Close your fingers for a moment.' He laid his hand on her thigh and leaned back on his pillows. 'I could die like this and ask nothing more of Heaven.'

She did not believe him. The flesh in her grasp trembled and strained. It put her in mind of a dog held fast by a shout but coiled and quivering to spring into a run at the first breath of a command. She knew what both duty and gratitude said she should do, but she could not.

They sat immobile, trapped in separate silences. At last, he gave her thigh a brisk pat. 'Time to sleep.'

She snatched back her hand and drew the coverlet up like a steel breastplate. He would not offer her a chapter of his story tonight after all. Nor would she ask.

'Thank you,' he said after a moment.

'You are welcome, sir.'

'My name is Philip. Now that you've touched my cock, perhaps you might care to call me by name.'

'Yes, sir.'

He laughed. 'Well. The babe needs for you to sleep.'

Sooner than she expected, he began to snore.

I'm not certain I can manage this, she thought. She felt lonely, as if he had deserted her and left a changeling in his place.

She slept badly. Woke once, but instantly pretended to be still deeply asleep.

He still had his back turned, but she had no doubt what he was doing.

I have driven him to the sin of Onan, she thought. I repay his kindness by endangering his soul. I consented to share his bed to save myself and John's child. I lie beside him almost naked. I can't blame him for not holding to his original conditions.

She curled on her side, which was now the most comfortable position, and wrapped her arms around the small tight fist in her belly. At least I have a time of grace. He is unlikely to press any further until the child is born. She lay rigid until he sighed and lay down again to sleep. She remembered that foxy smell, like a horse chestnut in bloom.

The triumph of the Hawkridge faction collapsed the next morning. The boy who fed the hens found Doctor Bowler behind the hencoop, still alive but senseless and bleeding. On questioning, the guards posted on the chapel confessed that they had decided to go home for an hour's sleep shortly before dawn.

'They must have posted a spy,' said Sam. 'To see when we left. We thought everyone had gone home to bed by then.'

The men moved Bowler's limp body onto Zeal's old mattress in the estate office while Arthur rode to Bedgebury for the physician. Meanwhile, Zeal tied a pad of linen onto the still bleeding wound in the parson's leg and bathed his other cuts and bruises with a decoction of fever-few and mallow. Mistress Margaret began to pound a fresh salve of marigolds, lanolin and honey.

Zeal wiped a crust of blood from Bowler's swollen green

and purple face. 'I think his nose may be broken,' she said. 'Dear God! Look at his poor hands!'

'Doctor Bowler!' she called softly to his senseless form. 'Come back to us. I need you to christen my babe.'

If I were a man, she thought, I would lie in ambush and slit the throat of the villain who could break the fingers of a musician's hand.

'They broke into his room through the chapel,' Wentworth reported. 'His fiddle is gone.' He stood silently while the women worked on the injured man, until Bowler groaned and fluttered his eyelids.

Sam and several of the other men wanted to set off for Bedgebury at once to retaliate.

'Don't be fools!' said Wentworth. 'How do you know who did it? Will you try to thrash the entire village? We shall find a better way.'

At dinner that day, Sir Richard shocked Zeal by ordering her to apologize to Gifford.

'But you know what he did!' she protested.

'And however much it grieves you, it was not against any law. Whereas, it seems that you pulled a tuft of hair out of his scalp and cut his lip so that he can hardly speak. He wishes to charge you with assault.'

'That's absurd! What of the attack on Doctor Bowler?'

'There's no proof at the moment that Gifford had anything to do with it.'

'This is madness,' said Zeal.

'But true, alas. He will withdraw the charge if you apologize.'

'Never!'

'I do recommend that you agree.'

'I cannot believe that you support him, Sir Richard.'

'I'd cheerfully whip him out of the parish, but I must also uphold the law. Which also involves trying to find Bowler's assailants. Apologize, my dear, and save us all a great deal of trouble.'

What happened next soon joined the body of local legend that quickly grew up around the Battle of the Bonfire.

No one heard what was said between the two men. But it became known across at least five parishes that, the next morning, Philip Wentworth marched into Gifford's church and up the aisle in the middle of a sermon, which the minister was valiantly delivering through swollen lips. Without a word to the startled congregation, Wentworth took the minister's arm, hauled him into the vestry, and locked the door. The members of the congregation who felt bound to defend their minister had first pounded on the door, then fetched an axe and swords, but the door had opened again before they could force it.

To their amazement, rather than stirring them to string up his visitor, Gifford assured his flock that all was well and that the wrath of God would strike any man, woman or child who violated the new and absolute peace he had just sworn to uphold. Furthermore, he meant to impose a severe penance on those who had taken part in the war of the night before last. And he ordered anyone who had so much as lifted a finger against the Hawkridge parson to deliver himself up at once to the parish constable. Privately, he withdrew the charge of assault against Mistress Wentworth.

Wentworth refused to tell anyone, even Zeal, what he had said to Gifford behind the vestry door. He allowed only that it had to do with a bishop, treason and Gifford's testicles.

In spite of a constant drenching November rain, Philip then disappeared for the next four days, as if he had exhausted all strength to deal with his fellows. He also sent word that he would sleep in the tack room again, to stay on guard at Hawkridge House in case Gifford had doubted his word. Though he had once again put himself out of reach of her curiosity, Zeal was relieved on another count. Fearing a renewed attack on the chapel, Bowler had refused to obey

her order to leave Hawkridge again for the safety of High
House.

'Doctor Gifford wanted our chapel razed along with the
other churches!' he protested.

As she did not wish to upset the little parson any further,
and Philip would now be within earshot, she left Bowler in
his old chamber behind the chapel, staring at his bandaged
left hand. He seemed not to notice that the Hawkridge family
began to attend prayers at High House.

After two more days, spent looking out of the window,
and falling over the other people kept within by the rain, or
else plodding through the downpour to Hawkridge, Zeal
decided that she, too, would move back to her own estate.
The little lodge at the top of the Hawkridge drive had a large
central chamber, which could serve as a parlour, two sleeping
chambers, one for her and one for Wentworth if he wished,
and a comfortable loft for Rachel.

It would mean finding other lodgings among her tenants
and labourers for the house women who had been sleeping
there. But though Sir Richard had been extremely kind, she
knew that so many extra people strained his modest household. When the coming winter kept them indoors for weeks
at a time, they would all be tempted to murder.

Zeal also wanted to be near Doctor Bowler, who had to be
fed like a baby and still needed opium syrup for the pain.
She felt very far from all her people sleeping in the estate
outbuildings. In any case, the half-hour walk between High
House and Hawkridge had begun to tire her, even without
the rain. And, though she still rode her little mare, Rachel
fretted that she would endanger the child.

'You should be riding in a chair, madam! I beg you.'

'And what excuse could I give for such feebleness?' Zeal
replied. 'I haven't been married long enough. I can't possibly
announce the child for at least another fortnight.'

The move would also relieve her from the constant scrutiny
of so many eyes. Though she had taken to wearing a sleeveless

coat, as if against the autumn chill, the lodge would offer more privacy than High House.

When she next saw Wentworth, he agreed at once with her plan. 'The tack room floor is hard on my old bones.'

Zeal gave him a sideways look. His talk of advanced years no longer deceived her.

He watched her counting eggs she hoped to sell at market to help pay for the new house.

'Three dozen and five,' she said.

'In any case, we will need the tack room to house a poor fellow I met in an inn near Basingstoke.' He looked at her expectantly, with his eyebrows raised, waiting for her question.

In an inn near Basingstoke? Zeal lost count of the eggs. He goes to Basingstoke at times when we all imagine him to be fishing somewhere on the river?

'Why are we housing another poor fellow when we have so many of our own?' she asked carefully.

'I think he might prove useful.' Wentworth picked up an egg and turned it in his hand. 'He's a discharged soldier. Reduced to begging for his meals. All he needs is a warm bed and better rations than he had with the king in Scotland.'

'How much longer can you contrive to string out the suspense?' she asked. 'Holding back information is clearly an unfortunate trait of yours.'

Philip Wentworth grinned. 'He's a former sapper, once a siege engineer in the Low Countries. We began by discussing the mining of the walls at Breda and arrived quite naturally at the nature of Hampshire rock.' He placed the egg to complete a half-dozen in the bottom of her wooden box. 'The weather is clearing at last. If we give him a rough plan of the shape and size of what you want, my Master Quoynt can level the site and begin to blast out the cellars. Clearing rock will give our young men something better to do with themselves than go to war with Bedgebury.'

As she sifted sawdust around the first layer of eggs in the wooden box, Zeal reflected that her taciturn husband seemed surprisingly happy to talk to strangers. It would not surprise her if the wily old man had not overheard the soldier talking and mounted a direct assault. She had begun to feel that things seldom happened to her new husband by chance.

22

Francis Quoynt arrived with assorted pieces of baggage on 13 November, barely noticed in the furore over Doctor Bowler. A thin quiet man, he had stayed out of the way in the tack room when he was not wandering purposefully on the slope of Hawk Ridge. Once he set to work a few days later, however, no one could miss his presence.

The cream jumped in the skimming trough. Dust fell from roofs. The explosive thud bounced back and forth between the ridges like thunder and set the estate dogs barking on their chains. A flight of white doves burst up from the paddock, followed by a panic of ducks from the ponds. The sheep bolted to the farthest ends of their fields. In the horse barn, the grooms held onto halters and talked to their charges. The dairy herd had been moved that morning into the Far, down river below the mill where the sound would be muffled by distance and trees.

'Begun at last!' Zeal hugged herself. All around her, voices cheered. Across the valley the cloud of dust and debris was just beginning to settle back onto the southern slope of Hawk Ridge. 'It looks as I imagine war.'

'With reason,' replied Wentworth. 'Master Quoynt is as gifted at bringing down a wall as he is at preparing to raise one.'

She stood bundled in a thick shawl outside the lodge beside Wentworth. Bowler sat nearby wrapped in blankets on a chair, guarding a line of estate children who had been warned by Wentworth under threat of a thrashing to stay put. All work on the estate had paused. Spectators crowded the near banks of the fishponds. Zeal could see the tiny figures of some of the younger men, from Bedgebury, High House and Far Beeches as well as Hawkridge, courting danger on the ridge above the site of the new house. The sky was filled with wheeling, crying black birds, crows, thrushes and sparrows. From the beech hanger came the harsh protest of pheasants and jays.

Quoynt whistled and waved a white kerchief over his head. Men from the estate, tenants and labourers alike, all hired for the day, ran down the slope to begin to clear the broken rubble from what was to be the fair-standing for her new house.

Before the end of the day, Quoynt had drilled holes for and set off six more charges. The labourers heaped the smaller rubble along muddy patches of the section of the parish high road that fell to Hawkridge Estate to keep in good repair. By sundown, Zeal was able to walk across a large flat space cut out of the hillside.

This must have been how God felt during creation, she thought. If He did not care for the shape of a hill, He could change it.

She was already forgetting how it looked before.

'I did not think this much could be done,' she said. 'Now it seems that anything is possible.'

'The only limit is in the imagining.' Wentworth was as excited as she. 'Another two days, and you'll have your cellars as well.'

The two of them stood looking back down into the Shir valley.

'Our backs and a hill to the north, our faces to the south,' Zeal said happily. 'It will be the most perfect house in England.' She would write to tell John about this first day of creation. He might even write back with suggestions for the new house, as if he were here to share the building of it with her.

Jonas Stubbs, the estate mason, had set aside a large pile

of boulder-sized rubble, which he was tapping in an exploratory way to discover which of them could be fashioned for use. Though Zeal and Wentworth had decided to build mainly of brick, the new house would need stone architraves, lintels, sills, steps, floors and hearths. And though the sandstone of Hawkridge was soft, it was strong enough and easy to work. It was also local.

'We'll get some good ones out of that lot,' said Stubbs. He clearly relished a greater challenge than his main job of repairing walls and carving the occasional tombstone.

Zeal studied the pile of stone with pleasure equal to his. The cost of transporting stone could often exceed the cost of the material itself. Even very small fragments of her own hillside might serve to make arch corbels, keystones or, at the very least, decorative masks to set above doorways.

'You were right,' she told Philip that night. 'There are more ways than I ever imagined to defeat the tyrant, Poverty.'

She set a candle to study the rough drawings she and Wentworth had made of the house, imagining its great H-shape against the hillside with a broad terraced forecourt in front, where carriages could stop before driving on to the stables. Then the green slope falling away to the river and fishponds.

Wentworth came to stand beside her. 'Who'd have thought Francis and his bangs would so lift everyone's spirits?' He laid a hand on her shoulder. 'New beginnings are good for the soul. If it's not still too soon, why not lift their spirits further with your news?'

23

Mistress Margaret clapped a hand to her mouth. Zeal saw speculation, then knowledge, blossom in her eyes.

'Will you stand for the babe at its christening?' she asked quickly, to ward off the questions that were sure to tumble out of the older woman's mouth.

Mistress Margaret had begun the day's baking when Zeal told her. When Agatha went out to the pump with a bucket to refill the kitchen cistern, Mistress Margaret leaned across the table. 'Forgive me, but I must know. Please, dearest Zeal, tell me! You were so quick to fall . . . Please! Can it be?'

'You must tell no one!'

'John's!' Mistress Margaret stood very still, cradling her ball of dough as if protecting it from attack. Then she burst into tears.

'Master Wentworth learnt of it and made me a most Christian offer. Otherwise I . . .'

'Why didn't you tell me? I was so unkind! Had such wicked thoughts!' Mistress Margaret pushed aside her dough and leaned across the table again to grip both of Zeal's hands in hers. 'My darling girl! I can't believe it! We shall have him still here with us, through his child. We'll have a young master again. God be praised!'

'I'm not sure He would want to claim any part in this matter,' Zeal said dryly.

At the sound of Agatha's returning footsteps, Mistress Margaret released Zeal and pushed herself upright. 'Master Wentworth is a king among men.'

'He is indeed. And generous in spirit.'

'The only true generosity. A Christian gives what he can and no one blames him if it's not more. Our Saviour, Himself, was known to distribute fish!'

They exchanged watery glances across the table.

As Agatha emptied her bucket into the copper cistern, Mistress Margaret wiped her eyes with the back of a floury hand. 'Who'd have thought? Our old sojourner . . .' she said with heavy meaning.

Agatha left once more for the pump in the stable yard.

Mistress Margaret lowered her voice. 'I don't suppose he'd agree to christen the babe "Nightingale"?'

'There will be gossip enough.'

'People have mean minds, but words kill no one. Oh, the wonder of it!'

She set her shaped loaf on a wooden board and covered it with a damp cloth. 'All the infants' swaddling clothes were burnt!' she said in sudden dismay. 'And the old cradle. It was in the long gallery with the silk table carpet John brought from Amsterdam, and those two walnut chairs with the . . . anyway, I will ask Todd to make a new one . . .'

She began to wipe the wooden mixing bowl with an oiled cloth. 'I shall bake a loaf with a softer crust, for Master Wentworth. He must need it for his old teeth.'

She won't be the only one to guess the truth, thought Zeal. But it doesn't matter now. Except that rumour might somehow reach John. I must make myself write again to tell him before he hears. But that means telling him that I'm married.

What if he doesn't believe me and thinks that the child is really Wentworth's?

A letter was such a fragile container for so great an event. But the longer she delayed, the greater the event grew.

I will wait until he sends the second letter he promised, she told herself. Until he replies to mine and tells me exactly where to send the next.

But his ship might have been sunk by pirates off the African coast. He had contracted a fatal ague. Been bitten by a serpent. His life seemed so much more fragile when she could only imagine it.

We will need to talk for five years to tell all, even after so short a time apart.

Before going to find Doctor Bowler, Zeal helped Mistress Margaret set the shaped loaves to rise on a shelf above the oven.

'The wonder of it!' the older woman said again.

Doctor Bowler now rose daily from his bed, but his face was still blotched purple and green with fading bruises. He could not use his swollen, distorted left hand to feed or dress himself.

In spite of the number of bastards he had christened and the number of unwed mothers he had tried to find it in himself to rebuke, he stared at Zeal in innocent delight. 'A babe at Hawkridge again! Of course, old Sir George never had any of his own, but John and then Harry visited as small boys. Oh, my dear! I should think Master Wentworth can't contain himself for joy!'

'He is very content.'

'I shall compose . . .' Bowler began. 'No. I shall do better than that.' He looked at her defiantly. 'I shall play at the christening!'

Zeal pinched her lips to keep from crying, then smiled brightly. 'No doubt you will.'

'I can't bear it!' she said to Wentworth later when she met him in the lodge parlour. 'Doesn't he understand what was done to him?'

'Trying very hard not to, I should think.' He was preparing to go out for a night on the river. 'I have another surprise for you, by the way. Now that you are officially with child, you will need help with the house more than ever. From someone who knows far more than I about how to keep roofs from falling down or how to marry a fireplace to a wall. I have arranged it.'

'Who is it? What will he do?'

'Surveyor is one title he bears. He is also the author of the drawing I gave you on our wedding night. You will have to wait to learn the rest.'

'I think you wanted a wife only so you could refuse to tell her anything!' said Zeal. But she knew Philip could see that she was pleased all the same. 'Another man who owes you favours?'

'As it happens, his father does.'

He wanted so much to take her into his confidence. He had forgotten the joy of shared purpose, though in his life, the purpose had seldom been so benign.

I could win her heart through this house, he thought, and the rest of her with it.

All the weapons of seduction lay within his reach – shoulder leaning on shoulder, shared glances, voices tumbling excitedly on top of each other as one thought built on the next.

Can't use them. Must not even try. Got myself into enough of a tangle with that unthinking bribe of the truth about myself. Have to be so careful with what I let myself give.

What the devil do you think you are doing, you old frog?

He allowed himself a chaste kiss on her warm smooth forehead before he left. He imagined that she leaned a little towards him.

The next night, when she took him by the sleeve after supper and told him firmly that the fish must wait on his long-postponed story, he found it hard to deny her. Nevertheless, he tried.

'I was born,' he said. He sat in the lodge parlour on one side of the fire, watching her face while she knitted a scarlet stocking on the other. 'I grew. I left home to become a soldier. I returned. I ventured again. Prospered. Returned. Ventured again. Returned. And here I am. What more can I tell you?'

She gave him a stony look across her needles. 'Were you wed? You said on our wedding night that young women had changed.'

'Did I?' He looked into the fire.

She knitted a few more stitches. Of course a man of his age must have been wed before. 'What was she like?'

'Fragile,' he said unexpectedly.

'Did you love her?'

'Not as much as she loved me, it seems.'

Zeal dropped a stitch and tried to hook up the escaping loop. Wentworth stood and brought his sempster's candle stand from his room, lit the candle and set the stand on a table beside her. The lens threw a magical oval of bright light onto her work.

'In what way did you love her less?' Zeal asked at last. In spite of the increased light, the loops of wool kept un-ravelling.

'I gave her what she wanted.'

'How were you at fault in that?'

'It killed her.'

She set her knitting down on her lap. Nodded once, blew out a small breath.

He was standing by the fire, watching her.

'What did she want?'

'Never to be parted from me.'

She bent to pick up her ball of wool, which had fallen to the floor. 'I can understand how a woman might want such a thing.'

'So much that she could not be without her husband, even for a night? So much that his next voyage would surely kill her, for she meant to kill herself rather than be left behind?' He left the fire and went to adjust one of the shutters.

'Yes, I can imagine that,' she said.

'Not one single night?' he asked angrily. 'Can you imagine weeping and clinging to his knees to keep him in the room? No, my dear, I think not.'

I fear I see where he is tending, thought Zeal unhappily. She felt him begin to pace in the shadows behind her. 'You took her with you on a voyage?'

'Being a weak fool, even knowing her weakness, I did.' He picked up one of his rods that stood beside the door, then set it down again. He remained by the door, as if poised to flee. 'That young man I told you of had a young wife weeping in terror in their cabin. She too felt the crucible at work. She feared the sea, but even more, she feared the changes she knew must come as the world around us changed from what she knew. She could not be parted from me, but she could not survive where we went and what it showed her about me. She hanged herself on St Kitt's. It seems that she could bear to be parted from me, after all.'

'Are you warning me?'

'Perhaps.' His clothing rustled. 'Are you not dissolved in tears at my sad tale?'

He had put on his cloak and taken up one of his rods again.

'I think it's sadder than you choose to make it sound. But I also think you're warning me not to try to follow you either, even in my imagination.'

Nor to follow John.

He took his bag from its hook and slung it over his shoulder.

'I'm not fragile,' Zeal said.

'I know. But I have learned to take care enough rather than love too much.'

From the door, she watched him disappear down the drive into the darkness. His story had made it impossible to call him back.

Damnation! Damnation! Wentworth thought as he strode angrily towards the river. That was not what I intended at all! How must I seem to her now? And how many other questions have I stirred up? At least I did not tell her all. I must think exactly what to say if she manages to catch me off guard again. I must be ready. And resolute.

24

Zeal lifted her head sharply at the cry of pain. She had waxed the balancing acrobat and dolphin finials of the first two pews and moved on to the leafy face of the wild man carved into the side of the next pew.

There was a second cry, a strangled yelp, followed by panting.

She moved warily to the back of the chapel. The sound could have been made by a wounded animal or by a human. Close by, not up in the family gallery. Whatever it was did not cry out again. Instead, it seemed to be holding its breath, as if it had heard her and feared detection.

The vestibule through which the house servants had once entered the chapel was empty. She heard a sharp intake of breath and pushed open the door in one side of the vestibule.

'Doctor Bowler!' She rushed forward into the little room which he used as both parlour and sleeping chamber.

'Don't touch me!' His tone was like a slap.

She stopped, shocked.

'Please,' he added. His face was grey-white under its green and purple bruises, his brow oily and damp. He trembled and sucked his breath in and out between his teeth. Tears stood in his eyes. He was sitting at a table with his left hand lying flat in front of him, without the bandages, which were tangled beside his hand. Two sturdy splints of firewood also lay on the table.

'The bones of the last two fingers weren't healing straight,' he said. 'I had to break . . .' He swayed on his stool.

'I'll be back at once!' She ran to the bake house kitchen as fast as her condition allowed and returned with a bottle of *aqua vitae*.

She held the cup to his mouth but had to steady his head. His skin was clammy and cold. 'Have you gone mad?'

'I mean to play again.'

She caught him as he fell from the stool. He shouted with pain.

'Lie there and don't move.' She covered him with a blanket from his bed. 'I'll fetch someone to help me lift you onto the bed.'

'I must tie the fingers straight first. Help me sit up.'

She wavered, then obeyed the astonishing firmness in his voice. She passed him the splints and bandages. When he had worked his fourth and little fingers into the desired line (a process which she could not watch and which he accompanied by gasps and whimpers), he allowed her to help him tie the splints into place.

'That will be much better, thank you,' he said, and passed out.

The following day, he dictated a letter for her to write down, to an instrument-maker in London asking the price of a new fiddle. Wentworth returned from a four-day retreat on the river in time to volunteer that he needed to visit a Flemish needle-maker in Basingstoke to buy more fishhooks. He would take Bowler's letter and arrange for it to be sent on to London.

He brought back not only his hooks but a fiddle and bow.

'It's old and not half so fine as your own,' he told Bowler. 'It's a second fiddle, in fact. Belongs to a tavern busker I know who prefers another instrument. On loan till you can get a new one.'

'What do you think you're doing?' Zeal demanded later of Wentworth. 'You saw how they smashed his left hand! It's the left that has all the movement over the strings. Why make it harder for him?'

'"Oh, ye of little faith!" . . . Don't, please . . . I didn't mean to make you cry.'

Bowler sent for the pale-haired, angel-voiced Jamie to help him with some mysterious task.

Two weeks after he had rebroken and set his fingers, Bowler took to carrying the borrowed fiddle with him at all times. Whenever there was a pause in his other activity, he tucked the fiddle under his chin and silently fingered the strings with his right hand, which had been bruised but not broken, miming scales and trills.

Zeal observed him with the heavy heart of a parent helplessly watching a child ride full tilt at failure.

'We re-strung it, Jamie and I,' Bowler explained jubilantly, as if re-stringing were the only obstacle. 'Not so hard as you might think with quick young fingers at work. And turned the bridge, of course. It's a looking glass fiddle, now, but I'll soon get accustomed to it.' He tucked it back under his chin and began the awkward, wrong-handed fingering again.

'Listen, you can just hear the notes.' He struck down on a string with his finger. 'Is it in tune, Jamie my boy? Then tighten it for me, there's a good lad.'

Francis Quoynt finished blasting out the footprint of the new house and left in the third week of November. Zeal had accepted tenders for work and engaged craftsmen to start in the spring. A roofed workshop was built for Jonas Stubbs not far from the building site. Nearby, he stacked the sandstone boulders, sorted by size and shape. The small broken rubble was pounded into the mud of the high road.

Though nothing more would take place there during the winter, the workings still attracted curious visitors, chiefly children but many adults as well. This interest stretched even further than the parish boundaries, for Zeal once spied an unfamiliar horseman peering down from the Silchester track at the top of Hawk Ridge. Instead of continuing down into the Shir valley, however, he turned back and disappeared again.

I can't think what they all hope to see, Zeal thought. Each morning, nevertheless, she walked across the muddy rock of the fair standing and peered impatiently over the protective wattle hurdles down into the raw holes of her future cellars.

She would not need as much knowledge of building as she had feared. When fine weather returned, a community of craftsmen would begin to play their own independent parts, as was the common practice, under the direction of Jonas Stubbs as master mason, and a master carpenter. Where she wanted a wall, the masons assured her they would raise one, turning corners as they saw fit. Where she wanted window openings and fireplaces, they would provide their own designs, chosen from pattern books, with her approval. She need only say, in the most general way, 'A staircase, there!' and somehow the master joiner and his men would accommodate one in the space created by the masons. Masons and joiners together would negotiate the exact nature and dimensions of a door. She need not concern herself with hinges and nails, they told her. By custom, many craftsmen even provided their own building stuffs, with the costs included in their wages.

'But how do I know these things will please me?' she asked.

'Well, madam,' said Jonas Stubbs, 'I expect you'll tell us if you want something different.'

In any case, she had to keep a grip on the costs. She had hoped to use Bowler as her clerk of works, to keep record of materials both needed and used, of wages and of costs. It was clear now that he would not be fit to add that burden to his own keeping of the estate books. The thought of hiring a stranger to sit at the heart of the project made her uneasy, even if she could have afforded his wages.

Each day, as she peered into the workings, she struggled with the problem.

I don't see how I will manage it myself, not with the estate, not after the child is born.

And though grown more sociable than before the wedding, Wentworth was unlikely to tolerate such unrelenting contact with others. In the short term, she must find the time and strength to do it. By the spring, when work began in earnest, Bowler might again by some miracle be fit to help. She was not certain what Wentworth's promised surveyor would do, but perhaps it might include being clerk of works. Or she would find some other solution.

If only John were here.

On these mornings, she also looked out over the valley as she and John had done.

We will need to carry the drive across the Shir, she thought. And she added a new bridge to the changes she must tell John about.

She held up her skirts and picked her way across the mud.

She must contain her impatience until the spring. Dried brown leaves now clung to the beeches in the avenue. Winter had suddenly arrived and turned life on the estate inward, into the shelter of roof and wall, wherever it might be found. A good housewife now bent herself to polishing, cleaning and cooking. To mending, knitting and needlework. To sorting and storing seeds so that mice and insects would not eat them before they could be planted. To inventories, lists and letter writing. To preparing for Christmas.

Christmas without John, she thought, as she knocked clods of mud off her pattens outside the lodge door.

As Zeal crossed the stable yard towards the tack room, one morning in late November, to look at a harness that Tuddenham said needed to be replaced, a raucous squawk came from the carriage barn, followed by the squeal of an inexpert attempt to butcher a piglet. She peeked through a window.

Bowler sat on a stool beside one of the carriage wheels with the violin braced under his chin. He had lashed his bow to the wheel. His useless left hand lay across his thigh, white and lumpy with bandages. As she watched, he swayed to the left, passing the violin under the fixed bow. The instrument squealed again. Zeal stepped back to keep him from seeing her.

'I mean to play at Gifford's funeral!' Bowler called after her.

She leaned in through the door. 'If you can play, I swear I will dance.'

But after two more days when, as far as she could tell, Bowler sat in his chamber doing nothing but stare into space and massage his bandage, he returned to the wrong-handed silent fingering.

Then he began to spend days in out-of-the-way rooms in the attics of High House, in the company of Jamie, with the ten-year-old serving as Bowler's left hand until his own had healed. Jamie's parents, both Hawkridge farm workers, seemed happy enough with his promotion to honorary house family. Then his father visited Zeal one evening at the lodge.

'We're very grateful for the honour, Doctor Bowler placing such confidence . . .' Jake Grindley was civil but determined. 'But we don't want him to go on wasting so much time with music. The boy must learn how to make his way in the world. It's not right to fill him with other ideas.'

'Let me speak to him!' said Bowler, when Zeal raised the matter as tactfully as she could. 'Jamie has an ear like none other! And if his voice holds with the years, and we encourage him, and he can be taught by better tutors than I am, he could earn them a far more comfortable old age than ever pulling turnips could! I shall go at once and tell them as much.'

For a time after Bowler's visit, Zeal heard no more from Jamie's father. She assumed that all had gone well, given what later happened at Christmas. In any case, Jamie Grindley was driven entirely out of her mind by the arrival of Philip Wentworth's promised surprise. The surveyor, who would help her to build the house, though she did not yet understand exactly how. The author of the Italianate drawing Philip had given her on their wedding night.

25

All her imagining had been wrong.

He's too young, she thought. What can he know of leaping the chasm between the imagining and the raising of walls? Then she saw that he was older than he first seemed.

Lambert Parsley had a smooth angel's face on a tall, broad-shouldered man's body. Though he was at least twenty-five or six, large, long-lashed blue eyes gave him the appealing air of a child. Red-blond curls lay so precisely on his high smooth forehead that they seemed carved from gold. His mouth, at which she could not help gazing, also had something of the child about it in spite of the glint of golden whiskers on his upper lip. He had a full, tender lower lip of a fresh colour. His ear lobes were a delicate pink. But what entranced her most was an alert readiness of both eyes and mouth, to be amused.

'Oh, Philip,' he cried. 'You did not tell me that she was so lovely!' Nor so young, added his eyes.

'I feared you might expire from anticipation,' said Wentworth dryly. He did not seem to mind the young man's over-familiarity.

'Forgive me, madam.' Parsley shone on Zeal. 'Your husband prepared me for such a painful task, warned me of so many difficulties – no money, difficult terrain, your impossible demand for perfection . . .'

Wentworth smiled and shook his head slightly when Zeal looked at him in protest.

'. . . that I agreed to come out of pure charity. But if it is you I am to serve, the charity falls the other way. Madam, I live only to become the extension of your will.'

Zeal glanced again at Wentworth, this time in mild alarm. He was watching the pair of them without expression.

'Look!' cried Lambert Parsley, unabashed. He stood beside Zeal, shoulder to shoulder. 'Same hair. Same eyes. Only a small difference in height. Could we not be Viola and Sebastian, brother and sister, twins, even?'

'Both equally handsome.' Philip now seemed amused.

'Your husband invited me, but my fate depends on you. Will you have me, lady?' Parsley's eyes gleamed into hers.

She flushed. 'If you will swear not to exhaust me with your compliments and enthusiasm. We're out of practice here with extravagant city manners.'

Lambert Parsley blinked and seemed for a moment to hang suspended.

I've offended him, she thought. When he is doing us a great favour.

'I see why you love her, Philip.' Parsley stepped a little away from her so that they stood in a triangle. 'I should have known it would take more than a fine eye to haul you out into the light again after so many years in the celibate wilderness.'

'A little more than a fine eye,' Wentworth agreed.

Zeal glanced at him but he was gazing at nothing in particular. What do you think you are doing, husband, bringing this young man here among us? And who is he to be calling you 'Philip'?

Then she saw that Parsley had retreated into watchfulness.

While she tried to think how to apologize for her sharpness, he said, 'I have done such things before.'

'Once,' said Philip. 'But that's once more than either of us. And then there's your experience of Italian practices. And your knack for drawing.'

'And my enthusiasm.' The amusement gleamed again.

I like him, Zeal decided. He makes me want to smile.

He was pleasing, like a beautiful horse or dog which you want to stroke. His only visible imperfections were curious raw patches on his skin, which encircled each of his wrists like a pair of bracelets. And now that she looked closely, a fading bruise lay like a faint shadow under the skin of his left cheek.

A marred angel. All the more interesting. If Wentworth could be an executioner, footpad or murderer, perhaps this young friend of his was a fugitive convict.

'I took the liberty of bringing you a gift from Italy, mistress. I had to have it the instant I saw it in Florence. And now I can't wait a moment longer to give it to you. Will you open it now?'

He called for his man to bring his saddlebag into the lodge parlour. 'You must sit down!'

Zeal glanced again at Philip, who did not seem to mind if another man gave orders to his wife.

Parsley laid a sacking-wrapped bundle in her lap. 'Take care, it's heavier than it looks. I do so enjoy this moment,' he said, as she began to pick at the leather thongs tied around the sacking. 'The anticipation! Before infinite possibility dwindles into a pair of embroidered gloves.'

She lifted the gift free of its wrappings. An owl made of a rough pale stone, into which the precise arrowheads of its feathers had been carved.

'Athena's owl. Do you like it? For an instant, when we first met I feared that I'd made a dreadful mistake in bringing you such a fierce little creature. And wisdom always has over-tones of darkness. Now, on better acquaintance, I think it's perfect, don't you?'

Zeal glanced up at his eager blue eyes then stared into the large round eyes of the owl, which seemed to look back right through her own into the depths of her thoughts.

'Bought in Italy,' said Parsley, 'but made in Greece. Born in the font of all perfection. Can you forgive me for bringing you an emblem of wisdom and not of beauty? I believe that wisdom must precede beauty in a venture like ours.'

The owl sat roundly in her hand, eight inches high, as

familiar as if she had seen it being carved. The weight of its immense age tugged her back through time. She looked up at Parsley and nodded, unable to speak, not sure of what she would say if she did.

'A fine thing,' said Philip.

Zeal shivered and shook her head to clear the feeling that her husband, for that instant, was the stranger, the outsider, while this newcomer was an old friend. He had known she would value wisdom and recognize its darkness, even while he was still in Italy selecting a piece of carved stone.

Perhaps Philip means to distract me from John, she thought. With someone closer to hand, whom he can keep an eye on. Then she had a thought so ignoble she could hardly admit it. What if Philip meant for Lambert Parsley to stir and excite her, so that she might be more open to his own advances?

She likes him. I was right to take the chance.

Philip Wentworth felt only satisfaction as he watched the two young creatures circle each other like puppies getting acquainted. He was not certain which of them he might be doing the greater service. Young Lamb, who was so very unlike his naval father, urgently needed a refuge, from himself as much as anything else. With luck, Hawkridge was far enough from London to keep him out of trouble.

Captain Parsley, that would-be admiral, now owes me a favour in truth, he thought.

As for Zeal, so improbably his wife, he enjoyed watching her whatever she did. Her shape and movements gave him pleasure. He was amused by the way her clothing always seemed to be rushing to keep up with her sudden surges of purpose. He delighted in her occasional steeliness, which he suspected might match even his own. The thought of a clash caused a quiver that was not entirely unpleasant.

Now, as always, he had to fight himself to keep from finding excuses to touch her. In this, he succeeded chiefly because he feared feeling her flinch. As she had made so clear, gratitude was not love, and he was not yet such a helpless pantaloon that he had lost all pride. As it was, he had nearly spoiled everything after the fighting on Bonfire and Treason Night.

Not helped by spilling the tale of my poor, wretched wife.

Now her face was bright with surmise and possibility, and he, Philip, had brought that about. Young Parsley would more than earn his keep. Might even distract her from grieving over Nightingale. Meanwhile the young man was being kept away from London. A happy conjunction of needs, all around.

He desired her again now. But that was his problem.

26

Christmas began well. Lambert Parsley entranced Zeal by his willingness to sit for hours, sketching and making notes while she described her vision for her house. He gave himself so totally to anticipating her wishes, to reading her moods and making himself generally agreeable that she was both flattered and uneasy. His instant, unstinting gift of spirit made her feel responsible in a way she could not explain.

He talked of nothing but the plans for the house, or the daily gossip of the estate. If he mentioned Italy, it was only to suggest a model for a portico, or bridge he had seen that would suit Hawkridge exactly. She sometimes found it hard to believe that he had left a different, mysterious self stored away somewhere else. But, of course, he had. When he was drawing, she often eyed the circles on the skin around his wrists, which slowly faded to the palest pink. When she knew him a little better, she meant to learn how he had come by them.

Perhaps he had been captured by Italian brigands and held for ransom.

Lamb, as he was soon dubbed, impressed everyone else with his fine manners, handsome looks and the enthusiasm with which he threw himself into any task in need of doing. He helped to deck both the Hawkridge bake house and Sir Richard's hall at High House. He bred festive anticipation by enlisting the smith, Mistress Margaret, and Todd, the estate carpenter, into an excited conspiracy.

'Go away!' Lamb shouted to Zeal when she hovered outside the locked doors of Sir Richard's upper gallery, drawn by hammering and the smell of hot glue.

'Just you wait, madam!' said Rachel, who was allowed to spy.

Doctor Bowler had recovered enough to conduct the morning service at High House. They ate a modest feast of roast goose, ducks, hams, ginger breads, chicken boiled with preserved gooseberries, a poached carp, quince cheese and pickled cucumbers, followed by nuts, raisins and a fine almond soup prepared by Mistress Margaret. The remains of this dinner were then served the next day as a general feast for the poor of the parish, along with other roasts, soups and breads made especially for the occasion.

'The number of the needy grows each year.' Sir Richard eyed the jostling mob in his great barn. 'I may soon have to ape my betters and escape the expense by spending Christmas in London.' He had his steward see off two men who were known to visit different estates in turn and stuff their pouches with any food they could not eat.

'We pay levies to keep such people fed,' said the old knight. 'Don't wish to do it twice over.'

Zeal tried to forget his reference to levies. Hawkridge still owed the last year's taxes. We just need a season to put things straight after the fire, she told herself. She suspected that Sir Richard might be deflecting the Crown agent as an act of charity.

As always, Philip Wentworth was absent from the feasting. On this occasion, however, he had been struck down by an ague, which he said had plagued him since his youth. He would not be budged from his chamber in the Hawkridge lodge and refused all attempts to nurse him.

'I've survived such attacks before. Let me be!'

Zeal had to content herself with appointing a groom to keep Philip's fire alight and his jug full of warm spiced ale. Though she had known better than to expect him at table, Zeal was sorry that he missed what followed the Christmas feast.

When the long table had been cleared and pushed back

against the wall, Doctor Bowler asked the company to arrange themselves on stools and chairs.

'Jamie and I have something we would like you to hear.'

Doctor Bowler stood facing them with his borrowed violin in his right hand. Jamie stood on a low stool in front of Bowler with his back against the parson's chest, holding Bowler's bow.

Bowler tucked his violin under his chin, placed the fingers of his right hand on the strings of his looking-glass fiddle and nodded. They drew breath at the same instant and began. Jamie drew the bow across the strings.

The violin squawked like a startled hen.

Zeal put her hand to her mouth. This was unbearable. The little parson had been driven mad by his misfortunes. She saw Rachel and Arthur exchange glances.

Jamie looked over his shoulder at Bowler who raised his eyebrows in comic dismay. Jamie giggled and they began again. Up, then down went the bow. Again the instrument cried and protested. Jamie frowned and fixed his eyes on Bowler's fingers. Again Bowler nodded. Again they drew breath. Suddenly, the sound came right. A rich confident note sang out of the violin, then another. Jamie frowned in concentration. Bowler closed his eyes.

A stream of notes followed. Zeal breathed out and felt her muscles soften with gratitude and relief. Bowler and Jamie were safe. They could not go wrong now. Like birds that wheeled in vast patterns in the sky, each knew exactly when the others would turn, exactly together, never colliding. She thought of the Gunpowder Treason dancing, then crossed her fingers to protect this dance from evil outcome.

Bowler and Jamie reached the end of the first verse of the melody. Then Jamie, while continuing to bow a simpler rhythm, also began to sing.

> 'O, sing unto the Lord a new song
> Sing praise unto Him with courage.

Make a joyful noise unto the Lord
All the earth, sing praise.

Sing unto the Lord with the harp; with the harp
And the voice of a psalm
With a trumpet and sound of cornet
Make a joyful noise.

Let the sea roar, the world
And they that dwell therein.
Let the floods clap their hands;
Let the hills be joyful together.'

When they finished, there was a total hush in Sir Richard's great hall.

'Now you must all sing,' said Bowler uncertainly.

'I wish you had heard us!' she told Philip when she visited him later at Hawkridge, in spite of his orders to the contrary.

'I swear I might have done.'

'We rattled the panelling with our cheers. Jamie grew at least five inches from pride and Doctor Bowler blushed the colour of beetroot. I thought he might weep . . . I know that I did.'

Philip smiled at her. He was sitting up in his bed, weak but cool again. He looked suddenly older and thinner.

'Then he taught us the tune and we all sang and clapped our hands. Jamie put down the bow and played the tabor while Doctor Bowler led us all. We were indeed joyful together! And then we danced . . .'

They looked at each other.

'I would like to dance with you again,' said Wentworth. 'After the child is born.'

'. . . without the fiddle, of course,' she hurried on. 'But the others all came and played. And Lamb was splendid. He taught us all the latest London steps . . .'

She did not tell Philip of the chill that had touched her unexpectedly at the sight of Lamb's golden head bent close to Jamie's silver one. Or of her unease at the over-excited abandon with which Jamie threw himself into the dance.

After Zeal left, Philip Wentworth took a tiny silk-wrapped parcel from where he had hidden it under the quilt. With fingers still a little unsteady from the fever, he opened the parcel. He frowned as he studied the six golden fishhooks lying on the silk.

He had meant to give them to her, as her New Year's gift. He knew, from searching her room while she was out, that she had bought him three reels of silk for tying flies. These hooks were proportionate to her gift and would not hurt her pride. At the same time, they were beautiful. And unique. He would not follow common practice and give her spices or a lace collar. He could not give her a string of pearls or a brooch.

Now the gift troubled him. She might read meaning into the hooks themselves.

And perhaps rightly, now that I consider it, he thought. How little we understand our own minds. Or bodies.

What had stopped him, however, was the certainty that she would not rest until she had forced him to relate how he came by them.

He picked one tiny hook up carefully, by its gleaming golden shank.

Is that what I want?

He had told himself she might have two of the hooks made into earrings. He now turned the hook so that it caught the light. The tiny flash illuminated a world hidden in his memory.

Quickly, he put the golden hook back with the others and wrapped them up again. When he had caught his breath, he climbed from the bed and replaced the parcel in his locked iron money chest.

I will give her one of my maps, he decided. Though even that is bound to provoke more of her questions.

Before going to bed, Zeal walked down the drive to the office. She put on John's coat over her own coat and scarf.

Where are you this Christmas time?

She watched her breath make faint clouds in the dark still air.

Where are you? she asked again. Please!

She buried her face in the collar. His scent was fading, along with the tang of smoke.

I must not put this on so much, she thought. I'm rubbing him away.

She hung the coat back on its peg and stood with her face pressed against the rough brown wool. The deck dropped away beneath her feet.

Only six and a half more years.

The child, who is both of us, will hold me steady.

The next morning, a banging on the lodge door interrupted Zeal's breakfast. 'Gifts! Gifts!'

Zeal got out of bed, where she had stayed for warmth, pulled her jacket around her and went out to the door.

'We're the Magi!' cried a muffled voice. 'Where are we?'

'Lamb, you fool! Have you elected yourself Lord of Misrule?'

'Help me, Rachel!' He beckoned to the maid, who had appeared at the opening of the loft, still tying the front of her gown. Together, they carried a shrouded, door-sized burden into the lodge parlour. It brought with it the smell of glue. Zeal stirred the coals in the parlour fireplace and fed kindling into the red quivering heat.

'Keep your back turned! Don't look yet!' Lamb ordered her. 'It's a surprise!'

'Why is everyone always bent on surprising me?' Zeal whacked a half-burned log with the poker. 'I'd prefer the delight of informed anticipation.' Surprises made her anxious.

'Surprises are a form of benign torment. And power. I have you at my mercy, just for a moment . . . You may look now.'

She turned and gasped. On the big table stood a miniature house, almost the length of her bed.

'I know that it's not exactly as you described,' Lamb said quickly. 'But you also said that you wish to build a perfect house. I have endeavoured to design one for you. More perfect even than the house designed by Master Inigo Jones for the Queen at Greenwich.'

Zeal bent close in wonder. 'I described only what I knew. I couldn't have imagined a house like this one.'

Shaped like a squared, rectangular letter 'O', it was perfect in every detail, made of oiled cloth on a wooden frame surmounted by a carved wooden parapet, with doors and roof leads of finely shaved wood like a lute-maker's leaves, and oiled parchment windows through which a golden light glowed. Lamb had painted one half in meticulous detail, from the gods and goddesses on the pilasters between the windows down to the single bricks. The other half, though shaped and modelled like the first, remained unadorned. Nevertheless, the two halves of the front reflected each other in perfect symmetry, whereas her imagination had clung to the collection of architectural accidents that had made up the old Hawkridge House.

Though this house was not in the H-shape she had imagined, Lamb had listened to her desires all the same. The house had a front wall of tall windows, just as she had asked, to let in the light. It had tiny iron window frames and lead water pipes as fine as wire. The windows had minute catches in the shape of dolphins. Her modest porch, which she now saw to have been very like the old Hawkridge House porch, still sat at the front but had grown here to a wide portico with four columns, each complete with dainty painted fluting and tiny wooden acanthus scrolls.

'Does it please you?' The uncertain child hovered behind his eyes.

'My wishes and far beyond. It resembles an ancient temple,' she said.

Lamb looked gratified. 'Because it follows the ancient rules for Perfect Proportion. And because a goddess shall live in it. Look!' Delicately he inserted a paint-stained hand between the columns and opened the miniature main door. 'The hinges are strips of my old riding gloves.'

She touched a tiny carved mask set above one of the first floor windows. It was flat. Its shape and shadows were illusions created by his brush.

'The masons and carpenters can take this model for their pattern, at one half inch to the foot,' said Lamb. 'I learned from experience in Italy that most men can't understand drawings and plans. I have even shown the exact number of bricks. The masons need only count them.

'And wait . . . !' He left and returned with a bundle of wooden rods marked with lines and numbers. 'Here! I have already made calibrated rods for builders. This one is for the main doors. This, for the upper windows. If you hold these against the model, they will translate it to the true dimensions. See, here on this rod? Where it says "two inches"? The "four" just above tells you to measure four feet on the ground. Now, come around to admire the back!'

She bent to peer through the open front door, and saw a painted hall and staircase. Up the wall of the staircase, so small that she could barely interpret them, Lamb had limned scenes from Olympus.

'I speak in figures, like the gods,' he said. '*Parlar figurato*. All is in perfect proportion, to reflect the perfect proportions of the universe. Shaped to the Platonic ideals. True beauty is mathematical.' He bent to see where she looked. 'For the joiners, I shall also make larger scale models of the staircases and fireplaces, an inch to the foot or more,' he assured her. He lifted off a section of the roof and re-lit one of the candle stubs behind the façade windows. 'I will be more than your surveyor. I will be your architect.'

She was a giantess, wondering what secret lives were being lived behind those glowing windows. She imagined she could hear the faint sound of a tiny fiddle. She bent again to look through the little door, as if she might be able to see the future life of Hawkridge revealed inside.

Lamb's perfect house felt like a talisman. His beautiful ordered mathematics, given earthly shape in brick and stone, would charm a similar order back into her life. She could not speak. Instead, she kissed him warmly on the cheek.

'And now for your more modest gift.' She gave him a pair of gloves, which she had embroidered with Greek-looking owls.

He said nothing when he first saw them. Still silent, he put them on, studied his hands, turned them over to examine the finely-worked gauntlets.

'Do you like them?' Or had he forgotten what he said when he gave her Athena's owl on the day they first met. She suddenly feared that she had misjudged, and had merely dwindled.

'You made them for me yourself?'

She nodded.

'I've never had such a perfect gift. To make me laugh and weep at the same time.' He threw his arms around her. 'Sweetest Zeal, I do love you so!'

'Lamb!'

He smelled of orange blossom, musk and fresh air.

'Philip and I both love you. You must know that. *Agape, caritas, eros*, any way you like. More of the brotherly *agape* in my case and not so much *eros*, but I'm sure Philip makes up for any lack. Lustful old goat!'

Zeal pushed away his sweet-smelling warmth. 'You're trying to provoke me or you're prying. And either will earn you a sisterly clap on the ear if you don't take care.'

Five days later, the steward from Far Beeches brought her a second surprise. He had overheard the messenger asking in Bedgebury for directions to Hawkridge Estate.

Feeling quite unhinged by hope, she put out her hand. The writing on the letter looked like John's. Gripping the paper as if it might dissolve from between her fingers, she just managed to thank the steward and send him to the bake house for a mug of ale.

She sat down on a stool and held the letter before her on the table, waiting for the letters of her name to stop jumping in front of her eyes and for her hands to steady enough to break the seal.

She felt the terror of those finally given what they most want, who must then look it directly in the face.

She stood and paced around the little parlour. Philip's heaviest pole was missing from beside the door. She looked from the window. No one was coming up the track to the lodge. She took the letter into her chamber and barred the door.

27

Dearest Heart, Darling Girl, My Own Sweetest Zeal . . .

Zeal began to weep. He was still alive. He still loved her. Or still did, when he wrote this letter. She wiped her eyes with the heel of her palm and read his opening words again before continuing.

. . . I reach for you in my sleep, in all my waking thoughts. I ache to be this letter, headed back to England and to you. Improbably, I find myself instead anchored in a creek on Hispaniola not an hour's sail from the Spanish capital of Santo Domingo. Don't fear for me at the hands of old enemies. Though the Spaniards rule this island, they have no battery guns and seem happy enough to trade with us in exchange for fresh water and provisions.

On a brief visit ashore today, I found the earth rather unyielding beneath my feet, which are grown used to a more fluid base. Birds must feel much the same when they leave their natural airy element and alight on a rock . . . Do you remember how we so often knew where the other was on the estate? Like birds linked in flight by an invisible cord, long before we dreamed we might be free to love. A pair of swifts flying together out over the valley.

I am building a house where we sat together in that imagining.

. . . I cannot wait to show you the birds here – flocks of perro-quetos exploding from the trees like red, gold and green fireworks.

You would also marvel to see pineapples growing wild. I fall asleep each night planning how we will make a life here together . . .

She faltered, then read on.

. . . I am assured that the ten pounds owed to me at the end of my indenture will buy us thirty acres of good growing land in Barbados, an island held by the English, with safer society for you than elsewhere.

Meanwhile, I face the future with confidence. I am told that true equality rules among all indentured labour, such as I will be. The planters are as content to employ their fellow English or Frenchmen in the fields, as they are the captive Caribs – who were the first inhabitants of these islands – along with black slaves imported in most devilish conditions from Guinea, and those called <u>mulattos</u>, who are born of whites and blacks, the <u>mesticos</u> born of Indians and whites, and the <u>alcatraces</u> who come from the slaves and Indians. The Spanish, English and French alone own the land and govern all the others. I shall tell you in time whether I take pride in being one of their number. Meanwhile, I am grateful for whatever protection that kinship may offer me.

So do not fear. Dream instead of the strange and wonderful creatures I will show you when you come. Giant lizards you might almost take for dragons, monkeys, agoutis . . .

She dropped the letter into her lap. I should have jumped, she thought. It would have been easier after all.

1640

28

Zeal's Work Book – 2nd January 1640

From Lamb, his list for the New House, delivered with model:

Purbeck stone, to make four columns, with plinths, and capitals. Also cornice. (Nota bene. Purbeck stone is too costly. Ask Jonas Stubbs to make assay of our own stone, to see if it will hold. Or use moulded bricks and plaster in place of stone?)

Lead for all roofs – (I do not expect enough to be salvaged. We must use Portsmouth slates instead)

Bricks – 200,000. From our own oven (And 43,000 from old house)

Burgundy glass from France for window lights. (Too costly. Settle for Norwich glass?)

Gypsum plaster from Dorset, being of the best sort. 7s. the load

Candles for heating solder, 200

Oil, three gallons   30s
White lead   29s iid
Four buckets of gold   5s ivd

Hire of Master Carpenter at 16d per day

Hire of Master Mason at 18d per day. (Persuade Lamb to agree to Jonas Stubbs)
Clerk of works, to be determined

(Set wattle fences around workings lest a child fall in.)

29

Zeal sat in her high-backed chair by the parlour fire in Hawkridge Lodge and set a hand on either arm, like a portrait she had seen of the old queen. It was the second week of January, not yet Twelfth Night.

I felt this coming on Christmas Day, she thought.

Jake Grindley ignored her offer of a stool. 'I'm taking my son home.'

The boy stood rigidly, his eyes on the floor, thumbs clamped inside white-knuckled fists.

'For how long?' asked Zeal, though she knew she was only delaying the bad news.

'He needs to get used to a plain life again. And to learn to work.'

'Surely you don't mean to keep him there?'

Grindley nodded. 'Yes, madam, I do.'

'I wish to keep him at Hawkridge,' she said. 'As a page.'

Jamie's eyes lifted to hers with a flash of hope.

'He's not for hire.' Grindley cast an eloquently dismissive glance around the little parlour. Not in a place like this, his look said.

'But did Doctor Bowler not tell you that Jamie has an unusual gift for music? And might make a good living at it?'

'All the more reason for taking him home before it's too late!'

'Too late?'

Grindley was a rent-paying tenant and she needed every penny that was coming in. She dare not threaten to turn him out. Wouldn't do it in any case, because of his wife and four other children.

'The minister says that that music is wicked idleness. And encourages other sins.' Grindley turned his hat in his hands. 'He says that you and Doctor Bowler persist in the ways of wickedness.' He gave her a malevolent look. 'I won't have my son singing mass!'

'He doesn't sing mass here!'

'Doctor Gifford says it might as well be.'

'The minister says . . .'

And who taught Jake Grindley to be so insolent to his landlord?

She wrapped herself in her warmest cloak, twisted a scarf around her neck, pulled a felt hat low over her ears, and set off to try to find Philip. He was not on the river after all. As she left the lodge, she saw his figure up at the new house, apparently pacing out distances.

Whatever is he doing? she wondered. But her present urgency drove the question from her mind.

'What shall we do?' she demanded, when she had struggled up the hill, which seemed to grow steeper every day. She panted in the cold air. 'Jamie doesn't want to be a farmer! He wants to be a musician! Doctor Bowler says. You can tell just by listening to him. And you should have seen him just now at the lodge.'

'His father is right, then. By his own light.'

'It's Gifford!' said Zeal. 'Using Grindley to punish Doctor Bowler for not giving in.'

'Perhaps Grindley is truly concerned for his son.' Wentworth hesitated, then continued. 'There's another point. While gutting a pike some weeks ago, I overheard him telling someone that he did not think Master Parsley was the sort of gentleman who could advance a boy's prospects.'

'I hope you stood up and put Grindley straight.'

'He may be right.'

Zeal glared at her husband but said nothing more. She had begun to learn that he often took his time to act, but when he did act, it was to considerable effect.

She trudged back to the lodge, trying to think how she would tell Doctor Bowler that Jamie was gone, if he did not already know.

There was worse to come, before Twelfth Night had gone.

The usual Twelfth Night celebration at High House was muted. Bereft of his bowing hand, Doctor Bowler could not play and did not feel like singing. The company, which was Sir Richard, Comer the parish councillor who had attended the inquiry into Harry's death, Lamb, the Wildes of Far Beeches with their four children, together with the combined house families of High House and Hawkridge plus Tuddenham and his brood, had to make do with the rough entertainment offered by a troupe of travelling mummers who knocked at the gate.

After miming the battle between Saint George and the Dragon with thrown squibs and sulphurous smoke, which were the high points of the evening, they juggled apples and brass cups, sang, and produced live doves from the ladies' sleeves. Zeal sat at the back, in case weariness forced her to leave. Even so, a boy wearing a monkey mask found her and produced a farthing from her ear. It was not until preparing for bed back at the lodge that she found the paper slipped into her apron pocket.

When Wentworth knocked on her door, with a rod in his hand and wearing his heaviest coat, she did not answer. He entered, saw her curled tightly on the bed and set his rod beside the door.

'Are you ill?' he asked urgently. 'Zeal, what is wrong? Is it the child?'

'I've had another letter.'

*   *   *

The same knife-slash strokes of the pen. The same venom. Both letters were from the same hand, Wentworth was certain.

'For lawless joys, a bitter ending waits.'

Though not particularly biblical, the words might still be Gifford's, but not the hand. Wentworth pulled at his lower lip and frowned at the paper on the table in his room.

And why would the minister write again now? Surely the removal of Jamie Grindley was enough of a victory.

He liked and trusted the scrawny, self-important little man no better after their confrontation in the vestry at Bedgebury, but he did not judge him to be a snake. He had known soldiers like him, good at the head of a charge, bad tacticians. Gifford liked to attack by the searing light of hell fire, with an audience if possible. He was a thunderbolt man, not a server of poisoned ice.

Some fanatic in the congregation then, stirred by Gifford's rabble rousing?

Wentworth sighed heavily and pinched the bridge of his forceful nose, as if starting a megrim. He had learned so well to avoid thinking unwanted thoughts. Now he felt he had begun to lose his grip on his thoughts entirely.

I believe this letter may be aimed in part at me.

Much as he wanted to be proved wrong, he thought he might suspect who could have written the letters.

If so, it proves that I was right in the first place to do as I did all those years ago, he told himself. Though that's no consolation.

He put the letter with the other in his locked chest.

But I've no proof. None at all.

He blew out his candle lantern and stood for a moment in the dark. Then he left his room, crossed the parlour and let himself into the opposite chamber.

He listened for her breathing.

Seems asleep at last.

Carefully, he eased into the bed and edged towards her

until he met a warm soft curve of hip. She sighed and settled back against him.

Dreaming of Nightingale, no doubt, he told himself wryly. But I'm the one who's here. He fell asleep stretched out beside her small warm body, his earlier discomfort wiped out by a deep and selfish joy.

30

Zeal's Work Book, The Lady Day Quarter Day – March 1640

Prepare hot beds in garden
Dig ground and mix in manure
Drive sheep onto common land
Leave eggs under brooding hens

Sow spinach, cabbages, coriander, parsnips, peonies and pumpkins
Transplant red cabbage

Begin the spring cleaning of bake house, brew house and lodge

Scour churns

For the New House:
  Dig cess pits against hiring of labourers, to be lined with poles
    and reeds, with sheds over
  2 cooking huts for same
  Clear level ground for their tents and huts
  Clean water supply for same

Water and trample brick clay and sift out stones

Agree lists with Lamb

By March, the salvage of building stuffs was well advanced. Most of the ash had been spread on garden bed and fields. Most charred wood had either been burnt on Bonfire and Treason Night, or further reduced to charcoal and burnt in the winter braziers. Teams of estate labourers had rescued much of the precious lead from the roof and down pipes, which, though most often found in deformed lumps, could be melted again and recast. Very little window glass had survived.

'We must find a way of making those windows of yours,' Lamb had declared early in the New Year. He had set off at once to visit an estate in Warwickshire whose owner had tried to build his own glass furnaces.

During the dark winter evenings, Lamb had calculated quantities of building stuffs and necessaries from his own plans and the model of the house. Bent shoulder-to-shoulder in the wavering yellow light focussed by Wentworth's candlestick, he and Zeal had drawn up tentative lists. They had invited written tenders for supplying glass, tiles, slates, and additional timber and stone to supplement what Wentworth could beg or the estate could provide. When those tasks were done, Zeal continued to describe her vision of the details of her house, and Lamb captured her words and thoughts in nets of quick, inky lines. Together, they had taken back from the craftsmen the control of the building.

By March, amber oak planks, sawn under cover, were seasoning in stacks. Casual labour, hired by the day from the parish poorhouse, had dug, and cast up to weather, great mountains of brick clay from a deposit on the edge of Far Beeches estate.

After discussions with Wentworth, Master Wilde of Far Beeches made a proposal that allowed Zeal to proceed with building for a few months at least. Not only would he buy the meadow with access to the river, he agreed to advance her the cost of building an oven on the site in April or May. He too needed bricks, to repair walls of his own.

Philip had undertaken to discover whether or not they would need a licence to rebuild. Of an evening, Zeal and Lamb, sometimes joined by Wentworth, would walk about the building site, discussing urgent matters like drains or where to build the encampments for the builders who would begin once warmer weather arrived.

Zeal ached to get on. So much preparation was needed before a house could begin to grow. She had imagined something more like a seed, which heaved up the soil, broke through, then uncurled upwards driven by its own internal force. Instead, three and a half months after Quoynt's first blast, she still gazed down into muddy trenches where the first heavy foundations now lurked damply, like teeth broken off below the gum.

'Winter always stops work,' Lamb reassured her. 'Later, you'll be grateful to have had time to ponder. By May, it will be all "Where exactly do you want this, madam?" and "You'll never fit those stairs in there!" and "This main beam went and split on us. What do you want us to do now?"'

Though she had not yet heard that he was safely arrived on Nevis, she wrote again to John, in the care of the tobacco planter, his master for the next seven years, whose name he had given in his first letter. She told him about starting the new house, but not who was helping her. She filled two pages with bridges, brick ovens, and the number of new lambs, without mentioning either the baby or her marriage. She avoided all topics that might even suggest them. She knew how dangerous the spaces between words could be. John would be as quick to read what she had left unsaid, as she had been to spy his peril in the words '. . . *whatever protection that kinship may offer me.'*

When they could look into each other's eyes, and grip hands, and hear the tone of each other's voices, they would put it all right again.

31

<u>March 1640</u>

'I must go to Basingstoke! It's the Quarter Day.' Trying to climb out of his bed, Philip collapsed onto the floor beside it.

'You're not going anywhere while your ague is on you.' Zeal called Rachel to help lift Philip back onto the bed. He was as hot as an ember and his eyes were bright.

'It comes. It goes,' he said. 'Don't concern yourself . . . Go saddle my horse, sir.'

Rachel looked at Zeal for guidance. Zeal gave her head a tiny shake and gestured for Rachel to go. She thought it best not to tell Philip that he had already missed Quarter Day, which had been the day before.

'I'll dress now,' said Philip. 'Must be there by noon!'

'In a moment, in a moment.' Whatever he wanted to do would have to wait. 'Drink this first, my husband.' She held the cup to his mouth. 'Why don't you sleep a little, to rest for the journey?'

He stiffened and looked at her in alarm. 'Journey? Where must I go? Never again! No journeys! The ship must sail without me.'

'Indeed, it shall.' She wiped his cheeks and neck with a cool wet cloth, then the insides of his wrists. 'You shall stay here with me.'

He seemed content with that, if a little uncertain who she might be.

When he had cooled and fallen asleep, she left Philip with one of the young house grooms standing watch.

'Send for me if the fever rises again,' she told the boy. 'And do not, no matter how he curses you, let him go out into this grey chilly day! I will be down at the old house with Tuddenham.'

Though her new house was still only foundations in a muddy hole in the ground, Zeal already imagined the painted fruitages and flowerages of wall cloths, and the subjects of the painted screens of oiled silk she would set in the big windows to stop winter draughts. She would set Philip's Christmas map, already traced, squared up and enlarged for transfer by Lamb, onto the floor of her new entrance hall. Made of inlaid stone or tiles, if she somehow found the money. But otherwise, painted wood would serve very well, and seemed far more likely.

She wondered where Lamb had gone, on yet another of his excursions after information or materials.

She tested possible names for the house, knowing that the right one already existed. It merely waited to be revealed, as distinct and unmistakable as a hen's egg discovered in a pile of straw.

Such were the thoughts with which she now entertained herself through the tedium of salvaging bricks.

'Hey, you! Girl!'

'Seven hundred and forty-four,' said Zeal, scratching another line on her tally sheet. As her pregnancy was now six months advanced, she sat on a stool and settled for keeping score. She did not look at the horseman who had shouted at her.

'You there, with the paper!'

Zeal glanced up as if at a buzzing fly, then back down at her paper. She rubbed her nose with a cold dirty hand. Lamb had calculated that to build their perfect house they would need at least two hundred thousand bricks, of which they must salvage as many as they could.

Tuddenham turned a brick in his hand, tapped it, then nodded. She made the satisfying diagonal line that marked the achieving of five and pinned down the previous four so they could not escape.

The horseman had come along the track that followed hedgerows from the garrison town of Silchester. They had noticed him as he crested Hawk Ridge, where the wintry yellows and browns were just pricked with pale green. For a moment, he reminded Zeal of the horseman who had gazed down on the workings of the new house before disappearing again. Then they lost him when he dropped down into the water meadows. His horse was wet to the girth.

He rode so close to Zeal that she could smell the damp leather of the saddle and the curdled sweat on his horse. The animal's breath clouded in the cold air.

'Philip Wentworth. Is he about?'

Zeal marked off the seven hundred and forty-sixth brick before she looked up. 'Are you asking me, sir?' The other men and women who had been helping with the salvage bent to their work with unnatural concentration.

The rider was a tall thin man, a little older than Harry. Perhaps in his early thirties, about John's age. He seemed to hum with suppressed rage like a hive of bees about to swarm.

'Who else might I be asking, Mistress Pert?'

Zeal heard Tuddenham give a startled sniff. She cast him a warning glance over her shoulder before standing up from her stool. To be fair to the stranger, she did not look much like the mistress of the estate in her heavy old skirt and a thick scarf around her neck and head, to keep off the dust as well as cold.

'I'm told he lives at Hawkridge,' said the horseman. 'But that doesn't seem likely, now that I see the place.'

'Are you a friend?'

The horseman smiled unpleasantly under his wide-brimmed felt hat. 'I don't believe I could call him a friend. Not that it's your business. Just tell me where he can be found, if not here.'

Zeal wiped sooty fingers on her apron and studied the square-jawed face above her. The eyes lay hidden in the shadow of his hat, but she did not like the set of his lower lip.

Philip had enough worry with his ague and raving. He could do without having this evil-tempered creature set on him, one of those who reserve civility for social superiors.

'If you tell me your name, I'll see that the message reaches him.'

'He needs no messages. He knows he left me hanging around like a looby at our agreed time yesterday. But, then, he's a master of broken promises.'

'Indeed,' said Zeal coldly. She dismissed any second thoughts about lying to this creature. 'Then we've nothing more to say to each other.'

'Who is your master?' he demanded angrily. 'I'll see that he teaches his people to respect a gentleman!'

'I have no master!'

'The more's the pity! He might beat some civility into you.' His hand tightened on his crop as if he considered doing it himself. 'Unless he's the one who fumbled you.'

'Get off this estate!' said Zeal quietly.

'You insolent little trull!'

Zeal drew herself up. She wished she were taller. Her hand found the knife that hung from her belt. 'If you don't go, I vow that the owner of this estate will have you driven off!'

He laughed. 'Old Wentworth would always rather consort with trollops, buggers and licensed thieves than with honest gentlefolk. Trust him to find them even here. Is it true that he married one of them?'

'Get off this estate!'

He shook his head in mock despair and struck his horse violently with the crop. The startled animal swung round so suddenly that its hindquarters knocked Zeal to the ground. She rolled to escape its hoofs, then scrambled to her feet, winded but filled with fury. He spurred his horse into a canter.

'Stop him!' she gasped. She gave chase, intent on pulling him from his horse. Her head thudded with white rage. She would ram his words back down his throat. Haul him up to the lodge and make him apologize to Philip for those ugly words.

But her right ankle gave way under her, as if the bone had turned to water. She stumbled and fell again. She limped to her stool, while two of the young men sprinted up the drive in hopeless pursuit.

'Are you hurt, madam?' Tuddenham bent to look at her face.

'Only my pride,' she said shortly. She brushed mud and soot from her sleeves and skirt. 'I was dirty before.' Her left wrist was hot with pain, while her ankle felt cold. A spike seemed to have been driven into her gut just above the pubic bone. 'Don't fret.'

'All the same . . .' Tuddenham was glaring at her with such intense concern that she flushed uncomfortably. She could see him biting back the suggestion that she return to High House to recover from her fall.

She stood up experimentally. Limped two steps. Painful but possible. 'I'd best go tell Master Wentworth what a delightful visitor he missed. You carry on with the tally.'

With honour satisfied all around, she set off up the long drive. Feeling Tuddenham's eyes on her back she tried not to limp.

I hope I did the right thing, she thought. Philip is too ill to deal with a man like that. I can't imagine what he wants with him even when well.

Nevertheless, her curiosity was aroused. If the former Philip had such associates, it was small wonder he decided to hide himself away and fish.

I've let him off his stories for too long. Distracted by the house, by Lamb, by exhaustion, and the growing child.

She decided to go to High House rather than the lodge. Philip would be sleeping now, and she wanted to report this stranger to Sir Richard.

A little uneasily, she recalled the stranger's mention of a missed meeting and Philip's urgent need to get to Basingstoke. On the track to High House, she stopped with a stitch in her side. While she waited for it to ease, she hauled up her skirts to examine a bruise that had begun to throb from knee to hip.

I shall tell Philip that it was an accident, if he notices anything wrong. Whatever's between them, there's enough bad feeling already.

The stitch grew worse, so she sat down in the grass. She also felt giddy.

After a short rest, she set off again. The ground was very cold.

Strong jaws closed around the base of her belly. Her hair prickled. Cold washed through her. When the jaws loosened again, she leaned forward, bracing her good hand against her knee, trying to regain her breath. She waited, heart thumping, but the pain did not return.

She limped a few more steps up the hill. All seemed well again. The skin still felt a little tight across her belly, but no wonder.

All will be well, she told herself. I must not allow that man any power over my body or my thoughts. Beyond her rage, he also filled her with unease.

He never came. When I get to High House, I will ask for some thyme water to wash him away. A man like that might very likely write poisonous letters. Or rather, someone like him who knows me enough to imagine that he has cause

Or that she has cause, Zeal reminded herself. We don't know that the letter writer is a man.

She stopped to rest again. Her eyes searched for a bright omen to replace the memory of the man on horseback. A single magpie dropped to the ground on the track ahead. The sharply defined black and white of its feathers seemed to belong to some other image, not the soft assembly of rusty greens around it.

She looked away. She could choose not to believe in omens, but the single bird still made her feel askew.

Half-way up the hill above the spring where she had made her wedding wish, she sat on an outcrop of reddish rock to rest her foot and calm her mind. The musicians had praised God in the field below her. The odd disorientation which had followed the fire wrapped itself around her again. High House seemed very far away. She decided to sit for a while where she was, cold ground or not. She cupped her hand over her belly and imagined that the child was sleeping. Best not to move and wake it. Perhaps Rachel could bring her dinner here.

The jaws closed again.

Suddenly, she knew that she should not walk the rest of the way up the hill and down past the lake to High House. That all might not be well.

'Rachel!' she screamed.

She pulled her knees up. Held her legs with her hands and tried to breathe. The cramp hit again, harder than before.

It's now, she thought. Too soon. Here in the pasture.

'Rachel!' she called again. 'Tuddenham!'

Wait! she ordered the child.

She could not draw enough breath to call again. When she tried, her voice came out in a frayed ribbon of sound. She felt as undone and shapeless as pond water without banks or dam. She became pain itself. Tried to hold the child and herself together, but pain invaded the space inside her body. It was crowding the child out.

She and the child both dissolved in the pain. Her reason turned to mist, lifted, blew away.

She fought the pain. Held. Held. Felt her grip begin to slip. Could not hold the child. With despair, she felt it slip away from her. She clawed up her skirts, lest they smother the baby. A boy, smeared with blood and a sheer white wax.

Voices. Hands. Rachel, thank the Lord. And a man. He shouldn't be here. Seeing me like this.

'Let me . . .' said a woman.

'I have him!' Zeal seized up her son. He could almost fit into one of her hands. 'Tie and cut the cord! At once!'

He was the temperature of her own skin. Too small. A miniature baby. Webs between his fingers. Long little legs . . . Oh, John!

She wrapped him in her scarf. His tiny mouth was no larger than the opening of a snail's shell. With a finger as huge and unwieldy as a tree trunk, she felt for a blockage in his throat as she had once seen a midwife do. She put her face on his and breathed into his nose and mouth.

'Madam, it's no use . . .'

She gave her son her breath gently, as if puffing away a tiny gnat. His chest rose and fell under her hand. She breathed for him again. Then again.

'Madam, he's not for this world.'

'LET ME!' cried Zeal, as fierce as a cat that thinks you will take away its bird.

Then she had to stop while the child's treacherous nest also slipped from her body.

'Madam, permit me!' Rachel, panting hard from her run to and from the hillside spring, held her cupped hands above the child's head. 'What will you call him?' She spilled a few drops of water from her hands. 'In the name of the Father, the Son and the Holy Spirit . . .'

'George,' said Zeal. 'For his great-uncle, who built Hawkridge.' She bent her head again to her son's damp face, only dimly aware of others around her, who waited while she blew into his lungs again and again. When he began to grow cold in spite of her scarf, she stopped at last. She let hands lift her from the ground and carry her, with her son still in her arms.

Once in High House, she asked for water and a soft cloth.

'Lady, you should be abed,' said Sir Richard's chief housemaid. 'Let me help you there. Rachel can look after the babe now.'

'Bring me water!'

The other two women looked at each other. Rachel shrugged and left the room.

'Come, mistress.'

'We're quite well here.' Zeal sat on the floor and leaned against the chair behind her. She felt that the floor was safer than the chair, in case she dropped him.

Someone brought a charcoal brazier and set it beside her.

I will learn his face, before it's too late. I didn't learn his father's face. I must press him into my memory before they take him from me forever. I think he's a little like John. His long legs. There's something in the set of the eyes.

She held him against her. A part of her still insisted that she could warm him again.

When Rachel returned with a basin of fresh water, Zeal washed her son's face, removing the waxy coating and smears of blood. His nose was narrower than the tip of her little finger. She washed the black hair that stuck to his head like wet down, then the new leaves of his eyebrows. She kissed his small forehead, then shuddered at the chill under her lips.

Then she began to wash his body, with long tender strokes along his arms and legs, and across his rounded belly. She stopped to study his minute penis and generous balls. She saw him as a man, as tall as his father, though with black hair instead of dark russet.

Don't be a fool. Many babies are born with black hair and lose it later.

She washed his genitals, his infinitesimally small toes. Then she began again with his face and hair.

'Please heat another basin of water.'

'Surely the poor creature is clean enough now,' said Rachel. 'Let me help with the winding. Then we'll put you to bed again, where you should be right now!'

Zeal's hands lightly enclosed the baby's frail ribs. 'The water's too cold.'

At that point, both Lamb and the midwife arrived.

'You've no business here!' said Rachel sharply.

Lamb ignored her and sank to his knees beside Zeal on the floor, bringing the smell of cold air and the outdoors with him on his clothes. She lifted her hands in a helpless gesture and let them fall again.

Lamb laid his palm on the baby's forehead. 'The skull has the same shape as his father's.'

She gave him a startled, questioning look.

Lamb winked. 'If one can't speak the truth in the face of death, when else?' He took off his hat and set it on the floor. After a moment, he observed, 'He is turning a strange but rather beautiful colour, like soiled ivory.'

'Sir!' Rachel stood at his shoulder. 'Please, leave. We have things to do. My lady should be in bed, not catching chills in a wet gown on the floor!'

'May I paint him?' asked Lamb. He reached out. When Zeal did not object, he gently took the body from her arms. 'Who'd have thought so small a thing could so resemble an entire person? I can see how he would have looked when grown. Do let me paint him.'

Rachel exclaimed in horror. 'Let her bury the poor thing and get on with mourning!'

'How do you propose to represent him?' asked Zeal from within the cold calm that followed her washing of the corpse. She observed in herself the deep-planted seed of a scream.

'Madam, don't let him.'

'I don't know yet,' said Lamb. 'A *putto* would be too obvious . . . perhaps as the infant Eros. The solution will come to me as I make the drawings. We must make a place for your son in your house as well as in the churchyard.'

'At the centre,' Zeal said. 'And also paint a miniature for me to take to show his . . .' She caught herself.

'Just as well the weather's turned cool,' Rachel muttered to Mistress Judd, the midwife. 'What shall we do about telling poor Master Wentworth? Anyone would think this young puppy is the father!'

'Give me my child again.'

Lamb glanced sideways at Zeal who had remained motionless since he took the baby. 'Not yet, my muse. If you let these good women settle you in bed, I'll give him back. Then I'll draw you both. You think you'll never forget, but in my experience, we hide such things away as fast as we can.'

'Wickedness!' cried Mistress Judd.

'My work here is to help capture truth,' replied Lamb. 'Most often, I chase visible truth after it has fled and have to make do with the greater, invisible truths instead.' He laid the baby on the foot of Sir Richard's great bed.

While Lamb went in search of pencil and paper, Zeal allowed the two women to strip off her wet and bloody gown, then wrap her in blankets in the bed. There, she cradled her child while Lamb drew and drew, until she finally slept.

'How did this happen? Who let it happen?' Philip raged at the far end of the chamber. 'He said that I missed him in Basingstoke? Are you absolutely certain?' He had come from Hawkridge wearing only a cloak over his night shirt and sleeveless gown.

'Not so loud, sir!' said Rachel. 'You'll wake her.'

'Why are you out of bed?' Zeal asked groggily. 'Is your fever gone?'

'Tell me!' Philip's voice cut like broken glass.

'You'd best ask Tuddenham.' Rachel crossed to the bed with a mug in her hand. 'And you, mistress, drink this down.'

'Where is my baby?' She was just testing.

'Our son,' said Philip. 'Oh, my poor, dear girl.'

Zeal thought that he seemed truly stricken. 'You married me for nothing, after all.' She watched him curiously, still too numb to feel anything much. How can he be mourning John's son? That's for me to do. She knew what lay waiting to ambush her. Not yet. Can't start that now. Will die. Later.

She woke in the night to see Philip asleep in the chair beside her bed with a candle burning on the chest beside him and a blanket wrapped around his legs. His eyes opened as she stirred.

'You're ill yourself. Go back to bed,' she told him.

'The fever is past.'

'All for nothing.' She laid her hands on her flat empty belly. 'I'm sorry.'

'Why? I wouldn't have missed Gifford's face when he saw the musicians in the meadow, for anything.'

She woke again near dawn, with the same awful plunge from warm sleep into knowledge. Wentworth was still there. When he saw that she was awake, he took her hand and rubbed it absently, as if trying to warm her.

'Please don't miss your early fishing on my account.'

He nodded. 'I'll go when those hordes of women descend again.'

The next morning, she clutched at her numbness while still climbing up from sleep. She clung to it, wrapped it around her like a thick cloak against icy winds. Clarity almost grabbed her once. Then she drank the potion Rachel held to her mouth and sank back into woolly calm again.

When she next woke, the light told her that it was afternoon. This time, Lamb sat by the bed, sketching her while she slept.

'You should have asked my permission,' she said crossly.

'Ingrate! Look how lovely you were in sleep.' He showed her several drawings.

'What of the others?' She dared not say the word 'baby'.

'I will show you when I am satisfied. Go back to sleep.'

As she lacked the strength to argue, she lay with her eyes closed to satisfy him.

After a while, he set aside his drawings and rubbed her bare feet. For some reason, this made her weep quietly, as if she had sprung a slow leak.

'What have I done?' she asked Rachel when her woman brought a savoury custard for her supper.

'Eat this and go back to sleep. There's plenty of time to talk later when you're stronger.'

'I don't want to sleep any more,' she told Philip, who was back in his chair that next night. Her face felt hot and her eyelids tight. She tried to sit up. The room tilted. The door and window frames wavered like reflections in water.

'I'm under orders to keep you in bed,' he warned.

She fell back and curled onto her side. She burned. My metal has begun to melt and combine into a new alloy. I am taking a new shape, a deformed lump of lead. John will never know me now.

A rocket exploded behind her eyes but the falling fragments turned to perroquets. She began to climb the rigging, towards a bright blue and red bird, which alighted on the very top of the mast. I can recapture it, she thought, if I take great care, and don't look down. The swaying mast carried her in a great arc through space. She felt sick. She had never been so frightened in her life, but she had to recapture the perroquet or die. She seemed to climb and fall for days. Sometimes the bird was there. Sometimes it had flown.

'I have not seen any of the birds, flowers or strange four-legged creatures that fill John's senses,' she said aloud when she awoke seven hours later. 'I know nothing of what is shaping him.'

Philip laid a dry warm hand on her forehead and grunted in approval. 'Welcome back.'

She looked at him in shock, then remembered that this was her husband. 'We must undo the marriage!'

'Why?'

The answer seemed too obvious to need words. 'Don't you wish to?'

'I don't think we could, even if we did wish,' he said.

All those clauses and hedges of words had been constructed only as a shelter around the child. But its death did not dissolve the words.

'You're trapped,' she said.

'As are you.'

'Don't you find it intolerable?'

'No. Do you?'

'But the reason is gone.'

'Friendship remains.'

'Yes,' she said bitterly. She laid her arm across her eyes. A moment later, she added, 'I'm sorry. I didn't mean that as it sounded. I'm very grateful to you.'

'But love for friendship is a poor exchange?'

She turned to look at him. 'You're as blunt as I am. I haven't grown accustomed to it yet.'

'Self-delusion is a waste of life.'

She did not reply. Even bluntness could not support her true thoughts at that moment.

Philip stood up and walked to the window. 'I'm an old man. That's your consolation. Mind you, I don't intend to die on demand.'

'Please! Don't say such things! I can't bear it!' She drew a shaky breath, then thrust the edge of the coverlet into her mouth to stifle a scream of despair. Then she began to cry.

'Zeal?' He walked back to the bed. 'Damnation!' he said to himself.

She sucked in long scraping breaths and sobbed them out again. The pressure of tears tried to push her eyes from their sockets. Her cheeks grew wet. Her nose ran. Still, she could not get her breath back. She was drowning in a black sea.

Philip sat on the bed. 'I didn't mean to set you off.'

She wiped her face with the coverlet.

'Why not use your sleeve instead?' he asked. 'I expect it's easier to wash.' His weight rocked on the mattress. 'Here's my handkerchief, if you like. A little used, I'm afraid.'

With eyes swollen shut with weeping, she reached blindly and felt him put the linen square into her hand. She blew her nose. 'You're all that's left,' she said, with astonishment. Then sobs shook her again.

'My dearest girl . . .'

Harry took her innocence and the nymphs. The house burned. John abandoned her. John's cat died in flames. Her son barely touched the earth before he left again. She was married, but not to the man she loved.

'What has happened to my child?'

'We set him in a vault in the chapel while you were ill.'

She said nothing.

Philip patted her shoulder. Then, abruptly, he climbed onto the bed and wrapped his arms around the small quivering hillock she made under the coverlet. For some reason, he began to hum, tunelessly. The vibrations in his chest reached her through the coverlet.

She took another deep breath. 'What tune is that?' she asked in a voice muffled by bedclothes.

'I have no idea.' But after a moment, he began to sing the Spanish words. '*Duerme no llores, hija de lagrimas . . .*'

She lay still curled and tried to steady her breathing. The ring of his arms held her firmly, so that she did not crumble like an unsupported pastry crust. Though she had thought that afternoon that she would never sleep again, she drifted slowly into a drowsy calm.

When she next awoke, the fever had left completely. It was dark, some time in the night. She felt bright and edgy. Her feet twitched. Her hands prowled like spiders. Philip still held her with arms as tight as a barrel hoop. Cautiously, she tried to free herself. His candle had burned down almost to the end.

'Can't sleep?' His breath was warm on the top of her head. 'Would you like a game of Angel-Beast? I have cards in my pocket.'

'Yes.' Keep your thoughts busy, she told herself.

But when he had lit a second candle and dealt their cards onto the top quilt, her mind refused to hold the details of the game.

The thing she had not known. Still did not know. Still an unknown danger.

'Who was that man?' she asked.

'I shall make certain you never see him again!' Philip replied savagely, without answering her question. He stared down at the long, slim cards. 'It was my fault the child died. If I had not been ill . . . if he had not come looking for me . . .'

She shook her head. 'No, Philip. Don't.' She shook her head again but dared not risk further speech.

They both sat looking at the cards.

'What does an agouti look like?' she asked at last.

'Is that one of those strange four-legged creatures you mentioned earlier?'

'Did I?' She had no memory of when. 'I suppose it must be.'

Philip gathered up the cards, straightened their edges against the quilt, turned the deck over several times in his hands. 'Imagine a giant rat,' he said at last. 'With long legs and a little nub of a tail.'

'What colour?'

'Dun, but a black tail.'

Soon after she arrived, John would call her to the window to see the creature for the first time. 'And perroquets?'

'Like tiny parrots.' He lifted his face as if watching them again in his mind. 'They fly in clouds, like blossoms blown in a storm.' He stopped talking and absently began to lay the cards out again.

'Thank you.' Zeal lay back down with her face turned away.

'Can you sleep now?'

'I don't know.'

He cleared his throat. 'If you can't sleep, shall I tell you of the most remarkable and fearful creature I saw during my own last adventure?'

'If you like.'

He gathered up the cards again, pulled off his shoes, stretched himself out on the bed and opened his arm for her to lie against his shoulder. 'Zeal?'

She turned back to him.

'I sometimes wonder now if the creature was real. At the time, I had no doubt.'

She burrowed into his slightly musty warmth. This time his arm encircled her lightly. She shuddered, sighed and lay quiet, waiting to receive fragments of John's new alien world, now offered again after she had almost given up asking.

32

'First we missed our island landfall,' said Philip, 'which we had urgently needed to make, for our fresh water had run out two days before. Then a sudden storm drove *The Golden Seal* towards the mainland coast. We dropped our sea anchor but gales drove us, helpless, closer and closer to the cliffs that our map told us must be hiding in the mist and blowing spume. The sun rose just in time to prevent disaster. In the first glow of light, we saw that we sailed straight at a curving beak of headland. Somehow, our captain steered us safely around into the lee. Though the waters there were still rough, we managed at last to drop anchor and send two boats ashore in search of fresh water.'

'Will you show me on your map where you were?'

He considered the question for some time. 'If you wish . . . I led the party in the first boat. We soon found a shallow stream, swollen by the rain, which spread out across the beach like a woman's hair across a pillow . . .' He hesitated for only a heartbeat, but she heard the tiny falter. Her senses snapped to full alertness. Her body stiffened. By that choice of words, that fractional silence, that merest hiccup of awareness, she knew that her time of grace was ending. As the silence lengthened, she knew that he had felt her understand his intent. The blood thumping in her ears almost drowned his next words.

'We followed the stream up into the jungle in search of a pool deep enough to fill our bottles and pails.'

They were still locked in their shared awareness though he pretended to think only of his tale.

I must tie myself to the mast like Odysseus when the Sirens sang, she told herself. And stop my ears with wax.

But not yet. When the time comes.

'The jungle soon closed around us,' he went on. 'Bulging walls of vine and brush overhung the banks and forced us to walk in single file through the shallow water. The air buzzed and throbbed with sounds none of us had ever heard before . . .'

'How did it sound?'

He whistled, then paused. Then, to her astonishment, he began to hoot, grunt, snort, and click his tongue. 'And rustling . . .' He rubbed his palms together. 'You must imagine all at the same time. If I were a hundred men, I might be able to demonstrate to your satisfaction.'

She thought she detected a dry edge to his voice.

'First, a wild pig came to drink, as rough as an old brush. It spied us and crashed away again. Monkeys followed us overhead, cursing and shouting out warning of our advance.'

'Could you see them?'

He turned his head towards her. 'Almost black, with flashes of white at their throats, like false beards. The size of large cats.'

'And what of the birds?'

'The parroquets were turquoise and cinnabar, and a vivid green . . . if you want me to describe them all, I shall never arrive at my encounter with that creature I set out to tell you of.'

'I bite my tongue.'

'I heard it before I saw it.' He gave three low, resonant barking coughs. 'I did not recognize the cry, but it stood the hair up on my arms . . . If I continue, you won't sleep at all. I'd best wait for daylight.'

'No!'

He laughed with delight at her urgency. 'Well then, imagine me standing there in the stream with clear water flowing around the ankles of my boots. As I listened to those unearthly coughs, I felt askew, as if the air had suddenly twisted like a veil around my head. I turned to see if my companions felt as I did. I was alone.

'They had vanished. I could not understand. I had not heard them go. In any case, they would never have turned back without me. The water ran as clear as if their feet had never disturbed it. Tiny transparent fish swam where their footprints should still have been dissolving away. I felt the air shift again and was suddenly giddy. Then the green wall on the left bank shivered and lifted. A shadow glided under the green hem of the jungle. Then the creature stood on the bank and looked straight into my eyes.'

He yawned. His muscles shifted under her head as he stretched.

'Philip! You can't stop there!'

'You're clearly out of danger now. Time for old bones to sleep.'

'I won't sleep!'

'I did warn you.'

She started to protest further, then remembered that he, too, had been ill.

He sat up and eased himself off the bed. 'I'll continue tomorrow night, if you like.'

'I know what you're doing,' she warned him.

'That's more than I do. Good night, my dearest girl.' He laid his hand on her head like a blessing and left.

Earlier that afternoon, Wentworth had questioned Tuddenham closely about the horseman and how Zeal had come to fall. Now he went to his own chamber and wrote a letter.

Sir,
If you ever again venture near Hawkridge, I will myself put a bullet through your heart. If I did not cling to some remnants of honour, I would also end our arrangement.

P Wentworth

If Zeal had died of her fever, could I have brought myself to killing him now?

Rather than try to answer this impossible question, he reached for his fishing rod.

I shall go see whether anything is biting in the High House lake.

An hour later, he returned to the lodge and listened at Zeal's door.

'Zeal?'

She turned restlessly in a dream but did not answer. With the silent expertise of a thief, he searched her room until he found a small locked coffer he had noted before. He took the coffer back to his own chamber and lit the candle in his sempster's stand, with the lens to focus and intensify the light. He opened the lock easily with his knife and removed John's letters from the coffer. He found his spectacles and sat down.

So, it seems that I have seven years. He refolded the first letter after reading it. Unwelcome intelligence. But learning the worst was vital to waging any successful campaign.

He rose and poured himself a glass of wine before opening the second letter. He had not known she had had a second one.

I wonder if Lamb knows.

He unfolded the letter and held it to the light.

33

Dearest Heart, Darling Girl, My Own Sweetest Zeal (John wrote) . . .

She has not told him, then, thought Wentworth. Or her letter has not yet reached him.

I reach for you in my sleep, in all my waking thoughts. I ache to be this letter, headed back to England and to you . . .

He skimmed quickly through the following details of Hispaniola.

. . . how we so often knew where the other was on the estate, like birds linked in flight by an invisible cord, long before we dreamed we might be free to love. A pair of swifts flying together out over the valley. I cannot wait to show you the birds here – flocks of perroquetos exploding from the trees like red, gold and green fireworks . . .

How did I describe them to her? Wentworth scowled at the paper in his hand.

I fall asleep each night planning how we shall make a life here together . . .

After reading that sentence twice, he leapt again over the next part and paused at the end.

. . . So do not fear. Dream instead of the strange and wonderful creatures I will show you when you come. Giant lizards you might almost take for dragons, monkeys, agoutis . . .

Wentworth poured another glass and drained it.

34

The next evening, after a visit from Lamb, Zeal lay waiting as darkness fell, afraid that Philip might change his mind about continuing his story and fish all night instead. After Rachel had gone to her own pallet in the loft, Zeal tried to stand. Though unsteady, she wrapped herself in her shawl and waited at the window until at last she saw her husband's stocky figure walking through the darkness from Sir Richard's lake. He saw her and waved a string of pale silvery fish.

A little later, he put his head through her door. 'Chubb for breakfast! I must clean them before I come to bed.'

'I'm too ill to torment like this,' she called after him.

Please come soon, she begged him silently. The darkness in the corners of the room crept closer, like an evil fog. She felt so cold and empty that she would scream soon, just to make herself present in the world again. The dead child sat on her heart.

At last Wentworth came to her room. She felt a pang of disappointment when he sat in his chair again rather than climb onto the bed and hold her in the circle of his warmth.

'Do you want me to continue?' He did not sound so friendly as he had the night before.

'I warned you once before not to play me like a fish.'

He smiled suddenly and his fists opened on the arms of his chair.

'The creature lifted its head, with water still dripping from the fur on its chin, and looked me in the eye with the terrible gaze that holds prey frozen in place. I had become a bird, a rabbit, a buck, staring back at my death.'

Zeal sat upright in the bed, watching him in the light of the single candle.

Resolve. That was what she felt in him tonight.

'At the same time, it was as beautiful as Lucifer. Its head was a triangular wedge of golden fur. Its eyes were outlined in black and glowed green in their dark frames as if the sun shone behind them. Its pelt was marked with spots, as if God had pressed his bunched fingers into the ink. Powerful shoulders and a wide chest folded down onto two great paws as wide as my palm. Its fangs were longer than my thumbs.'

She looked at the hand he held out before her, seeing the claws, the sleek flattened fur, the ridged sinews.

'It is crouching to leap, I thought, but I still could not move, not even to pick up my sword from the stream where my hand had let it fall. I felt an exquisite pleasure, which was entirely new to me – that of total helplessness. The end of all responsibility, all decision, all need to act.' He paused, somewhere on the coast of another continent. 'It tasted sweet.'

'That is death,' she said quietly.

Wentworth breathed in and out as if he climbed a steep track and needed to catch his breath. 'The creature lowered its head to drink again, as if it knew I was helpless to flee. It swept a long tongue across its jaw and yawned. Then it rose onto its hind legs.'

'Like a man?' breathed Zeal.

'In such distant parts of the world, God's laws reshape themselves. However much it wrenches our sense of what we think we know, we must alter our familiar world to make room for the wonders of these new laws.'

She stared at his hands, now contracted like claws. 'Did it spring?'

'It had more than a meal in mind for me. Did I say that the beast did not have rear paws like the front ones?'

She shook her head.

'Its hind feet were those of a man. I saw the bare brown

skin, five toes with flat nails as smooth as mother-of-pearl . . .' He reached under the coverlet and touched her bare foot. 'Very like yours.'

She shivered, trying to imagine him tasting helplessness. The young man, standing ankle-deep in the clear stream, skewered by the eye beams of a monstrous but beautiful beast, made her swallow against a thickening in her throat. An uneasy shifting took place just below her heart.

'Instead of attacking, the creature, still on its hind feet, half-turned back towards the jungle, and cast a look at me over its shoulder, as if to say, "Follow!" In the front, its naked-ness was that of a virile man, but a rope of golden tail grew from the base of its back.'

The image was both beautiful and shocking. 'Did you follow?' she asked quickly.

'I did.'

'Alone? Into the jungle?'

'Could you have refused such an invitation?'

Their eyes met with a shiver of shared understanding.

'No,' she said.

'Nor I. I felt a fierce purpose in the beast, as if it wished to show me something. As we moved through the jungle, the creature dropped onto four legs again, leaving me to scramble behind as best I could. I lost it, then saw glints of its pelt between the leaves. Sometimes it was no more than a shifting shadow. I began to imagine that I followed a phan-tasm. Once, I felt my own forehead, thinking I might be driven by the madness of my ague.'

'And did it prove to be so in the end?' She leaned back a little, preparing for disappointment.

'Wait and I will tell you.' He pointed upwards. 'Imagine now, that the beast and I climbed alongside the course of a waterfall that spewed through a break in the cliff high above us, then tumbled down a giant staircase in the mountainside. As I hauled myself up from boulder to boulder, slipping on the loose rock and moss, grasping at tree roots that came away in my hand, I was constantly brushed by veils of spray. My ears were thick with the roar of the falls. Twice, we crossed under a thundering curtain of falling water to continue upwards on the other bank.'

With her head tilted back to the bed canopy and eyes closed, she saw him, a tiny figure against the foaming water. He disappeared, so that she thought he had been swept away. Then he climbed into sight again, out of the mist.

'And then, at the crest where the water leapt into the void . . . Oh, my dearest girl . . . I looked down over the farther edge into a deep, deep valley, at a city of gold.'

He stood up. 'More tomorrow night, I swear.'

In the night, she thought that the golden beast with the head and tail of a jaguar and the genitals and feet of a man crouched on the end of her bed. She could not move. She was a bird, a rabbit, a field mouse under the shadow of a hawk.

The next day, she found that the golden spotted beast kept slipping between herself and other thoughts. She saw clearly what Philip had done. He might mean to distract her from her grief, but he had also taken his tales away from John and drawn her into his own story. Seeing this, however, did not lessen her urgency to hear the rest.

Philip Wentworth sat on a log above a gravel bank in a clear fast-moving stretch of the Shir. The cold spring meant a late spawning, and the fish still offered good sport. Through the clear water, he could see the long pointed heads of three large barbel eagerly scouring the river bottom. He closed his eyes. He had not even brought his rod. Had come here only for the solitude and to think.

He was playing a dangerous game with his young wife.

He dropped his head into his hands. Every word, every well-meant act tangled him more inexorably in his own net.

35

That night, he sat on the edge of her bed, still fully clothed. She was combing out her hair, which had grown tangled from lying so long against the pillows.

'Did you believe your eyes?' she asked.

He picked up a strand of her hair. 'Did you think that *El Dorado* was only a fable?'

'A great deal of what I read in travellers' accounts of travels may be fabulous.' She crossed her eyes to try to see a tangle over her forehead. 'Not all. While I'm sure that there are dragons, for we see their tiny cousins among our own rocks, I do doubt the reality of men who carry their heads beneath their arms.' She looked at him under her own upraised arm. 'How can the soul animate a body from which it is detached? It flies in the face of reason. Don't you agree?'

'I agree that you're right to apply the test of reason. Does my golden city pass?'

She pulled the ivory comb carefully through her hair. 'The existence of such a place has long been reported. The old queen herself, and the Spanish king both sent expeditions in search of it. I know that gold exists and I don't doubt cities. Therefore, it doesn't strain reason to imagine the two combined.'

'May I do that?' He held out his hand. 'There are tangles here which you can't see.'

She gave him the comb and turned her back to him. He worked in silence for a time, tugging gently, then stopping to unpick snarls with his fingers.

'I feel like a horse,' she said. 'It's quite pleasant.'

'Yes.'

She liked the idea that an old soldier, used to carrying a sword and commanding large numbers of men, now plied an ivory comb with such gentleness. When the word gentleness came into her mind, she was startled to feel tears well up.

'The tangles in fishing lines are easier,' he said.

'Why?' she asked gruffly.

'My fingers have never met threads so fine as these. Even the silk I use to tie my lures . . . even the green which I need for making my dragon flies . . .'

She cut him off. 'They won't work, you know.'

'The silks or the dragon flies?'

'These attempted distractions . . . ow!'

'Tell me when you mean to move.'

'What did you do after you looked down and saw the city?'

He gave her hair a pat. 'There. Now I think you should most probably lie down again.'

'It was my child who was weak, not I.' After two days abed, she ached to walk in the open air. 'I'd rather go fishing.'

'Lie down,' he said gently. He stretched out beside her on top of the quilt.

'You must try to understand what I felt, there on that mountain. That city was my own discovery. I knew that the Spanish, who controlled those islands, could not yet have found it, for their custom was first to plunder all gold and then to destroy any remaining objects of wonder, of fine or ingenious manufacture.'

'And not to take them as booty?'

'They dared not. Or else the "savage nature" by which they characterized the native peoples they conquered would be thrown into doubt. And with it would go much of their excuse for conquering.'

'Did you not go to conquer?'

'To trade. A subtle difference. We fighting men merely provided defence, against the Spanish, and pirates.' He gathered a handful of her loose hair into a rope and laid it across her shoulder. 'There. The finest gold I've seen for at least twenty years.'

'What happened to your creature?'

'When I lifted my eyes from the valley, it had vanished. Not even a quiver of leaf showed which way it had gone. I looked back into the valley. But the city still glowed there in the sun, a great pyramid covered in gold at its centre, with smaller buildings around, set beside a silver reflection, like a mirror.

'I descended the waterfall at once, meaning to gather my men, if they were still to be found in this world, and to return, to essay trade and gather intelligence.

'Back on the floor of the jungle, I followed my own tracks to the shallow stream.' He began to run his thumbnail along the teeth of her comb. 'I could hardly force myself to break out of the trees onto the beach. I half-expected to see nothing there. No men, no boats, no ship riding at anchor. Half-believed that I might after all be caught in a fit of madness. I didn't know which I feared most to find – an empty beach or a busy London street.'

'And?' She had propped herself up on her elbow facing him.

He smiled at her intensity. 'The ship was still there and so were my men. They pounded my back in relief and swore that I had disappeared just as suddenly as I felt they had done.'

'How strange.'

'Beyond reason?'

'I'll judge when I've heard the rest.' But she saw his golden city in the jungle so clearly that she knew it must exist, like one of Lamb's Platonic ideals, or else its ghostly image could not be so strong in her imagination.

'I confess, my conscience would have been easier,' said Philip, 'if I had told them fully where they went. I did not tell all the truth about my guide, for I still doubted it myself. And I did not want to stir their fear. In such strange territory, anything not understood becomes an insidious enemy. In semi-ignorance, our captain agreed to an exploring party. The following morning, I set out with over half the crew and a collection of needles, soap, knives and bolts of silk damask.

'I found the way back easily, as I had known I would. Hardly needed the barking cough that guided me from time to time. I knew that I had begun the great adventure of my life, that the compass needle of my fate had swung.'

He laughed without mirth and scratched the top of his head reflectively. 'Oh, yes, indeed it had. Well.' He looked at her, then away again when she could not share the joke.

'We lost only one man on the climb up the falls. The city still gleamed in the cleft of the valley. The men were both awe-struck and jubilant. We began the descent from the pass. Then disaster struck.

'The inhabitants of the city attacked, eight or more against each one of us. I soon found myself netted like a bird, so that I could not swing my sword. They trussed up the few of us who had survived the bloody fighting, hand-to-hand and foot-to-foot, and slung us beneath poles like hunted game. Then, two to a pole, they set off along a jungle track towards the city.

'Every step my bearers took jolted my joints apart like the rack. Every sinew was stretched beyond endurance. My hands and feet lost all feeling. My ribs crushed my heart . . .'

He rolled to the edge of the bed.

She caught his sleeve. 'Where are you going?'

'I no longer relish this account. Forgive me.' He pulled his sleeve away. 'I did not intend to toy with you. Truly, I did not.'

'Philip. Turn back to me.'

After a moment, he did.

'Is it so very painful to recall these things?' She ducked to look up into his face.

'And if I answer, yes?'

'Then I discharge you from any further telling. I withdraw my original terms for the marriage.'

'You'll survive without the truth?'

'I didn't say that. Only that I won't insist on any more of it.'

'Why?' He frowned and stuck out his lower lip.

'Do you think it gives me pleasure to cause you pain? Or even to listen to you tell of pain, knowing that I force you to revisit it?'

His expression was hard to read in the dim light. Then he tugged gently on the rope of hair that still lay across her right shoulder. 'You should never give ground so easily.' He leaned forward and kissed her.

His lips were dry, warm and brief. He placed one hand lightly on her arm as if to hold her in place.

'What I feel in recounting old adventures is not pain,' he said. 'Pain is of a different order altogether.' His eyes were on her mouth.

I was right, she thought. He does mean to make love to me, now that I'm no longer with child. When I am a little more healed. The air has just twisted like a veil about my head.

He left her chamber. A few moments later, he was back with two stemmed Venetian glasses and a flagon of wine. 'Thank you for that offer. You are kind, but I am a man of my word . . . Will you drink with me? I'm sure it will do you good.'

He poured wine for them both, then stirred the fire back into life. They sat at either end of a small oak table pushed against the wall. He got up again to bring her wool cloak and wrapped it around her. The night was so cold their breathing made little puffs of cloud in the air. She pulled her bare feet up onto the chair and tucked the cloak under her toes. She still felt giddy, but otherwise better than she had since the baby died.

'The city stood on the edge of a lake,' he said. 'The silver I had seen from the top of the pass was water catching the sun. My blood beat so thickly in my head that it half-blinded me, and I saw little of the city itself as we entered it. Our captors set down the poles in a large open place near the lake. They untied us, and then re-shackled us, with our hands behind our backs and just enough slack between our feet to shuffle a few inches at a time. By now, I was able to look about me again. I smelled smoke, animals and wet rot, as well as unfamiliar spices. But I had no time to wonder at the place itself.' He drained his glass and poured another.

'I forgot my fetters,' he said. 'Stood open-mouthed at what next took place. You must understand that I was already in a curious state of accommodating new knowledge into my old universe. Unlike you, I had doubted. Dismissed travellers' accounts of the golden land as the self-serving fantasies of adventurers trying to woo new patrons and to raise money for their expeditions. Now I learned how wrong I had been . . . Will you drink a little more?' He stood and leaned over the table to fill the glass she held out for him.

Wrapped in her cloak, she watched him, as still as a hunter in a blind.

'They were a mighty nation, these children of the jaguar. I heard the multitude before I could shake the red mist from my eyes. Even unbooted, their feet shook the ground. Accompanied by drums and high-pitched pipes, they wailed and cried out as if in grief. Not singing, but nevertheless, I heard the shape of music in their clamour.

'They approached the lake along the dusty avenue from the golden pyramid. Wave after wave of bodies, all glinting with gold at wrists, ankles and thighs. Some wore jaguar skins, still attached to the head, so that each man's eyes gleamed within the open snarling mouth of the beast. Their voices rose in a high dreadful keening but their fierce eyes showed more elation than grief. A strong perfume of musk and civet filled the air.

'Then I saw the musicians, also decked in gold, who played their reed pipes, not to draw out melody as we know it, but as if they had been running and now panted out their souls into their instruments. Behind the pipes, came drums, hanging on cords around the neck and struck with the hand.

'As the procession reached the shore of the lake, it divided. One column walked to the left along the shore, the other, right. Men in jaguar skins still advanced down the avenue. Then came a regiment of warriors with golden spears. Overhead disturbed birds wheeled and cried. The leaves of the trees quivered and dropped a bright shower of collected rain.

'The air was also filled with a faint metallic jingling. I looked for these other musicians, then saw that all the marchers wore strings of golden bells on their ankles, so that all their separate steps rang together like hail striking a vast metal plate.'

'I would like to see such sights!' said Zeal passionately. 'And hear such sounds.' And perhaps I will, she thought. John too might see the golden city and take me there.

She tried to imagine standing with him looking down into the valley, the jaguar with human feet at her other side. She glanced at Philip's intense, distant expression. His younger self was crowding out the indentured servant of an Antilles tobacco farmer.

Her husband stared into the bottom of his glass. 'When you hear the end, you may feel otherwise.' He poured again though her glass still stood nearly full. His hand jumped so that he spilt some wine on the table. He suppressed a curse, then dipped his finger in the puddle and drew a circle. 'Here is our lake, then, though it was not so close to the colour of blood. Its shores grew crowded with the multitude.' He conjured the image with his hands.

'After the warriors with their spears, came priests – or so I took them to be. In linen tunics and fragile crowns made of bright bobbing plumes that rose four or five feet above their heads. The feather tips dipped and waved as they walked, so that I could not see whether they were indeed men or giant birds. Some carried golden axes. Some, black knives, which shone like glass. All were weighed down with gold of every sort – necklaces, breastplates, bracelets, and short blunt rods of gold thrust through their ear lobes.

'When they had surrounded the sacred lake, they redoubled their cries and dropped to their knees. A single figure advanced towards the water. He did not walk, for a god's feet must not be allowed to touch the ground. And he was a god – or so it seemed that these heathens believed. He stood with easy balance on a palanquin borne on the shoulders of six men, his hands raised as if in blessing.'

Philip leaned across the table and took her hands in his. 'Feel how I still tremble at the memory. He appeared to be made all of gold. Wore a golden cap, short gold rods through his ear lobes and a golden collar. Breastplate, wide golden bands around his wrists and the muscles of his upper arms. A golden belt circled his waist. Golden greaves covered his shins. Every finger of his upraised hands flashed brightly. Otherwise, he was naked, and his skin too was covered in gold.'

Zeal closed her eyes to capture the picture. The beautiful golden god, riding his jerky palanquin with straight back and loose knees, as Muscovite riders stand on a cantering horse at a fair. She tightened her grip on the faint quiver she felt in her husband's hands. His fingers were cold.

'He glittered in the afternoon sun,' said Philip. 'For an instant, I was blinded by a flash of light off his breastplate. I wanted to weep with the force of what I had just understood. Then I wanted to laugh.'

He looked intently into her face. 'No one yet alive in England knows what I understood then and am about to tell you now.'

She held him steady in her grip.

'Though in fear of my life, I still presumed to feel triumph. Our party, or what was left of it, had found that which all men sought. Which countless expeditions had pursued. For which monarchs had commissioned searches, armadas had sailed, armies clashed. And though rich spoils had been taken, the fabled quarry had eluded all. In consolation, we told ourselves that we had perhaps misunderstood rumour. I had often said that we should be satisfied with smuggling tobacco or tin. Or with plundered cargoes of enemy ships. There, by that lake, I felt as I imagine St Paul felt at his thunderclap – ecstatic, terrified and humbled all at the same time.'

He still gazed into her eyes. 'You may not think it possible, seeing me as I am now. But all those years ago, I had arrived at the ultimate goal, and I understood that, like all those other venturers, I had been chasing the wrong prize. *El Dorado*, a place, a kingdom. Indeed, when I first looked down into the valley, I thought that I had found it. Now I saw that we should have sought a man. *El Rey Dorado*. The golden king.'

'Oh!' breathed Zeal.

'I would not wish the curse of finding what he seeks on any man.' He released her hands, stood up and began to pace. 'I'm afraid that understanding was only the first of my many tutorial surprises.'

He paused at the window to look down into the darkness at the track he had taken up from Sir Richard's lake.

'I was pushed to my knees, in imitation of the golden horde around the lake. The only sounds now were of birds and creatures in the jungle. An insect hummed near my ear.

'The palanquin-bearers lowered their burden to the ground beside the water. The golden king stepped forward, raised gleaming arms and unclasped his golden collar. He threw it into the lake.

'As it sank into the dark water, a cry went up around the shore. He removed his rings, his armbands, his belt, and threw them all into the lake. Then, when he had stripped himself naked, his attendants threw water on him until they had washed off even the golden dust.'

Philip came back to the table to pick up his glass.

'As he bathed, he seemed to grow weaker. Two priests half-supported, half-carried him into the lake. He stood in water up to his thighs, unsteady, eyes glazed, reaching out as if he might fall. Suddenly, he gave a cry and slipped down under the water. The priests hauled him back to the surface. Then, as if in a frenzy, the crowds around the lake began to strip off their own golden ornaments and throw them into the lake, as if to feed the virtue of the precious metal back into their once-golden king. A hail of gold rained into the water. The king stood unsupported but still reeled. All gold had been thrown. There was nothing left to give. He cried out again. A wailing passed through the crowd, back towards the golden pyramid. Their arms reached out as if begging for something more.'

Philip's glass slipped from his hand. He cursed under his breath as it shattered on the hard ebony floor. 'I forgot myself in my own tale.' He squatted down to pick up the shards, his broad back turned to Zeal, and set the broken glass carefully in the corner of the fireplace for a groom to clear the next day.

'I must go to my own chamber now.'

'Are you testing my resolve?' she asked.

He frowned. 'How so?'

'Not to press you against your will.'

'I'm not in full control of my tongue. Should not have brought you so far. I'm sorry. Despite my word, I've reached the end.'

'But tomorrow night?'

'What comes next is not for the ears of a woman.'

'You are cruel to tantalize me like this,' she said lightly.

'Don't use words you can't begin to understand.'

'Which one? "Cruel" or "tantalize"?'

He stared at her, from a great distance.

'Why not tell me?' she begged. 'I beg, rather than demand.'

'I would give all I own not to have been there for what followed. And I will not take you there with me. I should never have let you persuade me to blab so much already.'

'You seemed to find a little pleasure in the recounting.'

'A maundering grey-beard!'

'You know I meant nothing of the sort!'

He came to the table and set his large hands over hers, which she had bunched into fists. 'I do know what you meant. And I did want to tell you . . . I wanted, in my weakness, to show you something of my other life, which was more than tying flies and smoking by the fire.' He picked up one fist and kissed it. 'I wanted you to see me as more than I am now. As a venturer, a soldier. I fear that my vanity could not resist letting you know how much I am changed.'

'I like you as you are.'

'Ah, but just think how you might have loved the soldier!'

She avoided his eyes as he continued to hold her hands, but felt her face grow hot. 'Is our battle over?' she finally asked. 'I hate quarrelling with you.'

'"Battle"?' He smiled. 'That's another of those words, like "cruelty", which put on false domestic clothes.' He looked down. 'Do you still want to hit me?'

She quickly unclenched her fists. 'You can't abandon yourself on your knees in the jungle.'

'I can and shall. Good night, my dearest girl.' He did not try to kiss her again.

When he had gone, Rachel came down from her loft wearing the blank face of someone trying to pretend she has not overheard everything. 'Would you like a posset to help you sleep, madam?'

After Rachel had left again, Zeal lay fuming and turning in the dark. She had recognized finality in his tone. It had taken the loss of her child to shake his tongue loose again after the false start on their wedding night. What would it take to shake it loose again now?

Yet, I'm certain that he wants to tell me, almost as much as I want to hear.

She got out of bed again, pulled on thick woollen stockings and returned to stand at the window.

I'm worse off than I was before Philip started his tales, she thought. With my head now full of beautiful nightmares, John feels farther away even than before.

The sky had just begun to lighten to a thick grey. The long track up from the lake was empty. At its lowest point, it disappeared into a low-lying mist, out of which poked the top of Sir Richard's pavilion. Though the scene had a half-bewitched air, it felt solid and true compared to cities of gold.

But cities of gold already felt far more solid and true in her mind than an Antilles tobacco farm.

I am doing as Philip said – accommodating his wonders into what I think I know.

She tried to imagine John walking up out of the mist now, like Philip with his fish.

Write to me! she begged him. Let me know you are alive. Show me where you will be for the next six and a half years. I need images. I need your words sitting solidly on the page, even when I know how far short words fall from the truth. The cord that bound us in the air has snapped. The spider's web of my imagination is stretching beyond its strength.

She tried to think how to tell him that his child, about whom he had not known, was now dead.

I have waited too long to begin the telling.

As if on a secret signal, the birds began their pre-dawn clamour, like an entire village shouting all at once. She did not feel tired. She had slept too much in the past three days. Her heart was numb but her thoughts circled restlessly.

She took Philip's map from her cupboard, pausing absently for a moment over her small coffer, which seemed subtly out of place. Then she carried the map to the table and lit a fresh candle from the stub of the old.

The world, laid out like a ragged pelt, centred on the Caribbean, with the mouth of Hell near one edge, just off the Indian coast. And there was Nevis. A tiny inconsequential blob of ochre and green, floating on a lapis lazuli sea, in the belly of the island chain that curved from its sea horse head at Hispaniola to the tiny tail bones dangling below Barbados, near the Guyana coast.

She touched Nevis. John is here. So far as I know.

I will make Philip show me where he saw his city, she resolved. He can't deny me that. Otherwise, his adventures and John's will grow more and more jumbled in my head.

When the map was painted on her new hall floor, she would stand on the island of Nevis and imagine John. Then stand on that other spot and imagine the younger Philip, the soldier and adventurer, who had tried to be satisfied with smuggled tobacco and plundered cargoes. Each man in his place. Two separate places, not one.

A shutter quivered in its frame.

John?

She listened, poised as tautly as if she had called into a dark cave, and waited for an echo to say that something other than a void lay before her.

She felt no reply. Not even her own stubborn hope, busily explaining away the emptiness she felt.

I'm losing you. And how, given what has already happened, will you even begin to find me again after six and a half more years? I may no longer know myself.

If she ever believed that she had lost him forever and that they would never find each other again, she knew that she would simply sit waiting for death to come in his place. She laid her hand on the terrible new flatness of her belly, still soft from stretching around her child. She was suddenly in a panic to trap and hold who she was and what she knew at that moment.

She ran back to the cupboard and rummaged for Lamb's sketches of the child. She had seen her son for such a short time that she already distrusted her memory of his face.

The drawing was not there. Instead, she found Lamb's sketch of the old Hawkridge House, before the fire, which he had made one February evening from her description, for possible use in a medallion or decorative panel. She remembered insisting that the tendrils of some ivy had grown to the right and not the left. Lamb replied that it looked better as he had drawn it and therefore he better served the greater truth of the beauty she remembered. A small detail in any case. She had shrugged in unhappy agreement.

I was right to insist, she thought now. This drawing already falsifies the past. It was a tiny lie, but a lie all the same. Lamb must redraw this truthfully, as it was. I must have him record everything that I can remember, exactly as it was. Any house can hold the lives of the classical gods and ancient heroes. Mine will hold our own lives steady – mine, John's, Philip's – true in every detail, good and bad, including even Doctor Gifford.

It may be too late for some of the past. But I must begin to leave footprints. Then I, at least, can track myself back and remember the journey and who I was when I made it.

She studied the drawing of the old house, with the slope of Hawk Ridge rising smoothly behind it. No raw rock or spoil heaps.

And I will record each new change while it is fresh, leaving blank space for the future to fill. I must leave a clear track through time. I will make Lamb finish painting the baby's portrait, to show one day to John. The picture will tell him better than my words.

It came to her. The straw shifted and revealed the egg. Clear and unmistakable. The name of the new house.

The Memory Palace.

Feeling suddenly lighter, she slept.

36

'Like the ancient orators,' she explained to Lamb the next day. 'Who built houses in their minds, and placed imaginary objects in them, to remind themselves, as they walked through, of what must come next. But I want to place reminders of the past.'

Lamb was not happy, but he humoured her for a time.

At the end of March, as her first step in recording truth, Zeal moved her son's coffin. In spite of raised eyebrows and gossip, she had him set in the Beester vault beside the chapel, with his great uncle and namesake, Sir George Beester, who had built Hawkridge House.

She heard the whispers that the child had no right to lie there. And the other whispers insisting that it did, and how did she think she could get away with such brazenness, and whatever did poor old Master Wentworth make of it all?

She did not care. She set her son's plaque defiantly: 'George Alexander Wentworth, *natus et renatus est, 26 Martius 1640.*' John's son. Born and reborn. Taken from this earth and blessed in the next. Baptised with water from a pagan spring by a serving woman whose intent was surely enough to please God. Zeal was certain of that much and did not care a fig for the rest.

A sodden March gave way to an unseasonably hot April. The trees leapt into leaf. Zeal and Philip moved back into the lodge. She slowly recovered her strength though not her former fierce purpose towards the house. She thought of little but the child, nodded in distracted approval at the new brick oven, which Lamb had had fired while she was ill, and at the levelled ground stacked with seasoning bricks. All about the estate, the new house had begun to lie in pregnant heaps of its separate parts, waiting to be assembled into the whole. She was content, now, to leave that assembling to others.

She wanted only to direct Lamb in his new recording of her footprints. Hour after hour, she hung over his shoulder while he drew what she described. Her own childhood. John and Harry as boys at Hawkridge. Her own arrival on the estate as Harry's wife. The baby. Philip's tales, so far. As a start.

While she was still weak, Lamb obliged her without question. He sat with her and drew every moment when he was not needed at the building site. His hand became the extension of her thoughts. He re-drew Hawkridge House with the ivy growing in the right direction. For Jonas Stubbs, who would carve the mantles and for the smith, who would forge the fire-backs, he re-designed his original fireplaces, with real people in place of gods and the kitchen garden bounty instead of pineapples and pomegranates. He rubbed out basilisks in favour of pike.

'You will permit me to keep the acanthus leaves on my columns, I hope? Oak leaves would not be the same.' Though he seemed to jest, there was suppressed unhappiness in his tone.

She still felt too weak to let herself hear it. Working with Lamb, together with the pressures of spring, kept her just far enough ahead of her thoughts for life to be almost bearable.

Hens escaped their run, intent on making private nests. Cows dropped their calves. The sowing of pease and beans began in the fields. At the edges of the fields, young nettles and the tightly curled croziers of ferns waited to be picked.

In the kitchen garden, she oversaw the sowing of lettuces, gillyflowers, carrots, pumpkins, leeks, garlic and melons, the transplanting of autumn kale, and the setting of cauliflower in the hot manure beds. Orange pot marigolds bloomed a little ahead of their season, to be picked for soothing salves. Purple saffron crocuses began to drop their precious red-gold dust. Sea-green asparagus sprouts raced to shoot upwards into feathery, inedible bloom.

Then Philip found her in the garden one afternoon, holding a trug filled with violets for preserving in sugar, in helpless tears at so much unchecked life. He led her at once to the distractions of Lamb's studio, now moved from High House into one of the Hawkridge barns.

As the walls of the Memory Palace rose into sight at last, Lamb began to paint the panels that would eventually adorn them. To record Zeal's childhood, the death of her parents, her life with guardians, school and marriage to Harry, he painted plaster panels in muted tones of distemper, to resemble a faded tapestry. She meant for this series to line the upper hallway that led to her suite of chambers. Its final panel would be Lamb's picture of Hawkridge House, but in full, rich colour, unlike the others. Reds, ochres, blues and greens.

'For that's how wonderfully life seemed changed to me when I came here,' she said. 'That picture must stand at the top of the stairs.'

He made stretched leather panels for Philip's stories, to render in oil paints and gilding. These would replace the Olympian scenes on either side of the new main staircase, in spite of Philip's protests.

'Real gold for the golden god,' Lamb said. 'Gold for the treasures. Silver leaf for the lake.'

'And half of the panels left blank for what he has yet to tell me.' She eyed Lamb one evening. 'Do you know what happened to him?'

'Philip is my father's friend. I rarely saw him.'

'But you must have overheard something?'

He gripped a loose corner of a panel in a pair of tongs and pulled taut a faint dip in the leather. Then he reached for a hammer. 'As a boy I cared only for my paints, my dog and my horse. I thought all adults extremely dull.'

She huffed in frustration. 'Did you ever see his first wife?'

Lamb shook his head, his lips now clamped tightly on five nails. When he had banged them all into the side of the frame, he ran his hand across the leather. 'I know only that she was often indisposed. Suffered woefully from the mothers and feared to leave their house in Guildford. She never came to London.'

He once had a house in Guildford, Zeal thought. A crumb, but something at least.

Wentworth looked amused when she warned him of the blank panels. 'So few?' he asked.

Lamb also began a series of portraits of the estate residents, painted in watercolour on vellum stuck down onto card, the size of a man's palm, to be set into roundels above doors and windows. He worked on all these scenes at once, painting by daylight, preparing his grounds by candlelight.

He had not yet decided how to paint the child.

'I think I may go mad!' Lamb laid down his brush with a contained passion. While Zeal watched, he had been applying a green oily stain to what would become jungle on one of the leather panels. 'I have never lived for so long in the country. I sometimes feel . . .' He picked up his brush again and stirred it viciously in a mug of turpentine. 'And those workmen and their questions! Half the time, if they only stopped to think . . . As a master mason, your Jonas Stubbs lacks a grip on the broader view. And I've too much to do now, with all this painting, to be overseeing the likes of him and Todd!'

She was startled by his uncharacteristic vehemence. I should have seen it coming, she thought. But I was too caught up in my own concerns. 'What must I do?'

'Let me hire other workmen. I know an excellent Italian painter who could finish Philip's panels better than I ever will. And do the gilding, for which I lack the expertise. And we will need a proper sculptor. I'm sure Stubbs is a perfectly good hewer of gate posts and saddle stones, but an acanthus leaf seems to be beyond him.'

She felt as if his other self, stored away for so long in London, had suddenly arrived to take the place of the familiar Hawkridge Lamb. Who was doing too much, driving himself too hard trying to humour her.

'I wish I could afford the help you need, but in spite of our hours spent over estate accounts, Doctor Bowler and I have not persuaded cash to breed as readily as sheep.'

'There must be ways to find more money or else you may never have your Memory Palace.'

'Master Wilde is eager to buy the entire vale where the brick furnace lies,' she said unhappily. 'I could reconsider his offer. I've already borrowed from Sir Richard to pay the next three months' wages.'

Lamb finished cleaning his brush and paced the paint-spattered barn floor. 'You must trust to Providence, sister mine. It has always helped us squeak through before. Can't think it will stop now.' He sounded calmer. 'I hardly dare add that I also think we should build our own glass furnace here. And bring a Huguenot glazier from London to run it for us.'

'That is impossible! Providence notwithstanding.'

'I saw it done when I visited that Warwickshire estate in February,' he insisted. 'There's no other way you can have all that glass! Even if you could afford it, it would never survive the journey here by cart from Norfolk.'

'I can't afford either a furnace or your Frenchman!'

He glared at her in a fury of frustration. 'This whole project is mad. I wish I could tell you just how mad it is!'

'What else?' she asked. 'Beyond killing yourself with work. And Stubbs and slow-witted craftsmen?'

He shook his head and held up a pacifying hand. 'Forgive me. I need to escape. Just a few days. London, perhaps. I might persuade that Huguenot glazier at least to visit, and perhaps advise us without a fee.'

'He owes you a favour?' Zeal asked with a slight edge.

'Merely hopes I will put him in the way of patronage.'

She gazed about her at time recaptured and given solid form in oil, tempera and watercolour. All that diversion from his own original intentions and the great care it showed for her. 'Dearest Lamb, you must go when you like. So long as you promise to return.'

'To you, always!' But she saw that he was already flying away from Hawkridge.

Wentworth frowned when she told him.

Then Sir Richard, too, left suddenly for his house in London. After eleven years of ruling without Parliament, the king had recalled it at last. Before leaving, Sir Richard charged Wentworth in his absence to teach all able-bodied men on both estates how to use firearms and gave him the key to the High House armoury. Someone in London had finally noticed the scandalous disarray of most local militia.

'Do we know at whom they are intended to shoot?' Wentworth asked.

Even more disturbing was the arrival in the parish of a muster master charged with raising numbers in the county Trained Band. He recruited a half dozen young men from Hawkridge, and took them away for military training.

'If they aren't back soon, I shall have to hire labour from Basingstoke or Winchester,' Zeal told Philip. 'Stubbs wants to stack up the walls as fast as possible while we still have fine weather.'

'I can try raising labour from the Winchester poorhouse.' In Lamb's absence, Wentworth had involved himself again in the new house. 'On the bright side, we'll have fewer fools hanging about the work site, gawping and getting in the way.'

Lamb sent word that he was kept in London longer than

he had planned. While he was still away, in the first week of May, on her return from the mill, where she had been called to settle a dispute about the free milling of pig oats, Zeal found another anonymous letter shoved under the lodge door. She took one look at the characters carved onto the paper as if with a knife and thrust it under the squab pillow on her chair. She left it hidden there throughout the afternoon and evening, until she heard Philip moving about in his chamber on the far side of the lodge parlour.

Burn the thing without reading it, she told herself. Deny your curiosity for once. She examined the wax seal closely. It bore no identifying imprint. She broke the seal.

Whore, the fruit of your sin is rotten and shall perish like all other wickedness.

Wentworth came running at her cry.

'Not a subtle mind,' he said, turning the letter in his hand. His tone was light but the skin of his face had drawn tight against his skull.

'It must be Gifford!' insisted Zeal. 'Disguising his hand.'

'Perhaps. Though, as with that other letter, I would have expected a little more from his comprehensive knowledge of Scripture. A somewhat fuller orotundity of abuse.' He scratched his chin. 'Would you consider moving back to High House?'

'From fear?'

He raised a hand against the force of her scorn. 'I fear only for the life of the writer of that letter, if you should ever find him . . . or her.'

'You think the writer may be mad, and dangerous.'

'It's possible,' he admitted.

'I'm too busy to leave Hawkridge.'

That night, he came to her chamber in his night shirt and sleeveless gown. 'With your permission, I mean to sleep here every night.' He hung his sword belt beside the bed before taking off his gown.

'I don't need a guard,' she said.

'Need or not, you shall have one until I can teach you to defend yourself, as you once asked me to do.' He turned his back firmly and drew up the quilt.

When she woke in the night, as she always did now, she counted his soft snores until she slept again. In spite of her defiance, she found his bulk beside her profoundly comforting.

37

'We cannot permit such things!' said Lamb. He had returned the previous night, four days after the letter, restored to his old gleeful self and bringing with him a Monsieur Dauzat, who would advise on the manufacture of glass, free of charge against the right to sell a share of the eventual product. Now, just after breakfast, Lamb staggered under a large model of the main staircase. 'After dinner, I will go cut off Gifford's writing hand. Then perhaps move on to other parts of his anatomy.'

Zeal tried to smile, as she knew he intended. 'Philip doubts that it's Doctor Gifford.' She picked up her knitting. She had begun afresh on the scarlet stocking.

'Who could be more likely?'

Zeal shrugged. 'It's only words.' But she knew Lamb was not fooled.

He pushed the toy staircase across the floor to her chair and squeezed his buttocks onto the narrow bottom step, a giant fitting himself to a miniature human world. With his knees bumping his chin, he put on a miserable, yearning face. He was so close that she could smell his orange blossom, musk and fresh air.

'You do look ridiculous.'

'We both love you to distraction, you know. Philip and I.'

She smiled in polite dismissal. 'Philip rescued me. That's not the same as love. He's merely proud of my continued existence.'

'He feels more than that. I watch him when he looks at you.'

'We tend to like those who are indebted to us more than we like those to whom we are indebted.'

'Poor old Philip.'

'Don't mistake me. I'm most grateful.'

'But gratitude doesn't go very far in bed, does it?'

Zeal flushed and tried to think how to answer. She saw that she had knitted two stitches together by accident and threw down her needles in irritation.

'It should be me who lusts after you.' Lamb prised his buttocks out the step and stood. He spread his arms and turned in a circle, displaying his broad chest and narrow hips. 'Young, beautiful as Narcissus . . . but not half so vain.' He tossed her a wicked glance over his shoulder, a fallen strand of golden hair concealing his left eye. 'I expect I could, you know . . . in a pinch.'

'Lamb!' Dear Lord, I hope Philip has gone fishing! she thought. Lamb's renewed high spirits had a dangerously uncontrolled edge.

He raised a quelling hand. 'We bachelors have a duty to flirt with married women. I will not be derelict. First, Mistress Wentworth, I shall carry you off to the site of our glass furnace-to-be, where Dauzat's new English assistants are pretending not to understand his sign language but threaten to skewer him every time he tries to give an order in French.'

Before she could protest, he took her hands to pull her from her chair. 'When you have marvelled at my mastery of foreign tongues, you must then order Rachel to pack for London. I am charged by your husband with raising your spirits. I shall take you riding in Saint James's Fields, dicing in Southwark, to admire the lions at the Tower and to the theatre.'

'I can't afford to travel to London, nor to stay in lodgings. Every penny is needed for the house.' And to pay levies and rates.

'An acquaintance of Philip has room for us. Your husband and I are both agreed and adamant.'

To Zeal's amazement, when she saw him that evening, Philip confirmed the excellence of Lamb's plan. He even seemed eager to send his wife off to London with another man.

38

'I swear you're hard to please!' Continuing high spirits softened Lamb's irritation. 'Lord, how I love this place! Even its noise and smells.'

Zeal hated London. She found the lions at the Tower, which they had just left, to be as bleakly dispirited as any other prisoners. There were too many other horses in St James's Field to allow a proper gallop. The Southwark gaming inns, where Lamb stood erect and alert like a hound testing the wind, held too many hungry eyes and foul breaths. She refused to be entertained by watching any living creature die, be it cock or bear.

Zeal did not hate London for its noise and smells, as Lamb had suggested. Hawkridge at slaughter time could almost match the Fleet. And a jakes was a jakes, no matter where you set it. If you could cross a barn yard, you could cross a London street.

She disliked the city for its uneasiness, for the pockets of anger and sudden bursts of brawling which became battles, from which constables averted their eyes.

She did not understand the complex fault lines dividing Londoners from each other. The king's struggle with Parliament was the most easily perceived crack in the earth, but it was far from being the only one. A sense of suppressed violence puzzled and alarmed her. She saw fear in the eyes of women in the markets. Stepping out of the street to avoid a pack of shouting students and apprentices or a purposeful troop of militia, she felt that she stood upstream, studying a current that carried dark, hidden dangerous shapes towards her own clear, comprehensible waters.

Too many faces reminded her of Doctor Gifford.

'I don't know what's wrong with me.' This was only partly true.

'Let us see what you make of a play,' said Lamb with determined cheer.

They crossed London Bridge into Southwark, where he took her to see the King's Men play in an unroofed, public theatre not far from the bear-baiting pit.

'I should never have chosen a tragedy,' he said after they had left halfway through. 'I'm such a fool! Forgive me?'

'It was splendid, truly!' She wiped her eyes. 'Too splendid. Too truthful.'

'I didn't know there was a child . . .' He put a consoling hand on her shoulder. 'Shall we stroll by the river instead, then have a splendid supper?'

She took his velvet-sleeved arm. The Thames, at least was deeply satisfying, most of all at night, when the lanterns of the wherries criss-crossing the black expanse flicked gleams of light across each other's wakes.

'You'll be safe from all dangerous truth tomorrow evening,' he promised. He drew a deep breath. 'Ah, yes, tomorrow!'

It was too dark to read his expression. 'What then?' she asked, curiosity roused by the fervour of his tone. She also felt a tremor of unease.

'We are to see *Bellerophon Nikephoros* in a private theatre . . . in that great house over there, in fact. The middle one. A friend of my father.' He pointed across the Thames at a pale, ghostly shape. 'It will be improbable nonsense, I predict. No risk of true emotion, anywhere. Not in the performance, at least.'

Sir George Tupper, Lamb's father's friend, was a self-made man who intended to enjoy every privilege that great wealth and a purchased title could bring. These included being able to pay musicians, dancers, actors, singers, designers, poets, and artificers of the most ingenious sorts to astonish and delight himself and his many guests.

When they first arrived at the house, Zeal thought herself more interested in the lay-out of the terraces along the river, the number of the entrance steps and the grotesque masks set above the windows than in the play to come.

'Not a play at all,' explained Lamb with a touch of disdain. 'But a form of masque.' Nevertheless, he looked eagerly about the audience gathered in the great hall.

Zeal thought that he became suddenly downcast, but the performance began before she could ask why.

During the opening dance by various ladies of Sir George's acquaintance, all magnificently costumed as nymphs, she settled back on her chair in the fog of civet, rose-water, wormwood, sheep's grease and sweat that rose from the fashionably-dressed bodies around her. Lamb had been right. There seemed little risk of true emotion tonight.

The pastoral screen behind the nymphs parted to show the gardens of the Palace of Corinth. The king's wife entered with her women and trilled about her love for the hero, Bellerophon. Bitterly, she told how he had rejected her advances, and how she meant to be revenged.

Zeal was just reflecting uneasily on the subject of repulsed love, when the scene suddenly split again. She sat up and cried 'Ahhh!' with the other spectators when the gardens vanished as if by magic. In their place stood the interior of the palace, the king already sitting elevated on a huge and ornate golden throne amid columns and receding corridors, all illuminated by the jewelled lights of candles shining through bottles of brightly coloured waters.

Could I do the same with coloured waters at home? Zeal wondered, while the queen, with a most innocent look, told her husband that Bellerophon had made advances to her. When the king wrongly punished the hero by sending him to try to kill the Chimera, Zeal forgot coloured water and sat forward to see how they would represent that terrible monster, half-lion, half-goat, with a serpent for its tail.

But first, the throne room with its columns and corridors and jewelled lights suddenly seemed to sink out of sight. A cloud passed over the scene and lifted to reveal a thick wood filled with singing sprites, and a soothsayer's cave where the hero came to seek advice. With a great crash of music, the Goddess Athena appeared in a cloud of smoke and gave the hero a golden bridle. With another crash, she vanished just as suddenly.

Zeal clasped her hands against her mouth.

The woods at once transformed to a terrible rocky desert, with a dark jagged mountain touching the heavens at the back of the scene. Before Zeal could catch her breath, the hero entered carrying the bridle, and a huge white winged horse flew down out of the sky. The hero caught the horse, mounted it. Together they flew up again and vanished.

She felt weak with excitement and was grateful for the group of rustics who now began to sing of their terror at the monster that lived in the dark mountain and ravaged their land.

'A chance to catch our breath,' she whispered to Lamb.

He did not hear her. He was exchanging looks with a striking dark-haired youth who stood at one side of the audience, a late arrival, wearing silver cut-velvet and a single pearl earring. The youth left. Before the end of the first chorus, Lamb excused himself.

A chill invaded Zeal's wonder. I must get Lamb safely back to Hawkridge, she thought, without precise reason but a sense of understanding nevertheless. Then the performance distracted her again, with what she had been waiting for.

A band of demons dressed in fur and leaves attacked the rustics. Amid thunderclaps and lightning flashes, the mountain cracked open. A fiery cavern gaped. With a clunk and grinding of machinery soon drowned by more thunderclaps, a huge mechanical monster burst forth amid more clouds of smoke, casting out streams of fire from each of its three heads.

The Chimera, at last. It snapped its jaws and turned its heads.

A woman screamed, though whether in terror or delight was impossible to tell.

The Chimera's eyes glowed like hot coals. It took a grinding step, then another. The lion head roared and belched out fire. The goat jabbed with its horns. Weaving from side to side, the serpent spat sparks like a stream of venom at the audience. More women screamed. It was impossible that a mere machine should seem so alive.

As the beast advanced, the demons roared about the stage, waving fire clubs and scattering more sparks.

Zeal sat straight upright, her mouth a little open.

From the heavens, hero and winged horse arrived. They glided down on a long diagonal and landed with hardly a jolt.

Their fight with the monster filled the theatre with so much smoke that Zeal's eyes watered but she yearned forward, as if in prayer, breathing only in small incidental gasps.

All lies, of course, but with such an appearance of truth. And Lamb was wrong about the absence of emotion. She began to feel, without yet being able to put her thoughts into words, that he had brought her here for a larger purpose than mere distraction from grief. The intense wonder that filled her was surely as real as any other truth. It was a vital part of the truth.

Her elation did not ebb even when a spark from one of the fire clubs set alight the breeches of a spectator seated on the side of the stage.

When the play was over, Lamb still had not returned.

'Has he deserted you, then, for a darker pair of eyes? He won't have gone far.' With his long nose and crinkled hair, her host, Sir George Tupper, looked disconcertingly like one of her Wiltshire Horns. 'Did our performance please you?'

'I must have a theatre!'

'You liked it so much?' His broad smile made the end of his nose dip. 'Then come see how our magic is performed.'

At first, she thought that he had skilfully fobbed off an awkward guest. But after two questions, she saw that the man to whom Sir George had consigned her was the very one who had devised and built the wonders she ached to comprehend. For his part, Master Cobb, like any man with a passion, kept discovering more and more to show and tell to a new admirer of his skills.

'The thunder's simple, mistress,' Cobb said in answer to her eager questions. 'Just cannon balls rolling up and down this wooden trough. See, you can tilt it yourself, easy. But the lightning, now. That needs this metal case here, see, for setting the charge. The fire clubs? You pack the powder down into the end here . . . Take care! Hold it well away!'

'There you are!' Lamb exclaimed brightly, with the faintest hint of reproach, as Zeal rose up through the floor on the Goddess's trap. 'Are you ready to sup at my favourite Southwark inn?'

Zeal nodded. Her head was full of sliding shutters, powder charges, windlasses, pulleys and levers. Not to forget that cunning use of a mirror.

'If you would be content to travel back with Rachel and the groom, I think I shall stay on in London for a few days,' Lamb told her in the Red Hen, whose patrons would have kept Gifford on his knees for the rest of his days. 'Some urgent business has come up . . . my father . . .' He cut his roast mutton with great care. 'And, alas, one of us must go back to look after the building.'

'He's handsome,' Zeal said, coming back to the present with a bump. She felt sudden loneliness and a sense of exclusion. 'Like a fallen angel. And I don't mean your father. I don't mind what you do, Lamb, but don't lie to me.'

He put down his knife. 'Well then, I'm in love, dearest sister. As I never thought to be. In the purest love.' He looked

at her helplessly, more like the man-child she had thought
him when they first met than the competent young man who
designed houses, oversaw builders and conjured airy thought
into tangible form.

'Is he in the purest love, too?' I've known all along, she
thought. Or almost known. And of course, Philip knew.

'He . . . Ben, that is . . . is a coquette.'

She recognized that sweet, tell-tale relishing of a name on
the tongue.

'. . . "he's afraid" . . . the usual folderol. And he's only
seventeen, still unworldly. But surely, I could not feel such
warmth between us if he didn't share . . . Oh, yes, I believe
he loves me too. Or will come to it, given the chance. After
all, he agreed to meet me again tonight. Oh, sister mine, I
am transformed!' He took her hands. 'It's such joy to tell you!'

'Who is he?'

'Master Benjamin Neame. His father owns ships. My
sweetest Ben. We met the last time I came to London.'

She extracted her hands. 'But were you acquainted before?'

'Yes. But only to speak.'

And then Lamb's father bundled him off to Philip in
Hampshire.

It was Zeal's turn to cut her meat with unusual care. 'Be
careful.'

But Lamb had that odd, slightly ruffled radiance of someone
already far beyond reach of warnings.

Zeal set off with Rachel the following morning, still fired
by what she had seen in Sir George's theatre, but also
concerned for Lamb.

Lamb did not return to Hawkridge for another three weeks.
At his first supper back, he sat on his stool with the thump
of a man in a vile temper.

'What happened to your face?' Zeal asked in alarm. 'How
did you come by those terrible bruises?'

'No one should travel alone these days,' said Mistress

Margaret. 'Between footpads and soldiers and vagrant rogues who would kill you for your handkerchief . . .'

Lamb shrugged. 'I didn't have to leave London to find trouble.' He tore a piece of bread in two as if breaking a neck.

Zeal found him later on the wooden scaffolding that bristled around the new east wing. She remembered Philip standing at the bottom of the ladder, pretending not to care.

The warm April had led to a cool summer. A heavy dew had fallen. Even up here, the air held a chilly damp. She tucked up her skirts and climbed to stand beside him in the thickening dusk. 'I'm happy that you're back,' she said.

'Are you?'

'Stop that, Lamb. I'm your sister, remember?'

He nodded wordlessly and leaned forward to look down into the valley.

'Will you come down and drink a posset?'

'I won't jump.'

The masons had passed the second floor. The ground fell away beneath the walls. This scaffolding was high enough. She tried to think what to say next.

'I wasn't lying about staying to speak with my father.'

'How did you get those bruises?' she asked again.

'After you left father and I quarrelled ferociously. You can guess the topic. Then, in my distress, I decided to go for a walk, to purge my feelings. Walked all the way to St Katharine's Dock.' He spoke too quickly. 'Where I was set upon by footpads, just as Mistress Margaret said. My own fault, for paying no attention to where my feet led me.'

She nodded as if she believed his story.

'They're nothing to do with Ben!' he said angrily, answering her silence. 'And he would have met me if he could. I have his letter swearing as much.'

'Shall I bathe your bruises with mallow?' she asked after a moment.

He shook his head and seemed to pull farther inside himself. He tucked his hands into his armpits, but not before she saw the dark circles of raw skin on his wrists. He turned his head away, looking across the shadowy water meadows. She felt a small cold lead weight settle in her stomach. She had seen marks like that on his skin once before, when he first arrived at Hawkridge.

'My darling Lamb,' she said. 'Will you come down and talk somewhere warmer? Whilst we were in London, I thought how you can outshine Master Inigo Jones at all of his own games.'

'You're not usually so transparent.'

'I'm not trying to hide my concern for you. But that doesn't mean I'm not also telling the truth. I need you to design a theatre. I decided in London. Any perfect house must have a theatre.'

He sighed in the near-darkness. 'We have already moved some distance from my first perfect house . . . Take care climbing down. Let me go first.'

When they were safely on the ground, he said, 'You can't afford Purbeck stone for the portico columns or wages for Dauzat. How can you pay for a theatre?'

'Where is your faith in Providence?' Just in time, she avoided a dark puddle of discarded mortar. 'The west wing is still no more than cellars. If we put our theatre there, we will have months to plan and try to find the money. All labour will be bent on finishing the east wing for living in by Christmas next.'

'You're mad,' he said, but a speculative tone had reanimated his voice.

'Then so is Sir George Tupper.' After a few more steps, she added, 'He's one of the wisest men I know, to have both a kitchen and a theatre . . . is that a silence of disapproval?'

'Merely struck dumb.'

'Until that night at Sir George's house, I had forgotten the wonder I felt when I first came here. But that wonder was as real as the gloom that seems stuck to my feet now. I must revive it.'

'Sir George is a wealthy man. Putting on plays is a rich man's pleasure.'

'But we have Doctor Bowler. And Master Lambert Parsley. What other riches do we need to create wonder and delight?'

39

She was soon to lose Doctor Bowler, however. Her first warning came in the shape of the parson's anxious face at the door of the lodge one evening after supper.

'I'm sorry to trouble you, but . . .' He looked around as if he expected to be set upon at any moment.

'It's Jamie,' he explained, once safely inside. 'Came to find me just now. He has run away from home!'

'Where is he?'

'Hiding from his father.'

Bowler directed her to a derelict grain store on the High House estate, then followed by a different route.

'Jamie?' he whispered. 'I've brought Mistress Wentworth to help you.'

The barred door opened just enough for them to enter.

Jamie was a blurred shape in the darkness. Only his pale hair showed where he stood.

'Tell her,' said Bowler.

'I don't want to be a farmer,' said the boy. 'I'll kill myself first.'

'What do you want to do?' Zeal asked.

'Sing. I want to be an opera singer.'

'I fear it's my fault,' began Bowler.

'I want to go to London or Venice and study.'

'I should never have told . . . But a voice like his can't be . . .' Bowler's words trailed off. Then they suddenly surged back out of the dark. 'It's a crime against both God and Nature to waste such an instrument!' He subsided just as suddenly, as if startled by his own passion.

'My father forces me to go to Bedgebury church!' said Jamie, as if offering an incontrovertible argument. 'He agrees with Doctor Gifford about music.'

Zeal took a deep breath. 'I will see what I can do. Meanwhile, go back home and behave like an angel.'

'Is the boy truly so gifted?' she asked Bowler, back at the lodge.

'You have heard him.' Bowler looked away. 'His father is trying to beat all musical nonsense out of him. To please Gifford.' His voice trembled. 'The boy is going to run, with or without our help. Master Grindley has threatened to cut off half Jamie's tongue to prevent him from singing.'

Zeal heard suppressed violence in the parson's voice. 'I will try to think what we can do,' she said. 'It's no small thing to remove a child. I wish only that I had more money!'

After Bowler left, she went to Lamb's barn studio, where he was squinting in the candlelight, painting a woodland scene in *grisaille* on a pair of miniature theatre shutters cut from stiffened card. Since his return from London, he had taken to working late into the night.

'Of course, Jamie must go to Venice!' Lamb said at once. 'There's no finer place on earth for music! If I weren't so busy here, I would take him myself.'

'Bowler must take him,' said Philip. 'I wouldn't mind putting him out of Gifford's reach for a time.'

She had found her husband upstream near the higher weir with his rod beside him, not fishing but smoking a Dutch pipe and studying the start of the new cut that would carry water to the Memory Palace. She sat beside him on the bank.

'Many boys run away for worse reasons,' said Philip.

'And without such a sweet-tempered chaperon.'

'Legal guardian would be better.' Philip peered into the pale clay bowl of his pipe. 'But I don't see Jake Grindley giving his consent.'

'Bowler will be as eager to see Venice as Jamie,' said Zeal, shying away from the thought of Jamie's father.

'I shall send a letter with Bowler to a sea captain friend.' Philip put away his pipe. 'I'm sure he can manage free passage for our two runaways.' He levered himself to his feet and stamped to loosen his legs. 'Shouldn't sit on damp ground! As for living, young Lamb has a comfortable income, which he isn't spending down here. Let's ask him if he would make Bowler a loan.'

Lamb would. He also gave Doctor Bowler the name of an acquaintance in Venice who might offer cheap lodgings.

Once they had all agreed, Zeal began to wonder if the plan were madness. She did not want to lose Doctor Bowler. But if Jamie ran away alone, as he had vowed to do, his father would surely blame Bowler all the same and bring the wrath of Bedgebury down on the parson once again. Zeal knew that the next time, Bowler would not get off with merely a broken hand.

'We might meet Signor Monteverdi!' cried Bowler, suffused with a delight Zeal had not seen since before his hand was broken. 'Did you hear that, Jamie? Signor Monteverdi, himself!'

'Draw them both before they leave,' she begged Lamb. 'Capture them now!'

Two days later, Jamie finished digging early potatoes, washed, ate supper with his family, said he was going to set rabbit snares, and slipped away to Hawkridge. Lamb and Arthur rode with Bowler and the boy to Ufton Wharf, where they left them on a barge bound for London at dawn.

'Where's Bowler?' Jake Grindley arrived at the lodge after morning milking, having by then searched every place where he thought his son might be hiding. 'What has he done with my son?'

'I don't know where either of them is,' Zeal said truthfully.

But by dinnertime, she knew she had to tell at least some of what she did know, to console Jamie's distraught mother who wanted the millpond dragged. In the early afternoon, Zeal took the track past the Far to the farm Jake Grindley occupied as her tenant.

Mistress Grindley stared at her with wet eyes, trying to understand what she was being told. 'To Italy? Among foreign Catholics?' She moaned and pressed her apron to her eyes. 'But he was well? Unhurt? You swear he went of his own will?'

'He meant to run away alone,' said Zeal. 'I merely did what I could to keep him safe and well looked after.'

To her dismay, Mistress Grindley seized her hand and kissed it. 'Thank you, mistress!' Then she began to cry again. 'It's his father! I never saw the harm in a song, myself, neither.' As Zeal was leaving, Mistress Grindley said, 'If you don't mind, mistress, I think I won't tell Master Grindley what you just told me. You never know with Jake.'

'Grindley's telling all the workmen that Bowler has abducted his son,' reported Lamb at supper that night. 'And sold him to the Catholics to be gelded, to make him sing like a woman even when he's a grown man.'

'We must tell them the truth, then. That the boy feared his father and ran away of his own free will. Truth will kill the rumours.'

And I will try to think how to deal with Jake Grindley.

40

Letter from Doctor Praise-God Gifford to Mistress Zeal Wentworth. June, 1640.

Dear Madam, I write from deep concern to ask your denial of certain reports reaching me. The first is that you, as well as the man who calls himself your parson, are responsible for the disappearance of the son of one of my parishioners. I pray that there is some more innocent explanation for Doctor Bowler's absence and for Master Grindley's charge.

The second report is that you have put your youth and virtue in terrible jeopardy by viewing ungodly spectacles in pernicious company. I beg you to tell me that you have not been tempted to enter a theatre. If this latter report is true, you have exposed yourself to corruption by incontinence and lewdness, indeed, by the very pomps of the Devil. I hold you guilty by your nature of no more than arrogance and wicked pride. There is no sophistication that is not allowed by His Will to test us. But none is too great for His Mercy to forgive. I am willing to set aside all differences between us if only I can keep one of my sheep safe from the Eternal flames. You have accused me of wickedness, but like a shepherd, I must sometimes apply physic against the Great Worm.

I remain yours faithfully, P.G. Gifford.

41

Zeal replied at once. That man is the enemy of all joy, she thought. Just wait till he learns what I mean to do! Doctor Bowler shall have his own battlefield when he returns from Venice. And armies of gods and heroes and Amazon queens. And machines.

Sir: (she wrote) *Firstly, to my knowledge, Jamie Grindley ran away of his own will. On the second matter, thank you for your counsel. I did attend a theatre and now mean to build one. Yours faithfully . . .*

Then she threw Gifford's letter into the fire and smashed the ashes with the poker. Only when the letter had turned to floating dust did she suddenly wish she had kept it to read more calmly a second time.

I should have kept it to show to Philip, she thought. To ask whether this letter more closely approached the 'orotund profundity' he expects from the minister or the poisonous flailing of the two anonymous letters.

But if Gifford had not written the other two, who had?

On impulse, she sat down and picked up her pen again.

John, I miss you beyond describing. She wrote quickly, without letting herself think what she said.

When you left, my life began to grow crooked. I fear so many things now. I fear that you are lost to me, either dead, or in love with a new life. Or even a new woman. Sometimes I cannot bear to think of you because it gives me such pain. So I set you at a little distance, within sight but too far away to touch me. What will happen when you return? Will you still be too far away to touch me? Will you still want to? I am no longer the girl you kissed goodbye. The air is twisting around my head.

She stopped and crossed out that last line. *'Please . . .'*

She dropped her head onto her hands. How could she say, 'Please come back,' when his life would be forfeit? And how could she say, 'Please send for me, no matter what your circumstances are,' when she was married to someone else? After a time she burnt this letter as well.

She wanted him to tell her that there was nothing to fear. And how could he possibly do that?

Philip gave her a sharp look when he came to the lodge a little later that night.

She saw his glance and pushed aside her attempt to draw the system of ropes and pulleys that had moved the scenic shutters along their grooves in Sir George's theatre. 'I'm ready to learn to fight, as you promised.'

'What has happened?'

She shrugged. 'Nothing more than before.'

'Are you strong enough yet?'

'If I can survive travelling to London with Lamb, I think I can manage to lift a sword.'

He nodded. 'As it happens, the parish council have asked me to help tutor our local Trained Band in swords as well as guns, for fear they might have to go to war.' He was studying her with a cool assessing eye. 'I could use some practice myself. Are you ready now?' He put his coat over a chair and stood in his shirt and trousers.

He began to push all the furniture in the lodge parlour against the walls. 'I hope I can still remember a few tricks.'

'No tricks,' she said. 'Teach me to fight properly, like a man!'

His open amusement enraged her.

'Do you think I can't learn more than women's tricks?' she demanded.

'I'm certain you could learn anything you set your mind to. I wasn't thinking of women's tricks but the reality of brawling. Or an ambush. Both of which you are more likely to meet than you are to go to war. We will begin with a cloak and short dagger.'

'I would like to learn to handle a sword, nevertheless.'

The set of his square jaw and the detached working of his thoughts reminded her of the man who had overseen the removal of the statues. He looked like her Philip, but he was also someone else.

'If you insist,' he said at last. 'In that case, however, I insist on a rapier as a better choice of blade.'

'Because I'm too puny to handle a sword?'

'Because the finest swordsman in England once said that the short sword against the rapier is little better than a tobacco pipe.'

It seemed that he already had just the blade, three and a half feet long, with a sharp unguarded point.

'For thrusting with the point only,' he told her. 'Lighter and more mobile than a blade which can also cut.' His blade wore a padded button on its tip.

But before he would let her even touch her rapier, he put her through a series of exercises with her legs and arms, lunging, springing back, stretching, reaching, leaning.

Within a few moments, she was breathing hard.

'My skirt keeps getting in my way!' She stopped to untangle herself. 'Should I put it off?'

'Any true fight will most likely catch you unawares. Learn first to fight in spite of your clothes. Later, I will show you how to rid yourself of encumbrances whilst still engaged in battle. Now, take up your blade.'

He made her hold it straight out, then practise thrusting. 'Now, beat aside my blade as if you wished to strike past it at my heart.'

She moved her blade. His dipped beneath it and knocked hers aside instead. He then showed her this quick circular movement of the tip of the blade and made her practise it.

He showed her how to assume the *contra postura*, a position echoing his. He showed her again how to thrust. To parry. Above all, to watch.

By now, she was panting for breath.

'Watch me like a lover,' he said. 'Feel where I am in space. Where is my right hand? My left hand? Have I shifted my weight? Why? Am I about to attack? Yes? No? Do something!'

She lunged.

'Attack!' he ordered her. 'Don't tickle. A new-hatched duckling would terrify me more.'

'But I might hurt you,' she said.

He shouted with laughter. 'I fear that's the point.' He flicked his blade at her sleeve. 'But you won't.'

She lunged again, ferociously. Found herself suddenly thrown against the wall with his point at her throat.

'And that is the reality you face, unless you can practise rapier play daily, and with a tutor far more expert than I.'

'Does it please you to humiliate me?'

'No, puss. But to keep you alive, it's worth bruising your pride. Now will you let me also show you how to use a short dagger?'

They practised throughout the rest of the summer, in the evenings after the builders had left the house site for their homes, if local men, or the encampment if they had been hired from out of the parish.

During one week, Philip waited until dusk, and then full darkness, to show her how to work in diminished light.

One evening, Lamb drew them. 'For another panel somewhere,' he said. 'Though I don't think I'm likely to forget the sight of the two of you going at each other with cold steel.'

Sometimes Philip made her practise with Lamb, so that she

did not grow too accustomed to his own style.

After teaching her how to handle a short dagger, Philip showed her how to wrap a blanket or shawl around her left arm, leaving a corner free to snare an attacker's blade.

'Think always how to cheat,' he told her, again and again. 'Never fight fairly. The first and only rule is to stay alive.'

'That sounds like a true adventurer's rule,' she once said. She blew a lock of hair out of her face and wiped her forehead with her sleeve.

He laughed. 'Yes. And I am an adventurer again. Just for the evening. And you must imagine that from this moment, I am your enemy.'

'There have been times when I needed no imagination,' she said.

He smiled and laid down his rapier, beckoning her to the pushed-aside table. 'Now, let me show you a diagram of a pass in the Spanish style. You will need it . . .' Without warning, he was behind her, holding his knife at her throat.

. For a second, she could not move or breathe. She had misjudged him after all. Everything that had happened had been leading her to this sensation of cold steel against her neck. He had played her like a fish for the sport. All of it – marriage, house building, half-told tales. Such drawn-out pursuit was his only true passion in life.

'Remember this moment,' he said into her ear. 'There may be other times when it is just as hard to believe in your danger. And it will be real.' He moved the knife away and tightened his arm to hold her.

She nodded wordlessly.

'Did I frighten you?'

She nodded again. She knew he had felt her begin to shake.

He laid the knife on the table and turned her around.

'I'm sorry, puss.'

She stamped hard on his foot.

'God's Balls!' he yelled.

'That's for making me doubt you,' she said, near to tears.

Philip hopped to a stool and sat heavily. He tried to pull off his boot but winced with the pain. He tried again. Bit his lip. 'I think one of the bones may be broken.' With a sharp intake of breath, he began again, very gently, to try to remove his boot.

'Let me help!' She knelt in front of him and eased the boot down. 'Forgive me. Please! I didn't mean to stamp so hard.'

He set his foot carelessly back down on the floor and took her face in his hands. 'Kiss me and we're quits.'

His lips were firm, warm and brief. He pulled away and looked into her eyes. 'Remember this moment,' he said again.

That night, though she had half-expected him to stay and try to kiss her again, he went fishing as usual and did not return until close to dawn.

She did not know whether to be relieved or impatient that he was still evading his promised gift of truth.

Gifford did not write again. However, she saw him twice on his horse on the Silchester track. Each time, he left the track and rode across the high pasture to look down on the progress of the new house.

Trying to detect the first signs of my theatre, she thought. Perhaps it's just as well I can't afford it yet.

Though she despised the man, she could not disregard him. He seemed to have laid some claim upon her soul that she could not shake off.

She imagined once that she also saw the horseman who had come to see Philip and killed her child. She shouted for help and set off at once in pursuit, but he disappeared again towards Silchester.

'Mistress?' Tuddenham was panting from his run from the stable yard.

'I thought . . .' she said. 'But I'm sure it was only Doctor Gifford again!'

42

'What is it, Philip?' Zeal asked in alarm. He had slipped in after she was asleep as had become his practice. Now his silhouette sat up in the bed. It was the dark, heavy turn of the night.

'Old pains,' he said, rubbing his shoulder. 'Sometimes my body remembers old pains. Imagination punishes now, as reality did then. Nothing more. Go back to sleep.'

Twice more in what was left of the night, he shouted in his sleep and struck at the bed clothes, causing Zeal to roll in alarm to the farthest edge of the mattress out of range of his blows. The second time, he sat bolt upright.

'God forgive us!' he said. Then he groaned and curled tightly onto his side again.

'Philip?' she whispered. 'Sir? Are you ill?'

When he did not answer, she stroked the back of his neck.

He sighed deeply but did not protest, so she continued to stroke his neck and the back of his head until his breathing settled into sleep again.

'Your sleep was disturbed last night,' she said. 'I nearly feared for my life.'

The next evening, after supper in the lodge parlour, he had laid out the makings of a fishing fly on the table. Feathers, silk thread, a small horn box of shining hooks of different sizes gleamed on his table, set near the open window to catch the last of the sun.

Though she spoke lightly, he glanced up in alarm. 'I didn't hurt you? What did I do?' When she told him, he looked troubled. 'I would not leave the comfort of your bed for all the world.'

'Nor need you. You did no more than beat at the blankets,' she protested.

'I have heard of men who have strangled their wives while asleep, dreaming that they are old enemies . . .'

'Perhaps if you unburdened yourself while awake, your sleep would be less filled with dangerous dreams.'

'Are you pursuing my tales again to fill your blank panels?'

She looked firmly back. 'If the tales are where your troubled spirits arise. You spoke, half-asleep, of remembered pain.'

'I will not make your sleep as disturbed as mine, however ingeniously you tempt me.'

That night he slept in his old nest in the tack room.

'I'm too old for all the sword play,' he said the next evening. 'You must practise more with Lamb. And our valiant Trained Band would do best, in any case, to concentrate on becoming marksmen.'

'It's not age.' She had found him hunched over his table of flies, kneading his left shoulder with his other hand. 'You're stiff from the chill of the riverbank and the lack of a proper bed! Shall I rub on an embrocation?'

While she fetched the salve, Philip untied his collar and shirt strings and pulled off his shirt. 'Joints and muscles refuse to forget anything they have suffered.' He glanced up at her under his brows. 'The stiffness of age is nothing more than an accumulation of memories.'

She began to rub the sticky paste onto his back. She had never before seen him without his shirt. His shoulders were broad and the muscles still firm under his dry skin. Though stocky, he carried no excess flesh. 'Like the memory of being carried like slaughtered pigs under those poles?' She felt him go still.

She rubbed in silence for a time. At last the knots in his flesh began to soften under her fingers. 'I don't understand,' she finally said, 'why you still punish yourself so with silence. What did you do?'

'That's better!' he said. 'Thank you.' He reached over his shoulder briefly to capture one of her hands. Then he shrugged his shirt back on. When he turned back to the table, she pulled up a stool opposite him.

'You don't give up, do you?'

She shook her head. 'Never.'

'How alike we are, after all.' He began to split the tip of a pheasant's tail feather with his knife. He shaped the feather and laid it against the shank of a hook. Intently, he studied it, with his head tilted to one side. When he spoke, there was a tremor in his deep voice.

'A priest approached our small group of prisoners. He studied us in turn, looking each man in the eye, earnestly and for a long time.'

Zeal nodded as if he had merely offered an observation on the fine evening.

'At times, he stroked or prodded us, for all the world like a man about to purchase a horse, or a slave. He was civil, almost tender in his examination, but when he looked into my face, the hair stood up on my arms.' He tried to secure the beginning of his thread, dropped it. Began again.

'I tried to meet his eye bravely but could not. At the time, I feared that such cowardice might mark me out for death – for they were fierce people and valued courage. How wrong I was!'

Philip's hands began to shake so hard that he could not finish tying his fly. He set down the hook. 'And yet . . .' He gazed into the past with blank eyes.

At last! thought Zeal.

She was a hunter. She could see her prey clearly. Not John, not the odd double man who had begun to plague her, who was both John and Philip. Just Philip. With a sword at his side, not a fishing rod. Leading a body of armed men, not sitting alone at the water's edge. The man her husband had once been.

'Death might have been better than to have lived and be forced to remember.' He sank into thought.

Zeal picked up the bobbin of green silk and wound it slowly. She held herself still, became as invisible as a partridge in the bracken, lest she startle him out of the past.

'The youngest had to suffer,' he said suddenly. 'The priest pointed at last to the youngest of our party – James Dunne, son of our dead captain and nephew of Sir John Whitfield, one of the company of investors who had financed this expedition. Only nineteen years of age, with eyes as blue as yours, and golden hair bleached almost silver by the sun, like young Jamie, in fact. When the finger pointed at him, he stared boldly back but blanched white, knowing he had drawn the fatal lot . . . "God will send you to roast in Hell!" Those were his words as he was dragged away.'

Philip stared down at the table in silence. Zeal's fingers moved steadily round and round the bobbin of silk though the thread had ended long before.

Philip placed the four flies he had already tied in a line on the tabletop. 'Our golden boy . . .' He moved each fly in turn a fraction to the left, then moved them back again distractedly. 'I would like to say that I wanted to offer myself in the boy's place. But terror and desperation had paralysed my will. I could not act as I knew I should!'

She forgot to pretend to wind the silk.

'They took him away and killed him.' He inhaled. 'Cut out his heart, that is to say, while he still lived – as the French buccaneers were said to do with their prisoners.' His words raced to get to the end. 'Then they butchered him as if he had been a calf, cooked the choicest morsels over a fire and fed them to their weakened god. To restore his strength with that of the youngest and strongest of their captives, taken from a race which had so often vanquished them. When the king again sat up and showed that he had regained his strength, they offered us some left-over morsels to eat.' He arranged the eyes of the hooks in a precise straight line. 'It goes without saying that I refused as civilly as I could.'

She swallowed. 'Did all your men refuse?'

Philip cleared his throat. 'I feared that the savages would then fall on us in rage, but it seemed that they offered only from civility. To show that they bore us no particular ill will, apart from the purpose poor James had served. But when we declined to restore our own sadly-reduced strength, they themselves ate with gusto all that they had offered us.'

She watched in silence while he pushed the flies about on the table, making and unmaking various patterns.

He flicked a glance at her face. 'I sank low enough to thank God that my hair was black and not gold. And, as I have already said far too much, I will confess one last thing that haunts me more than all else – he smelled, to our starving nostrils, very like a joint of roast pork.'

Zeal drew a sharp breath. Small wonder he never came to the feasts of roasted meats. Nor ate meat of any kind.

'Not a glorious tale, is it? And telling old Whitfield . . . !' He looked up defiantly. 'Am I very changed in your eyes?'

'My imagination now holds things I had never thought possible . . .' she began carefully.

'Nor wished to!' He slammed his hands flat on the table. 'You asked me for a poisoned gift.'

'Let me speak, sir. I thank you for trusting me so far. But you should know that I had lost the old Master Philip Wentworth, the quiet fisherman, long before tonight.'

'Have I shocked you?'

'Yes, of course.'

'Do you despise me?'

Zeal blinked in surprise. 'Because you underwent such terrible adventures? My dearest husband, I admire you all the more! To have survived such a thing! The horror was not of your making!'

Philip closed his eyes tightly. For a moment, she feared he might be about to weep.

'Sir!' She laid her hand on one of his. It was cold. 'My

darling Philip, don't you understand how your candour moves me? To know that you might have felt such fear, at least for a moment, makes you a little more . . .' She chose her words delicately. '. . . sets you a little less high above me, a little more within reach of what my heart knows. Even so, I'm sure that I might have died of terror alone.'

Philip shook his head ruefully, as if he had not heard her. 'As soon as we returned, Whitfield insisted that we mount another expedition and go back to wipe out the murderers of his nephew. And Candish, my fellow survivor, was hot to go back and dredge that lake for golden baubles.'

'But how did you escape?'

He looked at her for a moment. 'More easily than you might imagine. After the sacrifice, our captors held a feast, at which they drank a great deal of some potent alcoholic brew. Even our guards drank, then slept. We helped each other slip our bonds, crept away and reached our ship the following day.'

Zeal could see the straggling line of men, sliding through the jungle, looking always over their shoulders for pursuit and listening for that unearthly cough. 'I can't think how you ended up here!'

'I wanted no more adventures. Never. I don't know if either Whitfield or Candish achieved his aim. I renounced the treasures that drove men to adventure. Lightened myself of worldly goods. Left London, determined to stay out of the way of excitements of all sorts.'

He began again to tie the fly, which he had abandoned at the beginning of his story. His whole bearing had lightened now that he was on easier terrain.

'And became a sojourner at Hawkridge?'

He nodded.

'Because you believed that no more adventure was ever likely to befall you here?'

He smiled thinly. 'Only that of encountering a bewitching young woman, and persuading her not to fling herself from a tower.'

'Did this place seem so abysmally safe?' Zeal insisted.

'It seemed a good place to think. And to lead a life where I could do no more harm.'

'What harm?'

'Oh, my dear child . . .!' he began.

'You returned safely . . .'

'Half-dead and without my men . . .'

'But with reports of treasure?'

'Enough to spur the investors off again.'

'Well, then?'

Philip stared at her for a long time. 'Don't you now see how impossible it was for Nightingale to take you with him, even if he had not been bound in indenture? Even if you are not fragile?'

'I understand why it would seem that way to a man.'

He gave her the fly so that she, with her keener eyes, could whip down the end of the winding thread. 'Arguing my rival's cause again. My wits are failing me, for sure.'

She took the fly to the window to catch the last of the light. She held it up, pretending attention, hearing only the word 'rival'. She felt him still watching her, as if he had given her a gift and she had not yet even turned it over in her hand.

What do I say if he asks whether I love him?

Neither spoke while she bent her mind to whipping down the end of the thread.

She gave him the finished fly.

'Young eyes!' he sighed. 'Perfectly done!'

She did see him differently now. The horror of his tale had lodged like a lump in her throat. But where some men might have used such accounts to try to thrill a woman, Philip had held back, to protect her. She quite liked this other man who blurred his familiar outline and gleamed at times from his eyes, although this other man also made her a little uncomfortable. The map of his heart was too strange. The darkness she glimpsed was too profound. And his vitality, which reanimated Philip's strong old limbs, echoed John's in an unsettling

way. Philip might jest about John as his rival. This other man
meant it. And something in her responded in startled surprise
– if only to a shadow of the past.

'Beautifully done,' said Philip again.

It was an odd thought, that her husband might be her
lover's rival.

'Will you sleep here with me tonight?' she asked.

He gave her a startled look.

The surmise she saw in his eyes made her redden. 'You
should not sleep on the floor.' She looked away. He had
mistaken her meaning. She meant only to comfort him.

'The tack room again, all the same. But first I may go onto
the river.'

'May I come with you? You have always wanted to teach
me to fish.'

He shook his head. 'Not tonight, my sweet. Of late, I have
been starved of solitude.'

She could not sleep. The moon sent a disturbing light into
the corners of the room. The beeches of the avenue whispered loudly in sudden gusts of wind. From time to time a
bittern boomed. A bird rustled in the lodge eaves. A pair of
foxes screamed. Ranter gave a single interrogative bark from
the gardens. The night outside felt lively and inhabited while
the room where she lay awake was cold and still.

In the stillness she saw Jamie, his golden hair bleached
almost silver, being led away by the priest. She heard his
dying scream, a high pure, dreadful music.

She rose, put on her shoes and a heavy cloak over her
smock. Rachel snored gently at the top of the stairs. Zeal let
herself out into the night.

As she had half-expected, the tack room was empty. She
looked down at Philip's nest of blankets. An empty glass stood
on the floor beside his straw-filled pallet. Both rods leaned
against the wall. He had not taken his sack. She sniffed the
glass. Malmsey.

I may have provoked him into releasing demons better kept in chains. Thought only of what I want, not what is best for him.

She would have worried less if he had taken one of his rods.

He was not by the fishponds. She crossed the sluice bridge and searched downstream, already knowing that he would not be there without a rod. She walked as far as the millpond, just to see that the surface stretched flat and silver in the moonlight. Even with the bright moonlight, she knew she could easily miss a man who did not want to be found. Or who had fallen and lay in shadow. An apoplexy could take a man of any age.

Why didn't I insist on going with him?

She searched the orchard and gardens. Then she hurried back to the herb garden below the chapel roof, feeling foolish for the surge in her pulse. But, of course, he was not there, neither above nor below.

I don't know where else he goes when he disappears, she thought. In truth, I still know almost nothing about him, except for a few tales and a liking for fish.

He went to Basingstoke four times a year, though she did not know why. He had another self who borrowed fiddles from strangers in inns and kept old friends who were siege engineers or owed him favours or had unneeded barns.

It wasn't much.

Lamb was right. I think he loves me. Otherwise, he would never have trusted me so far.

The thought made him suddenly so precious that she began to run upstream towards a pool he seemed to favour. She had to find him, before melancholy and evil memories could pull him down.

Her hair caught on an overhanging tree. As she pulled free, she looked sideways into the river, in case he had fallen and struck his head and now lay drowning in a few inches of water.

She saw a shadow hunched under a tree on the opposite bank. 'Philip?'

Then the branches lifted in the wind and the shape became a stump again.

When she had retraced her steps back downstream from the pool, she did what she should have done as soon as she saw that he was gone.

But the horse she had given him still stood in its stall, swaying slightly in sleep. The stable grooms and house grooms snored in the loft. Back on the bank of the pike pond, she tried again to think where he might have gone.

I have almost no map of him at all, she thought. After living together on this estate for three years and as man and wife for almost a year. She felt intensely angry with herself.

I did not pay him proper attention. Just as I let John go without memorizing him properly. Distracted then by anger and grief. Distracted from Philip now by this grand project of mine, which he has embraced with such generosity of spirit. And by my preoccupation with a lost love.

A sudden thought sent her back up to the lodge.

'Philip?'

When there was no reply from his chamber, she went in. She hesitated only a moment before opening the chest where he kept his unworn clothes. The pistol was still there.

At the door of the lodge, she looked across at the new house, but the rising walls and heaped building stuffs made the site impossible to read, even in the moonlight. She crossed the new bridge above the ponds, and climbed the slope of Hawk Ridge. She searched the strange city of stacked bricks, wheelbarrows, spoil heaps not yet cleared. Like an ancient ruined city, but growing instead of crumbling. The first pieces of two pale columns for the portico lay side by side on the part of the levelled fair standing which would become the main hall when money could be found to build it. Philip was sitting on one of the columns, staring back down into the valley in the direction of the lodge.

'Thank the Lord!' she cried.

'What is it, puss?' His hair and one shoulder were silver in the moonlight.

'I feared . . .' She sat beside him, still panting from her uphill run.

He sounded amused. 'Why? I'm in no danger. As you can see.'

She began to cry with relief.

'Hey, hey. What's this?' He laid his hand on her cheek.

'I don't want you to have those dreams alone. I know that you'd never hurt me, not even in sleep.'

He went very still, with his hand resting against her cheek. Then he stood and laid his cloak on the ground between the two columns.

43

After that night, making love always reminded Zeal of the smell of fresh mortar and earth. He had pulled her down with him into the sheltered gap, out of the wind and reach of prying eyes. Later, in the lodge, she fell asleep in his arms, feeling like a tiny precious kernel wrapped in a thick protective husk.

The next morning, he wanted to make love to her again, directly out of sleep. Still half-asleep, she acquiesced. But without her terror and the moonlight, she felt distant from the act. She did not recognize this intense man who laboured above and in her. This time, John was watching them. She had no excuse she could offer him. This was not rape. On the contrary. She had gone in search of Philip when he had fled from her.

When Philip rolled off her, she laid her arm across her eyes.

'My sweetest love,' he murmured. He stroked the bare skin of her belly. Even with John watching in her imagination, she shivered with pleasure. Then she moved away and felt Philip's sudden silence.

When he rose and began to dress, she could not meet his eyes. She stole glances at his strong sturdy body, his elegant ankles, the great sack of his testicles, and wondered how she could ever have thought of him as an old man, old enough to be content with mere friendship in marriage.

He gave her a slightly chilly look as he stood tying his collar strings.

She wanted to call him back to the bed, to make up for

the hurt she knew she had just done him.

'Where would you have me sleep tonight?' he asked.

'I don't know!' She stared at him as if he might help her find the answer.

He stepped into his trousers and buckled his belt. She watched his hands, which had so recently stroked her.

If he goes, he will not come back.

He pulled on his stockings, then his boots.

Zeal watched him, paralysed.

He held up his black coat and slapped at the hem, to dislodge a strand of dry grass.

He is what I have, she thought. John is dead. He has not replied to my letters, even to say that he arrived safely on Nevis. He will never come back. The tree told me but I refused to hear. I am clinging to my love for a ghost.

She imagined the door closing behind Philip, being left alone in the silence of the lodge.

'Here,' she said. 'Please lie here! I don't want to have my dreams alone, either.'

He stopped with one arm half into its sleeve. Then he removed the coat again and stood holding it uncertainly. He had pinched his lips so tightly that she thought he was still angry. Then he leaned over and kissed her gravely, without urgency, a ceremonial kiss. He kissed her as she had kissed John's glove.

Don't think even that, she told herself. She put her arms around Philip's neck to seal their new pact. The arrangement had ended, the marriage begun.

44

Philip knew that the letter had come. He had met the messenger by chance on the high road and brought the letter to Zeal. He read her as easily as he had recognized the handwriting.

'We hear at last.' He put the letter into her shaky outstretched hand. 'It came on the *Constellation*, docked in Portsmouth.'

One whole year (as far as Philip knew) since John had last written his second and last letter from Hispaniola, still on the way to Nevis. Why, in God's Name, did this one have to come now?

John is alive!

She knew that she should offer to show the letter to Philip. He had the right to know what another man had written to her. He was her husband. His warmth and smell lingered among her sheets. The feel of his naked body was crisp in her mind. With her eyes closed, she could still see him clearly while John had grown blurred, like one of Lamb's ideal forms, with the small flaws and complexities smoothed out.

She thanked Philip and put John's letter into her apron pocket.

Perversely, Philip did not fish that day but instead found tasks around the house site. He tied flies. Wrote at his table. In desperation, Zeal escaped along the Silchester track, looking back to be sure he did not follow her. She found her outcrop of rocks among the sheep, her place and John's, near the crest of Hawk Ridge above the new house. She set her back against it.

The letter was stained and spotted with damp. She touched it with the tip of her tongue. It tasted of salt. Having fretted to be alone to read it, she now sat with it unopened in her lap. She took a deep breath, as if about to jump from the roof.

My Sweet Love, Today I became an angel. If you remember how we imagined ourselves to be birds as we sat on Hawk Ridge, then you will begin to understand. But this transformation leapt far beyond the cage of our imagining.

I began with a most ordinary act. That is to say, I swam . . .

She suddenly saw him clearly again, poised to dive, taut and lean, as intense and eager as a young boy, his toes curled on the lip of the bank, his acorn-coloured hair already sleek against his head, with water tracing a rivulet down the side of his throat. The world had narrowed in his thoughts to the arc of his flight.

. . . pretending to want merely to cool myself while we lay at anchor off Nevis, waiting for the wind to shift so we could enter the harbour. In truth, a wavering dream teased me through the bright sharp facets of the surface and drew me down . . . Poor, striving words, my limping ambassadors. If only you had been there to become an angel with me, I could lie against you now, feeling the echo of my strange new temper in your heartbeat, and know that we need not speak.

I will try. Imagine, not the chilly layered greenness of our millpond but water as clear as fine window glass and as warm as blood, so that when I lowered myself off the ship's ladder, I could not feel where my body's envelope ended and the water began. I became limitless, a part of the sea itself. I ceased to exist, or rather, the tiny spark that still knew itself to be me floated amongst the other tiny particles that cast a haze here and there in the water, like dust motes hanging in a sunbeam.

I had imagined silence under the sea, and for a few moments I heard only the thundering in my own ears. Then suddenly, I heard a racket like a market fair. The sea throbbed with sound, with taps, clatters, squeaks, grunts, and an odd snapping sound like a thousand of my aunt all clicking their tongues at once in disapproval.

The water was so clear that I imagined I flew weightless in the air, amongst the other creatures that filled this strange liquid sky. They wheeled about me in flocks and schools, approached and fled. After being lost for some time in general wonder, I began to note the separate, distinct treasures. Our old sojourner fisherman, Master Wentworth, would never have recognized such creatures as mere fish . . .

'Old!' thought Philip when he, in turn, later read the letter in secret, after breaking into her coffer again. Well, young man, I may have a surprise for you.

. . . These were living jewels (wrote John). *Silver, gold, obsidian black, emerald, ruby, amethyst. Sea stars pricked with ivory knots. Rainbow crabs, lacy sea fans, corals as tall as trees, which proved to be the source of my aunt's admonitions. Sea urchins minced on purple needle tips. Other creatures grew like flowers, thrusting out their petals to feed then clamping shut again as tight as buttons. Every surface wore some treasure. Even the dark crevices and shadowy caverns were lit by the bright glassy eyes of eels.*

I soon acquired swimming companions, small fish of an enamelled blue and orange, which shone as if lit from within. Three hovered just below me. If I turned one way, they followed. If I turned back, they turned back with me. Whenever I was forced to the surface to breathe, I found them waiting when I dived again.

They were friendly, curious and most of all, innocent. Their innocence made me want to weep. They seemed not to conceive what I was, nor what my race might do to them. They were more innocent than the lion and lamb in Eden.

But this was not Eden. You and I both know that place well by repute and would most likely recognize it at once if we should chance to visit. I had entered a new, unforeseen paradise, which did not lack death but was nevertheless without sin.

Like an angel I flew through my new paradise, half-suffocated with exaltation. I soared. I glided and swooped. I hung like a goshawk. I dived, swam to the surface for air and dived again. I was an angel because I inhabited the sublime.

I hardly know how to express the deep, deep calm which began to invade my soul as I glided among these creatures, accepted, sometimes lightly bumped. Even nibbled by some of the smallest fish. A deep calm and ecstasy. I felt a great longing to breathe in, to join them and stay forever. I was so sure of this new wonderful world that I could not believe it would harm me. I felt it offer me its embrace. I knew that to give myself was death, yet I felt no fear.

Not yet, I told it. And devoured it with my eyes. The sea stars, the crabs, the luminous weed. Even when a pair of cruising sharks sent me back to the ship, reason rather than fear propelled me.

Many hours later I am still so full that I spill over onto this page. And unless you can feel a little of the truth behind my over-parted words, you will think me mad when you read what I write next. Even now, dry and returned to my fellows, and without any reason a sensible man could name, I am filled with a deep conviction that all will be well. I do not understand the nature of the manifestation, and I know nothing of what awaits me on Nevis, but nevertheless I believe (like Saint Paul) that we will be together to love each other in freedom and peace.

I have collected shells for you and a dried sea star. Think of me. Pray for me. Wait for me. I send more love and longing than a decent pen should permit . . .

Zeal moaned softly, pressed the letter to her face, then read again.

Your words have found me, she told him. I am with you, swimming with you like one of those enamelled fish. A spark of light drifting beside your spark.

She laid her hand on her breastbone and felt a deep, slow throb under her palm. She felt his calm, his ecstasy. As she believed he would have felt her death, she now felt his conviction. He had answered that letter she never sent. The one in which she wanted to beg him to tell her everything would be all right.

And I have betrayed you, thought Zeal. After only one year. Philip is my husband and I would not hurt him for the world. What am I to do now?

45

'There you are at last!' She took his hand to draw him into the room. 'You're cold!'

'Too much sitting alone and thinking of the past.'

'You've caught a miasma from the water,' she said severely. Philip shrugged.

'Or a chill from all that sitting on the ground after sunset.'

'Perhaps.'

Zeal looked at him in alarm. This acquiescence was not like him at all. 'My dearest Philip, you should try to grow fat like Sir Richard. A good quilt of flesh like his would keep you warm wherever you sit. All fishermen should be fat.' As she rattled on, she studied him.

He was not listening but stood at the window looking out into the night.

'Sir, what's wrong?' She began to fill a warming pan with coals from the fire.

'Ranter is too old,' he said. 'Far too amiable to keep thieves out of the gardens for much longer. His pup Bellman is nearly full-grown now. You should try him as night watchman.'

'And is that all that's troubling you? I expected something weightier . . .'

'Ranter is weighty. He's the size of a small horse!' He sat wearily on the side of the bed. 'Remind me to take the chub to Mistress Margaret first thing in the morning. They'll still do well enough for breakfast tomorrow but make a putrid supper.' One leg at a time, he swung himself up onto the bed. 'What progress does Dauzat report with our glass?'

Zeal climbed up beside him and pulled the curtains almost closed, against draughts. 'And what else troubles you?'

'Dear child, surely those are enough concerns for one night.' He reached out an arm and pinched out the candle flame.

They lay side by side in the dark. Zeal watched the shadow of his profile staring up into the canopy of the bed.

'Oh, Zeal, I feel so cold,' he said after a long while.

'Put your feet close to the warming pan and let me rub your hands.' She sat up and took his left hand in her own. 'You did stay out too long! You are a fool!' Her voice was gentler than her words.

After a moment, he reached up and pulled her head down so he could kiss her forehead. 'The cold was in my bones long before the frost got to them. And your hands are so warm.'

He lay back again and she heard him swallow. The silence grew longer and longer, while she continued to rub his hands. At last, she lay back down and folded her hands on her chest. She could see the silhouette of his feet against the hangings at the end of the bed.

Like a stone figure on a tomb, she thought.

No! She corrected herself urgently. Don't think that!

'Zeal?'

She heard intent in his voice and grew alert again, a little annoyed, as if she had been tricked into carelessness and inattention.

'Have you minded so much?'

It broke her heart. Philip so humble. So reduced in his own eyes. She felt a rush of protective tenderness. 'How can I mind when I love you?'

The bed clothes rustled as he turned onto his side to face her. 'Do you?' He had returned to his dry familiar tone.

Don't let the silence grow! she warned herself. Not with ears like his tuned to the void between every heartbeat. Just speak and trust your heart to guide your tongue.

'Yes,' she said. 'I . . .'

'Don't lie, Zeal. Please. I could not endure kindness.'

'Should I love you less because you are kind to me?' she asked sharply.

'But I am kind from love. I don't love from kindness. That difference can't escape your quick mind.'

'Sir, when you first asked me to marry you, did you ever think we would be lying together in the dark speaking of love?'

'Indeed not.'

'No more did I. And yet here we are, somehow arrived. I have never pretended not to love John. And yet I feel happy here with you. It gives me pleasure to lie with you. That may trouble my conscience but it does not change my feelings.'

'How cleverly you avoid perjuring yourself while you still protect my *amour propre*.'

'So ask me again direct.'

'Do you love me, wife?'

'Yes.' And it was true enough to slip out without discomfort.

'Oh, Zeal, my dearest girl!' He pulled her to him and drew the coverlet up. 'Even I know enough to rest content with that.'

She lay warmly against his chest, with his arms tight around her and his heart drumming under her ear. I do love him, she thought with surprise. If not as I loved John.

In recompense for this last thought, she reached up and laid her hand on Philip's cheek.

A complex man, with cruel edges, but always kind to me. And so generous with what he has. We are good friends, as he promised. And lovers.

She felt wrapped not only in his arms but in their hours of passionate planning, his surprises of building stuffs, his willingness to ask favours on her behalf. And to tell her, however reluctantly, truths about himself that he had shared with no one else.

'You are so very warm,' he said into her hair. He stroked her face, then let his hand settle on her breast. She pressed forward into the cup of his palm.

He pulled up her night dress.

What else can I give him in return? she asked herself. She opened her legs and placed her arms around his neck.

He sighed as he entered her.

I owe him all I can give. I wish to give him this. I do. Open, heart.

She closed her eyes.

'Zeal, Zeal . . .' he whispered. He groaned and shuddered.

He drew a hideous whooping breath. Coughed. His full weight fell onto her. His chin struck her head like a club.

She lay pinned under him, dizzy, barely able to breathe. 'Philip?'

She knew. She had known it since she saw the silhouette of his feet against the hangings.

She felt herself clamping onto her rock, closing down, becoming absent so that when realization arrived, it would find no one there to inform. As she had closed down at the age of six when she interrupted low, intense adult voices, belonging to strangers, standing in their London house where her parents should have been waiting, arms open, to greet her after their return from the Low Countries.

His right arm twitched.

'Philip!' she whispered eagerly. But his block-like head still pinned down her hair. She tried to draw breath, but his weight crushed her lungs.

Cold horror gave her the strength to heave him off. She yanked her damp night dress from under him. Then she smelled urine.

'Don't do this! No, no, no, Philip!' She shook her head. 'Don't you dare! I won't let you!'

She scrambled off the bed, lit the candle from the banked fire and took it back to the bed. He had rolled onto his back when she heaved him off and was staring at her so intensely that she thought for an instant he was still alive. His penis lay limply across his bare thigh.

I should have stopped you! I felt something askew. I think I knew! Why didn't I stop you?

I killed him.

She pulled down his night shirt, then made herself touch his cheek. Still warm. He still felt like Philip. Dry and warm. Grey stubble glinting on his jaw.

She bent her cheek close to his mouth, then set her ear over his heart. The silence in his chest nearly undid her but she closed her eyes and let the wave roll over her.

She raised her hand to close his eyes but could not bring herself to touch them while he still seemed to look out of them. They did not waver, but she now saw that they did not quite look at her. When she looked directly at him, her horror ebbed. She laid her hand on his forehead as if he were a sick child.

It had happened. There was nothing she could do to change it.

'In the morning, I will no doubt feel the truth of it. Right now, I just feel peculiar. Very still.'

She climbed back up onto the bed beside him and pulled the covers over them both.

He was still Philip and yet he wasn't. She smoothed his hair. Touched his fleshy ear lobe. Soon, she would call for help. Wake Lamb. Send for Sir Richard. Start up all that attend a death. Move him onward, into being a corpse. Begin the process that would hide him from her first in a coffin, then under the earth, and leave her standing on top of it. Stuck up there on the crust while he fell farther and farther away from her, into a place stranger and more unknown than any of the places he had conjured up for her to imagine.

For the moment, however, she felt him merely suspended, and herself with him, falling from one life into another, not yet entirely gone from the first nor yet arrived at the second.

She placed his hand against her cheek and sat with her eyes closed, rocking gently.

I should call Sir Richard, she thought. How very convenient to have a magistrate as one's neighbour. Then she remembered that Parliament was still sitting and Sir Richard was in London.

Philip's flesh cooled slowly against hers like water in a bath. She arranged him with his legs straight and his arms at his side, so that he might stiffen into a dignified posture. Then she lay beside him propped up on one elbow, to keep watch.

'I prefer the Italian design for the new fireplace,' she told him. 'That last one Lamb found. I hope you don't mind. And if Dauzat can't make us enough window panes, perhaps I should send to Norwich, after all. We could ship it by carriage to save the carters' fees. I can ride my horse in the meantime . . . we hardly ever use the carriage, and the glass might just survive such a journey.'

When she opened her eyes, the sky was pale grey, and she saw that she lay beside a dead man.

By supper, she was in a rage at him.

How dare you? She glared at the sunken face of the stranger he had left in his place, now laid out on the dining table at High House. How dare you leave me?

'Where has she gone?' Lamb interrupted Rachel as she was banking the bake house fires. 'I can't find her anywhere.'

'I think she went fishing. At least, she took one of his rods and his sack.'

Lamb found her below the mill. He watched but did not approach her. She was sitting on the bank of the river, holding the rod, staring into the water.

Zeal saw Lamb. She turned her head just enough to put him out of sight. When she looked again, he had gone.

All clear, she said. Just the two of us now. Where are you?

Tiny splashes marked fishy attacks on the minced cheese she had thrown. There was no bait on her line.

A seed pod popped near her elbow. Upstream and downstream, the dark, cold water chatted and gurgled. The surface in front of her swirled in a long whispering curve. Dried nettle stalks rasped at each other in each slight movement of the air. A thin glassy fringe of ice hung above the water on shadowed stretches of the bank.

Where are you? she asked again. I know you must be here on the river. After so many years, you must have left a substantial ghost. Just whisper something. Tug on the line. As you know, I won't give up, so you might as well speak to me now. You hadn't finished your stories. You must have something more to say.

As indeed he did, but he would tell it by other means.

46

The sky declined to act as an oracle for the day. As Zeal rode to High House for the reading of Philip's will three weeks after his death, she looked up at the grey veil above her head. It hung damply but glowed nevertheless with a hint of possible sunlight to come. Dried grass bent under the weight of a light frost. Seed heads stuck to the fetlocks of her horse and strands of cleavers fringed the hem of her gown.

She pulled up her horse on the ridge above Sir Richard's lake, remembering the double line of children, and her own blind walk through the same meadow.

When she threw Rachel's silver pin into the spring and made her wedding wish, a chilly lump of flesh had ticked in her chest in place of her heart.

Her horse dropped its head and pulled at the grass.

I believe that my wish came true. To my astonishment and past my deserving. I was loved. And in the end the old soldier trusted me and let me comfort him.

She looked for John, seated in the meadow, waiting for her. She wanted to ask his forgiveness for this grief over another man and needed to see understanding in his face.

She pressed her hand against her mouth and squeezed her eyes tight shut.

Women love men for the power they give us over them as much as for the power they imagine they must exercise over us, she thought. Dear, wily double man.

She looked across the lake at High House with dread. He was already slipping from her, pushed away by images of his coffin and burial, by images of dust and decay. Today would

307

push him farther with papers and legal language. With a lawyer's face, black gown and smell of musty wool.

Sir Richard was waiting at the front door of High House.

'Need to speak, my dear.' Whatever it was clearly made him uncomfortable. 'Now, if you don't mind.'

Startled by his uncharacteristic abruptness, she handed her reins to his groom, climbed the shallow stone steps and followed him into his small parlour at the front of the house, just off the hall.

Sir Richard glanced up at the ceiling with what could only be described as alarm. 'Still don't believe that Philip . . . In any case, instructions from him about his estate . . .'

He thinks he has bad news for me, she thought. If he only knew how low my expectations are, what my real reasons were for the marriage. And how much Philip has already given me.

'Had to send word to . . . a gentleman he named.' Sir Richard pressed two fingers against his temple and rubbed. 'Roger Henry Wentworth.' He waited in unhappy expectation for her response.

'And who is this Roger Henry Wentworth?'

'His son,' said Sir Richard.

'His son?' She felt she had walked into a tree that was not there a moment before. 'But Philip said he had no . . .'

'No children who are alive to me,' was what he had said, in fact.

'Did he tell you he had a son?'

'Not a squeak.' Balhatchet raised his head and listened to the sound of feet marching back and forth overhead. 'Then, he didn't say he did not, neither. And the man is here.'

'His son,' Zeal repeated, numbly.

'I had to offer him lodging last night, of course. And his wife.'

Zeal at last noticed the pacing feet. And heard raised voices. Now she began to understand Sir Richard's wretchedness.

'And is he very angry with us for not calling him to Philip's deathbed? Did you explain how unexpected his father's death was? And that I did not know enough to send for him?'

'I don't believe that's what is agitating him . . . God's Teeth! I think he's coming downstairs!'

The parlour door flew open. This time she saw that he resembled Philip. A little taller, a little leaner, but Roger Wentworth had the same beaked, slightly fleshy nose, the same square jaw. His father's pugnacity and edge were now distorted into quivering rage.

Her mouth fell open. How did I not see it then? she asked herself. My step-son. She had to look away from his angry face while she fought to control her voice.

'It was you!' he exclaimed. 'The wife!'

'If you'll allow me, mistress,' said Sir Richard, 'I would like to introduce Master Roger Wentworth.' His voice, however, made it clear that he liked it not at all.

His hat. The sun in my eyes. But even so, I should have recognized his father's bass voice. The man on the horse.

'I suspected as much at the time,' he said.

She stared at this almost-Philip, this terrible distortion. I've lost something of great value, she thought, if this is what is left behind.

The muscles in her face began to jump.

Did Philip know that his son killed our child? And from what he just said, did it knowingly.

Roger Wentworth turned and left the room again.

Together, Zeal and Sir Richard watched him march back up the oak staircase. After a moment, they heard voices overhead again.

'He can't hope to inherit Hawkridge Estate, can he?' she asked, suddenly cold from scalp to toenails. 'As Philip's son? He'll be disappointed.'

Unless I misunderstood those documents Philip was so keen to have me sign before the marriage.

'I have the deed of gift, secure!' she said.

309

Unless I misjudged Philip, as I misjudged Harry.

'Whatever he might hope, he brought a lawyer,' said Sir Richard with considerable edge. 'To be certain that I deal properly with the will.'

'I suppose I must be an unpleasant complication.'

'A lawyer!' snorted Sir Richard. 'To ensure honesty!'

Wentworth's lawyer was much younger than Zeal had expected, given the weight of his responsibility. He had only recently qualified, he explained when summoned by Sir Richard for brutal questioning. Had known Roger Wentworth at university. Yes, Wentworth was older. Had been sent down, then returned some years later. He himself was here as a favour to Roger. Who was a hard man to stop when his mind was set. Here, the lawyer tried, without success, for collusion with his alarming host.

'Too bad old Forwyth died,' said Sir Richard. 'Best legal man I ever knew. Never knew him to be anyone's tame puppy.'

The young lawyer blushed and toyed with the minced egg that Sir Richard had insisted he consume to fortify himself.

They gathered in the small courtroom at the back of High House where Sir Richard dealt with parish cases. It had its own entrance so that those on court business need not enter the house. The small holding cell just beneath the courtroom saw few occupants except an occasional vagrant taken in the parish before removal to Winchester, or the odd violent drunk being kept away from wife and family till he sobered up again.

To Zeal, who had never seen the courtroom, it seemed very plain to be a seat of justice, even at parish level. Undecorated stone surrounded the door. The walls were flat panelled. The windows held clear glass. Only the county arms above the door and a flag beside it told her that she was not in a stone storage barn.

Sir Richard took his chair behind a square oak table, with

a manservant standing by to fetch fresh ink or pens. The lawyer set his writing chest on the end of the table to Sir Richard's left. Wentworth, Zeal and Wentworth's wife sat on stools facing the table.

The woman had taken her introduction to Zeal with no apparent emotion except curiosity.

She's not happy, Zeal thought, glancing at her now. And who can blame her? At a less distressing time, she might have studied more closely Mistress Wentworth's fashionable high-waisted jacket, plucked hairline and heeled shoes.

Sir Richard rumbled through a formal explanation of why they were there and skipped briskly through the opening sentences of the will. 'All the usual assurances, sound mind and so on . . .'

'Sir . . .' interjected the lawyer.

'You can see for yourself when I've done. Ah, here we come to the meat . . .' He bent his round white-fringed head more closely to the document. 'I'll be damned!' He read on, as if alone in the room. He chuckled.

He's having one of his lapses, thought Zeal unhappily.

'Sir!' said the lawyer firmly. 'Might you wish to share the reason for your amusement?'

Sir Richard handed him the will, leaned back in his chair and crossed his arms. 'I beg you, share away!'

The lawyer read aloud:

'. . . I will firstly that my wife, Mistress Zeal Elizabeth Wentworth, shall keep and use my tools so long as she doth use my trade . . .'

'My father was a gentleman!' Roger interrupted. 'He had no trade!'

Zeal smiled. 'He means his fishing rods. It was a jest between us. He was convinced that their use led to a special state of grace, from which he feared I fell short.'

Roger shrugged and glanced at the lawyer. 'Continue.'

'All other chattels, properties, bullion and coin, loan deeds, live-stock, holdings of any kind and all other estates of all sorts, without restraints of any kind in addition to all jointures settled by either of *us on the other at the time of our marriage, I also leave entirely to my wife . . .'*

'No!' Roger Wentworth knocked over his stool as he rose. 'Let me . . .!' He tried to seize the document. His wife bent her head onto her hands.

'Surely it does not matter,' said Zeal. 'It's only words.'

'The lawyer slapped his hand down on the will. 'Please sit down, sir. I will not continue otherwise.'

Roger picked up his stool. 'The will is false.'

'She may . . . You, his wife, that is,' explained the lawyer, looking at Zeal. *'. . . She may, at her will and best judgement allow such persons as presently inhabit my houses, to remain as tenants or she may turn them out to find other . . .'*

'"Such persons"!' Roger leapt to his feet again. '"Such *persons*"? He means by that his own son! And "turn them out"! He never wrote that!'

His wife lifted her head from her hands.

'The imprint of two witnesses say that he did.'

'Then his wits were gone. Or that trollop twisted his thoughts against me. To speak so coldly of his own begotten flesh and blood!'

'I don't understand . . .' Zeal said. A jolt of intimation froze her tongue even before Wentworth could.

'Oh, don't you, madam?' He stood over her. 'I'm certain you understand far better than any of the rest of us!'

'Then we're all mired in ignorance,' she said hotly.

'Sir Richard!' Roger turned to appeal to their host. 'Witness how she insists on her deceit!'

'Sir!' Zeal rose to her feet.

'". . . such persons as presently inhabit my houses . . ." He means to say my own house! Where my mother lived all her married life, and where I was raised and have lived in full and proper expectation that it would be mine.'

'What house?' demanded Zeal.

'Your house?' asked Sir Richard. 'Have you the title in law?'

'Morally! In God's law . . . !'

'WHAT ARE YOU ALL TALKING ABOUT?' When she had their attention at last, Zeal sat down again.

'Your late husband's property, I believe,' said Sir Richard gently. He pressed his right temple with the heel of his hand. 'I wish you would all let this young gentleman on my left get on with it.'

'Are you saying that my father proposes to give this woman the right to turn me out of my own house?'

'In law, unless you have the deed, it's not your house.' Sir Richard gestured to his manservant to bring glasses and claret. 'Calm and civility. The only way forward.' He looked at the young lawyer encouragingly.

'Did he truly leave all to this deceitful little trull?' demanded Wentworth.

'No. He has left you an allowance . . . Let me find my place again.'

'Why is there such uproar?' asked Zeal. 'Of course, I wouldn't throw you out of your house, even if it were mine . . .'

'How generous! How saintly! You scheming trollop, you female crocodile . . . !'

'SIR!' Now Balhatchet was on his feet. 'I will not . . .! Not in this house! Just shut your mouth or I will cuff you round the ears.'

'Did you say, "houses"?' Zeal asked the lawyer. 'How many?'

'Four!' Wentworth said tightly. 'And a London lodging house. And two shops. As if you didn't know.'

'I did not! Your father lived modestly on Hawkridge Estate. As quiet as an ancient hermit. Why should any of us imagine that he owned four houses? And a London lodgings, and shops?'

'Claim what you will, I know that you played on my father's spite towards me . . .'

'I didn't know you existed!'

'. . . and trapped him into a false marriage. It's easily done

313

with old men once their pricks start to droop. Pantaloons! I shall set about at once to have this will declared false, the product of deceit and cold calculation.'

Zeal caught the lawyer's eye. 'What is the total worth of my husband's estate?' Her voice trembled slightly.

He sifted through the papers in his hand. 'You will have to examine these inventories in detail, madam, to calculate precisely. And they must all be proved. But the total will be considerable.' He rose and gave her a sheaf of documents. 'The houses have tenancies and land. One has a lavender farm. And there are also docks near Norwich which bring good mooring fees, and some rights to customs farmering. And two tracts of forest, producing timber.'

Timber. She felt the intimation of a landslide of understanding.

She glanced at the first inventory, which was fixed to the seal on the deed with silken threads. From one of the houses. Her mind stumbled and slid across lists of acreage, outbuildings, carts, doors, windows, locks, shelves and other carpenter's work. She lifted the top sheet and saw joint stools, tables, silver spoons, half-headed beds, trundle beds, full-headed jointed beds, table carpets, wall-curtains. Feather beds, quilts, sheets. Washing tubs, copper water cisterns, latten bed warmers, leather fire buckets and pierced steel lanterns.

'Has he left me anything at all?' asked Wentworth.

'There is a letter here for you.' The lawyer passed it via Sir Richard. 'And the allowance, of course.'

Wentworth broke the seal.

The room was absolutely silent while he read. Zeal watched the enraged purple of his cheeks fade to grey.

'Will you read it to us?' asked the lawyer.

Wentworth threw the letter onto the table and stared down at it. 'He has always disdained me. Taken all I valued most. What more harm can he do?'

Balhatchet leaned forward and pulled the letter to him.

'*Sir,*' read Sir Richard. '*As you showed no kindness when I*

*would have set aside our differences and given you all, I took it back
again to be administered by a gentler, more generous heart than
yours. When I turned to you for forgiveness and for respite in which
I hoped to heal my soul, you would have turned me out, sold my
estates for your own profit. I thank God only that you betrayed yourself before I placed my final seal on the instruments of my own self-
destruction.*

'*Your hot temper and greedy self-concern so disgusted me that I
looked into my soul for the causative taint in my own blood. Having
found enough there to dislike myself even more than I dislike you, I
set out to do penance in a life of simplicity and denial. This intended
mortification, however, has failed to serve my intent. Instead, it
brought me true peace beyond my deserving and, finally a joy I
thought I had long left behind.*

'*When you disobeyed my orders and pursued me to Hawkridge,
you did damage beyond your comprehension, compassion being absent
from your soul. You also killed all last temptation to relent, which
had been prompted in me by the remnants of paternal feeling . . .*'

'Hah!' said Wentworth under his breath.

'*. . . I willingly grant you one gift: the chance from which I was
fortunate enough to benefit – to honour my wife, as young as she is,
and to learn to husband your soul according to her example. You
owe her a measureless penance, which I fear she will be too kind to
extract.*'

'It can't be,' said Zeal quietly.

Wentworth lifted his head. 'She admits the truth at last.'

'Take care, my dear,' said Sir Richard. 'I see what you mean.
I knew your Philip too, but today I must listen with legal
ears. So, I do not think that you meant to say, in absolute
fact, that the letter is not properly written in Philip
Wentworth's hand.'

'May I see it?'

Sir Richard passed it to her.

'Looking with legal eyes,' she said at last, 'this is his own
hand.'

'There is a letter for you, as well, madam,' said the lawyer.

'A serpent for her, too!' exclaimed Wentworth. 'Read it to us, madam.'

Zeal broke Philip's seal and unfolded the paper. 'Oh,' she said faintly after a moment. 'I don't think . . .'

She handed the letter to Sir Richard. 'There's nothing here of legal import, but look for yourself and reassure Master Wentworth that no deceit is being practised on him.' She inhaled to steady herself. She refused to weep in front of that detestable *simulacrum* of a good man. Philip had written only a single line from *Ecclesiastes:*

A feast is made for laughter, and wine maketh merry; but money answereth all things.

'What my father has done is against the natural order,' said Wentworth. 'In turning against his own child, he has turned traitor to nature.'

'May I beg paper and pen?' Zeal asked the lawyer.

'Take care what you set down,' said Sir Richard. 'I should reflect before I did anything, if I were you. There's much to consider.'

'Is your name truly Wentworth?' she asked the son.

'Beyond doubt, madam! What's your meaning?' A look of understanding widened his eyes. 'If you mean to claim that I am not his true son . . .'

'Will you make a fair copy?' she asked the lawyer when she had finished writing. 'Then I will sign it before you.'

'May I just see it before . . .'

'Don't fear, Sir Richard.' She let the old knight read what she had written. 'You will see that I have merely settled on Master and Mistress Wentworth the right to live in their present house during her life time, so long as she wishes it. But upon her death, he must quit it.'

One question at least had been answered. She was indeed Mistress Wentworth, not Mistress Something Else.

'Does it give you pleasure to humiliate me further?' asked Wentworth. 'You're not content with robbing me?'

'Roger,' protested his wife faintly.

'Be still!' he shouted at her. He turned back to Zeal. 'I don't believe he ever married you. My mother was his only wife. Yours was a false marriage! A sham! I know your wanton history, madam! You cannot deceive me. I have sought intelligence!'

Afterwards, Zeal remembered only that she stood, grew as tall as a tree. Her throat swelled with rage. She feared that she might have roared.

Wentworth had stepped back. Closed his mouth. Looked away.

'Don't ever say such a thing to me again.' She was in control of herself once more. She spoke carefully, remembered to breathe. 'Thank your wife and my concern for her future comfort that I don't take back the right I just gave you. But one more word of false marriages, and I will throw you out as your father gave me the power to do!'

Wentworth's jaw shook before he could manage to speak. 'Now I see it! How you mean to entertain yourself in the future! "Oh, sir, you may stay. Oh, no, sir! I've changed my mind. You must go." Well, madam, I will not tolerate life on such terms, subject to the whims of a . . . !'

'Please!' cried his wife.

'I fear you must either learn to tolerate it, sir, or live elsewhere,' said Sir Richard.

'No,' said Wentworth. 'I won't learn to tolerate it. I shall take it to court!'

'Sir! I am the court.'

'Then I shall find another that is not so clearly skewed in favour of my enemy. You are small fry, Sir Richard. I intend to see you, madam, at the quarterly assizes.'

'What can he do?' Zeal asked Sir Richard later. He had asked her to stay to dinner and now they sat together in his small parlour. 'Can there be any question about the will?'

'Tight as a drum. And the allowance will work against him. Shows that Philip hadn't lost his wits and merely forgotten him. He might have tried that . . .' The old knight paused. His natural ruddiness darkened several shades. 'There's no question he could raise about the marriage, is there?' He avoided Zeal's eyes. 'Consummation, and all that?'

Zeal smiled. 'No. No question like that about the marriage.'

Forgive me for misjudging you, she told Philip. I thought that male pride alone urged you to insist on my bed and on the charade of blood on the wedding sheets.

'Then I can't think what charge he can make stick,' said Sir Richard.

Zeal interlaced her fingers into a small solid structure on her lap.

How many more surprises do you have for me? she asked Philip silently. Her mind was too full to consider the question now, but sooner or later, she knew the landslide would bury her.

'Do you swear you did not know his true estate?' she asked Sir Richard.

'I trust that I would remember if Philip had told me.'

'Nor the crime for which he so clearly tormented himself?'

Sir Richard shook his head.

She unlaced her hands, stood up and took her leave. There was another whom she must question.

She found Lamb among the fragrant amber stacks of oak planks by the plantation saw pit. Wet sawdust made a soft acrid carpet under her feet.

'Did you know?'

47

Lamb did not bother to pretend ignorance. 'He swore me to secrecy as condition of my employ . . .'

'Your employ?'

'I am truly sorry . . .'

'He employed you?'

'The favour was also true. I did need to escape London.'

'What were your wages, that let me imagine friendship?'

'The friendship was not imagined!'

'How do I know? How do I know to believe anything? The source of those gifts of timber seems clear enough now. May I hazard, too, that Quoynt was not a beggar grateful for a warm bed? Did Dauzat truly settle for a share of the glass? What about that barn Philip claimed to have been given? And all those supposed favours? Where else was I blind?'

Lamb looked away. A flush dawned above the rim of his collar.

'Even Bowler's second fiddle! I wager it was bought, not borrowed at all!'

'Bowler did not know.'

'You made a fool of me,' she said. 'The pair of you. But Philip most of all.'

'From love. He did it from love.'

'So you say.'

Behind them, a sawyer bent down towards his partner in the bottom of the saw pit. The saw rasped through the log set across the pit. The sawyer straightened to haul up his end of the eight-foot saw again. She took Lamb by the sleeve and pulled him out of earshot.

'What else don't I know?'

Lamb rubbed his nose vigorously and looked her in the eye. 'You know that Philip did not confide in anyone unnecessarily.'

'And you were more necessary than I?'

'Don't be a fool! I already knew him . . . though not well,' he added hastily. 'My father knew him. Philip wanted to please you and to ease your life enough to risk exposure after all those years in hiding. Swearing me to secrecy was a small matter against that risk.'

'I feel such a fool!' she said again. Suddenly, everything was put in question. 'He didn't also pay Sir Richard for his old barn? I could not bear it!'

'That was a true gift,' Lamb assured her. Then he heard the knowledge he had revealed and grimaced in mock agony.

She turned an icy eye on him. 'I think that you and I must explore the full extent of Philip's need to confide.'

Later that evening, she sat wrapped in her cloak on the steps of the lodge looking across the valley at the brick walls which had risen that summer and autumn from the hole in the side of Hawk Ridge. Winter rain and freezing weather had again stopped work until spring.

What of the brick oven and Master Wilde's advance payment of the building costs? she asked herself. Did he truly buy that meadow? Or did he collude with Philip too?

Can't ask him without exposing my own pitiful ignorance.

And those ships' timbers? And that friendly barge owner who transported sand for such an amiable fee? The Record of Works told her only what had been spent, not where the money had come from.

She heard footsteps from the drive above the lodge.

'It's you,' she said coldly.

Lamb sat beside her, forcing her to shuffle sideways or else find herself sitting closer than she wished just then.

'Are you still enraged with me, darling sis? You should

know that I mean to drown myself if you don't relent. I need a good excuse to drown myself. My only difficulty will be deciding whether the carp or the pike will best harmonize with my attire.'

'Go to Hell, Lamb!'

He sighed. 'Implacable harpy.'

'I killed him, you know.'

'I don't think so.'

'I did. I should have stopped him. Instead, I led him on.'

'No one led Philip Wentworth anywhere,' Lamb said firmly. 'I didn't know him as well as you seem to fear, but I'm certain of that, at least. I never saw a man who by doing so little could have so many people running around doing exactly as he wished.'

'Including me?'

Wisely, Lamb kept quiet.

After a moment she said, 'He saved my life.'

'Then why are you so angry with him? He also left you a wealthy woman. You can do as you like now, with your house. You can afford your theatre at last.'

'Yes. I must think further about that,' she said grimly. 'As you say, the possibilities for imagination are much increased.' After a moment she asked, 'Did you also know his son?'

'You can be sure at least that Roger most likely deserved his harsh treatment at Philip's hands.'

'Why?'

'Met him once. I was told to be kind because his mother had died. He was eleven. I was six. Let him ride my horse and he lamed it. Then he told my father I did it, and I got a beating.'

'Didn't you tell your father the truth?'

Lamb shrugged. 'My horse knew. And that was the only opinion I cared for.'

'You must know more of him.'

'Didn't want to.' Lamb returned to diplomatic silence while they gazed across the valley. A small figure appeared among the low walls.

'Oh!' Zeal put her hands to her mouth. 'My eyes are deceived by distance. It's only a boy. For a moment, I thought that was Philip! He used to prowl the site of an evening.' She looked up as if studying the weather. 'I can't trust even my eyes. I don't know if I know anything, anymore.'

The day Philip was buried, Zeal had gone into his chamber and sat on his bed, hugging a linen shirt that he had left lying on his stool.

Philip?

She sat very still, waiting, with his shirt against her face.

I'm sorry my eyes were closed when you left me.

The room was dark, and cold without his fire burning in the grate. Mice rustled behind the panelling. Outside, a loose gate bumped its post in a small surge of wind. Inside, the air was so still that she heard her own breathing and the tiny rearrangements of her clothes.

He was not there.

Nevertheless, she forbade Mistress Margaret to have the chamber cleaned.

After talking with Lamb on the day the will was read, she went into Philip's chamber to uncover his secrets, if she could. She entered like a thief.

His smell still hung in the air like a physical presence. Polished leather, lemon balm and the mustard he had applied to his stiff joints. She pressed her face against his pillow. The not unpleasant smell of his sweat still lingered, underpinned by a deep elusive maleness that made her think of warm earth in the spring. She opened his press, but his presence here among his clothing was too strong to permit prying.

She closed the press again and eyed various small boxes and chests. She picked one up and tried to turn the key. Suddenly, she felt the lash of his rage, as she had never felt it in life.

She dropped the box and fled.

You will have to permit me such liberties, she told him when she was safely outside his door in the lodge parlour. It will take more than that to stop my curiosity now, my dear husband. You may have eluded me in life, but now you suffer the disadvantage of being dead.

But for that day, she had had enough.

Shortly after midnight, she sat up straight from sleep with a further thought.

What of Philip's stories? Had he created a true world for her or were his tales all lies too? Where did his false shaping of her world end? Did she sail on imaginary seas and plant her feet on sands as insubstantial as fog? Had John vanished into a limbo of mists and fable?

The room around her seemed no more than a hallucination. The quilt crushed in her fist might be merely a feverish dream. Her teeth began to chatter. For a flash of time, she knew with absolute conviction that the world outside her chamber had disappeared.

I lie here and vanish as well, she thought, or I learn the worst. Whatever it may be, I must hold on to something solid.

She first unrolled his map, his Christmas gift to her, which she would have painted on the floor of the hall. She had to hold the candle close to see in the dim light.

She touched Nevis, which John had not yet described to her. Then moved her finger to Nombre de Dios, Maracaibo, La Conceptión. Vera Cruz. San Juan de Ulúa. Cartagena.

How do the courts ever discover the truth? How do those wise men learn to weigh evidence?

She heard Philip's voice again, singing 'Duerme no llores . . .' But then, any London ballad seller could learn a Spanish song.

This time, back in his chamber, when she unlocked the first box, she felt nothing from him. Not even a draught of cold air.

You can stay, she told him. Earlier, I didn't mean for you to leave. It's just that I must know.

The first box held business papers. Receipts, for that first load of Portland stone, among other items. Letters of tender. Copies of her lists of required building stuffs, on which he had made notes in a heavy-lined, impatient hand. All were to do with Hawkridge and the new house.

She slammed the box shut.

The next box was empty and gave no hint as to its former contents.

The next held his collection of unguents and salves.

A small chest held all his fishing gear.

Another box was filled with small notebooks, each labelled with a year, in which he had kept meticulous record of his catches, the numbers of fish seen at the time, the effects of flood water and drouth. Good spawning years, bad spawning years, recipes for bait. At the bottom of this box, she found six golden fish hooks.

She picked one up. She had seen steel hooks, bone hooks, hooks made of thorns. She had never seen a golden one.

If I were a magistrate or lawyer . . . She imagined herself to be Sir Richard seated behind his table examining this extraordinary object as a piece of evidence.

The golden hook did not prove the truth of a golden city in the jungle, but it did suggest the possibility.

She looked at the boxes around her on the floor.

Have I misjudged you again? she asked him.

Otherwise, she had so far added nothing to what the day had already taught her. In truth, she did not think that he had obligingly written down what she most wanted to learn.

Nevertheless, the least detail would feed her hunger to know. There was also the illicit pleasure of prying into someone else's belongings, with the full right to do so. She thrust her arm into his press and found a ring in a casket at the back of his linen undershirts and drawers.

The poisoned ring bought in Italy, perhaps. Its heavy intricacy supported that likelihood. He had shown her the broadsword and buckler. She had used his dagger, now hers.

More corroboration. Mere detail to be sure, but cheering nonetheless.

Folded into his old frayed black coat, she found his personal account books. She pulled these out and set them on the bed to take to her own room. A quick glance at one page showed reference to the income from the London lodging houses. Among his debits, she saw the regular presence of his son's name, each time set against the same generous sum. With the account books was a small bundle of letters.

She opened the first of these with a surge of excitement. But it was from his agent. He seemed to have left his business affairs in other hands and merely recorded the results. Among these letters, however, was one written in John's hand.

Dear Philip . . .

Confused, she read the salutation again. John had written to Philip. Philip had not told her.

. . . I beg your help. I believe my life here to be at risk. I will say no more than that M. Baulk considers the lash to be the mildest punishment his labourers deserve, followed most often by a bath of lemon juice applied to the bleeding stripes and standing under the noonday sun. I beg you, do not tell Zeal, for I would not have her fear for me. But none escapes his impatience. A man died only four days ago after a second helping of such improvement. I mean to bolt before I am too weakened by hard labour in this unspeakable heat to take any action at all. I am ignorant of all places in the Indies but this plantation, and lack opportunity to learn more. I need only a name, one man or place, which might still endure since your experience here. A church, a minister, a hospital, a merchant – anyone or anywhere I might throw my first grappling hook to begin to save myself. I pray God this reaches you. I hardly need say that M. Baulk has our letters read before he gives them to us. I am trusting this to a woman among his house slaves who has treated me kindly. Your grateful servant – John Nightingale.

She read the letter again.

John was going to die. He was dead already. That was why he had never written from Nevis. He was living among wild beasts, hiding from pursuers. She saw him bound to a post, his back cut open by a whip, bleeding to death under a hot sun. She saw snakes in the tobacco fields. She saw swinging machetes. She saw monster perroquetos swooping like the eagle that tore out the liver of Prometheus. He had left all worlds she knew. She could not even see his dangers clearly.

She had by chance laid her hand on an adder. Here was a truth, at last, and she wanted only to fling it from her.

She was too distracted to deal with Doctor Gifford as she might otherwise have done, when he came to call the following day.

'Mistress Wentworth, my deepest sympathy,' he said at once and with great force, as if to forestall her attack. He was standing at the door of the lodge, while a groom held his horse outside the gate.

What does that man imagine he is doing here? she wondered.

'The devil often offers solace to those in distress. I wish to offer the true consolation of the Lord's . . .'

'Thank you,' she said absently, cutting him off. 'I have an excess of truth just now.' She stared at him and did not invite him to enter.

Gifford's left foot beat a small tattoo on the stone step. 'Satan will tempt you with the promise to relieve your grief . . .'

Zeal closed the door in his face.

48

Zeal's Work Book – November 1640

Dig new beds outside walls and clear of stones (for sowing in March with extra cabbages)
Sprinkle lettuces with chimney soot against snails
Set strawberries, leeks and garlick cloves
Harvest saffron
Slaughter lame bullock and four killing rams
Grind pig oats
Hang woollen curtains against winter draughts in Lodge and stable loft
Fill lye dripper with new ash . . .

Lamb – Order from Italy, engravings of statues for possible setting about fish ponds
Make Christmas gifts to all master craftsmen on my behalf

Send for lawyer to draw up deeds, for Jake Grindley, to give him his farm outright, to console him for loss of Jamie's labour (and in hope of diminishing his bile)

Send for Francis Quoynt to enlarge cellars of west wing for theatre
Order a clockwork nightingale that sings

49

Although the estate was in the full panic of late autumn tasks, Zeal had to leave them all to it. The final settlement of Philip's estate waited for the inventories to be proved. The new owner had to make a progress around her properties.

Before she set off on this progress, however, she sent for Jake Grindley.

He replied with the message that he would never set foot in her house, so she sent the lawyer to him. Grindley did not refuse the farm.

Accompanied by Rachel, Arthur and a lawyer's clerk, Zeal began with the lavender farm in Norfolk. As the early November rains had eased, she chose to ride on horseback whenever they could not go by water. From Ufton, they went by shallow draught boats down the Thames to London, then up the coast to Yarmouth, Breydon Water and the Yare. Near Norwich, she hired horses, still astonished that such costs, like that of their lodgings, need no longer trouble her.

The lavender farm, now so improbably hers, seemed muddy and drab in early December but promised fragrance and profit in July and August. The tenant assured her that the London market for the herb could never be satisfied.

She moved on to the equally unlikely warehouse and quays back at the coast, with customs farming rights over various goods imported from the continent. Next came the Suffolk estate, and its twelve tenanted farms. Then more quays, the lodging house, two tenanted houses, a shop, and a slaughter-house in London, all bringing large rents and licence fees.

She accepted an agent's sworn statement on two tracts of forest, north of London, which, she now knew, must have provided most of those beams. Though they told her how wealthy she now was, none of these properties told her anything further about Philip, the man.

She dined with Sir George Tupper in London on Christmas Day, watched a masque in his private theatre, and engaged Master Cobb to help construct her own theatre.

The next day, she visited a Hebrew gold merchant in Clerkenwell with whom Philip had lodged two large money chests. In these she found sacks of golden angels, quarter angels and pound coins, all carefully accounted. A peck of golden unites worth twenty shillings each. An Arab dagger with an emerald set into the hilt, gold rings, a small coffer of loose pearls. Numerous silver candlesticks and pieces of plate. A golden mask.

Though she was by now numb to any further astonishment, Zeal lifted this last from the chest and studied it closely. Wide lips parted to show sharp teeth. Short rods had been thrust through the golden earlobes.

She set it as evidence beside the golden fish hooks.

After London, she at last turned south to Guildford, where Philip had once lived with his first wife and where his son now lived on her terms.

A man's house must tell tales on him.

Though she dreaded meeting Roger Wentworth again, she was eager to see Hunden Hall.

Half an hour's ride from the town, feeling a little breathless, she drew up her horse at Philip's former gate. Once a large half-timbered farm house, Hunden Hall had grown wings to enclose a courtyard and acquired the dignity of an ornate twin-towered gatehouse built of local sandstone. It might once have had a cheerful workaday aspect but now its roof timbers sagged, and weeds clogged the remains of an old moat.

I don't know what I expected to learn, she thought. Philip has not lived here for more than nineteen years. Even so, her heart speeded again as she knocked on the door. What she saw within told her much, but nothing that she wished to know.

The high, vaulted entrance hall was as bare of furnishings as a barn. Eyelets still in place showed where tapestries had once hung. Where Zeal would have expected to see a brace or two of hospitable, carved and padded chairs, stood a single rough stool. Rectangles on the wall panelling outlined newly-vanished picture frames. Only a single portrait of a pale, dark-haired young woman remained.

Zeal was eyeing it greedily when Mistress Roger Wentworth appeared and greeted her in confusion.

'My husband is, alas, forced away on matters of urgency.'

Not in the least surprised by this news, Zeal gave the woman a slightly vulpine smile. She glanced at a window ledge where a clear circle in the dust gave away the recent removal of a pot or jug. Her first disappointment at finding so few clues to Philip's past was giving way to the astonished realization that his son was selling off the house contents and pocketing the proceeds.

She followed Roger's wife to the small parlour off the hall, which still held a pair of chairs and a small table. She accepted a glass of elder flower cordial and a plate of almond biscuits, produced by Mistress Wentworth in a fluttering of feathers but with watchful eyes.

'I'm sorry about the child,' the woman said. She was sincere, but there was also a pleading note in her voice.

Zeal saw for the first time in her life that she held true power. She glanced back through the parlour door at the ghostly rectangles where pictures had hung before Roger Wentworth sold them.

'Thank you for the kind thought,' she said. 'Do you have children?'

Mistress Wentworth pinched her lips. 'Alas, no.'

After a moment of silence, Zeal asked, 'Do you have so few pictures from religious conviction?'

The woman touched her lace collar uneasily. 'We do have some pictures. You saw the one of my husband's mother in the hall.' She sat hunched as if braced against a blow.

'The one,' Zeal agreed. There was another silence.

'Please, madam! I beg your understanding!' the woman burst out desperately. 'Roger has . . . moments. He feels lacks. He was mistreated terribly as a boy.'

'By whom?'

'Left alone in England when his father took his mother away. Without a thought for the dangers to a fine gentle-woman. Or of what it might mean to the boy when she never came back.'

'That is indeed terrible for a child.' Zeal put down her glass a little harder than she intended and went back into the hall to look at the portrait again.

'She was always delicate,' said Mistress Wentworth behind her. 'Roger made himself her page as soon as he could walk. So she would never grow too tired. Then his father carted her off on a sea voyage, for his own male purposes, Roger is certain. Can you conceive it?'

She was far more beautiful than I, thought Zeal. A nymph or dryad. Not as commonly imagined in stone or marble, but as such creatures must truly be, wisps of mist or flashes of movement seen in the corner of your eye. Both Philip and Roger must have loved her very much.

She felt a rush of compassion for Roger Wentworth. His beautiful mother had chosen his father over him.

I would never have left my son.

Then Zeal could think only of her own child, who had left her behind. Like its father. And its stepfather. She rose to flee.

The clerk who had accompanied her returned to the hall from his room-by-room audit of the house wearing a grim expression. 'Madam, I think you should know that I am finding great discrepancies between the inventory lists and . . .'

'I am satisfied.'

He looked at her, astonished. Opened his mouth, closed it.

'We need stay no longer. I wish to leave at once.' She did not want this unhappy house nor anything in it.

'Thank you, madam!' Mistress Wentworth's right hand leapt to her own mouth, her cheek, settled at her throat. 'Thank you.' She unclenched her left only to raise it in farewell.

Zeal had been away from Hawkridge for seven weeks. By the time she returned in the new year, winter rains had made lakes in the new cellars. She wrapped up against the wind and shoved her feet into iron pattens to keep her shoes above the mud. Breathing hard from the climb, she stood on the top of Hawk Ridge with Lamb. Together, they looked down at the new house with the wind whipping their hair into their mouths and eyes.

'Thank the Lord, you're back,' he said. His mood fit the grim weather. 'No Philip, no you! Not even Bowler struggling with his second fiddle. Sir Richard in London helping to sort out the Scots and who knows what else. And Mistress Margaret runs away at the sight of me lest I infect her with a fatal Italianate fancy for art. At Christmas I almost expired from tedium.' He hesitated as if about to say something more, then seemed to decide against it. 'I do wish we had managed to enclose the house so that work could continue under cover.' He looked at her silent face. 'I suppose we can always hold skating parties in the cellars.'

'I have had long hours in boats and in the saddle,' she said. 'To think.'

'And?' he asked cautiously.

'I must reconsider everything.'

'Your life?' asked Lamb. He pulled his cloak tighter. 'Ah, yes, sister mine, so must I.'

'The house.'

He looked away, down the valley, as if he had not heard.

1641

50

After leaving Lamb on the hill, Zeal went to look at Philip's nest in the tack room. Someone had folded the blankets and rolled up his straw mattress but left them there for another sleeper to use. She went to the office and touched John's coat.

Later, Zeal tossed in the empty bed in the lodge and cried out in her sleep.

She ran her fingers over the letters carved into the stone wall of the vault. In the foetid darkness, they shone with their own light. She smelled cold brass, polished leather and something like a sweating horse.

She read:

'I am come out of Egypt, out of the narrow place, into the nothingness. I am no longer where I was, but I have not yet arrived where I am going.'

The voice found her before she saw the speaker. 'I have been waiting for you,' the creature said. 'Here in the darkness at the centre.'

She cried out and beat away the quilt.

She could make out a shape in the dark, but nothing more. Larger than a man, but like a man. Except for the head.

'I have nowhere else to go,' it said. 'I am already there. All my journeys are done. I am frozen here, my life achieved, without possibility, without movement. Finished. Hungry.'

She began to back away.

'I can hear you,' it said. 'Come closer, fresh blood. Young strength. Unlike me, you can still take another step forward.'

Her stealthy foot felt backwards, slowly, slowly. Hit a wall.

The tunnel through which she thought she had come had vanished. She felt behind her, felt solid stone as far as she could reach. Cold stone pressed at her back, pushed her towards the beast, forcing the soles of her feet to slide across the stone floor.

'Yes,' said the creature. 'Come, join me in the still centre of everything, from which there is no escape, only waiting.'

She struggled to stop but slid helplessly forwards.

'I will not eat you, lovely child. Oh, no, I won't eat you. Everyone lies about that. They tell such lies! I want only to put you into my place and take yours for myself. Then I will teeter on rusty feet, delirious with reborn possibility, back into the world, following the trail of light that you laid as you came to me.'

She raised her golden rapier.

'Ahhh,' breathed the creature. 'A fight! Nothing would please me more.'

She saw the shape more clearly now. It had the legs and arms of a man, but pointed ears and a tail. The shoulders were massive, like a bull. Sharp white teeth gleamed briefly as it smiled.

'I hunger even for struggle. I long for our limbs to clash. You might find that you like it too. I will seize you and hold you close against me. Then, as bone snaps or flesh is breached, my frozen senses will be dislodged into the ecstasy of unbalance.'

Its claws fastened in her hair. Too close for her rapier's point. The thick fur of its chest suffocated her. She could not inhale to scream when it pulled out a hank of her hair.

'My golden rope,' it said. 'It will twist like a trickle of fire around the corners and folds of my prison, to lead me back to the sun.'

She fell through the darkness as the creature released her. She stumbled and scrabbled for footing among the golden cups and plates that littered the creature's den and fell heavily onto the black floor. The creature's pelt had come away in her hand. She clutched it to her breast.

'But how shall I find my way out?' she screamed after it. 'I've lost the map! Don't leave me here!'

She was on her knees on the floor, with the coverlet twisted in her hand, breathing hard.

Don't leave me here!

PHILIP! She reached for him in the darkness.

With relief, she saw the brighter shape of her window, and the shadows of her bed hangings.

Not real. Thank God, not real.

But she still heard her own voice in her head. Don't leave me! And heard again the creature's delight when she appeared.

What did I feel as it held me?

Would have killed it. Yes.

But there was something more, just beyond reach of her reason. Now that she had begun to wake, the dream did not seem so terrible. Not good, but not entirely filled with horror neither.

She climbed back onto the bed but not to sleep again. Her heart still pounded with an emotion more complex than fear. The thick air of the tunnel still dragged at her lungs. Propped against the pillows, she imagined that she still felt the wall pushing at her back. Heard the creature's voice suddenly break the dark silence.

I don't understand it at all.

Even so, she recognized it as a messenger dream, hedged about with ambiguities and confusions, but as inarguable as an angel. She rose again and stood at the window, where she could see the balanced geometry of the new house rising against the shadows of the ridge, the beautiful, perfect geometry found only in Heaven.

Though wide awake, she still felt heavy with sadness, as if she had not yet finished the long journey back from the dream. Whatever it might mean, it belonged in a different world of deception and shifting truths, in the world after the Fall from Grace, where the heart of the truth is found in the tangles and confusions. Where something always remains unknown. Where all maps are hopeful lies.

She sent for Lamb to breakfast with her at the lodge. The previous evening, she had been too preoccupied to notice that there were unfamiliar bruises on his cheek, now faded to a subtle tone of palest yellow green, which he would no doubt have appreciated had he been able to see it clearly. Dark circles still underscored his eyes as they had before she left.

'What is wrong?' she asked at once.

'Nothing. Should something be wrong?' He touched his cheek and looked at her defiantly.

'What happened to you while I was away?'

'You sound like my father.'

She frowned at him thoughtfully. This was clearly not the best time to tell him what she had decided, but the matter was urgent. Given fine weather, work on the house might begin again in a few weeks. 'I meant what I said last night.'

Silently, Lamb cut a slice of cheese and began to carve it into narrow strips. As always, his nails were rimmed with ochre and ultramarine.

'I cannot build your perfect house.'

He set down his knife and pushed himself back from the table, flushed and pale at the same time, so that his face was splotched red and white. 'What are you saying?' His voice trembled slightly.

'What we are building is too beautiful, too smoothed, too ordered. It's a beautiful lie.' She met his eyes squarely. 'The house must be the sum of my very own truths. A map of my world, my *mappa mundi*. Since Philip died, my view of the world has changed. I cannot continue to build a false map.'

'But beauty is a greater truth than vulgar daily human truths! It is the ideal truth.'

'We must reflect the reality of deception.'

'Well,' he said. 'I see. Or rather, I don't see. You can't have

338

understood what I tried to teach you about Platonic beauty . . . perfect proportion . . .'

'I believe that I understood, but I now see things differently.'

He blinked several times. Then he leaned and gripped her hands. 'Sister, if we do not believe . . . do not insist on the reality of beauty and order, what is left to us?'

She was startled by the fear in his eyes but clung to her new resolve. 'Like it or not, we're left with Truth, which is often not beautiful. And is often hidden. You, more than anyone, must understand that.'

'If we turn our backs on beauty, all that is left to us is the abyss.'

'And we would be cowards not to acknowledge both.'

He released her hands and leaned back. 'If I keep my eyes closed and don't look down, I might not fall in.'

'If you watch where you are going, you might avoid the brink altogether. Anyway, I won't let you fall.'

He smiled darkly and shook his head. 'Not even you, dearest sister, can spin a rope strong enough to hold me once I go over the edge.'

'Is that a threat?'

'Merely some of your precious Truth!'

'Then you must go farther and tell me what sort of rope you need.'

He dropped his head onto his arms.

Irritation warred with a deep concern at his misery. 'Will you help me reflect the present tenor of my thoughts?'

'And what of all those memories I have already recorded?' asked his muffled voice. 'Lies? Do I scrub them out? Slash the canvases? Take an axe to my panels?'

'Some may still be true. But I've lost the knack of knowing which. I know only that we must find a way to express their unreliability.'

'Please don't do this!' He looked so desperate that she almost changed her mind, just to ease him.

'Don't you see?' she begged. 'Every decision I have made so far, every instruction I have given, was based on a false understanding. How can the result be the microcosm of my true world?'

She imagined trying to live in the present Memory Palace. 'It will still be a marvellous prodigy house. More marvellous than any other. We will merely push our conceit a little farther than most who build.' When he did not reply, she added gently, 'Lamb, it is my life in the house, not yours.'

He looked up at her as if she were a crocodile that had crawled from one of the fishponds. 'But the house is also a part of my life. You know that it's to be my means of making a solid place for myself. My master piece. My introduction to English patrons. My fresh start.'

'It still will be.'

'Not if you insist on a reflection of ugliness and deceit! I have already changed it almost past recognition to suit your previous whim of recording your life. I replaced gods with your tenant farmers and centaurs with pigs! And I didn't protest then, but I do protest now.' He jumped up from the table, knocking over his stool. 'You'll make me a laughing stock!' He left the stool where it had fallen and crossed to the door. 'No matter! I will go back to London and pursue another hopeless cause. If you don't want my plans for your house, you don't want me.'

'Don't be an ass!' Her face was now as splotched as his. 'I need you more than ever!'

He slammed the door so hard that Philip's fishing rod, leaning on the wall beside the door, quivered and fell.

Hellfire and damnation! She stared after him, trembling with anger and astonishment. I knew I should have waited. He never rages like that. Something is badly amiss. But I must make him understand, nevertheless. And keep him from London if I can.

*   *   *

She found him at High House, directing his manservant how to pack his things. 'Please stay! We must not quarrel! Your work is the outward shape of my thoughts.'

He handed his man a red wide-brimmed felt hat. His face was blotched and swollen with weeping. 'Will you raze all that we've built so far?'

'I never said I meant to.'

'A glimmer of light,' he said bitterly. 'Which lies will you keep?' He began to gather a mess of scattered drawings together into a pile.

'We keep the outward appearance of perfection,' she said. 'That which we all strive to show. The façade. Your portico and columns . . .'

Briefly, she remembered making love with Philip for the first time, between two of the columns, when she had foolishly imagined she was beginning to know him.

'And the memories in the halls and staircase, if only to record my credulity. The domestic offices and kitchens, so that we may sleep and eat. But behind it all, nothing must be as it seems.'

Lamb dropped the drawings into a small oak chest. 'And the theatre? The painted shutters, which I have begun to shape? Will you recall Master Quoynt to blow it all up? The theatre deals in beautiful lies, for sure!'

'Don't you see that the theatre and its lies now become the very heart of my conceit? How can we better express the unreliability of the world? We shall make solid rock crack open. The earth must shift under our feet.'

'You're mad,' he said. 'Destroying my only chance to show English society what I can do, merely because your humour has darkened. Because Philip died and unexpectedly made you a rich widow and, instead of rejoicing in your good fortune, you now see the world as some sort of devilish fair ground full of illusion and deceit.' He slammed down the chest lid. 'I can't imagine what you now mean to build!'

'I won't build a monument to your ambition.'

He threw back his head and glared down his beautiful nose. His eyes glittered. 'I never before thought I could dislike you.'

'Because I have never before denied you anything.'

'You think I'm a spoilt brat? You hid it well, madam. All that time I thought you valued my work . . .'

'I still do! Just because I have changed my . . .'

'Indeed, madam! You have changed!'

'Lamb, stop this nonsense!'

'I shall!' He held up a large drawing of a portico column, tore it in two, then dropped the pieces on the floor. 'I shall stop, indeed! I resign. From this very instant, you no longer have a master surveyor. And good fortune to the poor fool who takes my place! I only wish I could watch while you tell the craftsmen what you intend. I see now that you never wished to build my house. Will you keep the original model as a monument to our lies?' He picked up half a column again and crumpled it viciously. 'Madam, you have left me with nothing. Now, please go!'

As he was beyond reason, she went.

51

From Zeal's Work Book – February 1641

Finish trenching and mucking garden

Sow:
  Orach
  Cabbage
  Spinach

Set tarragon slips: and garlic cloves . . .

Fine J. Simms and H. Bull, 2s each, for brawling with M. Dauzat
To M. Dauzat, 5s for torn shirt

Commission a finer nightingale. Engine to start it running?
Cannon balls to make thunder

Hire new masons
Engage new painter, limner and gilder

Write to Master Webb, master builder, to seek his services as master
  surveyor and architect

52

By good fortune, Zeal had kept more of Lamb's work at the lodge than he had at High House. For the next week, she sat each evening turning over his drawings, admiring his light, quick line and noting his taste for feathery curves and dramatic sweeps that warred with his purported goal of perfect proportion and simplicity.

'You have left me with nothing,' he had said.

We see with the same eyes, more than you want to admit, she told him. My poor, dear brother, I fear that things are not going well with your pure new passion. If only you will listen to me, I believe I can restore at least our more innocent passion.

Though she did not entirely understand his bruises, she suspected that he must seek them out for reasons of his own, and that they spoke of danger for him.

Any rope she could offer was better than none. At the least, it might delay his fall.

She wrote to Sir George Tupper in London, though not for a bed. As she owned two lodging houses, she would seize the chance to see for herself how well or ill they were managed.

Sir George accompanied her to three theatre performances, *The Fair Anchoress of Pausilippo* at the Blackfriars and two private masques. What she saw confirmed her belief that theatre was indeed the key to what she now intended.

I must persuade Lamb to rejoin forces. Not only for his sake. I fear that Jonas Stubbs and my master joiner are not equal to my new ambitions without more guidance than I can give them.

'Had the king still had his players at court,' said Sir George later, over supper at his big house on the Thames, 'I might have been able to arrange for you to attend. I myself was fortunate enough to see the last performance of *Salmacida Spolia*. You've come just in time, I fear. Many fierce Puritans want to see all playhouses closed.' He shook his head. 'What will all the poor players do then?'

Zeal nodded, struck by the sudden image of a closed theatre, playing without players, all the same. 'I must speak to your Master Cobb while I am in London.'

'Will you still build a theatre in your new house in defiance of the killjoys?' asked Sir George eagerly, a spiced chicken wing between finger and thumb and a fine linen napkin tucked into his collar. 'An act of admirable courage! But we who know the value of art must fight to keep it alive, don't you think?'

'I had not thought of my ambitions in quite those terms. But, yes, I still mean to build a theatre.'

With his free hand, Sir George raised his glass to her. 'To poetry and illusion!'

'And to music.'

'To all enemies of the new barbarians!'

As Zeal drank the velvety claret, she considered how following one particular purpose can, before you know it, ally you with other purposes you never imagined or intended.

'I would be grateful for directions to the house of your friend, Captain Parsley.'

Sir George grew suddenly sober. 'Young Lamb's father? A friend no longer, I fear. Thinks me a pander for merely entertaining his son. I shall take you there myself in my carriage though I won't descend. I imagine they will be very pleased to see you.' He held out his glass to be refilled. 'Poor Lambkin. It's sad how those sweet fellows often seek out their own retribution.'

Zeal stood appalled, trying not to show her dismay. 'Thank you for agreeing to see me,' she said at last.

Lamb nodded without taking his eyes from the window, where he sat looking down into the street.

His father, an older, paunchy, raddled version of his son, had indeed been pleased, if a little startled to see her. 'Mistress Wentworth. I feared that my son had quarrelled fatally with you, his best friend. Indeed, I don't know . . .' He had stopped distractedly. 'Damnable boy!' Then, with effort, he smiled.

'Are you still angry with me?' Zeal asked Lamb.

He was pale. His red-gold hair had lost its gloss, so that it resembled ravelled orange rope.

'Father didn't tell you?' He gave her a quick glance then turned his eyes to the street again. 'But then, I don't suppose he's telling anyone, unless examined on the rack.'

She could not bear to see him like this. She crossed to stand beside him at the window. 'Darling Lamb! What has happened?'

'You must have guessed that my love affair was broken off.'

She nodded.

'And I've now had such a quarrel with my father!' He turned into her arms and burst into tears.

She stroked his head where it rested against her waist.

He quivered. 'Broke off before Christmas,' said his muffled voice. 'Whilst you were away. I'm afraid I deserted Hawkridge for a few days. Now *his* father's causing terrible trouble. But Ben begged me so prettily . . .'

In time, she got the tale straight.

'With those huge dark innocent eyes,' said Lamb bitterly. 'But he kept pressing me to show him . . . things I had done before I met him. He was excited by the thought of danger, of meeting those low, rough types . . .' He looked up, testing her response. 'I told him I had turned over a new leaf because of my love for him, put all that behind me . . .' He paused, then began to cry again. 'I should never have agreed to take him . . . !'

She continued to stroke his hair. 'Had you been allowed to see him again?' she asked carefully.

He shook his head against her waist. 'But we managed to meet.'

'Whilst I was away at Christmas?'

After a moment, he said, 'And once or twice before.'

Ah, she thought, thinking of those sudden, apparently fruitless, trips in search of lead or pigmented earth.

'I'm a weak swaggering fool . . . I gave in.'

'What went wrong?'

'Matters got out of hand.' He drew a deep shuddering breath. 'He lost his nerve. Struggled too hard. By chance one of his eyes was crushed like an egg!'

He felt her stiffen and lifted his head. 'Now you think that I'm weak and wicked, and deserve to die, just as his father says!'

'His father's wrong.'

'I've also ruined your bodice front.'

But she was not to be diverted. 'What does his father say, apart from blaming you for corrupting his young son, as I've no doubt he's doing?'

'The man has most likely buggered all his pages since the age of twelve,' said Lamb. 'But he means to bring charges against me for the same crime. Treason against Nature, it's called, when the wrong man is caught at it.'

Zeal swallowed. Her mouth was suddenly dry. Lamb was talking about a capital offence. Like it or not, he was looking down.

And I promised not to let him fall, she thought with despair. 'Do you need money to defend your case?'

Lamb shook his head. 'It's enough just to speak with someone who neither swoons or shouts. But thank you. Father is trying to negotiate with Ben's father. My chief hope is that neither is any keener than the other to attract public notice.'

'You must come back to Hawkridge at once!'

'They will find me there, if they want to.'

'It feels farther from the abyss.'

'Zeal, I'm already over the edge.' He looked at her bleakly.

'How can you climb back out?'

He shook his head. 'The chasm is deeper than you can possibly know.'

'I know the pull of the edge,' she said. 'And the seductive ease of giving up.' She began to circle the little parlour. 'You do not deserve to die. It would be a terrible waste of your gifts, apart from all else.' She went back to him and set her hands on his shoulders. 'What sort of rope would you need?'

'I told you. There's none stout enough for me. Only a respectable married man, preferably with a string of children to prove his capacity with a woman would stand a chance in court.'

Zeal swallowed and took her hands away. Her heart began to race. I can't! she told herself. Or I unravel all my last stubborn hopes for John.

But he has been gone for a year and a half. I have seen his letter to Philip. Glimpsed his real perils. Begin to understand the odds against him.

Philip saved me, with the gift of himself. I may have been saved in order to save Lamb.

She paused in front of the blur of a tapestry, as if studying it. What shall I do? she begged. I feel that you're still alive, but no longer close. Where are you?

After those first three letters, nothing. Except his conviction that all will be well. Against the threat of Baulk's lash, or trying to escape recapture and almost certain death.

She clasped her neck with both hands and rocked slightly.

In the side of her eye, Lamb, by the window. Her twin, who had bought her the owl of dark-edged wisdom before they ever met. The brother she had never had, who received her thoughts and gave them outward form. She imagined herself among the friends who hung on his feet, desperate to speed the slow terrible strangulation by the noose. His severed head rolled to stop at her feet, still trying to speak.

He is what I have.

'I came to beg you to reconsider our differences over the Memory Palace. And persuade you that theatre might deserve your talents as well as architecture does.' She stood beside him for some time looking down into the street before she could make herself speak again. 'Would it help if I married you?'

53

For The New Memory Palace:
Master Quoynt to enlarge cellars
Also to make channel to carry water from river above weir to turn
*   an engine wheel*
Also to make new holding tank and pipe to house. Required height
*   above house?*
Also enlarge receiving lagoon
Also, his advice on small explosions
Build fences around his workings and set guards to warn off
*   gawpers*

Timbers to make pipes
A water closet on model of Sir John Harington's Ajax. A goodly
*   cistern to hold water for discharging, to move impurities away by*
*   water*

Stone for arched entrance to theatre, from gardens
Remind plasterers to set eyelets in walls for hanging

A Signor Paroli, painter and gilder – engaged by Lamb from Italy,
*   to complete leather panels in great staircase with scenes of Philip's*
*   escape, as first related*
*   And shutters for theatre stage, following Lamb's designs*

Engage 2 Flemish stone carvers, to be chosen by Lamb
Also 3 Italian woodcarvers, to travel with Signor Paroli
Also 1 assistant to Signor Paroli

22 pounds, 4s. to M. Dauzat, for making mirror glass. Estimated need: 1,500 pieces

Hire assistant to Dauzat who can speak both French and English

Also hire new Clerk of Works

Send to Master Cobb for model of proposed sinking trap (1 inch to 1 foot)

Accept his tender and plans for counterweight system, to work without players

Write again to Master Webb, to say that I no longer lack the services of a surveyor and to thank him for taking trouble to respond to my first letter

54

Back at Hawkridge that spring and summer, Lamb drove himself in a way that alarmed Zeal, who, after a simple witnessed exchange of vows, was now his wife. Marriage had changed nothing in their relationship, except that Lamb moved from High House into Philip's old chamber in the lodge. After some thought and with Lamb's permission, Zeal explained the match to Mistress Margaret, Sir Richard and Rachel. As Lamb had said about his horse, those were the only opinions she cared for. She closed her ears to the rest.

For whatever reason, Lamb had capitulated to her new wishes with what seemed to be a whole heart.

'Men will come to Hawkridge to wonder as they now visit Venice or Rome!' he said more than once as he proudly showed Zeal yet another set of plans or drawings.

To his own surprise, if not to hers, he seemed to relish the freedom from the mathematical constraints of architecture now allowed to him by the fantasies of theatre design. He thrived on the intricacies of masque and pageant.

'You were right,' he told Zeal. 'I shall easily out-do Master Inigo Jones, the designer of masques, if not Master Jones, the architect. That man hasn't an original bone in his body. I saw most of his stage designs in Italy five years ago.'

The tricks of theatre soon escaped the actual theatre in the new west wing and spread through the new cellars. Surprises and illusions also sprang up throughout the house, amongst the memories. A mechanical moving tableau in the hall from Master Cobb replaced the painting of John's departure. Clockwork birds arrived from Italy, including a nightingale that at last satisfied Zeal. A musical fountain was planned for the forecourt. Lamb conceived a wonderful false sky for the ceiling of the hall, to be filled with clouds and flying birds.

'And that deception, dear sister-wife, will arise from pure art, not mechanical tricks! And Paroli is just the man to execute it. I know my own limits.'

'From time to time,' Zeal agreed dryly. 'Do you know a man who can also make the birds appear to sing? One can have joyous deception as well as alarming surprises.'

'Even in your Underworld?' he asked. 'For that is what we are now building in those new pits made by Master Quoynt.'

They still clashed from time to time, but carefully. Lamb was resolved, for instance, that in her Underworld of deception, which had grown beyond the limits of the original theatre, she must make a labyrinth, a single twisting path that arrived inevitably at its goal. Zeal insisted on a true maze, full of misleading turns and dead ends.

'Mazes are out of fashion among the *cognoscenti*,' he said. 'When life is so disordered, where is the pleasure or entertainment in yet more wilful misdirection and confusion?'

'In the satisfaction of reflecting truthfully the plight of the human soul,' she retorted.

'You must include a little hope! We must believe that one foot placed in front of the other will get us there in the end.'

Rather than deny him the possibility of hope, she agreed to consider further before making a final decision.

In late May, Lamb's father sent word that his negotiations had failed. Master Neame, Ben's father, had decided to press charges after all.

Lamb began to draw every day and into the nights, using Philip's candle stand. He designed sliding shutters for her theatre. Profiles for the posts in her new interior maze or labyrinth, whichever it proved to be. Designs for further painted leather panels in the great staircase. Corbels, arches, cupboards. Banisters, shelves for the new kitchens. Window latches, mirror frames. Paroli and his assistant even painted panels pretending to be windows with cats or flowers on their ledges, or mimicking half-open doors, for the attics, to cheer the grooms and maids who would one day sleep there.

Lamb had friezes made for the hall and corridors. For both speed and verisimilitude, he had the plasterers experiment with real tree branches as a base for moulding the relief of a plaster forest, which would one day grow in the new entrance hall.

He designed a small pavilion for the new bridge across the Shir. 'A place for elevated reflections,' he said. 'In which to recover from your fiendish house.'

He also made drawings for figures to set around the ponds. He sent to Italy for engravings. But none of these possibilities seemed right to Zeal.

'It's like trying to replace a lost lover or child,' she said, pushing aside a set of The Muses. 'Everything else is a poor substitute.'

The Muses had been taken from her. How had John felt, she wondered, when the king took back the land he had given, the first land John had ever owned, after so many years of serving others.

She frowned briefly at a pride of fantastical beasts, then pushed them aside as well.

But, unlike her, John had earned his land. His reward for multiplying the king's money by a successful venture in tulip bulbs in the Low Countries. And with the land, he had earned and then lost the right to be called a gentleman. Far worse than losing mere statues.

Slowly, she began to turn over a set of exotic figures from distant lands, a Moor, an East Indian princess. She paused at an engraving labelled 'The West Indies – a Native Carib Woman'. A half-naked female figure with long flowing hair, her skin delicately cross-hatched to show that she should be carved from dark stone.

She's strange but beautiful all the same, Zeal thought uneasily.

'How does it feel to love John Nightingale?' asked Lamb, with one of his accurate sideways leaps that delighted Zeal. 'Tell me how true love feels.'

Zeal thought for a long time. 'Easy,' she said. 'It felt easy.'

I used the past tense, she thought unhappily. It doesn't feel easy now.

'Then I was up to something else,' said Lamb.

Their eyes met briefly in the unspoken fear that time might be short.

The arrival of Paroli, with his assistant and the three Italian Catholic woodcarvers had provoked Jonas Stubbs into resigning as master mason.

'Hiring England's enemies! This is an ungodly house you're building! And I'm not alone in thinking so,' he told Zeal. 'Old Sir George . . .' He shook his head. 'Not even Master John would have tolerated . . .'

Although increased wages for Stubbs and his team of masons overcame their moral and political objections, the episode left Zeal uneasy. 'I should have foreseen such difficulties,' she told Lamb.

When Francis Quoynt had returned in May, he and his explosions had attracted almost as many onlookers as on his earlier visit. The parish was soon divided on what was thought to be happening and what was thought of it. Stubbs and his men no doubt contributed their own opinions. Zeal's guards often had to see off those determined to invade the building site to see for themselves.

'Don't you understand that you could easily be injured?' Zeal demanded of four Bedgebury boys who had been marched to the lodge for a scolding.

'Not me,' said one eleven-year-old. 'My mother gave me a charm against the evil eye.'

55

Letter from Zeal Parsley to Doctor Bowler, May 1641.

My Dearest Friend, I take great pleasure in telling you that I am building a small theatre in the new house, which is now dubbed the Memory Palace, for reasons which will become clear to you when you return. You shall have a temple dedicated to music and to all the other Muses who make life tolerable in the times of greatest darkness and sorrow. It will be, however, much more than a simple platform for players. You must wait to know more. I, too, can torment with surprises.

Meanwhile, England is become an uneasy place. Though I miss you and your music, I would not have you rush back before you have quenched your thirst for opera and all the other wonders of Venice. I hope only that the wonders are not so great that they will keep you from us forever. You and I can both take a little satisfaction in knowing that Jamie is at last where he belongs. I am pleased that you have found him such a good teacher and that his voice seems not to be breaking. I pass all his news privately to his mother. His father still glares and spits whenever he sees me. Which seems small gratitude for the gift of a freehold farm, but I dare say he does not understand that his son was lost to the soil long before we are supposed to have abducted him.

Have you yet enough money? Your loving friend, Zeal . . .

She hesitated, then wrote 'Wentworth'. There would be time enough to explain the complexities surrounding her new married name after Bowler returned.

56

Also in May, Sir George Tupper wrote from London to Zeal, with whom he had continued to correspond as his ally in the battle against the new barbarians.

My Dearest Madam, I can bear to listen only to sombre music, such as Dowland's 'Tears'. My own stage is now kept as dark as those of the court. The king signed the death warrant of his chief favourite, Strafford. The man's head is already off. Whilst I do not mourn him as a friend – he put down the Irish most violently while governor there – this death fills me with foreboding. None of us is safe when a man of note is sacrificed by his sovereign to appease the mob. Though you know how my sympathies lie, I am nonetheless shamed as an Englishman to hear a mob howling for the blood of any woman, even though she be a Catholic and foreign-born. And I am shamed for a monarch who sees no solution but to hand over a faithful servant to save his wife.

I hope your small theatre continues to progress well, in defiance of London. I visited Master Cobb's workshop on your behalf and inspected your sinking trap as well as the engine of ingenious displacement. The man is a genius. Italy does not hold finer. When your project is done, I shall beg an invitation to visit and see what you have wrought. If we place not our faith in kings, will poets, players and composers serve instead, do you think?

57

'Have you a portrait of Nightingale?' Lamb asked one day in August.

'Why?'

'Never you mind. You'll learn in time.'

Zeal lent him a double portrait of John and Harry, painted when John was fifteen and Harry twelve. In it, Harry, blond and rosy-cheeked, posed as if about to draw his sword. John, taller and darker, stood holding his horse, one hand resting lightly on its muzzle, looking squarely into the painter's eyes.

'Take care,' she said. 'It's my only image of him.'

'I must do you a triple portrait one day. To make your *mappa mundi* complete.' He flicked her a glance. 'Harry, Philip and me.'

'But I still have you.'

There was a small silence.

'And so you do, for the moment,' said Lamb. 'Though I don't know why you want me.'

'Don't speak like that. I could not bear to lose you too! And you have your master piece to finish.'

That September, John had been gone for two years with no further word. Five more years of unease to be survived. She did not know if that was a short time or eternity. Since Philip died, she had felt more and more that she experienced life as if lit by flashes of lightning. Between these clear, unnaturally sharp glimpses, she trudged forwards through the demands of each day, each like the one before and the one to come, with her head down, looking only at her own feet, trying to stay on her chosen path. She felt a crack opening in her world that she had no power to mend. In spite of what she had said to Lamb, she had begun to fear what she might see if she looked down over the edge.

Shortly after her marriage to Lamb, another anonymous letter had been shoved under the lodge door, addressed in the same writing as the others. She had almost been expecting it. Neither she nor Lamb needed to let its words into their heads. She left it lying on a window ledge for two days. Then she put it in the fire, unopened. As it flared, she felt a small sense of victory. If she burned them all, from now on, sooner or later the writer must grow weary and leave her alone.

She had to lift her head again when a foraging army unit made the first raid.

58

The king's quartermaster gave her a list.

'You can't take all this,' Zeal protested. 'We'll have nothing left to feed ourselves this winter!'

'Bring it, or we'll forage for it.'

Sickened, she took him to Tuddenham and handed over the list. 'What we don't have, we don't have,' she said. The steward nodded without meeting her eye, but she was certain that he understood. What they had was what could be seen. It did not include the sheep on the far side of Hawkridge, nor the hens in a second run, built upstream above the falls, in a clearing above the water meadows. Nor the bales of wool in the loft above her chamber, which she was keeping under her own eyes. However, it did include the forty loaves that Mistress Margaret had just baked, twenty bags of flour and the yeast sponge.

Zeal made a second list while the carts were loaded.

'I need a receipt,' she said, as the last two bleating sheep were heaved onto a cart. Two bullocks jittered on their tethers at the tail of another. The four carriage horses had already been led away up the drive.

The quartermaster laughed. 'What good will a receipt do you? I don't give receipts.'

'I want a receipt,' she repeated. 'For the estate accounts. And because I refuse to believe that the king is a thief. I'm certain that once he has restored civil order, he will want to make good his debts.' She held out her own list. 'Please see that this is correct. And then, sign it.'

The man scratched his ear, shifted his weight, then decided

to humour her.

When the soldiers had gone, Zeal went to the bake house and stood looking at the empty shelves, which had recently held forty loaves of bread.

'Have they gone?' asked Mistress Margaret, peering through the door.

Zeal nodded. 'The bread is nothing. We could bake again. But they left nothing for us to bake with, either.' She sat heavily on a stool. 'I must go ask Mistress Wilde if she can spare a little yeast. And Sir Richard's steward might give us some flour until we can mill more of our own. Unless his has all been taken too.'

Mistress Margaret hobbled into the kitchen. 'Close your eyes.'

'Another one who likes surprises,' said Zeal. 'I would like some comfortable certainties.' But she obeyed.

'Smell!' ordered Mistress Margaret.

Zeal inhaled the scent of raw yeast and opened her eyes.

Mistress Margaret beamed and managed to look crafty at the same time. 'If they take flour, they take the yeast. As soon as I saw them coming, I took half the sponge under my shawl and hid it along the track to High House.'

Survival is the sum of such small victories, thought Zeal. Then she trudged on through the rest of the autumn, until Christmas, when everything changed again.

59

In mid-December, Sir Richard had returned in a gloomy mood from London, where Parliament had now been sitting for just over a year.

'Stay away from the place,' he warned Zeal and Lamb. 'No more visits to the theatre. Not even you, young man. It's a bad place to be just now. Armed bands roaming everywhere. Mobs. Saw some of those fine *caballeros,* who claim to ride for the king, charge at a group of unarmed men and women, just for shouting abuse. And that's all I care to say.'

'At least those fine *caballeros* don't tear down paintings and smash statues and the organs in churches,' Lamb muttered under his breath.

Sir Richard also brought word from Lamb's father that Neame's case against him had been delayed by the political confusion.

'Thereby extending my exile.'

To Zeal's ears, Lamb spoke in earnest.

Over Christmas dinner at High House, after much wine, Sir Richard's tongue loosened enough for him to allow that in November he had joined in a fierce debate in Parliament.

'I merely asked the man if he meant to curb the king or bring him down, and he tore off my scarf in rage.' He drained his glass and held it out for more. 'So I grabbed him by the hair, an insult that he could not return.' He ran a hand over his glowing bare dome.

Zeal's mind seized onto the words '. . . bring him down . . .'

'Whatever was the cause of such terrible rage?' asked Mistress Margaret.

'Pym!' exclaimed Sir Richard, as if the name were an exple-
tive. 'Hampden, Holles, Strode and Hazelrig!'

'Friends or foes?' Zeal asked, suddenly uncertain what
those words might mean.

Sir Richard glared. 'The curs wanted to try the queen for
treason as a Catholic!'

'And did they prevail?'

Sir Richard laughed darkly. 'Someone shouted
"gunpowder!" and all those brave ministers of Parliament
trampled each other in their rush to escape. But at least we
guaranteed that we meet! The king can no longer play his
old trick of holding us at bay.'

Zeal stopped trying to work out where the old knight stood
in his loyalties. She kept repeating to herself, his earlier words
'. . . bring him down.' She had not thought until now that
the king might ever fall.

She wanted to leap up from the table and run home to
Hawkridge to look with fresh eyes. She had to be certain that
she had not, from hopelessness, lost track of her earlier
purpose in making the Memory Palace, that of leaving traces
of her journey from one self to another.

Lamb is right. I must create a labyrinth, with a single path
leading from start to finish, with no risk that the pilgrim will
lose his way, if he chooses to proceed.

Slowly, she warned herself. Don't jump ahead of the facts.
But at that moment, Zeal declared firmly and irrevocably for
Parliament, even if some of its members tore down pictures
and destroyed church organs.

Perhaps, if Pym, Hampden, Holles, Strode and Hazelrig
have their way, she might not have to wait seven years after
all.

I don't suppose I'm the first to turn traitor to my king from
love, she thought.

That night she saw John again. Underwater, smiling and
mouthing at her.

Why have you left me for so long? she asked him. Why have you not answered my letters? Have you somehow learned of Philip and Lamb? Please come back!

She could not hear him, nor make him understand her, but she clearly saw his long naked limbs languidly carving the water. Enamelled orange and blue fish swam around him. She reached for his hand to try to pull him out. He was too deep. Then she rose, or else he sank. The distance between their hands grew greater and greater.

'Swim!' she screamed. 'Swim this way! Catch hold of my hand.'

He smiled and sank out of sight. When she woke, she was sobbing.

Zeal and Lamb now pressed the builders to work even faster, leaving the delights of the theatre and the Underworld, for the moment, in order to finish the domestic wing and sleeping quarters. Zeal used the unfinished parts of the new Underworld cellars as temporary storage for food, ale and wool, disguised by random piles of brick and timber. She also wanted time to consider what further changes she might make to the house, knowing that John might perhaps return after all, to read her map.

She kept one dark thought locked away in a chest. She did not even let herself look at the chest. But inside it, crouched the terrible, inadmissible possibility that Lamb might still be tried and executed.

If John returns, and still wants me, she told herself, I shall simply run away with him as if I weren't married at all. Who in Barbados or Nevis would ever know?

1642

60

Sir Richard came back again unexpectedly early in January 1642 to set up his falconnet so that its range of fire covered the drive from the main road to High House. When Arthur brought Zeal this astonishing news, she visited at once.

'War has begun in the London streets,' said Sir Richard, who was in a large closet off the courtroom, making an inventory of the High House armoury. 'The king invaded Parliament and tried to arrest some of the Members. They escaped but you can't imagine the furore. You should have heard the shouts of "Traitor!" directed at the king himself!' He shook his head in disbelief. 'On my way home, I was almost scalded by a pot of boiling water meant for some of the king's soldiers. There are barricades across the streets. And cannon.'

He frowned at a stook of muskets and sat down on a stool to wipe his face. 'I do wish Philip was still here.' He looked at Zeal. 'Oh, my dear, I fear I must raise a company of men.'

'To fight on which side?'

Sir Richard tugged his handkerchief by the corners. 'It challenges a man's ingenuity to try to stay a loyal Englishman.' He twirled the kerchief into a rope, then untwirled it again. 'I think it must be for Parliament until the king comes to his senses.'

Perhaps because of this war, the court in London at its Easter sitting threw out Master Neame's charges against Lamb.

'Free to return to London, at last!' Lamb smiled at Zeal's expression. 'Don't worry, sis, I won't desert you before the house is done.'

61

On the 22 August 1642, King Charles raised his standard at Nottingham against Parliamentary forces.

'He's been badly advised!' cried Mistress Margaret when the news eventually reached them weeks later. 'War against his own people! It's that French queen of his. Send her back to France, I say!'

Sir Richard, when they saw him, which was now seldom, had begun to look thinner and pinched in the face. 'Oh, madam,' he said on this occasion, having, in fact, been the source of the news. 'I would it were so simple.'

'Where do you stand now?' Zeal asked him bluntly.

Sir Richard pulled his side-whiskers. 'With Mistress Margaret on the matter of advisors, at least. Many of the Parliament forces want only to rescue the king from those Catholic traitors who have misled him . . . as good as abducted him, I'm told. But we'll soon have him safely back, you'll see. Before Christmas if only we had better generals.'

Gifford now attacked the king openly in his sermons, as an enemy of England and the English people. The death of his wife from a canker seemed not to soften him but to increase his rage.

Before he next left for London, Sir Richard gave Zeal the key to the High House armoury, kept in a large closet off the courtroom.

'Not much left in it,' he said. 'A few old pikes and half a dozen muskets. But you never know.'

Zeal looked at the floor and prayed for Sir Richard and

his friends to fail still in their rescue plans.

She almost forgave the cost to Hawkridge of the king's war, in the continued loss of precious food and supplies to both foraging armies. Even more disastrously, the men and boys were taken to fight. She had enough money to survive the time it would take to replace food and supplies, but had no one to do the work. By September 1642, Hawkridge had lost two house grooms, two kitchen grooms, four shepherds, two cowmen, one stable boy, both of the under-gardeners (one of whom had also served as fish man) and Tuddenham's son, Will, who was being groomed by his father to take over as steward of the estate. Bedgebury village and the Wildes at Far Beeches fared just as badly. Sir Richard had already mustered all his own able-bodied men.

That's my single consolation for John's absence, thought Zeal. If he were here, he would be called to fight.

Those who escaped mustering did so only for a reason. The head shepherd was fifty-four and losing the strength in his left side. The smith was rejected for lacking two fingers. The head joiner, likewise, had the traditional carpenter's short ration of digits. The Hawkridge mason, Jonas Stubbs, swore that he could not see beyond the reach of his short muscular arm. But Arthur was taken, to fight for Parliament, and for a time, Zeal feared that she might as well have lost Rachel as well, through distraction.

Work on the new house slowed to half pace, even with the hiring of more foreign labour. She lacked men to keep watch over the workings at night to deter the curious. Only Dauzat and his enlarged army of Huguenot glaziers marched steadfastly forward. By September, they had set glass in all windows on the first two floors of the east domestic wing. Freed from his furnace by Zeal's purchase of a quantity of Norfolk glass, Dauzat also busied himself like an alchemist with experimental brews of silver and of mercury salts to use for making mirror glass.

Lamb drove the remaining masons, joiners, plasterers, tilers and white smiths to close in and make habitable the domestic wing, with its several sleeping chambers, a first floor parlour, numerous places of easement including Sir John Harington's Ajax incarnate, the kitchens, and the domestic offices. Sir Richard, and others, had already given beds to the needy for two and a half years. Over-crowding did not grow easier to bear with time.

'We must be accommodated in the new house by Christmas!' said Zeal. 'Another winter like the last two and everyone will go mad.'

Before living again in her own house, she had to replace the house grooms, Geoffrey and Peter, and the two kitchen grooms, as well as the laundry maid who had married an alien mason and moved all the way to Windsor. While not needed to help look after a large house, Agatha had gone to a niece in Portsmouth. She had written in July to say that her niece's husband had joined the king's forces, and that she herself would stay on in Portsmouth until the latest child was born.

Meanwhile, sheep developed scab, hay rotted uncut, the mill turned only part-time, holes in hedges expanded, and all the autumn sowings and transplantings were late. In the absence of the men, women had to turn their hands to unaccustomed work.

Then, even for his enhanced wages, Jonas Stubbs refused flatly to work any longer with Lamb, whom he accused of insulting him, or with any of the increased number of Italians, Flemings and French who now crowded the workmen's encampment and stirred up alien smells from their cooking pots. After negotiating bitterly with Zeal, he left with what he was owed but no more.

It's just as well that I'm replacing muscle with engines in my theatre, Zeal thought. There will be no one left to operate the mechanisms.

She imagined how it would ease her problems if she could discuss them with John, as she had done when he was helping to run the estate. Lamb was distracted by the house and the need to replace mustered workmen. Often he did not hear her when she spoke to him.

Then he made a trip to Southampton in search of a particularly fine sort of sailcloth. When he returned empty-handed but in the dangerously high spirits that she remembered from their visit to London, she told him, 'You're mad!'

When he merely laughed and did not ask her what she meant, she knew she had guessed right.

62

Zeal's Work Book – September 1642

<u>*For the training up of new maids*</u>

<u>*House maids:*</u>

Shake feather beds and air them against dampness, each day
Note stitching on same and make good all that is loose or undone
Shake all table carpets, some each day
Strew green herbs on floors (tansy, mint, balm, fennel) and rub well all over floor with hard brush. When dry, sweep off greens and rub well with polishing brush. Each morning do some part of floors as they grow dirty exceedingly fast
Each day, remove all grease blots with fuller's earth, as you find them
Every Saturday, whisk all window curtains and bed hangings
Every Friday, brush all places dust might settle with goose wing or soft brush. Not forgetting above the doors. Brush picture frames, but not the paintings
Each Wednesday, help laundry maid to fold linens
Each morning, sweep down soot when fires have been lit
Each morning, empty pots in all places of easement, into slops bucket and give this to under-gardener. Keep mop in cupboard with pot and use warm water to wash pots clean
Sweep attics three times a week
To church each Sunday. Thereafter tend to own affairs

Kitchen maids:

Keep the fires small until needed. Guard against taking of embers
  except by cook
Help with baking on Wednesday and Saturday
Scour cooking pots well with sand or horsetail
Keep great cistern full from pump in yard
Fill hog pails with leavings from table . . .

Zeal or Mistress Margaret would have to read these lists out to the new women. She made two notes before they slipped her mind:

Also, dairymaid to help with milking until new cowman is found
All women to help in gardens and fields when not needed elsewhere

It's all impossible, Zeal thought. I allowed for everything but war. And for Lamb. She had a sense of unravelling and could not hook up the running stitch again.

63

Letter from Sir George Tupper to Mistress Zeal Parsley, 12 October 1642.

My Dear, I send this with a loyal fellow whose discretion I can trust. We must take care now how we expose ourselves in the written word. This is a temporary farewell. As I am too old to fight, and like neither side better than the other, I shall leave England for Italy in a very few days. The barbarians have broken down the gates. That is to say that a little more than a week ago, by Parliamentary Ordinance, all plays have been banned. The play-houses are closed. Poor, poor Melpomene, Thalia and Polymnia! I fear, too, for their sister muses.

I confess that I also fear for my household, as my poor old cook was badly beaten in the streets for the sin of feeding me, a declared and notorious sybarite, and some of my windows have been broken. I mean to send my people, with what little they can carry by way of pictures and other effects to the relative safety of my house in Kent – if they can escape the barricades which now enclose London. I pray that you will be kept safe and do not lose heart nor faith in the spirit of man. We are but flies to the gods, but I mean to die in my own time as a fly of discrimination and taste. I remain your faithful friend, George Tupper.

64

'I've decided. I must go to London again.' Lamb squared the edges of his papers.

'But you read what Sir George wrote,' Zeal protested. 'Remember Sir Richard's warnings.'

'I shall wear my soberest Protestant face.'

'Will you try to see Ben again?'

'Again?' He looked at her in challenge. 'I'm forbidden to see him. Had you forgot?' He had not answered her question. 'And his father's charges against me were dismissed. There's no reason why I shouldn't go.'

And what if his father is doubly aggrieved by his defeat in law? Zeal thought. And suspects that you are still meeting his son. What if he still seeks release for his rage, like Roger Wentworth?

'What if you are enrolled as a soldier?' she asked.

'Then I could please my father at last by dying a valiant death.' Lamb stared from the window. 'In fact, Sir George's letter decided me. This may be my last chance. I can bring back any finished work from Master Cobb. And I must buy more ochre and turpentine, and new brushes for Signor Paroli. And I shall tell my father how well married life in the country is suiting me.'

'We can survive without ochre and turpentine.'

'You might be able to,' he said. 'Paroli and I will die.'

'Be careful!' she begged him when he prepared to ride away two days later. 'I could not bear it if anything happened to you.'

He's what I have left, she thought as she watched the beech

avenue swallow him. Then she remembered saying exactly that to Philip, and went to the office to lean her forehead against John's coat for luck.

1643

65

My Dearest Doctor Bowler (Zeal wrote) *In reply to your joyful report of your operatic adventures in Venice, I wish I were not forced to send the sad news that our darling Lamb has been killed. Whilst in London – against all advice . . . I can hardly bear to write it . . . he was beaten to death. Although one of the constables swears that it was no more than a common brawl, his father insists that he was murdered by hired ruffians, to settle a personal score. The guilty villains have been neither named nor arrested and seem likely to escape.*

The estate seems unbearably quiet without him, or Philip. Sometimes I feel that most of all I miss your music. We all miss the music, and both your voices. After you left for Venice, Doctor Gifford might have been tempted to claim a successful rout of the Antichrist from Hawkridge, had he not been distracted by the iniquity of the king. He is more sour than ever since the death of his wife – with a canker, I believe, though I do not enquire of the man and he no longer essays correspondence with me since that last visit after Philip died.

The new house and its theatre now stand almost finished as a monument to Lamb's genius, and to the generosity with which he applied it. I will say no more but that the plan is somewhat changed since you last saw the model. When you return to us at last, dear friend, I think you will understand very well the new antic face that now hides behind the original Olympian posturing. And you will wish to help me fill the terrible silence that is now its only shortcoming as a true reflection and microcosm of the world.

There is still no word of John, though I now dare hope that, with our new disorders of war, he might dare return to England if he is still alive. Please give my warmest greetings to Jamie, and my congratulations on his elevation to chorister at San Marco. Lest you find yourselves in need, or Jamie requires a new gown or livery, I enclose a bond written in your name and the address of a Venetian goldsmith who will honour it. Your most loving friend – Zeal Parsley.

It has happened again, she thought as she read the letter over before sending it. Another man I loved has died.

66

First, she gathered together Lamb's paints and brushes, his stacks of papers, his Italian pencils of *piombino* wrapped in string, his pens and inks. She began the pile of what she would keep with a portfolio of engravings and drawings from Italy.

Doing the easy part first.

She opened his clothing press. Yet again, she inhaled the scent of a man who no longer existed. His true odour, faint under the insistence of orange blossom and musk, curled out of the press, a miasma trying to assume a shape that no longer lived on the earth.

She stacked his shirts on the bed to give to any males still employed on the estate, to wear or to sell as they pleased. His manservant would have the green silk suit and perhaps the workaday woollen breeches as well. She touched his hats, his razors, scent bottles, gloves, collars, sashes, belts, stockings and boots. She had told his father's messenger that she did not want the clothes in which he had been killed. Captain Parsley had insisted, however, that all the pictures and statues collected by Lamb in Italy but stored in London, were also now hers, as well as his large collection of books, his annuity, three horses, and share of an investment in an East Indian trading voyage.

She suddenly felt too weary to continue. She picked up the small bronze figure of David, set it down. She gazed at the painting by Buontalenti, which was now hers. Then she touched the model of the ideal house, which he had given her with such pride.

His big oak cupboard held the tiny working models of her machinery. The gifts of a generous spirit, eager to forgive and to give again. She lifted out the first version of the singing nightingale, whose grandchild adorned the entrance hall. This one now looked ungainly, and its wings refused to open. She pulled the pin of the small scale sand trap, one fifth its final size and watched the flow begin, that would finally tilt the mechanism into delayed action.

Next she took out a model of Cobb's sinking trap, felt the wooden flap fall away beneath her fingertip. Watched the opening close again as the counterweight fell.

Lamb, if you weren't dead, I'd kill you myself for being so careless with your life.

I think I saw it coming.

She had known her husband better than anyone imagined.

You had too much that you thought you did not deserve, and not enough of what you truly wanted, which I could never give to you, no matter how hard I tried.

That look in his eyes, reserved, amused and dark. Even with her, his sister-wife, he was still lonely.

Now there's a truth for me to chew on.

She shook her head and gave a quick 'hhnh!' of unhappy laughter, so that a passer-by might have taken her for one of those mad wandering souls who argue aloud with themselves. Now she saw the models, like all of his last feverish work, as Lamb's apology to her for making her not enough.

She set his boots on the floor beside the bed so his man-servant could take his pick. His rapier and dagger she kept for herself.

His money chest was locked. When he was killed, Lamb's pockets had been picked and his keys taken from his belt to make the attack look like simple robbery. After a few moments of pulling at the iron straps, she sent for the smith to remove the hinges.

The chest held only a small purse containing some gold angels, an ivory fan, a box carved from a soapy black stone, and a long pewter box which held two dozen Italian matches. Under those lay a small watercolour portrait of Benjamin Neame. There was also a sheaf of letters with a pressed rose, not yet fully dry, inserted carefully under the blue ribbon.

Her hand went to the letters at once. She turned them over. Sniffed. Civet and rose with an undertone of cinnamon. The writing on the top letter looked fresh. The paper had not yellowed.

What he had hidden from her now sat in her hands. Things she did not understand.

'*Merde!*' she said.

After another moment, she took one of the matches and burnt the letters in his fireplace.

The black stone box held a small lumpy linen-wrapped packet and another letter, addressed in Philip's hand, to her. On the back, lightly written with one of Lamb's Italian pencils but in Philip's hand was the note: *I leave it to your discretion, PW.*

For a moment, she was angry again at their conspiracy to keep her in ignorance. Her anger included John's terrible letter to Philip. Then she began to read.

My Dearest Zeal, My Wife, My sweet Friend, I must tell you all. Yet if I myself cannot live with the truth, how can I ask you to show more courage than I?

Her eyes raced ahead, skipped, stumbled. She folded the letter and tucked it into her sleeve. With eyes down and face set to tell anyone she met that she was not to be stopped, she left the house and climbed the hanger to the Lady Tree. She had no further expectations of the estate oracle, but knew that the tree was sure to be deserted in daylight. She wanted perfect solitude for what she already knew was to come.

. . . I fear you will hate me . . . no, I fear that you will feel such profound revulsion that all your tender memories of me (which

383

are my best monument on earth) will turn to horror. The worst – that you will wipe all traces of me from your mappa mundi.

She had delayed by deciding just where to sit. At last she chose a coppiced stump from which the young sprouting poles had been harvested on one side only so that it grew like a chair of grace, half-surrounding her with delicate walls of green just turning to copper. From her throne, she could see the bones of the bird still white against the grey bark of the Lady Tree. Even then, she delayed, convinced for a time that she had been followed.

. . . In the end, I choose the truth, because I know that you will hate me more if you should ever discover that I deceived you further. Also, you seem to have released in me a secular urge to confess. I have asked Lamb to hold this letter back until the heat of your first response to my death and its aftermath has passed.

Some of what I told you was true, in those delicious evenings with your head on my shoulder and the scent of your hair in my nose. What I told you of my first wife was true. Thereafter, in the manner of all travellers, I both embroidered to make a good story better and borrowed from other men's experience. But the bones of my story still stand. We were driven aground, however, not anchored, and took to our pinnace. We found a native city very near where I showed you on the map, and we took away gold. Only in one matter did I . . .

Here, he had written and crossed out so many attempts to capture the exact word so that the paper had turned black with ink.

Only in one matter did I lie. There. 'Tis said. I shall pause here and write empty words while you decide whether or not to continue with my confession. If you would keep whatever good opinion you might still have of me, stop reading now, I beg you.

What did he imagine I would make of that first great lie about his very life?

Or did he imagine that vast wealth would serve as a draught of the River Styx and make her, like the newly dead, forget all that had gone before? However benign his intentions, and however grateful she might be, the fact remained that he had injured her faith in her own ability to judge the truth.

Rather than lose what I have left of him as a man, I shall take him at his word and stop reading.

She tore the letter in half. Then she smoothed the two halves on her knee. She lifted her head. Something had moved in the corner of her eye.

A bird dropping from a branch, she decided. She set the two pieces of paper side by side again.

Our capture was much as I told you. The golden pageant beside the lake could well have been as I said, for I saw the several parts of it played out in different places on earlier ventures – through which I also made my fortune. El Dorado lived. His minions wore golden breastplates and greaves, just as I told you. I saw such head-dresses. The rest, I was told by reliable witnesses. Only the final sacrifice took a different shape.

It was common knowledge throughout the New World that these Indians offered human blood to their gods, but I never saw it. An innocent feast was planned for the night of our capture, as I told you. We took advantage of the confusion of the preparations and the amounts of liquor drunk by the revellers, to snatch some booty and escape. Twelve of us achieved freedom, including young Master Dunne, Sir John Whitfield's nephew, whom I said falsely had his heart cut out to feed the god.

I don't know how to proceed . . .

Our ship had broken up on the rocks. However, the pinnace remained on the beach. We took to the sea in it.

We were desperate men, fleeing north along an unknown coast, in a craft too small for our number, hoping to reach the Floridas, and then to follow that coast north until we reached a French or English settlement. We had no guns, no means of hunting. We tried to catch fish with our bare hands, sucked the shells of sand crabs, made ourselves ill by eating strange leaves and roots. Four men died and were left in shallow graves where we could find sand to dig. Then two more died. In all our minds were the tales of other expeditions, when men walked the same sharp edge of desperation. We accepted that none of us would survive without some great change in our luck. When the next of our number died, we cast a vote. There was no dissent as to how we might use this chance to bend our fate. We cooked and ate him.

But what comes next will at last answer your question as to why I hid myself from the world and cut myself off from the man I had once been. We ate him and with renewed strength, made good progress. With the wind at our backs, our pinnace cleared the rocks and whirlpools of the Florida Straits and set us on the last leg of our journey. A long leg, to be sure, bedevilled by storms and equally devastating doldrums. We lost our sails, most of our oars and depended utterly on the current to carry us. As I told you, two of us survived. I have killed men in the course of duty, but none of them troubles me so much as young Master Dunne. You may surmise the rest, for even in my confessional humour I cannot write it.

Forgive me for making you my confessor (in the non-Catholic sense of the word, I hasten to say, in case any other eyes than yours should read this. I fear that the time may have come when a man can burn for his vocabulary.) You gave me a gift at the end of my life that I neither expected nor deserved. I have learned that the best of life can be as ferocious as the worst. And that healing is not a slow, gentle process, as many would have it, but a leap into belief of both body and soul. I came to Hawkridge in search of the slow healing. You were my leap.

Your loving and grateful husband – Piscator.

She left her green throne and climbed higher to sit on the ground with her back against the Lady Tree, where she had thought to take root the night she accepted his proposal of marriage.

I always knew, she thought. Or something of this magnitude. Now she saw all the evidence that she had wilfully ignored. His refusal to come to table. That he ate no flesh, but only fish. His flight from the wedding meats. His troubled study of Jamie before accepting the wedding crown.

An executioner, a murderer. He had claimed both roles for an adventurer.

She had known that no trivial transgression would drive a man of Philip's force and keen wits into self-imposed exile in his own country.

I'm so sorry, she told him. I suspected, yet was still merciless. In my ignorance, I was excited by the sense of dangerous mystery.

How he must have suffered, knowing that in trying to satisfy her hunger for truth, he committed the one sin she would not forgive.

How clever you were, my love, to show me just enough indignity and guilt to make me trust the rest.

Looking back, she saw how often he himself had questioned the reality of what he told her, and how fervently she had explained why it must be true.

Suffering or not, you did worse than deceive me. You induced me to collude in my own deception.

She wiped her eyes. Then she sat staring into space, thinking of the blank panels on the staircase. She had Philip's truth and did not know what to do with it. She felt it already re-shaping something in her, as it must also reshape the Memory Palace.

I know already that I will have an inscription set over the entrance to the new forecourt: *Homo vult decipi, ergo decipiatur.*

Man wishes to be deceived, and so he will be.

She had still one more piece of evidence to examine.

She returned to the lodge and opened the lumpy little parcel. It was a tiny golden jaguar.

A slip of paper fell from the wrappings. *The people who made this*, wrote Philip, . . . *believe that their healers, whom they call in Spanish, <u>curanderos</u>, assume this form to consult the gods. It has always belonged to you.*

She gave a little moan and held the creature against her heart.

67

Zeal's Work Book – March 1643

A Giant Mask of stone for Philip's Grotto Below, to my own design. Take stone from our own quarry. Trust local masons?

To Master Quoynt, for shaping waterworks and over-seeing the laying of new pipes in grotto, 30 pounds, 12s
Also for shaping of a new passage in Underworld

Ask Master Paroli to paint walls of new passage, according to my own design. Have made a key for him, to secret parts of Underworld

Engage a second theatre artificer to help Cobb with new devices and illusions (if such a man can still be found in London)

Begin at last to move belongings into east wing

With Sir Richard, discuss fining of J. Simms and F. Bull for brawling again with Dauzat's glaziers

68

Zeal also asked the old knight's advice on how best to deal with the increasing number of evil rumours about the new house, spread in part by Jonas Stubbs and other workmen dismissed for one reason or another. Lamb's death had stirred up still more, being seen by some, particularly among Gifford's congregation, as an act of God, punishing Master Parsley for any number of possible crimes. In addition, Jake Grindley was now suggesting that Jamie had not run away at all, but had either been killed or was a prisoner serving as Doctor Bowler's slave.

'We are besieged by the curious,' she told Sir Richard. 'They try to creep in and see for themselves the depravities they think to find there.'

'Fools! All of them!' Sir Richard stood up. 'Don't trouble yourself, my dear. Just go and have a good sleep as I now mean to do.'

Three weeks later, she was forced to take action. One of the things she had most feared happened at last. The charm against the evil eye worn by that inquisitive Bedgebury boy failed to work. After particularly heavy rains, he was found drowned in the new water tank on Hawk Ridge. He had wriggled through the fence and could neither swim nor climb back up the straight sides. Five different people told her of an angry meeting in Bedgebury.

Zeal called together Tuddenham, the smith, her clerk of works, the new master mason, and four tenant farmers whose opinion she respected. They met in Lamb's former studio in the barn.

'I am told that a delegation has been formed to visit and confront me about the boy's death,' she said. 'Only their inability to decide exactly what they wish to achieve has delayed them so far.'

'Don't fear, madam,' said Tuddenham. 'You tried to prevent such a mischance. People will pry, no matter what you say or how much you warn them. Nothing like that house has been seen in all of England, let alone Hampshire.'

'Invite them all to come have a good gawp, then,' said the smith curtly. 'Show them where the boy forced his way through the fence. They'll see how it happened, easily enough. Let them in here, too, so they can see that illusion is only brushes and paint.' He looked around for the support of the others. 'Let them look all they like. Then they'll have no more excuse to pry. Or anything else. My best tongs were stolen last week.'

'If you invite them all to come here as your guests,' said Tuddenham, 'it might take a little of the wind out of certain persons' sails.'

'The parish didn't celebrate Bonfire and Treason night, last November,' offered a farmer.

'And small wonder!' said the smith.

'People might like a small bonfire,' the farmer persevered. 'And perhaps a little ale.'

'A celebration so soon after the terrible death of the boy?' asked Zeal.

'We all know it was his own fault,' said Tuddenham. 'I warned him off more than once. And I'll say so, too.'

'A bonfire might be welcome, madam,' said a second farmer. 'Lift our spirits out of the winter dark.'

69

Zeal had braced herself. She had had a bonfire built ready for lighting on the grassy slope between the fishponds and the old house, with three roasting pits already aglow nearby. She set up kegs of new ale on trestles in the new forecourt, and jugs of cordials in the hall. The pits held only apples and squash, as she had no sheep to spare. Without Doctor Bowler, there would be no music.

She had announced the occasion as the quickening for the new house, welcoming the parish into the new home of the Hawkridge family, occupied at last. She had locked off her private Underworld. Nevertheless, she quailed at the straggling parade of the curious that crossed the new bridge in the late afternoon and climbed the drive to crowd into the Memory Palace.

She greeted and welcomed. Accepted respects, smiled into a good many stony faces. Moving from group to group, she listened. Good mingled equally with bad.

'Look! There's your Abigail, true to life!' one woman cried in delight, pointing to a plaster frieze of Bowler's choir of children on one wall of the hall.

'She's more than twice the size now,' said her mother. 'And isn't that one Jamie Grindley?' Their voices dropped too low for Zeal to hear.

She watched a pair of farmers hunched in amused perplexity before a small self-portrait of Lamb painting his own face, looking into the spectators' eyes as if into a mirror, with the tip of his brush just lifting from the outer corner of his smile.

Still more visitors arrived. They stopped to peer at the mechanical ship at the entrance. Then they gawped up at the bird-filled heavens on the ceiling of the hall. A voluble group shifted and jostled around the brightly coloured picture of Hawkridge Estate at the top of the stairs, where people looked for their own miniature selves in the painted fields, or among the painted outbuildings.

'I believe that's my mastiff!' exclaimed a farmer. 'Caught him just right. Always scratching himself.'

'. . . hens!'

'All these windows,' she heard a woman say as she looked about her. 'They feel like eyes spying on us all. Like the house has eyes.'

'A devilish house, painted like the face of a harlot.'

Her choices, exposed and judged.

She watched people stare at the gilded and painted leather panels of Philip's Staircase, then frown in puzzlement at the blank panels at the bottom of the stairs. She watched them search for England on the map on the floor of the entrance hall, treading thoughtlessly over Nevis, picked out in red oxide, *terre verte* and gold against a lapis lazuli sea.

'Hell's own Mouth!' exclaimed a Bedgebury woman. She jumped back to stand on the greyer seas off the Indian coast and stare as if Satan himself might emerge from the painted floor.

'. . . full of marvels!' Zeal heard someone else say. Then the reply, 'But not worth killing a child for.'

'Did you know that Doctor Gifford is here, madam?'

Zeal set the mechanical nightingale into motion to delight a group of children and to try to shake off that last overheard remark. 'Keep him away from me, I beg you! Feed him. Take him to Aunt Margaret for condolences about his late wife. Or ask Sir Richard to start a debate on who should be the next parish constable.' Her attention was then distracted by two Bedgebury men standing behind her.

'Those must be the real trees under there, that we heard

tell about,' said one. 'Real branches under the plaster. Near enough the real thing but for the colour.'

'And aren't those birds up there true to life as well?'

'And those children, too.'

Then Gifford stood before her in a musty-smelling black coat and thick knitted scarf. He doffed his black hat and stretched his lips at her. 'I hear that your house is a most curious place, over-filled with colour and vanity.'

She did not even try to smile. 'I hope you will warn your congregation against tale-mongering and false witness.'

'Nothing I have seen yet today disproves anything I have heard.' He left it to her to decide whether the gossip or the house was at fault. 'You wrote to me yourself, madam, that you meant to build a theatre. But I do not see it. Where is it? Do you not display it with the rest?'

'Would you have me put these people's virtue into such jeopardy?'

'I wish to inspect it.'

'I'm afraid you must be denied the very pomps of the devil,' Zeal said blandly. 'My theatre is closed, like all the others.'

Gifford gave her a searching look. 'Only while you are observed, I fear. I know you, mistress, and your taste for rebellion.'

'Sir!' She mustered all her indignation. 'I have always been direct with you. Why should I begin to deny my actions now?'

'Nevertheless, I would see it.'

She glanced past him at the three large men from his congregation standing behind him. His wreckers, no doubt. 'Remember that you are my guest today.'

'I am also your shepherd.'

Eye to eye, they engaged in a silent struggle. In the end, Zeal shrugged inelegantly and led him out of the house, around the front of the west wing. They descended a short flight of steps in the slope of the hill, to a paved walk running along the side of the new half-cellars under the wing. The three men followed.

'The entrance to my theatre.' Zeal gestured politely at a high arch set into the wall. The arch was solidly bricked up.

Gifford drew a sharp breath. 'Must you always flout me?'

'On the contrary, I would have spared you this frustration. But you insisted on visiting my theatre, which I assured you was closed.'

'Is there no other entrance?' Gifford asked suspiciously. He jiggled on his toes in irritation. 'How did the workmen go in and out?'

'At the other end of the house is a small door giving access for matters like clearing out the pits of the jakes. Hardly the way to introduce either players or audience.'

'There's no other door inside the house?'

'No door,' Zeal assured him with absolute honesty and a mendacious heart. As Gifford did not ask about any other style of entrance, she felt no need to tell him how one might still go into the Underworld where the theatre stood.

Though off-balance, Gifford would not give up the attack. 'What of the sinful waste? Have you not entombed a fortune in labour and stuffs behind that door?'

'Do you have spies among my workmen?'

'Not I!'

But she had broken his gaze. 'Who is watching, if not you?'

'People talk, madam, as you well know.' He waved his followers away and leaned close to Zeal to speak in confidence. 'I will hazard that today you hoped to satisfy gossip with the food of what you see as the truth.'

She looked away, lips pinched. His face was far too close to her own. She could see every curling rusty wire of his eyebrows, smell the damp wool of his black suit. She clasped her hands tightly together on her best lace apron lest she give him a violent shove.

'I see that I hit home. But I fear that you may have misjudged, just as all who see dark as light are blind to their own error. Others will see more clearly.'

She gazed up the river valley towards the setting sun. She

had overheard some of those others and felt too weary to fight him today. 'Doctor Gifford, why will you not leave me in peace to face my own damnation?'

His nostrils flared. 'Because, madam, not one sparrow is forgotten before God, and you are my least sparrow.'

She walked away, down the steps into the new forecourt and then on down the drive to the new bridge. On the bridge, she stepped up into Lamb's little pavilion, which he had persuaded her to build.

'Suitable for elevated reflection,' he had said, and been childishly pleased by his own word play.

Standing at the rail in the pavilion, she looked down at the dark water breaking against the pilings of the bridge. Imagined Gifford floating out of sight downstream, his mouth twisting with inaudible words. Then she dropped a number of his parishioners in after him. The owners of the pinched lips and narrowed eyes. And Jake Grindley, who had not come today, though his wife had touched Zeal's sleeve in greeting.

That's how much I mean to let you all trouble me, she thought.

A gust of fragrant smoke blew towards her from the roasting pits by the ponds. The babble of voices was as cheerful as she could have asked. She reminded herself of people's delight at recognizing themselves in the pictures, woven into the fabric of the estate's past. But she still heard the mutter, 'Not worth killing a child for!'

She looked up at the house. Lamb's four columns marched across the front, pale and elegant in the last of the light. His speaking in figures. His mathematics of proportion given form in Purbeck stone as he had wanted, at last. Her life journey arrested in moments along the way, however misleading. And beneath that outward show, lay her secret Underworld, which told the truth, meant to be read by John alone.

Shadowed figures strolled in the portico. A single figure stood alone in the dusk, looking down into the valley.

Though it proved to be only the Wilde's dairyman, she felt a catch under her heart at the sight of him. What will I do when the house is quite finished? she asked herself. How will I survive then?

The wood of the bridge resonated with trotting hoof beats. She ran to meet the rider with the new hope that had infected her at the onset of war. But it was Sir Richard.

'Back from London so soon? Though I'm delighted to see you any time. Will you come up and have some . . .'

He cut across her. 'Stay here. We need to speak apart.' He began to dismount. By the time he had swung his leg over and eased his bulk slowly down from the saddle, his groom had dismounted and was at his side to steady the final quick slide.

'Leave me be!' Sir Richard waved the youth away irritably. 'Over-solicitous pup!' He handed over his reins. Then he stood looking for so long after the two horses as they clopped on across the bridge, that Zeal feared he had lost his thread. She and Mistress Margaret had spoken together not long before, of their growing concern for the old knight, who seemed to lose his thread more and more often.

'My dear . . .' he said at last. He stopped and pulled glumly at his lower lip.

The air twisted about her head. All other movement of the universe stopped with a jolt. 'John is dead!' she said.

'No. Nothing like that.' Sir Richard looked startled. 'Haven't heard a tittle from him. Since . . . can't remember when.'

They strolled slowly back across the bridge away from the house.

'It's that damnable man!' he said.

'Doctor Gifford?'

Sir Richard shook his head vigorously. 'Not him. That other one!'

'Jake Grindley?'

'No!' he cried impatiently. 'No . . . Roger Wentworth! Got

397

him! I'm so sorry, my dear. That creature has made a deposition against you at the Winchester Assizes!'

'Wentworth? Why? What does he want? I thought you judged that the question of the marriage had been settled beyond doubt.'

'Not the marriage. He never did get anywhere with that. Worse, I'm afraid.' Sir Richard looked up at the sky, then tapped his temple. 'A few plums short in his pudding, that one. Can't think how Philip got him! Wife probably, you know . . . while Philip was off junketing around the Caribbean . . .'

'What does he charge?'

'Happens all the time. Some low . . .'

She caught his sleeve. 'Sir Richard! Please.'

'Well . . . murder, in fact. As it happens . . .'

'Harry? But surely you dismissed that charge yourself!'

'I did. But it wouldn't stay dismissed, would it?'

'How can he raise it again?'

'New charges. Philip died. And then Master Parsley.'

'You don't mean to say that he claims I murdered both of them as well as Harry?'

'I'm afraid so.'

Zeal laughed. 'This is even more absurd than saying I bewitched Harry's horse.'

'And I might as well be blunt and be done – the child, too.'

She stopped laughing. 'He says that I murdered my own babe?' She wrapped her arms around herself. 'Now we know that he is mad.'

They paused at the far end of the bridge.

'What will happen now?'

Sir Richard pulled at his lower lip again. 'As it's a capital offence, the court returned his deposition with an attached writ of *a certiorari*. That is to say, Wentworth was charged to provide more detailed evidence to support his accusation.'

'But he won't find any!' A capital offence, she thought. That means I die if found guilty.

'He thinks he did. Seems that he responded with a list of

witnesses he says will be certain to expose the truth.'

Is it possible that I am to be punished for my most secret thoughts? she wondered. For my rage towards Harry. For fearing that John might come back and find me married to Philip or Lamb. Even though I didn't know that I wished them harm.

'Who are his witnesses?' she managed to ask. 'All liars! They must be!'

'Me for a start.' Sir Richard snorted. 'That's how I know. Just had the summons to appear in Winchester for examination. And your woman.'

'Rachel? What does he expect her to say against me?' Then she gripped the railing of the bridge. I did not know Philip, she thought, though I was his wife and shared his bed. How can I presume to know my waiting woman?

She had built an underworld of uncertainty into her house, to represent what she knew to be true.

'Am I called?'

'Not until the magistrate is satisfied that you have a charge to answer.'

Did I do anything that might be twisted? Can thoughts I didn't even know myself to be thinking have taken shape, to testify against me? If nothing is certain, nothing is impossible neither.

70

Winchester, Midsummer Assizes. Extracts from clerk's <u>verbatim</u> notes for the examinations of witnesses concerning the deaths of Sir Harry Beester, Captain Philip Wentworth, and Master Lambert Parsley (for later transcription into the court records).

<u>*Examiner and Roger Wentworth, gentleman, of Hunden Hall, nr. Guildford, Surrey*</u>

Examiner: . . . Did stepmother and father ever quarrel?

R. Wentworth: Who knows what goes on behind closed doors? Do not call her my stepmother.

Examiner: You assert that this young woman seduced your father, then caused his death by witchcraft in order to steal his fortune. (*Examiner's Note: the soundness of Captain Wentworth's will, which excluded plaintiff, being already proved and not an issue in this case. Likewise, Mistress Wentworth, now Parsley, was judged fit to inherit.*) In evidence, you offer the death of Sir Harry Beester, as a previous murder by witchcraft. Was a charge not made against your stepmother at the time and struck down *nolle prosequi*? (*Clerk's Note: records of that case attached.*)

R. Wentworth: But she has now killed again. Making three. Sir Harry, my father and Master Parsley. Three husbands! Surely even the dimmest wit can see that the death of three husbands goes beyond unfortunate coincidence!

Examiner: Coincidence does not prove cause. Can you offer good reason for your claim?

R. Wentworth: Her greed.

Examiner: What was her gain by Sir Harry Beester's death? (*Examiner's Note: that marriage voided, joint consent, by decree a vinculo matrimonii. Deed of gift made to Mistress Parsley in settlement. Accused had no further interest in Sir Harry's estate at the time of his death.*)

R. Wentworth: Why don't you ask her?

Examiner: I mean to. And how did she profit by Master Parsley's death? Her fortune being as great as, or greater than, his.

R. Wentworth: My father's fortune, not hers. Amazed that you need such assistance in understanding simple facts. She's no fool, to let her reasons appear so baldly a second and third time. But when has greed ever had limits? I have intelligence of her wanton and wicked extravagance in building her so-called 'palace'.

Examiner: Has your intelligencer brought evidence of murder, however?

R. Wentworth: She defies her minister in all his counsel. She has built a theatre when all theatres are ordered closed. She consorts with foreign Catholics and offers them haven in the guise of workmen. She is accused by an honest man of abducting his son. Another boy died on her estate. If you take close look, I vow you'll find she had as good reason to kill Master Parsley as she had to kill my father. Such a woman may do anything.

Examiner: A close look is indeed my intent. I ask again, have you evidence of murder itself? Can you, for example, produce the footpads you say she hired to kill Master Parsley?

R. Wentworth: Ask your constables to find them. I'm a country gentleman. The lowlife of Southwark is outside my experience.

Examiner: But you say that it is within Mistress Parsley's experience, as country gentlewoman?

Examiner and Sir Richard Balhatchet, Magistrate and MP, of High House, nr. Bedgebury, Hampshire

Examiner: Good to see you again, Sir Richard.

Sir Richard: And you, you oily old courtier! (A line is drawn through this exchange.)

Examiner: Sir Richard, in deposition you reject both charges. Why?

Sir Richard: Because Philip Wentworth was old, in failing health, and in love with his juicy young wife. No need for murder or witchcraft to explain his death in her bed.

Examiner: Did it occur to you to refer the witchcraft charge to church court?

Sir Richard: It did not.

Examiner: I've just been informed that a boy died on her estate.

Sir Richard: Accident! The pup broke in where he had no right to be and drowned himself. What's it to do with this case, anyway?

Examiner: Are you not swayed by friendship with this young woman? A close neighbour, I believe, and long-time guest at High House.

Sir Richard: My dear James, I was acquainted with Philip Wentworth for seventeen . . . no, I make it sixteen years, before I ever met the girl. And in all that time, that son of his took his allowance readily enough but never came near, not even when his father was ill . . . Philip suffered from a recurring ague. Contracted in . . . place escapes me. She, on the other hand, looked after him tenderly once she took him in hand. Warmed his last year. Turned him from an unsociable old hermit into a happy old man. Son never made a squeak till he learned he wouldn't inherit. Now he won't rest till he proves her guilty of some charge to make the estate fall back to him. I see human greed and jealousy in this case, and neither of them is hers. That man's wasting our time with his bile. If I were you, I'd put him on charge, not her. And you can refer that case to any court you like.

Examiner: Thank you, Sir Richard, I will keep your advice in mind.

Examiner and Doctor Praise-God Gifford, minister, Parish of Bedgebury

Gifford: . . . She is immoral, lewd and lost. She delights in outrage and rejects all good counsel. Nevertheless, in my estimation, she is not a murderer. She is too given to an unbridled excess of life . . .

Examiner and Rachel Whitefoot, serving woman, of Hawkridge Estate, nr. Bedgebury, Hampshire

Examiner: Don't you think the coincidence of numbers does begin to strain reason?

R. Whitefoot: Sir?

Examiner: Does it never seem strange to you that your mistress has lost three husbands?

R. Whitefoot: I know that more often it's the husband who loses three wives. But I doubt, all the same, that she's alone in this misfortune.

Examiner: Did your mistress ever quarrel with her first husband?

R. Whitefoot: Not that I heard.

Examiner: What of their witnessed quarrel beside the pond, just before he died?

R. Whitefoot: You must mean Sir Harry. But he was never her husband. And I thought everyone already agreed she never killed him. If you're asking about her first proper husband, she never raised her voice to Master Wentworth, nor he to her. I was against the match at first, because of their difference in years, but soon saw how they loved each other.

Examiner: What of Master Parsley?

R. Whitefoot: He and she were like twins, joined in all their ventures. They could debate all night about the shape of a fireplace, but that was shared passion, not rage.

Examiner: You make her sound like a paragon of female forbearance.

R. Whitefoot: She's a good-natured creature, if that's what you mean.

Examiner: We know what she gained from Master Wentworth's death. What do you think she gained by the death of Master Parsley?

R. Whitefoot: Loneliness, sir.

71

'Hey, *nolle, nolle, nolle,*' sang Sir Richard. 'All of you sing!' He beamed along his table at his dinner guests. 'With a hey, and a *nolle* . . . What ails you? You won't even be called for examination. You must celebrate!'

Zeal and Mistress Margaret exchanged uneasy glances. To their knowledge he had so far drunk only one glass of wine.

'Will Wentworth rest content now, do you think?' Zeal asked. 'With the court's judgement against him?'

'Got no choice.' Sir Richard shook his head fervently. 'No choice, however much he may shout and rave. Unless you oblige him by killing someone in truth. You won't do that, will you, my dear? Otherwise, he's holed below the waterline. Holly, nolly!' He waved to a serving groom. 'He's sunk and drunk, in a dead man's trunk! Who wants some *oporto* and *prosequi*?'

'I knew she'd never be found guilty!' said Mistress Margaret.

'A toast to Justice!' Master Wilde raised his glass.

We need Doctor Bowler back again, Zeal thought. To lift our spirits with his music. While smiling back at her host and his other guests, she wondered briefly whether the little parson was regaining the use of his left hand.

And I would so like news of Jamie.

But the heart of her disquiet sat in his chair-of-grace at the centre of the table, now frowning into his wineglass as if he had spied a drowned fly. 'The man's barmy! Barmy in the army!' he said with dark relish.

She had believed he would always be there, an amiable

shield who knew how the cards were dealt in the greater world.

There will soon be no one left, she thought. The higher ranks have fallen. After Sir Richard, I will be left in command.

After the judgement, Zeal began to think about death. Not in the desperate fearful way she had confronted it on the chapel roof, but more as a friendly darkness, a dark cape under whose hem she could slip and hide. Having at last mellowed enough to accept help in ordering her world, from both Philip and Lamb, she told herself now that she had been right all along.

If I had not grown accustomed to that luxury, I would not miss it so much now.

In other words, she was profoundly lonely.

Death took on the aspect of a companion who was always there, not insistent on joining her but waiting patiently just outside the door until called. And while she did not yet feel impelled to call and lift that cloak hem, she did have a small chamber built into the walls of the west wing above the theatre, stealing more space by turning a small retiring room into a corridor.

She hired still more Italian workmen, who would soon depart again and take the secret with them. The new chamber could not be reached directly from the public part of the house. Indeed, anyone walking among the sleeping chambers and private parlours on the upper floors would not know that it existed. The only entrance was through her private *mappa mundi* of the Underworld. If John neither returned nor sent for her, the room was to be the last memory in her story.

The floor was square, eight feet to a side. She had a door made thick enough to stop all sound. And because they represented a future she did not yet know, she left the plaster walls bare, apart from John's coat, hung on a peg.

My Last Resort, she called it privately.

There remained the problem of the lock.

She must be able to lock out the world and its unreasoning hatred. She also needed a lock with which the final turning was the leap from the roof.

At first she thought she might have a lock devised that closed forever once the mechanism had engaged. To test this possibility, she pretended that she had entered the room for the last time. She swung the great door closed. Even without a lock and with a strong rope handle in place for the moment, she felt a rush of overwhelming terror and hauled the door open again.

She had imagined John, returned after all. She had not heard him. Did not know he was there. Had locked herself inside to die while he bloodied his hands trying to tear down the door.

She wrote of her dilemma to Lamb's Italian locksmith in Florence. Some weeks later, he replied. She had challenged his genius, but he had triumphed in the end. The solution required not just a lock but a much larger mechanism. However, it would be much more costly.

'I can arrange so that you cannot open from within, once the mechanism is set. One can open easily from the outside but only if knowing the trick. When entering, therefore, you must ensure that you always disarm or you will be trapped inside . . .'

His price translated to forty-six English pounds, plus the cost of shipping it to England, so long as she took full responsibility after the arrival at the London docks.

She wrote back at once commissioning him to proceed. If she understood the man correctly, she might be saved after she had closed the door for the last time, but only by someone able to look beyond appearances and understand how truth might lie hidden within deception like the seed inside an apple.

To balance the lock, as an earnest that hope had not yet entirely died, she leaned against the wall of her secret room the painting of her child, which Lamb had finished at last shortly before he was killed. In fact, it was a triple portrait showing Zeal with John, imaginatively aged from the double portrait with Harry, and the child. Lamb had chosen in the end to paint the baby in Zeal's arms, just as he had drawn him while she was refusing to give him up, but with rosy cheeks and open questing eyes, like those of both his parents. The baby reached up to touch Zeal's cheek. Only very close examination showed a tiny wing budding from one dimpled shoulder. In the upper right corner, a flock of fully-fledged infants stretched down their hands in welcome.

72

Letter from Zeal Parsley to John Nightingale

'John. My Sweet Love, where are you? (Zeal wrote the same night she commissioned the lock.) *If only I could feel your breath on my cheek, or touch your hair, I might not go mad. I move my limbs with effort. Some other hollow creature goes about the daily business of the estate. I know that you must have died, for my own soul feels dead, and if you were still on this earth, I believe I would sense some faint humming in my bones. I have made a final refuge for myself, if you should never come nor send for me . . .*

I know that we loved, but can no longer remember how it felt.

Yet I cannot give way. Doctor Bowler is gone to Venice with Jamie Grindley. Your aunt limps bravely but is losing strength. Sir Richard is returned to cheerful infancy. Only I remain. I am almost done with my sustaining project. My house. My mappa mundi nears completion. The Memory Palace. Conceived when I still hoped that you might return to follow the rich traces I have left for you. To read the journey I have made . . . To find me again . . . Yet I myself do not yet know where I go. I cannot see the track ahead. I hear wolves among the trees.

She covered the writing with savage inky strokes to cage that indulgent self-pity behind bars of ink. She crumpled the letter and threw it on the fire.

73

Letter from John Nightingale, addressed to Zeal Beester, of Hawkridge Estate, near Basingstoke, November 1643.

Dearest Love, if you still exist,

I think of you all the time. Not quite all – not while I'm doing things I would rather you did not know of. Things I fear you will not forgive. If we ever meet again, you must feel free to ask and I will try to confess . . . I begin to think I have invented you to keep myself steady and am in danger of writing as if the real Zeal (if she exists) will never read my words. Write to me. Reassure me that my words and actions will have consequence.

What is taking place in England? The rumours that reach me are too terrifying to contemplate. I imagine the worst. Have you had soldiers billeted on you at Hawkridge? Which way does Sir Richard lean? Has there been fighting near you? Is my aunt well? Arthur? Write. I must know that you are still alive. I am no longer employed as I was – you will understand what I mean. As I move about a great deal, a letter may take some time to reach me but if you send to The Dovecote, Tortuga, care of a villain by the name of Bouton, your letter may . . .

Let me not pretend. A letter will never reach me. There's no man in the Dovecote I trust not to use a letter to wipe his arse. I may not live to collect it.

I imagine your rape. Your hair is a beacon. I know now what groups of men will do. I imagine your death. Fighting in London. Scarborough. Banbury. Hull. England seems dissolved into madness.

The skin of your breasts is as velvety as the muzzle of a horse, or a moth's wing. Or the tender belly of a mouse. You smell of honey and rosewater. Also, at times, of yeast or sun-warmed grass. As for your bush . . .

You will never see this, so I may write what I like before I burn it.

A confession. In England's disorders, I spy a kernel of shameful selfish joy. If the king should fall, I can come home . . .

74

'We've nothing left to take!' Zeal tried to close the office door on the quartermaster who stood on the gravel of the old fore-court. 'No food. No men.' She glanced in dismay at his half-empty wagon. 'Your lot have taken everything already! Go away! Leave us in peace!' She had been collecting papers to move to the new office in the domestic wing of the Memory Palace.

'Are you Mistress Parsley?'

With resigned despair, she held out her hand. 'Let me see the list. I'll tell you what we have.'

'You misunderstand,' he said. 'I'm delivering. You're fortu-nate that London's in Parliament's hands. The king's dainty *caballeros* might have taken a fancy to what's in it.'

Curiously, she watched two of his men lift down a large parcel lashed into a canvas coat. It appeared to have been opened and carelessly re-packed.

The quartermaster asked for her signature on his bill. Then the wagon lumbered away again, towards the Parliamentary garrison at Southampton. The soldiers' route had pointed them past Hawkridge on their way southwest from London, and a quick-witted shipping clerk at the London docks had seized the chance to save a cartage fee.

'From Italy,' Zeal told the curious crowd which quickly gathered. 'Or so he said.'

The thick padding inside the canvas proved to be lengths of brightly striped silk smelling of fish, which they unwrapped like bandages. Then came folded panels of creamy Venetian lace.

413

'We can see now why the Parliamentary army let it through,' said Rachel.

At the centre, like the stone of a very large plum, sat a curious contrivance of wood and metal, painted to resemble a small cathedral, with a crank at one end. There was a letter attached.

'It's from Doctor Bowler!' Zeal waved the letter over her head. 'He has sent us a gift to sing for us until he returns!' She returned to the letter, then cried, 'Wait! Take care! Let me read the doctor's instructions before you leap upon it!'

She elected the smith, as the largest and steadiest, to carry the box-shaped instrument on a strap hung around his neck.

'You first, madam!' cried several children. 'Then us.'

Tentatively, Zeal turned the crank. Three musical notes sprang into the air, like startled water drops.

The smith braced his feet. She turned the crank with greater force. More liquid notes were plucked somewhere inside the instrument, this time blending into the first implication of a tune. With conviction, she began to crank away steadily, and unrolled across the forecourt a *canzonetta* by Signor Monteverdi, or so Bowler's letter said.

She looked around at the open mouths and wide, disbelieving grins. 'Doctor Bowler says that Jamie has learned to sing this tune.'

'Shall I go fetch my drum?' asked the smith.

When everyone had taken a turn at cranking, and they had tried to sing the tune, and had discovered how, by shifting a little lever, to make the organ sing two other tunes, Zeal locked it into her new secure store cupboard.

She knew that this delightful new arrival would need guarding. The Antichrist had returned to Hawkridge.

75

The best gift of that Christmas and the New Year of 1644, however, was the return of Arthur, limping from his long walk from Southampton and much thinner. 'I never knew it,' he said happily, when Rachel had at last released him. 'I'm blind as a bat after sundown. And don't hear too well neither.' He took Rachel's hand. 'Amazing what you learn in the army!'

'I could have told them you only hear what you want to.' Rachel's tone was dry, but her voice shook very slightly.

'Welcome back,' said Zeal. 'You must learn to read if you're turned too deaf to hear instructions. We badly need another useful man about the place.'

Arthur cupped a hand behind his ear and grinned. He later told Zeal in private that he had not been able to stomach the idea of fighting fellow Englishmen.

'Foreigners, yes. And I might stretch to the Scots. And I'm not alone,' he said. 'The colonels have their work cut out. Most men are refusing to fight except to defend their homes.'

They celebrated that Christmas in the new house. Master Cobb came back twice to check measurements for the sinking trap, which he had almost finished in his London workshop. The saddler was still seeking hides large enough for Zeal's purpose. The mason who had replaced Jonas Stubbs still chipped away in the secret Underworld, and Francis Quoynt had yet to make a final test of his extended hydraulic systems that would power Master Cobb's counter-weighted machines.

However, the east wing of the Memory Palace with the

domestic offices and most of the sleeping quarters was now roofed, glazed, and had working fireplaces. Light filled the rooms, as Zeal had planned. From her own chamber window, she could look down as she and John had looked down, although the scene was somewhat changed. On good days, she could sometimes still remember the exact weight and warmth of his arm around her shoulders as they sat side-by-side in the grass. Arthur's return sometimes made her dare to hope that John's angel letter was finally coming true and that all had at last begun to go well.

She rejoiced for Rachel and Arthur, while fending off her own loneliness in deciding the exact curve of the soffit under a final arch and whether or not to apply a sixth coat of paint. She even felt flashes of joy and wonder when she wandered about her new house touching the wooden flower-ages and fruitages that Lamb's Italians had found lurking inside clumsy blocks of timber and set free with their chisels and saws.

Every evening, she set off from Hampshire on the map on the hall floor and walked across the seas to stand first on Hispaniola, then on Nevis, the red oxide, *terre verte* and gold island in its lapis lazuli sea. So few steps to make such an immense journey. She closed her eyes and tried to think how he might have been changed by experiences she did not yet know of.

But you did not tell me about your troubles, any more than I've told you mine.

She gazed up at the paintings of Philip's Staircase and the saga of Hawkridge Estate at the top of the stairs. Then she looked across the world to the mouth of hell, near the Indian coast.

I fear we've done each other, and ourselves, a false kindness, she thought. Our trials reshape us more severely than our joys.

She had laid a trail for him, but it might lead to places where he would not care to follow.

Please come back! she would beg him. Before it's too late for both of us.

She had tried throughout the autumn to reassure herself that the growing disorder she felt merely reflected the more general uneasiness of war. The small thefts of building stuffs, the more frequent brawls between English workmen and Dauzat's Huguenots or Lamb's Italians.

On her way to bed each night, she passed the blank panels of her own story that she had asked Lamb and Paroli to leave unfinished, to be completed in seven years, however the story might end.

But Lamb was dead, and now so was Paroli. At Twelfth Night, four staunchly Puritan carpenters, outraged by the invasion of French and Italian craftsmen, had set upon the Italian painter as a treasonous Catholic enemy of England and a spy. As none of them would admit delivering the fatal kick to his head, Zeal had been forced to charge all four with his murder. The four men had spent Christmas awaiting trial in the Basingstoke gaol. The family of one, a Bedgebury man, had asked Gifford to challenge her charges.

Zeal's Work Book – April 1644

Send to Florence to Mistress Paroli, sixty pounds, being her husband's last wages of 6 pounds, and some relief against her losses by her husband's death. Also his brushes, tools, sword and boots

Send deposition in reply to magistrate at Basingstoke with details of Sr Paroli's murder

Set locking bars on inside of all doors

Locking gate for kitchen yard, of a sort not to be climbed

M Dauzat, sign off his contract. Wages, (three weeks) and cost of his passage home

Also 2 pounds and a pair of silk stockings for loyal service

When last man is gone, fill cess pits and set fruit trees above

Visit High House daily to see that Sir Richard's people keep him clean and well-fed

Harvest asparagus shoots and marigolds

Sow whatever spinach seeds, radishes and carrots remain

Beg garlic cloves from Mistress Wilde to replace stolen stock. If she has any

Hide all food as fighting is now very near, at Alton before Christmas. Both armies now reported at Arlesford

At the end of April, the king was reported to have removed his queen to Exeter for safety and gathered his armies around Oxford. Parliament now controlled London. When Zeal, cresting Hawkridge on her mare, saw a single horseman crossing Lamb's bridge, she knew without doubt that it had to be John. She turned her horse straight down the hill and kicked so fiercely that they nearly fell. By the time both had regained balance, she could see that the rider was Doctor Gifford.

She reined her mare away again, towards the back of the house and the entrance through the new kitchens.

'I tried to turn him away!' Mistress Margaret said vehemently. 'He just smiled in that superior way of his and refused to listen! What was I supposed to do? Send for a constable to arrest the parish minister for making a call?' She added with a triumphant smile, 'But I did leave him standing in the hall staring about him like a looby. And without refreshment!'

Zeal took off the wide-brimmed black hat in which she rode. 'I wonder how he dares come here uninvited. Let him stand!' She went up the back stairs to her new chamber to change from her riding boots and skirt into a black silk mourning dress.

'Mistress, did you know that Doctor Gifford is in the hall?' asked Rachel, when she answered Zeal's call for assistance.

'I thought The Sword of the Lord had given us up,' said Zeal. 'Go tell him that I refuse to see him.

'He won't go,' reported Rachel a few moments later. 'Says he must hear his dismissal from your own lips.'

Zeal frowned at a letter from the London saddler explaining the unforeseen additional cost of obtaining hides of the size she had required. She still could not believe her new freedom to create as she pleased and not fret over the money. She went down the back stairs to the new estate office to write telling him to proceed.

'He's still there,' said Mistress Margaret as Zeal passed.

In the office, Zeal looked down from the window towards the fishponds and the looking-glass view of the old stables beyond. Then she watched two masons building the first pier for a gate at the entrance to the forecourt. Her mind could not settle with the enemy still inside the walls.

Call Arthur and have him removed, she decided. But curiosity got the better of her. In any case, it is always better to know what your enemy intends.

'Mistress Parsley!' When she appeared in the hall doorway, Gifford bared his teeth in what Zeal took to be a smile.

'Have you ever before smiled at me?' she demanded.

Gifford missed only a single beat. 'If not, it is not for the lack of good will.'

'I'm sure you have not smiled. Why begin now?' She advanced a little into the hall.

'Enmity rusts the soul, madam. I have been praying and reflecting since my last visit. I would like to end the needless enmity that seems to have arisen between us. Set aside our differences . . .' He took a step closer and wiped his palms on the skirts of his coat.

'You call what lies between us "differences"?' she demanded icily. 'I call it vile and despicable.'

Arthur passed through the hall, eyes straight ahead. He paused fractionally at the door, to give her a last chance to call him.

Gifford reddened. He did not try to smile again. Nevertheless, she felt him digging in. 'Madam, I will overlook such hyperbole in view of your loss. But do not fault me for wishing to act as any Christian might and offering consolation to one who is now alone in the world.'

'I have Sir Richard's parson for that . . . in the absence of Doctor Bowler.'

'I don't make myself clear . . . could we withdraw to somewhere we could speak more privately?' Gifford glanced at the door through which Arthur had disappeared, then upward at the painted sky full of wheeling birds. The final version of the clockwork nightingale sat on a carved plaster bough above his head.

'Say what you have come to say right here, or else leave still carrying the full burden of your words,' said Zeal.

Gifford cleared his throat and smoothed his rusty terrier hair. 'Mistress Parsley, it won't have escaped your notice that we are both now returned to the single state. You will know that I lost my dear wife more than a year ago. And as marriage is God's prescription against sin, it occurred to me that . . . you wanting the guidance of a man, and I lacking the solace of a wife . . .' He looked at her with raised brows.

She was startled by her lack of surprise. Even so, his blind effrontery left her unable to speak.

'It's true that you are rich in earthly estates, but I offer you far more – the Kingdom of God.'

She shook her head in disbelief. 'I should have known it would come to this. Philip was wrong. Those love letters came from you, after all!'

Gifford looked dumbfounded. 'Love letters, madam? I never wrote you love letters!'

'Poisonous love letters! Foetid oozings of an obscene imagination!'

'Are you raving?'

'The vile rantings of a diseased madman!'

'How dare you suggest that I . . .?'

'And how dare you come near me? How dare you presume? Haven't you drooled enough over my imagined sins?'

Gifford's face turned as dark as a fresh bruise. 'Madam, remember who I am in the parish!'

'A toad! A viper! Hypocrite! Your God will pitch you down from Heaven before you can even knock!'

Gifford dropped to his knees and raised his arms to Heaven. 'Dear Lord! Aid me in this my final battle in Thy . . .'

'Get out!' she screamed. 'Now!' She grabbed a Delftware jug and threw it at his head. It struck his shoulder and smashed on the floor.

'You're a vicious, dangerous woman! Not worth saving, after all!' He scrambled to his feet and began to back towards the door, the rims of his lips white with rage. 'I had hoped to be strong enough to lead you out of the darkness. Even offering my own flesh as Our Lord . . .'

'Go!'

'. . . but you won't have it! Not you! For years, you have resisted righteousness. You insist on your own damnation! You spurn your last chance to save yourself, through me. When retribution comes, madam – from both God and man, as it must . . . accusations are being made and you will have to answer them – just remember, I tried to give you a way out. Whatever happens now, you bring it on yourself! You and your obscene house!'

For two days after Gifford's visit, Zeal could not work. She could not even think.

I wish I could have made the earth open and swallow him! That would have sobered him!

But such vengeance still attended on the London saddler, on Master Cobb and on Francis Quoynt's theatrical artificer, who had promised to finish his part within the week.

Again and again she tried to unpick the meaning of Gifford's parting words. Clearly, he was threatening her with a retribution more immediate than damnation. She knew that the showing had not stilled the mutterings in the parish about the house, but they came chiefly from men she had dismissed for one reason or another. Their reasons for complaint must be clear to any reasonable man. The families of Paroli's murderers, too, were understandably upset, but surely no one else blamed her or the house for the men's arrest when the killers themselves had boasted of their guilt. And people had seen for themselves the circumstances of the boy's drowning.

The arrival from London of Cobb with his sinking trap finally distracted her. The saddle-maker followed a few days later with his large and costly hides, from which he constructed a giant curving tube of leather, large enough for Zeal to sit in up-right, wearing all her skirts. Then Cobb and the saddler tackled the marriage of their two creations. Quoynt tested his water-powered engines and showed her how to set a slow fuse. Cobb pronounced that his counter-weighted system, driven by Quoynt's engines rather than men, now worked perfectly. The new mason finished his work in the Grotto and returned his key. For most of May, Zeal secretly tested and re-tested the workings of her theatrical Underworld, which no one but she could now enter unless she arranged otherwise. Her *mappa mundi*, for the journey so far, was now complete.

For a sixth time she arrived in her theatre as John would arrive, if he ever should return and still wanted her. Though she was prepared for it, the new descent into her theatre still took her breath away. She shook her head to clear it and opened her eyes.

The word 'GOMORRAH' had been painted across half of a woodland scene.

She felt sick. Her blood pounded in her head. She recognized those slashes, their madness as clear in brush strokes as in the dashes of a pen.

The writer has not grown weary after all nor decided to leave her alone. Was no longer satisfied with mere letters.

She had sealed off the public entrance before the showing. No one had known how all the parts fitted and worked together, she was certain. The masons knew the shape of the foundations. The smiths knew the contrivances of iron. The joiners knew the sweet intricacies of boxes and corners and staircases. Quoynt knew the footprint. He and Cobb understood the machines and devices. But surely only she and Lamb had understood the purpose and workings of the whole.

The word had not been there last time she visited, and she now had the only key to the workmen's door.

Could it be one of my own house family?

But she had kept everyone except Cobb and the saddler away from the final work.

Has someone been spying on me when I enter?

But she had been careful. Arthur might know, and Rachel and Mistress Margaret. No one else.

And yet, that word testified that there had been an invader in her secret part of the Memory Palace. One who had examined her most private thoughts without her leave or knowledge. This trespass was worse than the accusation it made, worse than burglary. It boasted of the secret power to violate her privacy at will.

You should not have come here, she thought. Now I will discover you and grind you into powder and feed you to my pigs.

Thinking of false appearances, she crossed to the walled-up arch of the former public entrance and pushed against the stones. Solidly in place, of course.

Then she suddenly thought, Paroli's key!

She had given the Italian a second key, to lessen his need for contact with Jonas Stubbs. In the furore over his murder, and because nothing else of his had been stolen, she had forgotten his key.

I must set a guard over the workmen's door and send at once for a new lock.

But she was not given time to change the lock. Before her letter could even have reached her London locksmith, Rachel discovered the first shape of Gifford's threatened retribution.

427

78

By preference, Rachel was late to morning prayers. Or absent, if she could find good enough excuse. But today she was early, even before Sir Richard's chaplain had arrived from High House. She was hoping for a few moments alone, without someone's eyes always on her. To think. This self indulgence made her the first to spy the bundle in the chapel porch.

Another one for the parish, she thought. Common enough. No surprise, given the penalties for bearing a bastard.

Her keen eyes searched the ranked gravestones, the shadows around the Beester vault, the short grass over Philip Wentworth, who, Zeal had insisted, could not be confined in the chapel. She probed the orchard dropping its bloom beyond the low stone wall. The mother often stayed hidden, to see that her child was safely found.

A pair of finches picked busily at the moss on the wall. Rachel looked back down at the baby.

The little bundle was tied round the middle with twine like a bale of gloves, with a letter tucked under the twine. Hands on hips, Rachel stared down for a long moment. Too still. Not even a sleeping new-born twitch.

She felt a rush of rage. Should have left it to be found sooner. Or better yet, done something before the thing took on human shape. There were ways.

She laid a hand on her own flat stomach. She had not told him. You don't present a child to a man who wants only to chase after his master like a dog. A man who imagines that you must leave home to have terrible adventures.

I won't be your drag anchor, my man! Not me. And you won't pull me up by the roots, like he wants to do with her, and try to plant me in some foreign earth, where I'll rot or dry up or be eaten by something worse than sheep or deer.

She stooped down and folded the blanket back from the tiny face. The baby was sticking out its tongue and peering at her through sly, red eyes. The tiny tongue was purple and swollen.

Rachel exclaimed, leapt back, and then stood staring down, stroking her heart as if soothing a dog in a thunderstorm. When she bent at last to touch the waxy blue face, her fingers met a chill that made her shiver like a bad dream. She tried to lift the nub of its chin with her thumb, but its neck was stiff and unyielding. She looked more closely. A hemp cord had been drawn tightly around the neck with a hangman's knot.

Not much could rattle Rachel. At six, she had survived the small pox that killed her mother, and later tried to be grateful that the scars had saved her from the sin of vanity. When she was twelve, her father was forced out as tenant of his farm. Homeless, with his family and without work, he had died soon after in an accident Rachel thought anyone could have seen coming. From that time, she had looked after herself very well, thank you. Even dead babies could be dealt with. Murdered ones were another matter.

Her usually quick-moving thoughts stumbled over each other. Though she knew it was too late, she tried to loosen the cord. She had to sit down on the shallow step beside the baby. Hands trapped between her knees and rocking slightly, she looked at the hangman's knot.

However bleak life could be at times, it had patterns. You could rely on hard work, for example. You could rely on the plague in the summertime. You could rely on men to try to lift your skirts. You could rely on bacon after the autumn slaughter and peaches if the sun and rain obliged. You could rely on war.

Rachel liked patterns. They let you prepare yourself for the worst, when it next came round, and taught you to make the most of the good while it lasted.

She did not like any of the patterns that began to settle around this dead baby with a hangman's noose around its neck.

She pulled the blanket back over its face to see if she could think any straighter that way.

You hide an unwanted babe, all the more urgently if it's dead.

She closed her eyes against the memory of the little mulberry shape she had secretly buried.

It's a message.

She lifted her head at the sound of distant voices then pulled the letter from under the twine and strained her eyes at the inky slashes on the page. Though she could not read, her young mistress had taught her enough to know the letters 'Z. . .E. . .A. . .L. . .' when she saw them. She refolded the letter.

I'd rather not be able to read. Then words like these have no power over me. I can leave them stuck right there where they are on the paper, thank you very much, and not let them into my head!

She stuffed the letter into her sleeve and hid the baby in the long grass behind a gravestone at the far end of the grave-yard. She was back on the chapel porch by the time the High House chaplain, two dairy women and the fish man came through the gate.

Bury it! Burn the letter, she told herself.

Even as Rachel decided, she changed her mind. Don't be a fool. Someone clearly wants it known. Wouldn't have left it here for the whole world to fall over otherwise. That's a fine wool blanket, not a dairymaid's rag. Someone intends a vile mischief. I smell it. My lady must think how to protect herself. How to protect me, for that matter!

Rachel had already been questioned once and had not cared

for such close proximity to the law. Better to be unknown, invisible. Particularly now that Sir Richard, poor man, could no longer offer much protection.

She stared into the questioning face of the young woman who now stood before her. If she's accused of anything more, it might be the last straw. They might change their minds about the past. They might say that I helped her. Who is closer to her than I am?

But how can I tell her what is being said? A girl who does only good as far as I can see, though I sometimes want to thump her to make her sit down for a moment. She has enough to deal with already, doesn't need a murdered baby added to her account.

Though Rachel's imagination was limited, it was quite able to conjure up a gibbet. She had seen a few, and with women kicking the air under them.

I have to tell her.

Her mistress might be young, but she was quick. Just the flick of the eyes as they went into the chapel was enough to tell her something was up.

Zeal saw panic in the eyes of her steady, dry, sometimes humourless Rachel. If Rachel was afraid, so was she.

A cold, tight fist gripped her.

It was getting closer now. Hard to breathe.

Don't know exactly, but I know all the same. This is the one.

Can't breathe. 'Our Father Which art in . . .'

I'm so weary!

'. . . our sins as we forgive . . .' Precious little forgiveness around . . .

'Go in peace,' said the chaplain.

Zeal straightened her shoulders and rose to face whatever waited for her.

Before she could speak with Rachel, however, she had to decide how many of the few, precious, remaining chickens to kill for dinner the next day, who would churn . . . please God, let Tuddenham not start on seedling hot beds and manures!

Numbly she looked where Rachel pointed in the long grass. She stooped and examined the little body as Rachel had done. She noted the hangman's knot. She put out a fairly steady hand for the letter Rachel offered. Unlike Rachel, she recognized the writing. Even invading her Underworld had still not drained the writer's bile.

'What does it say, madam?' asked Rachel after Zeal stood silently staring at the paper for a very long time.

Zeal fainted.

A copy of the letter was posted that same morning in the Bedgebury market square. Arthur was the unhappy messenger, having walked to the village early, before prayers, to try to buy eggs. Zeal, who might once have gone for the pleasure of the bustle and company, now avoided Bedgebury for fear of meeting Gifford or members of his congregation, or, unwittingly, her invader.

That evening, Geoffrey Comer, newly elected to head of the parish council, arrived with the parish constable who, after eyeing the little mechanical ship set near the entrance, began to study the ceiling of the hall with open-mouthed astonishment.

Comer was a tall thin man, on whom all lines flowed downwards like the branches of certain pines or weeping trees. In his plain black, narrow coat, he seemed to extend upwards forever.

'I suspect you know what brings me, mistress.'

Zeal looked at him a little wildly but took comfort from his calm civility. 'Arthur told me that I could save sending.'

'As our magistrate, Sir Richard, is unwell, I thought it best if I dealt . . .' Comer hesitated.

She managed to find words to invite the two men into the

little parlour to the right of the entrance hall and to offer refreshment. She sent Rachel to bring the dead baby, which had begun to bloat in the warm early summer weather. She showed it to Comer along with the letter that had accompanied it.

Comer inhaled sharply, then asked the constable to take the child away.

'Yours is a copy of the letter I saw in Bedgebury,' he said.

'I have some others I should perhaps have shown you long before.' Zeal sent Rachel to bring the other anonymous letters. 'But Sir Richard knew.'

Comer spread all the letters on a table.

'The same hand,' he agreed.

'I thought at first that they were from Doctor Gifford.'

'Gifford?' Comer raised his eyebrows in astonishment.

'He and I have our differences,' Zeal explained hastily. 'But Master Wentworth was certain the writer was someone else. And I came to the same conclusion.'

Comer nodded, again studying the letters. 'I'm relieved that you're not accusing a man of his standing and influence in the parish.' He lifted a single eyebrow. 'In any case, though our minister can be extreme in his fervour, he strikes me as more likely to seize you by the throat than to work in darkness like this.'

'Philip said just that.'

Comer touched the most recent letter with a long knobbed finger. 'Did you do it?'

Zeal's head jerked as if he had slapped her. 'Have you come to arrest me?'

'Not unless you did it.' Comer looked down at her steadily.

She shook her head tiredly. The letter still made no sense. Still made her head swim.

This babe was murdered by the woman who now calls herself Mistress Parsley. In the same way, she killed her own bastard and two husbands. Look no further for reason than the devilish deceptions of that abomination of extravagance she calls the Memory Palace. It is there that she practises her black arts. It is there that she charms and destroys her victims. If you would find the bones of others whom she has sacrificed to heathen gods, you will find them used to model the obscene simulacra of infants and children among the other images of idolatry and wickedness.

It is widely known, too, that she consorts with Catholic traitors and has welcomed these enemies of England to live amongst us. If you search, you will still find a theatre in that place, though theatres are banned. And most damning of all, a hidden priest's hole, final proof that this woman is an agent of the Antichrist and sister to the Great Whore of Babylon.

'Who can hate me so much?' she asked.

'None of this is true?'

'I never killed anyone. And the courts have agreed. The rest is a wonderful confabulation of half-truths and rumour.'

Comer watched her coolly.

'I never used, or caused to be used, the bones of any creature in the making of my house. That last accusation may have been inspired by the use of tree branches under the plaster in some of the friezes, to give verisimilitude. I was inspired there by the example of the Countess of Shrewsbury at Hardwick.'

'And the theatre? The priest's hole?'

'Nothing plays in my theatre, I keep no players – and I haven't heard yet that theatres must be destroyed as well as closed. The so-called priest's hole is in fact a goodly-sized closet reserved for my own private contemplation and study.'

Comer picked up and refolded the letters. 'I must take these with me to show the magistrate in Basingstoke.' He waved away a mug of ale, which had finally arrived.

'What will happen now?' asked Zeal.

'I can't speak for the magistrate. In your place, I would pray that he detects an act of malice against you. By a person who may or may not also be guilty of infanticide if you are not. Praise God, that's not for me to discover.'

She walked with him to the front door. He frowned up at the painted ceiling, then at the map on the floor as they travelled across South America, then at the walls.

'An officer may need to return to look at those friezes, and perhaps your closet.'

She nodded.

'Mistress . . . a warning.'

She looked up the long distance to his narrow face.

'Old scores get settled in bad times,' he said. 'The war has set the devil free in England. Ugly rumours are being put about.'

'Uglier than the murder of a babe?'

Comer glanced away. 'And also, someone is paying those carters of Sir Harry's to spout their stale accusations again to anyone in the parish who will listen – and there are always those who will. Stay close to home for the moment.'

Later, Zeal stood before the blank panel in the hall outside her chamber, as if its oiled surface might suddenly shiver and reveal the future like a diviner's mirror.

If not Gifford, who can hate me so much? she wondered again. And what do they hope to gain by proving me a murderer?

Jake Grindley?

But the letters had started long before Jamie ran away, with her marriage.

She could think of only one other old score to be settled.

She remembered Sir Richard's voice four years earlier, saying, '. . . unless you oblige him by killing someone in truth . . .'

79

The mob turned into the beeches at the top of the drive.

'The bones! The bones!' Their shouts were muffled by the trees.

Zeal threw open the window of her chamber to see without the distortion of the window glass. The deputation had come, at last.

A horseman rode out of the beech avenue towards the new bridge. The light was going and he was still too far for Zeal to see his face clearly, but she knew the shape of his shoulders, and his horse. The first of the mob boiled out of the trees close behind him. Their sticks and pikes tossed like the horns of cattle. Half a dozen people carried torches.

Burning torches.

This is what Gifford had meant.

'Sweet Lord in Heaven save us!' cried Rachel, looking over Zeal's shoulder. 'There's Mistress White as well as her husband!'

Besides five of Sir Richard's pikes, Zeal counted two scythes, six clubs and lost count of the staves.

She did not see Comer nor the constable among them, only the man she had feared to see. Who had hated her enough to kill her child.

Roger Wentworth moved at the head of a strange, shifting beast, which stretched and re-coagulated like a swarm of bees as it moved down the drive. Almost hidden among the trees lurked more women and some older children.

'The bones! The bones!' they shouted.

As the mob crossed the bridge and climbed the drive towards the new house, Zeal began to make out their faces.

Four militia men, all from Bedgebury, armed with muskets. Five of the joiners, whom she had dismissed. Jonas Stubbs. And the two masons who had attacked Dauzat. The six men who had come with Gifford to the bonfire. And Jake Grindley. At the back rode Doctor Gifford.

Zeal held tightly to the window ledge.

This battle may be too great for me to fight, she thought. If John is still trying to come home, he will be too late.

I'm sorry, she told him. I tried.

She recognized the families of three of the men likely to hang for Paroli's murder.

Wentworth saw her in the window and gave a shout. He kicked his horse up to the foot of the wide pale steps. 'Whore!' he shouted. 'Murdering witch! We have come to uncover your sins!'

The crowd gave an approving roar. Someone began to chant 'Let us in! Let us in!' The others picked it up. 'Let us in! Let us in!' They banged the ends of their weapons on the ground. 'Let! Us! In!'

Zeal looked around at her defending army, who had come rushing to her chamber. Mistress Margaret, Agatha, Rachel. Two chalky-faced grooms.

'Arthur's gone to ring the bake house bell for help,' said Rachel.

They all watched in silence, as Zeal took Philip's pistol from under her pillow and his rapier from his sword belt hung beside the bed.

'Shall we get our staves, madam?' asked one of the grooms.

'Yes,' she said. 'Then I charge you to stay here and guard this gentlewoman and her companions.'

'Zeal, don't!' Mistress Margaret tried to grab her sleeve. 'Oh, please, don't!'

'What should I do instead? Please bar the door.' She went down the great staircase into the entrance hall.

In the illusion of endless blue sky, her birds sat frozen in silent readiness. The little ship waited at the dockside. She had another choice.

She could go now, before this sweet, false imitation of worldly order gave way to the chaos that pressed in on it. Her means of escape lay close at hand. She stood on her map, which pretended that geography could be tamed with meridians. She looked down at the floor. She could vanish, flee into her secret room in the elbow of the tower and close the door behind her. And rest at last. She could abandon her people. Abandon her *mappa mundi* to those who wanted to destroy it.

She opened the door and stepped out into the portico.

The crowd gave a jubilant yell. A stone struck one of Lamb's columns.

'What do you want with me?' she shouted. The hair around her temples was dark with sweat and her eyes were fierce. 'Jonas Stubbs! Are you after a commission for my tombstone? And Jake Grindley! I'm surprised to see you here. Is this how you repay me for your farm?'

'You stole my son!' he shouted back. 'And sent him to live among foreign whores and mountebanks. Then tried to buy me off like he was a bullock or shoat.'

'Unless she killed him too!' screamed another voice. 'How do we know he's not dead too? And in there with all the rest!'

'I've killed no one! All honest men know that!'

'She lies!' cried Wentworth. 'As she lied under oath to the courts!'

'You know that all charges were knocked down before matters ever went so far! I was never called to court!' Just keep them out of the house, she thought. Or Mistress Margaret's heart will stop with terror.

'See how she tries to turn you now as she turned the others!' cried Wentworth. 'Close your ears to her sweet dangerous words.'

Gun, useless. One bullet. So many of them.

She walked forward to the edge of the top step, dropped Philip's rapier and gun. 'If you mean to violate the laws of both man and God, kill me now,' she shouted. 'Or else act in a more neighbourly fashion. With more warning that you were coming to call, I might even have been able to offer you refreshment.'

The crowd subsided slightly. The bake house bell began to toll.

'Though you set the law on others, you think that you're beyond the law!' Wentworth rode to the foot of the steps. '"But, be sure, your sins will find you out!" We shall raze Gomorrah!' Holding her eyes, he waited for her to grasp the totality of his triumph.

She had to look away. The hatred in his face scattered her thoughts like a blow to the head. It filled the air between them as thickly as water, stole the breath from her lungs. 'You wrote the letters!'

'Yes, madam! I admit it with pride.'

'And the babe?'

'A virtuous deception to expose the truth. I have you now, madam. You may have hoodwinked the law, but you'll find me and these others harder to charm than that whey-faced Winchester magistrate or old fool Sir Richard who can't take his eyes from your dugs!' He wheeled his horse so that he half-faced the crowd again. 'Murderess!' he shouted. 'Triple murderess. Whore! Witch!'

More than a deputation . . . private angers spurred on by a wilful, unreasoning malice.

'Hang her now and be done!' screamed a woman's voice from the trees.

'Do you put yourselves above the authority of the courts?' Zeal shouted back. But she had lost all hope of quelling the mob with reason, when unreason rode at its head.

Gifford kicked his horse forward to join Wentworth and raised his hand to still the mob. 'A man's conscience now has as much authority as the courts.' Unlike Wentworth, he did not shout, but his voice carried like a trumpet. 'When civil authority is divided against itself, where else can we then turn if not to our own conscience?' More quietly, he added, 'I did try to warn you, madam, but you chose to reject my help. Let God's will be done.'

'No more words. Let us in!' cried Wentworth.

'Into the heathen house!' cried a man's voice from the back.

'In!' echoed other voices.

A stone crashed through one of the windows. 'Put out its eyes!' screamed a woman's voice. 'Put out all its eyes!' More stones smashed through glass.

'Seize her and keep her fast while we search the house,' Wentworth ordered. 'Then we will deliver justice at last.'

Zeal looked past him in the thickening darkness, at a dark man with a musket who stood silent at the back of the crowd.

Now that she had seen him, she could not look away from him, even though the crowd below her shouted and pressed forward.

Death has come for me, she thought. She felt his gaze calling her. His stillness sucked at her. It pulled her towards him, over the tossing waves of the mob. He was the true heart of this moment.

'No!' she shouted at him. 'You won't have me. Call off your dogs!'

'We will have you, mistress!' yelled one of the masons. He brandished his pick. 'We'll dig out the bones of the murdered babes and children you had your Frenchmen and Spaniards conceal in your walls! Then see what you have to say!'

'The human bones in your plaster figures. Your heathen sacrifices!'

'My son!' shouted Grindley.

'Is this your doing?' she cried to the silent man. Wide-brimmed hat, ragged beard. Gleam of eyes. 'Are these your lies?'

'Not lies, madam!' Gifford stood up in his saddle so that he might be clearly heard by all. 'A clear light will at last burn away the darkness of your sins.'

Gifford was a cloud, a gnat. Death stood at the back of the mob, the still centre of the world.

She thought she saw eyes like sparks blown into the darkness from a fire, searching for new tinder. She was a dry leaf, withered grass, a dead branch about to snap. She felt the heat of his danger. Felt the dream of fire before it flared. In her imagination, she was already singed. If only he would speak. Or move. Make some small human gesture. She wanted to challenge him again but her throat had closed.

Look away before it's too late.

The tossing horns of the mob hooked at her. Their boots poised to trample her. But the true fear flowed in a cold stream from the silent man at the back. The mob turned to mist, swinging ghost horns, a stampede of wraiths.

I am going mad. Must think how to save myself. Save us all. The house and all who live in her.

Hatred beat at her feet like the tide.

I am dreaming. Seeing phantoms. An Indian woman, as Philip had described. Polished black ropes of hair hanging on either side of her head. In her arms, the phantasm of a small child, bronzed and oiled like a sword. Black eyes. So many eyes, no, only four, but bright darkness. Darkness can glow. The glow burned her. Still the man did not move.

The woman and child were not clothed in gold. They wore ragged smocks, the woman, a brightly striped shawl.

Now, when she needed to act more than ever before in her life, she felt as empty of will as she had in her secret chamber.

Another stone glanced off a pillar. A chip flicked across her wrist. She looked down at the thread of blood that sprang out on her skin. The sight woke her.

The danger below her was real. Her flesh could be torn, cut, burned. Her spirit stamped out like a fire.

'You'll find no bodies in this house!' she cried.

'The murdered babes!' screamed a woman. 'Killed to feed her devil house. Uncover their bones!'

'A place of idols and darkness!' Gifford waved the mob forwards. 'We must earn God's Grace. We must beat off the forces of Satan destroying England! To survive, we must purify!'

'In! In!' roared the mob.

'You will not enter this house!' She felt them pressing forward. Wentworth's eyes had fixed on her like claws.

'Tear down the walls!' shouted a man.

I can't hold them!

'The bones!' prompted Wentworth.

'The bones! The bones!' The chant began again.

I am about to die, she thought. She felt too heavy to run.

She heard the shot but felt no blow or pain.

The crowd turned to look back.

A mere man after all. He still held his musket raised into the air while the echoes of the shot bounced back and forth across the valley of the Shir. She saw him clearly now, without the veil of fear across her eyes, as the smell of the burnt powder reached her.

He wore filthy leather breeches and stained pigskin boots. In his belt, he carried a butcher's knife. A floppy, wide-brimmed leather hat cast a shadow over the top of his face while a beard of the same leathery colour hid the rest. He held his four-foot musket aloft in his right hand. His left hand was thrown out as if to protect the Indian woman and child. The child clung tightly to the woman's neck.

'Stay out of this, whoever you are!' shouted Wentworth.

'If you are a Christian,' shouted Gifford, 'you'll help us seize her.'

The barrel of the man's gun dropped to point at Gifford's chest. 'Whom did you say she killed?'

'Her own babe,' said Wentworth when Gifford turned suddenly silent.

The gun barrel dipped for a second, then returned to its original angle.

'She killed a babe?' the man asked quietly. 'You say she killed her own babe?'

442

'And others not her own.' Gifford regained his nerve and waved his arm to draw an echoing roar of agreement from the mob.

'A heathen blood sacrifice,' added Wentworth. 'The blackest witchcraft . . . I have a witness to her practice . . .'

'And don't forget the two husbands!' shouted Jake Grindley.

'Three! If you count Sir Harry,' cried another voice.

'Several babes and three husbands, you say?' The man sounded suddenly and unaccountably relieved. He looked at Zeal again across the heads of the crowd. Showed white teeth in an unlikely smile. 'A woman of great dispatch, I must say.'

Zeal gasped.

'I heard a contrary rumour that Sir Harry's executioner was his horse.' He took a step forward, his gun held casually in his hand but still pointing at Gifford. The crowd parted to let him through, with the woman behind him. The child stared wide-eyed at those they passed, its grip tight around the woman's neck.

'She charmed his horse so that it threw him,' said Roger Wentworth angrily. 'I have witnesses who saw her cast the evil eye. As for my father, Master Philip Wentworth . . .'

'Wentworth!' exclaimed the man. 'Philip Wentworth the fisherman? Is he dead then?'

'And young Master Parsley.'

'No sooner married than dead,' said Gifford. 'All of them.'

'John Nightingale too, I swear,' said Roger Wentworth. 'Even if he wasn't a husband, good intelligence had him in her filthy bed. She put it about that he left England on the sly but none of us saw him go. I dare swear we'll find his bones in there as well!'

'You swear she killed them all?'

'It's clear to all but gullible fools like that doddering old knight, Balhatchet,' said Wentworth. 'There are too many deaths for chance alone to explain.'

Zeal heard none of this exchange. The machines of her

being had begun to shift and churn so that nothing was properly hooked up. Thoughts froze. Breathing paused. Muscles refused to take orders. Her strength drained out through the soles of her feet.

Not like this! Dear God, not like this!

She stared at the woman and child, then back to the man's face.

'I vow you won't find Nightingale's bones in the house,' said the man. 'And aren't much more likely to find the rest.'

'Sir,' said Gifford. 'You are a stranger. Beware of meddling where you are ignorant.'

'With respect, sir, you must trust me on the one point at least. I'm John Nightingale.'

Zeal found herself sitting on the stone floor of the portico.

John reached the steps, climbed halfway and turned. 'I don't much care for this welcome after so many years away. Come back tomorrow when I've had a chance to trim my beard. We can talk then, man to man, in a more civil fashion.'

Some on the edges of the crowd had already begun to sidle away, some muttered among themselves, while others pushed forward in eager disbelief.

'Master John, by God! Alive and all!'

John took the child and set it on the top step. 'Whoever the pair of you may be,' he said to Wentworth and Gifford, 'I'll shoot one of you if you don't leave now – and I'm not saying which I favour most.'

'No need to choose,' said Tuddenham.

Zeal turned numbly, to see the estate manager beside her on the porch. He had picked up the dropped pistol. Four of the Bedgebury men had now gathered uncertainly beside John, while eight of her tenant farmers and Arthur stood behind Tuddenham, armed with two muskets and staves.

But, oh, not like this!

'You may be alive, sir,' Jake Grindley called. 'But what of the babes and Wentworth? And Sir Harry? And that London bugger she married last?'

'I meant what I said. Call off your dogs,' John told Wentworth and Gifford. He placed the spade-shaped stock of his gun against his shoulder. 'Someone take the child out of harm's way.'

'Wait!'

Startled faces turned to look at Zeal.

'Let a half dozen of my accusers come in and seek proof of what they say I've done. I want this matter settled beyond all doubt.' She had to look away from his face or be overwhelmed again.

The child's black eyes stared up at her, the accused murderer of babes.

80

Two men from Gifford's congregation stood either side of Zeal, holding her by the arms lest she disappear in a cloud of fiendish smoke or suddenly mount a broom and fly away. Gifford called for ladders, more torches and lanterns. His wiry body danced from one foot to the other as if a spring in him had been over-wound.

While the masons climbed up with picks and hammers to crack open the plaster children in the hall frieze below the painted sky, John stood with the Indian woman and child against the wall farthest from the destruction. After seeing the work started, Wentworth went to lean against another wall with the drained elation of a man who has at last arrived on his mountaintop.

Each blow of the hammers rattled Zeal's bones. She watched the masons carefully. Though they did dreadful damage to the frieze, they did not harm any of her mechanisms. Nor did they reach as high as the clockwork birds.

The sounds of destruction brought Rachel and then Mistress Margaret to peer fearfully into the hall. The two grooms, clutching their staves, advanced on the wreckers, albeit uncertainly.

'These men have my leave,' Zeal called to them, 'but I thank you for your courage.'

'Ha!' cried a mason. 'I've struck something! Send up more light.'

Wentworth stood up away from the wall where he had been leaning. Gifford ordered a second ladder put beside the other, to add another pair of hands to the uncovering. He stretched his neck again and again and clasped himself in his arms. Then swung his arms in unwitting imitation of his wreckers above him. His face darkened with impatient emotion.

'What do you see?' he cried.

While the masons were chipping at their discovery, Zeal felt John's eyes on her and knew that he sought signs of guilt. How could he not, in such circumstances?

'It's only a piece of tree, sir.' The two masons yanked the branch free of the wall and sent a blizzard of plaster flying down on Gifford and the others below. The shallowly moulded boy who had been sitting on the branch fell apart into chunks of plaster and rags. One hand broke off entire and shattered softly on the hall floor.

'But that is the principle!' said Gifford triumphantly. 'Plaster modelled over the reality it purports to imitate. Truth at the heart of illusion!'

Zeal looked at him sharply, but the minister seemed unaware of what he had just said.

And he would not welcome my pointing it out, she thought.

'There's nothing else here,' one of the men called down at last.

'She's too clever for you.' Wentworth spoke for the first time since the search began. 'You forgot the figures on the pillars. Search them all. Don't let her escape yet again!'

'Crack open that likeness of Jamie first,' said Grindley. He closed his eyes as the masons attacked.

Again, they found nothing but plaster, rags and horsehair.

'Your intelligence said the bones were in the frieze in the hall,' protested Gifford. 'Would you have us search the whole house?'

'I know the bones are here.' Wentworth touched one ravished wall. 'You must believe me.'

By the end of the night, the searchers had destroyed the

friezes in the hall, the great parlour and the gallery on the top floor of the maze wing. Chunks of plaster littered the floor and the tops of tables and seats of chairs. A fine grey dust floated like smoke after the fire. Zeal, like the searchers, soon tied a handkerchief over her mouth and nose. With each failure to uncover a skeleton, Gifford's face grew redder and his lips pinched tighter.

'There is nothing here,' said Gifford at last. Plaster frosted his rusty eyebrows like ground sugar. He stirred a heap of rubble one final time with his foot. 'It seems that Master Wentworth's intelligence was wrong.' He glared accusingly at the masons as if they had been the source, and directed the men to sweep up the plaster as best they could.

Gifford turned to Zeal. His face, now as dark as a boiled beetroot, contorted in apparent agony. 'We have found no evidence of murder.' He held up a hand to stop her reply. 'I still do not hold you innocent, madam. This house, at the very best, is a shrine to heathen worship, filled with obscene and ungodly images that should be destroyed. It harbours worldly delusion as vile as that found in any playhouse in Sodom, and I hold our work here tonight to be a cleansing pleasing to God. But we have not proved murder.'

'Where is your friend to echo this handsome retraction?' John interrupted.

Roger Wentworth had gone.

'I too have a retraction to make.' Zeal's voice shook. 'Do you remember those letters I accused you of writing?' she asked Gifford. 'I too was mistaken. Roger Wentworth wrote them, as well as those letters falsely accusing me of killing the babe. You heard him admit it earlier before you and all these other witnesses.'

'He intended the deception to uncover the truth.' But Gifford looked uneasy.

'And yet you still trusted his claims to true intelligence? And were willing to encourage such mortal damage to me?'

Gifford breathed harshly in and out but said nothing.

'And if he wrote those letters, did he not most likely also kill that foundling babe in order to lay its death on me?'

Gifford's eyes widened. 'I . . .' He clamped one hand to his head. Zeal thought he staggered slightly.

'I fear that you were duped by an agent of the Antichrist,' she said, past caring what further rage she might bring down on herself. 'He has gulled you into the terrible sins of wrath and wanton unlawfulness. Doctor Gifford, I have thought you to be many things but, until now, never a fool. You have proved to be a false shepherd leading your sheep full tilt into the slavering jaws of Hell.'

'It . . .' Gifford, for the first time in his life, had difficulty finding words.

'It seems clear to me,' said John, stepping forward, 'that you are his confederate in raising a hanging mob in defiance of the courts. A court may find it just as clear that you share his guilt for murder.'

Gifford swivelled his eyes onto this new speaker. 'I . . . uh . . . !' A look of terror and confusion now twisted his face. 'I . . .' He stared at Zeal in appalled surmise. Closed his eyes. 'I . . .I . . .'

'Something ails him!' said Zeal in alarm. 'He's never been at such a loss for words.'

Wild-eyed, Gifford nodded. He toppled and crashed to the floor, sending up a cloud of plaster dust.

She knelt beside him. 'Doctor Gifford, can you understand what I say?'

At the sound of her voice, he held his hands up to her in terrified appeal.

'Can you answer me?'

'I . . .' He made a gesture of despair.

Zeal stood up. 'You must take him home and send at once to Basingstoke for a surgeon,' she told his followers.

Everyone trouped back down to the hall as Gifford's men carried him away.

'Hardly a fulsome retraction,' said John when the door at last closed on Gifford and his wreckers. 'But retribution was astoundingly swift.'

'The Sword of God snapped,' Zeal said absently. She wanted only to study John's face. She thought that he seemed as uncertain with her as she was with him.

'An apoplexy!' announced Mistress Margaret. 'I've seen one before. Caused by an excess of blood. A boiling choler.' She surveyed the wreckage left in the hall. 'However will we get all this clean again?'

'We all need refreshment,' Zeal told her. 'Take Rachel to help you. Bring it to my small parlour.' That room, decorated only with painted leather panels had not been touched. 'And see whether any of our gallant defenders are still on duty and in equal need.'

At last she was left alone with John and his small family.

With the charges of murder dismissed there now remained only the explaining of two husbands when she had sworn to be true.

And the woman and child.

I have no right to question anything he may have done, but I fear it will kill me all the same, she thought. He should have shot me when he fired his gun.

'Thank you for your timely arrival,' she said.

'Not what either of us expected or planned, I don't imagine.'

The child woke from sleep, tied against the woman's back in her shawl, and began to grizzle, as if more upset by the tense silence than by all the shouting and crashing that had gone before. When John lifted her out of the shawl, she grabbed his beard and thrust her copper face and shining black hair into the curve of his neck.

Where I once rested my head in the illusion of total safety, Zeal thought.

'My daughter,' he said. 'Two and a half years old.'

Zeal nodded. Then she smiled brightly at the woman, who

had retreated against the wall as if she wished to escape through it. 'And is this your wife?' With her hands extended in welcome, she pressed herself onto the blade of the woman's dark-eyed stare.

'Tesora's nurse,' said John. 'The mother died.'

The woman hid her hands behind her, as if terrified of Zeal's touch.

Zeal nodded again, tried to smile. 'Welcome, mistress. I hope we can offer hospitality of a better quality than your welcome.'

The woman glanced at John, who translated Zeal's words.

She wondered if he had heard the sudden joy in her voice at the news of another woman's death. 'I'm sorry,' she said to John.

'She deserved a better fate.' He turned his head and kissed the child's hair. 'I try to atone.'

Zeal could not think what to say next.

81

Between dawn and end of morning milking, Zeal washed herself out with tears, beat herself on the rocks, and flung herself over the bushes to dry.

She had found a room for John, the child and the nurse all together, as the little girl would not be separated from either adult. John took the bed, the little girl slept in a hammock he slung between two heavy chairs, and the nurse had a pallet under the hammock.

There had been at first a difficulty in finding food not too strange for the child, but an apple and piece of bread sufficed in the end. Zeal left them speaking together in their shared alien tongue.

This cannot be the way our journey ends! Zeal thought as she lay listening to the already busy day outside her window. She felt bleached clean of the events of the past night. A cloud of blankness hovered over her thoughts, threatening to close in like fog.

I'm not ready. There has been too much.

But, ready or not, he was back.

Not dead. Come back to her. With all his limbs and senses, as far as she could see.

But does he still love me? He would have returned to Hawkridge in any case. I cannot assume he has come for me.

At the least, I'm farther on than I was that dreadful night at the Lady Tree.

Take this impossible situation by the scruff of the neck, she told herself. Shake it until it yields, one way or the other. Whether happy or tragic, resolve it! Don't lose your grip now.

She got out of bed and went as far as his door. She imagined him lying warm and tousled among the sheets, breathing quietly, one bare arm bent above his head. It's too soon, she thought. They still need to sleep. She returned to her own chamber.

When Rachel brought her morning ale a half an hour later, however, she took her mug with her and knocked on his door.

He emerged with a finger to his lips. 'She's still asleep. A late night for her, last night. And the travel back to England was tiring.'

'Do you hate me?'

He looked shocked. 'I would say that you have more cause to hate me.'

'You accept all my protestations of innocence without question?'

'Of course.' He smiled a familiar smile. 'Or, rather, my understanding of the word "innocence" has broadened.'

'Poor "dogged struggling words".' She looked away from his mouth.

He was barefoot. His feet were very brown. He had already trimmed his beard. 'That doesn't mean that I'm not filled with questions. As you must be.'

Zeal felt a humming in her bones. Not quite a trembling, more like the beginning of an ague, but not unpleasant. 'You need breakfast.'

'Among much else,' he agreed. 'Such as the belief that I'm back.'

'Are you?'

'I don't know where "back" is yet.'

'No.'

He took her hand, turned it over, ran his thumb across her palm. 'I often feared I was inventing you.'

The line traced by his thumb was a trickle of cool water. She stared at the thin scar that circled the base of his thumb. Then she saw how rough from work her hand was and wanted

453

to pull it back and hide it under her apron. 'Did you think of me when you were with her mother?'

He released her hand. 'Are we ready for this conversation yet?'

'No, but I would like to rehearse it a little.'

'Give me time to arrive first!'

'So long as you steer for the right port.'

To her surprise, he laughed. 'Land, ho!' He took her hand again and kissed it quickly. 'Oh, blessed, familiar cussedness! She was far less contrary than you. A house slave on the tobacco plantation. She helped me to escape. And I never loved her. I'm not proud of it. But I do love our daughter, beyond my life. Is that enough for now?'

Zeal swallowed and nodded. She had asked for it.

After breakfast, which John took in his own room with the child, Zeal walked with him about the upper, public part of the Memory Palace, playing hostess to his guest to buy them both time. Aware of the exact distance between her shoulder and his, she stopped on the broad steps of the great staircase by the painted and gilded wall panels of Philip's story. She saw now that all of the many miniature Philips were far too clean and finely dressed, if judged by John's appearance.

She looked at him sideways. 'He married me to save our child – yours and mine.' She heard John's intake of breath. 'Lamb brought an Italian painter here to help execute this memorial for me. The narrative ascends one side and descends on the other.'

'A grand memorial, and at the very heart of the house,' he said neutrally. She saw him glance at the blank panels at the bottom of the stairs.

Together they walked down the stairs, studying the images of a golden city that surrounded a great gilded pyramid beside a lake of silver leaf. Near the top of the stairs, a golden god accepted the gift of a cabin boy's heart. A few steps further down, following the story backwards, the same naked golden god washed in the silver lake and fell through a dark hole in the glittering surface. In the panel below that, he rode a palanquin carried on the shoulders of eight tiny men. Then came an endless procession of figures in jaguar skins and tall, feathered head-dresses marching towards the silver lake, carrying slivers of spears and playing reed pipes the size of apple pips.

'After Philip first told me his tales, I tried to capture the reality I believed they showed me.' She spread her arms. 'And here they are, where all the world can see them and be entertained, as I think he meant to entertain me.'

They reached the beginning of the story, the beast with the head of a jaguar and the feet and genitals of a man, followed by toy ships being driven ashore by a storm.

'I urged him on.' She took a deep breath, not looking at John. 'To tell me about the world I believed you occupied. Thinking that if I could imagine that world, and capture it in images, then I could imagine myself there with you. And you would not grow strange to me.'

'I fear that you will be disappointed. My tale lacks all glory. These are wonderful fables you show here, but fables all the same. I mean no offence.'

She looked back at the small painted figure that stood ankle-deep in a shallow stream, staring directly into the eyes of a jaguar crouched to drink. 'I learnt later how to decipher Philip's version of the truth.'

'And do I see your conclusions anywhere here?' He glanced again at the blank panels across the staircase, where the end stood opposite the beginning. 'Or were you too kind?'

She looked into his eyes for the first time that morning. 'My private thoughts on all matters are elsewhere.'

'Do you mean to show me? To help me to steer for that port.'

'You might hate and despise what you see.'

'So might you, when you know more of me and what I have become in order to survive.'

She nodded wordlessly.

'We're alike in that, then.' He touched her shoulder, then retreated. 'Both of us, afraid.'

They descended the last three steps into the hall in silence.

'Zeal, did you love him?'

She knew whom he meant. 'I believe that question belongs in the conversation you don't yet wish to have,' she said lightly. 'Let me show you how Lamb and I entertained ourselves. I did love Lamb, as it happens, but as a brother.' She led him to the little mechanical ship set into an alcove in the wall by the main door.

'Turn that crank,' she said. 'This was our first attempt to trap the past in motion. We grew more subtle with experience.'

John turned the little handle and laughed aloud when a tiny replica of himself jerked out of a dockside shed and up the tiny tongue of gangplank onto the ship.

She watched his eyes as the anchor chain wound itself around the capstan and the sails hoisted themselves, spurred on by the waving arms of tiny sailors set about the deck and glued to the rigging. Whatever else had happened to him, he had not lost his capacity for delight.

'And now this one.' She pointed.

John turned the second handle. The ship pulled slowly away from the dock, jerking and squeaking along a track hidden behind two rows of heaving painted waves. As the vessel slowly departed through a slot in the wall like an actor reluctant to leave the stage, the miniature John stiffly waved one arm at a tiny red-haired woman left behind on top of the hill that formed the backdrop to the harbour.

He sighed deeply and turned to her. 'Zeal. How far apart are we?'

She led him onto the map. 'That tiny spot is Nevis. Go stand there.'

With his brows only slightly raised, he obeyed. 'Will you now stand on Hawkridge?'

'No.' She crossed oceans with a few strides. 'My place was here.' After kicking aside a shard of plaster rubble, she stepped onto the island near the coast of India.

'The mouth of hell,' he said quietly. 'Did it swallow you?'

'That will be for you to say.'

'And is the private world of your thoughts a map of hell itself?'

'Nothing so straightforward.'

'Like life, then. For both of us.' He pointed at one of the ruined friezes. 'What traces were represented there? I was too distracted last night . . .'

'The children of Hawkridge, making a joyful noise unto the Lord.' Hymen on the lake had been smashed with the children.

John opened his mouth to ask another question, but closed it again.

Zeal seemed fascinated by the ruined walls. 'I want you to be clear about my intent in making all this.' She gestured at the walls, the house itself. 'It has some bearing on what happens to us next.

'After the baby died, I told Philip and Lamb I wanted to turn what we were building into a prodigy house. But not a mere memorial to my vanity, like a house in the shape of my initials, nor a cross as evidence of my faith. I wanted a prodigy of memory. To imitate the Greek and Roman orators, who constructed buildings in their fancy to help them remember what to say next. Placing a statue of the emperor at the foot of the steps, for example, to remind the speaker of formal greetings and reverences . . .'

'But you wished to hold open to memory the past, rather than the future.'

She gave him a look of startled delight. 'Exactly so.'

'Did you hope that I might yet return to see it?' He left Nevis to stroke a wooden sheep in the border below the ruined frieze.

Some of the clenched tightness left her body. 'So much

took place so quickly. I feared I was losing my way back to what I had been, and would not know how to tell you to follow.'

'So you laid tracks for us both! When will you set me on the trail?' He pointed back to the staircase. 'Those travellers' tales will lead us both astray.'

'I must share the blame for them. I think he told them just to please me.'

'Knowing Philip, I doubt very much that he was so innocent. He would have had his own reasons to sing his siren songs.'

Zeal felt heat rise up her neck into her face.

John smiled tightly. 'Philip Wentworth was not born to a fortune, he acquired it. And he did not do that by letting himself be deceived. You should not trouble yourself on his behalf.'

'He showed me only kindness,' she said hotly. 'Whatever the truth proved to be, he showed me only kindness and good will.'

'I'm glad to hear that, though not surprised. He also had a decent heart and I owe him much. Nevertheless . . .' He turned away to study a pair of wooden cats, who stretched tail-up and nose-to-nose in the place of a classical swag.

She pinched her lips and stared into a corner of the room. 'I do know by how much he lied.'

John tilted his head in ironic belief.

'Philip himself told me. After Philip's death, though still recording the past, I began afresh, subverting Lamb's ideal Olympian designs to fit the darker theatre of my own heart. That staircase is also my first memorial to deceit.'

'Ah,' said John.

In silence, they looked back up at the progress recorded on the walls of the staircase, then up into the sky above their heads.

'I see public posturing everywhere else here,' he said. '. . . Of the finest sort, I hastily add.'

He had lost none of his sharp-eyed quickness either. 'Yes. You detect the hand of my darling Lamb. For him the posture had to be perfect, but also public, or it had no meaning.'

'Is there nothing of you here at all?'

'Only the will to build, which underpins it all. And a few details of daily life.'

John crossed the Indian Ocean to take her hand again. 'Zeal, do you see anything familiar in me?'

His palms were warm. His long fingers enclosed her whole hand. She felt the ring of his thumb and middle finger around one of her wrists like a hot metal bracelet.

'After almost six years . . .' She turned her head away. She had imagined for an instant that she saw something of Philip in his eyes.

'Do you?'

'I want . . . I imagine . . . but how can I know?' She tried to withdraw her hand in order to think straight.

'Someone has returned,' she said at last. 'But he doesn't look much like the gentle man who left. In those leather breeches, with that great knife stuck in his belt. And a child on his arm.'

'That's all you see? You terrify me now.'

'I may think I recognize you, but you made one journey and I a very different one. Who can tell where we have each fetched up? You stand there, I here, only inches apart, but for all I know, we're not in the same place at all.'

'Then show me your private map. I will attempt to draw mine for you. I have always found you before. Tell me what I must do to find you again!'

'You truly want to?'

'Can you doubt it?'

'I can doubt anything now.'

'Show me.'

She pulled free and crossed to one of the pilasters that marked Lamb's perfect intervals around the walls of the hall. As she looked back at John's bewilderment, she pulled the little pin and heard the first whisper of falling sand inside the pilaster. She returned to her former place beside him.

Above their heads, the nightingale began to sing. A liquid, fluting 'piooo, pioooo' growing slowly more intense.

'Look!' She pointed upwards. 'One of the details. Now you must try to put yourself into my place.'

The automaton stretched its wings, opened and closed its beak. Its liquid song poured down, fluid and clear as the water that powered it.

With her arm still raised, Zeal disappeared.

82

A reasonable man with worldly experience doubts such things. Nevertheless, as John Nightingale stared at the spot where Zeal had been standing, he fancied he might smell sulphur in the air. Under the bird's song, he had heard her clothing rustle, the faint creak of what he thought was the whalebone in her bodice, then a muffled thump. He had not heard feet crossing the gritty floor.

'Zeal!'

Nothing dreadful has happened, he told himself. This is her own doing.

One minute she was there, within reach, white-faced and jittery as an unbroken colt, but still as beautiful as he remembered. He had wanted to seize her in his arms but held back. She was in no fit state to be rushed.

Now she was gone again.

Why didn't I grab her while I could? Is that what she wanted me to do?

A heavy weight of foreboding settled on his chest.

I let her go again. Lost her a second time.

He had been flattered by the mechanical bird, and absurdly cheered that she had set up his namesake to sing in his absence.

'Zeal?' he called again. This was impossible.

'. . . ealealeal?' replied the dome of the ceiling.

She had not had time to escape up the staircase. Hardly time to reach the bottom step. He had not heard a door open and close. He took three experimental steps. He would most certainly have heard her crossing the remains of last night's rubble.

He began to feel both frightened and angry. That is to say, he began to feel frightened and foolish, and that made him angry.

'What the devil do you want me to do now?' he shouted. And how can I do it, if you don't tell me what it is?

I could call her bluff. Leave her to her game, whatever it might be.

He looked up at the clockwork nightingale and felt even more foolish. It was, after all, here with the public posturing, her first monument to deceit, and the pretty lies.

I am to be dismissed then?

But angry and foolish or not, he knew that he must find her to be certain. Otherwise, it was already over.

Pure terror jolted through him.

'Tell me how to find you again,' he had said. His last words, before she vanished. Oh, brave words! And he had thought that she was then about to reveal her private map.

What had she said?

'. . . you must try to put yourself into my place.'

Haven't I been trying to do just that, remaining so unruffled by the news of the two husbands? He knew nothing yet about that 'London bugger'. But old Philip Wentworth! Already married, while he was writing of his own desperate hope and love.

To say nothing of biting his tongue about not being told of his dead child!

Zeal ran through the dimness, setting mechanisms, striking light. All she could think was what she might do if he had not listened.

What else had she said?

She had pointed up. '. . . put yourself into my place.'

He leaned forward suddenly, then squatted on his heels to examine the floor where she had been standing. On Hell's

Mouth, on an island near the coast of India. He ran his fingertips over the floor.

'Oh, my dearest love,' he said aloud. 'Most wonderfully
precise.'

He stood and stepped exactly into her place.

83

Though he had prepared himself, he staggered nevertheless when the earth opened under his feet. The floor, which he had expected to sink, tilted instead. He fell back, slid downwards on his arse, helpless, into a black sloping tunnel, kept sliding in an uncontrolled rush, curving downwards through darkness and the improbable smell of polished saddles. He tried furiously to reverse his fall but still kept sliding helplessly, blindly. Twenty feet? Thirty feet? Farther. He lost all sense of distance, gave himself up to the black rush.

He spun around a sudden, steep dizzying spiral and shot out into the light. Landed softly, on the smell of feathers. Shook his head to clear it and saw that he sat looking down a short hall at a small but splendidly painted stage.

His throne was oversized and well-padded with feather pillows.

A deep rumbling began, muffled by stone walls. And the sound of running water.

Drowning.

He had had too much water. He turned, but the hole that had admitted him from the leather chute had closed like the iris of an eye. To his left, he saw a stone arch, but the opening had been walled up.

He looked back at the stage. Though there were brackets to hold torches, enough faint daylight fell from somewhere overhead for him to see the painted screen across the front of the stage. He leaned forwards and peered.

A bosky woodland, a tumbling river that spilled into a distant sea. Water nymphs disported themselves on the riverbanks. In the half-light, they seemed to move.

The missing Hawkridge nymphs, unless he was very mistaken . . . another question he had not yet asked. Yes, there was old Nereus, leaning on a rock beneath the overhanging roots of a tree with his dolphin now on his crown. On the highest bank, in a bower of ivy and vines two forest divinities sat in warm embrace, gazing into each other's eyes. He wore John's face, or a fair attempt at it. She was unmistakably Zeal.

John unclenched his muscles. Apart from the fact that no water had yet entered the chamber, the happy scene did not suggest that Zeal had nursed a secret vengeful rage.

A new lighter rumbling now joined the earlier sound. John just had time to note that one of the nymphs had lost her hand. Then music began to play, a limpid yet complex stream of notes like a giant musical box. The stage screen cracked down the centre. With a grinding not entirely masked by the music, the two halves began to slide apart.

A little ahead of him, out of breath, Zeal stopped to listen. If he had followed her he would be in the theatre by now. She could not tell whether the rumbling machinery marked her passage or his.

The parting shutters revealed a scene in three dimensions. Billowing clouds and a shining, illuminated golden sun swayed in the heavens. John recognized Hawkridge House before the fire, almost like the painting at the top of the stairs, but subtly transformed here in placement and scale. On every ledge and rock around the house sat or lay paired creatures of all sorts, sheep, pigs, magpies, and dogs, but also lions, monkeys, and two rat-like creatures which might have been agoutis. Painted children played among the trees. All together in harmony, as in God's peaceable kingdom in Eden. Then he saw the pregnant Zeal, fecund but solitary among the others. The music flowed on like a small clear brook.

So far, a play without players, he thought. And nothing required of me but to pay attention.

He studied the scene for any clue to her desires or purpose, relieved that she seemed to intend such straightforward exposition. After the opening game with the map, he had feared she would set him a more veiled quest.

His breathing began to steady. His heart slowed a little. This secret world of hers, where he must now find and reclaim her, was not proving to be as obscure or fearsome as he had expected, given what he had already learned in his arrival and could surmise.

With a muffled wooden clunk and a metallic rattle, the sun above Hawkridge House jerked and slid behind a cloud. He heard thunder, like cannon balls rolling across a deck. Lightning flashed. And flashed again while the thunder still pealed. A bolt seemed to strike the house. A wisp of smoke rose. Then a black cloud boiled up from the house. Through a dark veil of smoke, he watched Hawkridge House go up in flames.

For a moment, the flames were real. Sparks bit at his hair as he staggered across the steep bake house roof, beating at the fire. Zeal on the ground watching. He felt her holding him safe with her will.

This is merely theatre, he told himself. He wrinkled his nose at the sharp smell of sulphur and saltpetre. All trickery and illusion. But he was clutching the arms of his chair nonetheless.

In the flickering orange light, the burning house seemed to collapse and sink into the earth. Deep within the smoke, still to the sound of heavy rumbling, the Memory Palace began to rise in its place through a veil of flames. The paired creatures had gone.

I think I still follow your narrative . . .

The thump of an explosion struck him like a piece of heavy timber. He threw himself sideways onto the floor. After a moment with his ears ringing and without breathing, he lifted his face from the cold stone floor. No rush of flame had seared off his hair or sucked the air from his lungs. No lethal fragments of rock had struck him. None littered the floor around him.

Just another theatre trick. If perhaps a little overemphatic.

He cursed and rose cautiously to his feet, unsure whether he was angrier with her or with himself. He turned to glare through the pungent, smoky air. Where the Memory Palace had been, he now saw nothing at all. A gaping cavern in the earth filled with smoke and darkness.

Zeal heard the dull thud with profound relief.

He understood and chose to take the first step. Chose to follow me.

John stepped forward cautiously. Took two more steps. Then two more. Nothing but chilly darkness. He felt into the smoke. Still nothing. The stage itself had disappeared. Suddenly he doubted everything he had thought he knew about where he had found himself. The entertainment of theatre had become something else.

He advanced a little further, then stopped. He did not like darkness. He wiped his palms on his trousers. Darkness meant locked cells. Helplessness. Secret coffin-shaped crevices among a ship's cargo where an overheard gasp for air meant death to a fugitive.

But I never wrote to her of such things, he thought. *This is her darkness, not mine.*

Then he thought he saw a faint light, deep in the earth. No more than a single candle. A shadowed figure stood as if waiting for him. He peered through the smoky darkness.

'Zeal? Thank God!'

She seemed to tilt her head for him to follow. He strode eagerly after her.

Sick disappointment punched him in the gut.

A painted image of oiled cloth on wood. A decoy, he

thought angrily. I've seen the same trick played with cannons and false men. He took the candle from its iron sconce and leaned close to the questioning look on her painted face.

Then he turned and saw that the walls had closed behind him. Now he was forced to go forwards.

He was turned player.

Through my own actions but not by my choice.

He stood for a moment, thoughtfully. Then, holding up the candle, he moved past the painted Zeal and found himself in a roughly dug underground passage.

Or so it seemed. Assuming nothing now, he touched one wall.

No illusion here, after all. Solid earth and stone.

He looked back. Seen from behind, Zeal was an ugly frame of raw wood and unpainted canvas.

He moved on, around a bend. Turned again. Then he lowered the candle and paused to let his eyes grow accustomed to the new dimness.

Light reached this passage through mirrored shafts, which seemed to have been punched through from the surface, several feet above.

Slowly, he began to see where she had led him.

He stood at the end of a curving passage carved into the earth, irregular in dimension, its roof low enough to touch with his hand. The floor of the tunnel heaved and subsided like the back of a serpent. The walls, which blended without definition into the floor, also undulated and heaved. In places they had been smoothed with plaster or mud daub. In other parts, they were naked stony earth. So might the inside of Jonah's whale have been shaped. He looked down. And felt the world shift. He was walking on stars. Fish swam above his head.

Slowly he moved down the passage. He began to make out images painted onto the plaster of the walls or picked out in tiny stones. Animals drifted upside down among swimming fish, falling into the sky beneath his feet. A horse, a black bird, a flock of familiar-looking, goat-like sheep. A ginger cat tumbled slowly. A naked man – drowned or swimming? Near the ceiling, a red-haired woman drifted among ballooning skirts. Birds flew, or fell, or swam past his ankles.

What he took at first to be a rough fan-vault ceiling proved to be the roots of trees growing upside-down into the space of the passage. Among one set of roots, hung a tiny Hawkridge House, which had just begun its long slow fall.

The muscles of his thighs weakened. He forgot to breathe. This was no longer stage spectacle and tricks. She had let him in. He did not understand all she meant to say, but he recognized the terrain of the private mind. He touched the images as if they might yield their meaning to his fingertips. Beyond the next tree, he stopped to study a drifting lion. It half-turned as it fell, or flew, holding the sun in its jaws as delicately as if the celestial orb were a kitten or an unbroken egg. Then he saw that the tree was a branching coral.

The passage began to curve. He heard running water again, closer to him now. He felt its deep pulse and bump in the earth. He looked down at the sky and saw that the heavenly constellations beneath his feet now looked like sand stars. He gazed up and saw the underbelly of a shark. Shoals of fish swam on the walls and above his head. All doubts about what he now saw vanished as he rounded a buttress of rough stone.

In a pool of light from one of the shafts from the surface, he saw himself and his orange and blue enamelled swimming companions.

He was under the sea. His sea. In a world turned upside down.

I asked only that you try to imagine the things I wrote. I never expected this.

His sea, his sky, his paradise, here, a part of her life.

Against his expectation, it seemed that his words – mere dogged words – had carried his soul to her after all, and she had read them with full understanding. She had swum through this sea, where he had known without reason but beyond all doubt that all would be well. Though this was no longer straightforward exposition, he could read it clearly enough.

You can't be far now, he thought. Together, we will make all well.

Remembering that unreasoning ecstasy, he moved boldly to the door at the end of the tunnel. In spite of the wonders of the passage, he half-expected the door to be another trick, and not to open. But it did open, onto a long tiled passage that led to another door, ornate and panelled, left standing just ajar. A crack of light showed down the side. Light picked out a tapestry hanging on the wall and leaked along the polished black and white floor. The way out.

He cursed even before his hand tried to grasp the painted knob. He had reached the door many strides too soon. The lintel reached no higher than his forehead. A painted door. The light shone through oiled cloth. He felt suddenly unsteady on his feet.

He retraced the false, painted perspective with a sense of moving far too fast, and stepped back into the undersea corridor. The door closed itself behind him.

He heard more of the mysterious grinding and thumps that he had heard before in the theatre, like the internal rumblings in the belly of a giant beast.

After a moment of thought, he went to the door again. The light behind the false door must have had a source. If he cut through the painted cloth, he might find a real window or door.

Have I guessed what you mean to tell me? he asked her. Did you have to find the brutal way out? Believe me, I have shared that need!

He opened the door again and froze.

Holding the door so that it could not close once more, he stepped back a little and studied the rough passage wall on either side. He frowned and turned his head gently, like a man just dazed by a clout on the ear. The tiled passage, with its false perspective and false door, had vanished.

Ahead of him now, in the light falling past him from the undersea passage, he could just make out the top of a set of stone steps twisting down into shadow. He stepped back yet again, and cautiously explored, to be certain he had not been mistaken and opened a second door. But there was only this one. For a moment, he doubted his sanity.

If I am in her place, then she must once have been in the place I now find myself.

He shook his head.

I read too much reassurance into that sea of mine, he thought. The story may have just begun.

All thought of enjoying a battle of wits had gone. He did not care for the darkening turn in the game.

He hesitated for a long moment before closing the door behind him.

The arched roof above the steps was low. The deep bumping in the earth grew louder as he descended, joined by the sound of running water. At the bottom, he froze a second time.

A stone mask made up one entire wall of the dim, irregular subterranean grotto where he had arrived. The mask loomed four times taller than his height. Distant light shining through its eyes gave it a bright demonic glare. Water ran from its mouth and tongue into the shallow pool beneath its chin. Thin streams of water ran from its hair, its eyebrows, fell ten feet, and splashed John with a fine constant spray. The deep watery pulse bubbled up from the pool.

John stepped forward cautiously.

The face smiled in a friendly fashion. Its gaping mouth was the only way forward out of the chamber. It looked very like Philip Wentworth. Lest there be any doubt, John now saw small carp and pike caught in the tangles of its brows and a tiny red-haired woman lying in a stone curl of its hair.

Whatever did I leave her to?

He crossed the small pool on the stepping stones and ducked his head to enter the cavern of the mouth.

She has gone mad after all, he thought. Grief for her, grief for the pair of them, and cold unreasoning fear warred in him as he stared.

The tongue was a table, a single stump of a tooth offered a seat to the diner, for whom had been set a glass, a knife and a plate on which lay a human hand holding a heart.

84

Zeal paused in the dark antechamber beyond the grotto. Something moved just ahead of her. Even before reason could reassure her that it was another rat, or some other creature like the barn cat that once found its way through the walls, she saw that it was a man.

She tried to speak but could not. She had entered her dream. The beast waited at the centre of the labyrinth.

He stood quite still. The whites of his eyes gleamed in the light from a candle lantern set on the floor. 'So, you've come to me. I had begun to fear I'd be lost in this hell for weeks before I found you alone.'

Roger Wentworth. Holding his unsheathed sword.

'Here again?' she said. 'We wondered where you were when Gifford apologized.'

Go back and hope to reach John in time, she told herself. Philip was right – the need to fight most often catches you unawares.

'A man could lose his soul in this mire of deception and confusion,' Wentworth said. 'This monstrous house grows worse than I imagined. The grotto . . . the viciousness is clear. First you murder him, then you defame him. When I show the others, they will see why you must never go free again!'

She took a step back. Wentworth stood between her and the way forward. 'How did you get in?'

'There are no secrets among your workmen. Nor loyalty neither. Did you imagine that there would be? Don't try to run.' He shifted his weight.

She tried to remember what Philip had told her that might mean about a swordsman's intent.

Feel where he is in space, whispered Philip.

Wentworth's dagger still hung at his belt. Her own knife hung on its chain. Her hand moved.

'Don't!' He raised his sword point.

'Guile,' she heard Philip whisper urgently. 'Don't fight unless you must.'

Delay, she thought. Keep him talking until John arrives.

If he arrives.

'Who let you in through the workmen's door?' she asked. 'Who gave you Paroli's key?'

'A God-fearing man who wants to see your corruption stopped as much as I do.'

'Gifford?'

Wentworth snorted. 'Him? An over-nice, lily-livered smock when it comes to anything more than shouting!'

'Who was it then?'

'Why don't you ask instead what I intend?'

'Because I know.'

She heard his breathing and the faint sound of a pleat in her linen trembling against the velvet of her bodice. No sounds of John coming up behind her.

'Cheat,' said Philip urgently in her ear. 'Never fight fairly. The first rule is to stay alive.'

His son's boot creaked as he shifted his weight again.

Soon, she thought.

She began to unhook the top of her skirt from her bodice.

'What are you doing?'

'Nothing dangerous, as you can see . . . Look!' She undid the chain holding her knife. The blade rattled onto the floor. 'Now you have nothing to fear from me.' She unhooked as far as the back of her waist on one side and began on the other side.

'Stop doing that!'

She heard the change in his voice. 'But you believe me to

be a whore . . .' Her fingers slipped on the hooks.

'I know you to be!'

She kept her eyes on him. Reached back to untie the last strings. They knotted. She yanked and broke them. Pushed down her skirt.

'Witch!' he whispered.

The black silk creaked and hissed as it fell. She shook her petticoat free and stepped out of the black circle. 'I often wonder if you don't ask yourself why I gave myself to the father . . .' She stooped to pick up the skirt. '. . . instead of the son.'

As he lunged, she ducked aside and flung the skirt up from the floor around his sword arm, as Philip had taught her. Gave the massed fabric a twist, and hauled with both hands, swinging him with her entire weight. Unbalanced, he staggered and landed hard on one knee. In that instant, she was through the far door.

She reached out for one of the rusty fragments of light. Her hands met a smooth, chilly wall. Dauzat's maze.

A cry of rage followed her. She moved fast. Here she had the advantage. She knew exactly where she was. Turned, turned again, doubling back, reversing herself, slipping through sudden gaps. Trying to be quiet. Stopping to listen.

He was close behind, but blundering. Cursing.

Then she was at the centre. She climbed.

'Where are you?' His voice was suddenly very close.

His hand brushed her ankle. Found it again and seized hold. She took her full weight on her hands and kicked at his head.

He gave a roar of rage and began to climb behind her. She stamped on his fingers, hauled herself up the last three feet and threw herself forward onto the floor of the room above. She rolled away from his grasp, stumbled to her feet. Ran the final yards to safety and slammed the door of The Last Resort. He could not get at her through that heavy door. Then she saw what she had done.

She tested the door, but she already knew that in her haste, she had forgotten the locksmith's warning. She had not disarmed the lock. Wentworth could not get in, but she could not get out.

85

He could go back. This time, no shutters had closed behind him. He could retreat to the dreamlike passage where happy endings had felt possible. He could choose not to be a player.

He touched the pale hand on the plate. A delicate woman's hand. Marble.

He remembered the handless nymph on the painted screen. There was surely a story there, if he ever had the chance to ask and she was in a fit state to answer. The heart was carved from a bright, slightly soft red stone, which felt unnaturally warm to the touch.

To go back might be physically possible, even if it meant breaking through the theatre walls and cutting his way back into the leather chute. In every other way, it was now impossible.

The stone palate at the back of the mouth curved into darkness. John felt with his hands and found a small opening near the floor. He would have to crawl to get through. He knelt and looked at where he knew the opening to be. Blackness. Not a glimmer of light. Not the slightest crack of a door or shuttered window. No apparent end. Soft, infinite, terrifying darkness.

Sweat prickled on his neck. A band tightened around his chest. He could not make himself crawl through that low narrow hole into blind infinity.

My darling Zeal. If you wanted to set me a test, you found it. This I cannot do.

He went back and sat on the tooth, where light from the grotto still fell. The fine mist reached him even here. He looked again at the heart on the plate, then at the silver salt cellar beside it, and rubbed both hands over his face.

The two objects were eloquent, but in a strange tongue he did not yet understand. The weight of their import was clear. What eluded him was whether this eloquence told him that she was mad, or that she saw the world as mad instead.

Whichever it is, she fears I might stop here.

He held the heart in his hand until it warmed to the temperature of his skin, while he remembered stories he had heard while hiding from bounty hunters on the outlaw island of Tortuga.

Can't abandon her again. Won't. Never.

But the alternative was to crawl through that hole.

He replaced the heart on the hand and went back to the low entrance. He imagined that he had passed through it. His body went icy cold, as if he had dived into a half-frozen pond.

Until that moment, he had managed not to remember a time he had been trapped in similar darkness, with the sound of rising water in his ears. He clutched his knees and rocked.

I can't do it.

He lifted his head. He thought he had heard a voice. A second later, he heard it again. A man's voice shouting in anger. The voice was muffled, but it was reaching him through the dark maw. He drew a deep breath and plunged into his nightmare.

He arrived in a large dark room without windows, so thickly planted with slender columns that it might have been a grove of young trees. A shadowy figure stepped towards him. It hesitated.

'Zeal?' he whispered.

The figure stepped forwards again and stopped when he did.

He squinted through the dim twilight that fell from above, light that might reach the back of a hayloft from a small window at the front. He slapped his hand to his sword.

The figure did the same.

He stepped forwards again and saw all around him an army of imitators. He turned his head. Bits of himself slipped out of sight and others appeared. He advanced on the closest self. On all sides, he saw himself vanishing into the shadows, scattering like a shoal of frightened fish. His stomach shifted as it had when a ship first rolled under his feet. He reached out to touch his own hands, met a shock of chilly glass. He swung to his right and cracked his forehead against more glass. His own eyes peered back, very close, watering slightly and indignant.

He drew a long breath. Felt walls of glass on either side of him, angled to meet each other, each wall made up of leaded panes set into a gilded frame. He stepped forward. The gap between the walls narrowed so that a man could not squeeze between them. They sprang like fins from the columns. What he had thought was a complete column was merely a small section, given the illusion of a whole by its reflections.

He turned, set his back into the narrow angle where the mirrored walls met and opened his arms as far as they would go to either side. He saw himself offering to embrace an army of selves. Full-face, in profile, half-seen from the back, left ear, front of right ear, looking squarely into his own eyes.

A man rarely had the chance to see himself as others did.

He didn't care for what he could see in the dimness. Rough, ragged, with stubble high on his cheeks, lines, embedded grime. One shoulder drooped a little lower than the other. He could not tell which. An old scar dented his beard. The line of his thighs, which Zeal had stroked with such delight was now masked by leather trousers polished slick with blood and dirt. In quick succession, he spied a suddenly youthful curve of one cheekbone (right or left?), the glint of cold, weary eyes, a strange shell that was the rim of one ear. The wizardry of mirror multiplied all these ills into a host of evils. One such man was already too many.

He moved away from the column. Fragments of self swam

around him. His stomach shifted again. He had already lost the way he came in.

With his eyes closed, his stomach settled and he could unscramble his thoughts.

It seemed that an excess of self-contemplation interfered with reason.

There's nothing here but more trickery, he told himself. No magic, any more than before. Just tricks with mirrors. He had seen such things in gardens in the Low Countries and later in the Bermudas, placed at junctures in a maze. Tricks meant for pleasure, to stir a quick trembling of false hazard while a glass of wine and sweetmeats waited to reward the triumphant return.

Oh, my dearest Zeal . . . He steadied himself on the nearest reflecting wall. How shall I read this one? What new illustrative trial have you prepared for your would-be knight? I hope you are waiting with my reward for confronting my many selves!

He shook his head and set the world in motion again. He had opened his eyes, without thinking. On all sides, entire and fragmentally, other heads shook in a pattern as intricate as the scales on a fish.

It was at least clear that . . . He stopped. In truth, nothing was clear. He had met nothing but deception and illusion in her underworld.

Except for my sea. Don't lose sight of my sea.

What did I write?

He could no longer remember his own words. Only that peculiar suffusion of joy as he looked down on the pair of clown fish swimming two feet below his navel. Whatever they had been, his words swam now on the walls of a grotto in Hampshire, like the other end of a broken thread, waiting to be picked up again.

Now, my man, think how to get out of this place and find the perverse little creature. If she has told you one thing clearly, it's that she wants to be found. That passage tells you so. Believe that! All that is truly being tested is your will.

'Put yourself into my place.'

There's no rejection in that, surely. A plea, perhaps.

I don't mean to disappoint her ever again.

A man who could escape indenture, then make his way from Tortuga to St Christopher's and back to England, in the teeth of decreed exile and with a woman and child in tow, should be equal to this theatre of confusion.

No more knocks on the head from blundering about like a trapped animal. A maze most often had a rule if only one could discover it.

He began by testing the right-hand rule, turning always to the right. Came nose to nose with himself against a gilded column. Then he tried turning always to the left. Then he tried turning first left, then right. Then the converse.

Surely so many of us must be equal to the task! he told the double self which blocked his way. Walls of green yew had seemed more friendly and fathomable than this splintered, infinitely repeating world. In a green maze, you could at least see the path, even if you weren't sure which turning to take. Here there were no visible paths on the stone floor, not even false ones. He found no inscription, no secret sign, no emblem that he might interpret.

Only myself. With all my sins.

He stopped with a sense of revelation. How can such a man not understand and forgive everything? Whatever it might prove to be? And if I am now in her place, then by reason, she has been in mine. And therefore means to forgive me. He was still lost in thought when he imagined a flash of movement among the reflections.

'Zeal?'

A scarlet sleeve vanished like a mouse down a hole. He looked at his own sleeve as if some sleight-of-hand might have transformed it. Once green, it was now black with smoke, the sweat of his horse, ship's tar, blood stains and the general filth of living.

'Zeal! Don't tease me!'

'She's a murderer, Nightingale!' A man's voice.

He decided that this place had muddled his senses. I thought I heard a real bird sing. Why not hear false voices now?

'She killed three husbands,' said the voice. 'All her denials are lies.'

He let out his breath. He was not mad. Had not imagined. It was indeed a man's voice, muffled but undeniably real. He felt he should know it. But that man could not be here.

'Nightingale?'

The ancients had placed ears of brass around their theatres to fling the actors' lightest murmurs out across the air to the most distant spectator.

He looked into the gloom for sign of such a device.

'Nightingale?' The voice was now closer, though John had not moved. Then he heard the grating of a boot heel on the stone floor. Then a thump, followed by an oath.

This was sounding more and more like an actor of flesh and blood. And not one who knew the maze, either.

'Nightingale, can you hear me?'

He stared at himself, infinitely multiplied in the act of listening. Watched his many mouths open to reply and then close again.

What use to me are so many ears if not one of them can say where the voice is coming from?

His eyes skated over the glassy walls but still found only himself.

'Three husbands buried. And she means for you to be the fourth.'

If this is a test of my love, it's a brutal one, he thought.

'Nightingale? Answer me. I know you're there.'

If I can't find him, then he can't find me, unless he is part of my lady's tricks. In which case, he will find me whether I wish or no. But, whoever he is, he does not feel like her confederate.

'What do you want with me?' he finally called in return.

'It is you, after all,' said the voice with satisfaction. The sound of boots moved nearer.

He had fallen for one of the oldest tricks.

Zeal, my love, I fear this man is no attendant sprite. I know his voice now.

'I want to do you a service.'

This time John stayed silent. *On my left,* he decided.

He followed the mirrored wall on his right with his hand until it ended abruptly. His own puzzled face, a few feet away ahead of him, turned a little to beam its question back to its source.

There had to be a pattern. The human mind could not build pure disorder without ordering it at least to some degree.

He set his belly to the point where the wall ended and turned back on itself, stretched his arms forwards along both walls. With his right hand, he then followed the new mirror into the narrowing point of a corner. He pressed his back into the corner and again spread his arms along the walls to either side. Less than ninety degrees, more than forty-five. A flash of clarity eased the disorder in his mind. He stood at the centre of a hexagon, with its centre post now at his back, the hexagon cut into six slices like a pie by the mirrored walls.

The voice followed him. 'Don't waste your baubles. Her commodious purse will swallow all you have.'

There was no mistaking the malice now. John forced his thoughts back to divining the trick of the maze.

'I've no doubt she swore to be faithful when you left,' said Roger Wentworth's voice. 'And I'm sure that you, a willing fool, wanted to believe her.' There were more sounds of someone moving amongst the mirrors. 'What if I tell you that my ancient father had bedded her before your ship had cleared the Canaries . . . Can you still hear me?'

Like Odysseus, John wished for wax to fill his ears and deafen him.

'Her gate is open to all comers, Nightingale. And her garden is filled with poisoned herbs.'

Sick with haste to escape the voice, he followed the right-hand mirror to the next outer corner.

'She casts spells as potent as Circe. Sir Harry tried to escape but she silenced him before he could expose her.'

As I mean to silence you, my mad friend, when we're out of here and I can see where you are.

He followed his hand into another narrowing point. Another slice of hexagon. He listened again. The infinity of selves rolled their eyes and tilted their heads. Then, suddenly, pattern replaced chaos in his mind. He was lost in a honey-comb of mirrors.

'Then she induced my father to belly-bump himself into his grave.'

He heard sounds of movement again.

'She robbed both him and me.'

And I understand you now, all too well.

John's zig-zag path into the centre of the hexagon and out again was taking him in a circle. But there must be gaps, or else escape would be impossible.

But what if there is no way out? What if she had never meant for me to follow and find her after all? There is no escape from temporal hell, after all.

Was that the message of this otherworld she had built? That grotto might contradict his sea.

His next right turn brought him closer to Wentworth's voice, but he had to test one rule to the fullest before trying another.

'Did she tell you about the one who came after my father? That degenerate boy. Master Parsley, a rare putto, a puss pleaser, and with a fortune almost as great as my father's. I've no doubt my young stepmother cuckolded my poor father before she killed him. If she mourns anyone, it's that boy. You must ask her about him. He helped her lay waste to my father's money by building this devilish place. Did you know that? Our present confusion is the fruit of their evil union.'

John found the corner. Felt around it.

Empty space. Wide enough to pass through. The first gap. He scratched a cross on the floor by the centre post he had just left so that he would know if he doubled back on himself. He looked around the corner and saw what he had always seen, himself, entire, at angles, moving in contradictory directions all at once. He repeated the entire pattern of moves and found himself beside another post, with no cross on the floor.

'Who do you think will help her spend your fortune?'

Don't let his words in! But he felt a red pressure inside his eyeballs, as if they would burst.

'He followed my father into her bed.'

Don't listen to him!

'. . . even more swiftly than my father followed you, who was simple enough to trust him, and her.'

They were suddenly no more than a few feet apart with no walls between.

The shock of the man's nearness matched the force of the sudden return of reason. He was no longer a demonic voice but a half-familiar set of jaw and ears. A scarlet coat soaked black at the armpits. The animal stink of high emotion came off him in hot waves.

The pressure inside John's eyeballs eased. 'Your father was my friend,' he said quietly.

'That harmless old duffer who abused your hospitality for so many years?' Wentworth answered at last, in a more conversational tone. 'Let me tell you, no man is harmless until he's dead. Nor woman neither!'

'Why are you here spewing poison? Is that the service you offered me?'

Wentworth smiled. 'Let me replace my father as your friend. A truer one than he ever was. He betrayed both of us as much as she did. I offer you our revenge.'

The multitude of Johns drew their swords. His hair prickled like a dry thistle. 'How do you mean to do that?'

'It's already done.'

86

Behind the thick door, Zeal could not hear whether Wentworth had followed her. He might be standing outside, waiting for her to venture out. He might have let himself out again through the workman's door with Paroli's key.

Was Jonas Stubbs the traitor?

Stay calm, she told herself.

She felt her way in the darkness to the shelf on the wall. Her fingers found the candle, then Lamb's match. Then the rough striking stone. She had only one chance. If she bodged the stroke, or if the match failed, she must wait in darkness to either live or die.

She steadied herself and struck the match across the stone. A fragile flame blossomed. She held it to the wick. She set the candleholder on the floor and sat beside it.

She faced Lamb's triple portrait, which leaned against the wall. In the dim light, her face and John's and the child's all grew animated. Their eyes seemed to move.

I want to live, she thought. Whatever other confusions remain about John's return, I know I must live to try to sort them out.

She got up and pushed on the door. She still disbelieved that she had closed it irrevocably on herself. She did not let herself push again. If she did, she would lose control and begin to fling herself against it and tear at it with her hands.

She put on John's coat and sat on the floor again. Pulling the coat around her, she tried to imagine that he occupied it, not she. That her head was his head thinking her thoughts.

I have asked too much of him. He will see that I am mad, and stop his search. What if he finds my *mappa mundi* merely laughable? What if he no longer loves me enough to persevere?

She wondered where Wentworth would come upon him.

I may never know what happens when they meet.

John went cold. 'You killed her?'

'When magistrates and judges are made fools, someone must do their work for them. She was guilty!'

He felt too weak to lift his sword. 'Do you mean that she has been tried and acquitted of whatever charges were made against her?'

Wentworth stepped backwards and was swallowed by the mirrors. 'By blind men dizzied by her whorish scent.'

'How did you keep such clear sight?' Around the next mirror edge.

'By the grace of God and some experience in the world, I know a scheming cunny when I meet one.' Wentworth's fractured figure retreated in all directions.

John turned the next corner, shifted his sword to his right hand, and lunged at the shape in front of him. His blade struck hard glass and nearly jumped from his hand. A blade slashed past his shoulder, from behind.

He spun round to see scarlet fragments scatter and vanish.

'Don't turn murderer to save a stinking pole-cat!' shouted Wentworth.

'It's not murder to kill a murderer.'

'Oh, she's not dead yet. I confess, I tried. But matters have worked out more neatly than I had planned. God stayed my hand and saved me from the stain of murder.'

'Where is she?'

'Please do attack me again. I would welcome the need to defend myself.'

'What have you done?'

'All I need do is to detain you here. One crippling blow will do. The rest will take care of itself.'

Zeal's thoughts flew like bats. Wentworth had killed John. They had left together and were sharing a jug of ale, toasting John's escape.

She was a witch but did not know it. Three men dead. Two babes. And now she had put John in danger.

And I may never know what happened.

The air was growing thick in her lungs. She thought that the candle flame dwindled.

Time doubled upon itself, slipped, stretched, suddenly condensed. She had been there for an hour, for four, for less than half an hour. A night. Perhaps it was already the next morning.

If he survived Wentworth, John would not be able to guess the secret of the lock.

John glared at the wild man blocking his way. He smashed the face with the hilt of his sword. His reflection shattered. The leads holding the mirrors snapped. The crystal shards tinkled to the floor. He swung to his left and broke the second wall of mirror. He had to pound four times to break through both faces of the wall. At last, he looked through the empty frame. The horizon leapt a few feet farther away. Some of his many selves retreated.

He stood panting, tight with thought.

Zeal was close ahead of me at the start, so Wentworth must already have been waiting for her. If he had followed after her, I would surely have heard him ahead of me. Therefore he most likely came in by a different route. A secret entrance.

He listened for Wentworth's boots as he tried to think straight.

The workmen. This place had been constructed by masons and joiners, like any other building. They must have used a way in and out through the wings.

The wall to his left smashed into fragments as a sword struck it. Wentworth had circled round and attacked from behind.

John put the nearest corner between them. 'What's the secret of this place?' he called.

'You won't need to know.' Wentworth stepped into view, or appeared to do so. 'I've never before tried to kill a man who did not dare to kill me.'

'Where is she? How do I find her?'

Wentworth vanished. His coat flickered on all sides of John. He reappeared, in the flesh. His sword stirred a breeze near John's ear. 'That's just to let you know that I can find you any time. I have visited before.' He vanished again.

'Who gave you the key?'

'What if I said that it was your sweet lady herself? That she whispered it into my ear as I fondled her naked breast? Like father, like son, you see.'

John smashed the nearest wall with his sword hilt. Stepped through the frame over the sharp edges that remained and smashed the next wall of the hexagon.

Wentworth turned in surprise as the top half of the mirror between them crumbled. 'Give it up, Nightingale. She's as good as dead already.'

'If you bedded her, I want only to die.' John held out his arms to the side and dropped his sword. Wentworth might overlook the ocular evidence and mistake him for a gentleman.

With a triumphant cry, Wentworth lunged with his sword, overreached, staggered. John took a step back, ready to grab Wentworth's sleeve. He placed his other hand on his concealed dagger. Wentworth tried to step over the half wall of glass between them. Swung one leg across. His boot slipped on the broken glass on the floor on the far side, slid from under him. He screamed as he landed.

'Who let you in?' John squatted and peered at the top of Wentworth's leg where the glass had sliced it.

'Get help!' gasped Wentworth. 'I'm bleeding to death.'

'How do I get out? How do I find her?'

'The door . . .' Wentworth pointed, but his eyes were fixed on the dark flood that was soaking his breeches. 'The master mason had a key. Need the key to get out again . . .'

'Where is she?'

Wentworth shook his head. 'For the love of God, fetch help!' He took hold of John's sleeve. 'Don't let me slip!' He lay back onto the floor.

John propped Wentworth up again against the pillar. He took off the man's scarf, made it into a ball and placed the pad over the pumping wound, with Wentworth's hand on top. He pressed down. 'Can you hold that in place?' He bent close in the dim light to try to read the man's face. 'Where did you leave her?'

Wentworth's eyelids fluttered.

John quickly searched Wentworth's clothing for the key, then stood up with an oath. He crashed into a wall. Unbuttoned his shirt, pulled out the tail and wrapped his bleeding hand. With this slight protection, he began to smash all the mirrors, one after the other, to clear a straight line, find an outside wall. Then he would beat his way around it until he found the door. Kick it down, if need be. The basket guard of his cutlass began to buckle under the repeated hammering. He squinted and turned his head aside with each blow. Glass flew into his beard, his belt, caught in his collar. Impatiently, he removed the largest shards and began smashing again.

Was Zeal, too, bleeding to death? Suffocating in a locked chest? Lying face down in water?

He thought of going back to ask Wentworth how long he had in which to find her. Instead he smashed through another wall. He could now see far enough to spy a break in the beehive pattern of hexagons. He thought he saw a ladder. He stepped forwards. The ladder disappeared. He stepped back and changed direction. Two turnings took him from reflection to reality. He had found the heart of the maze.

It was empty. No reward awaited the successful pilgrim. No wine or sweetmeats. No maiden at the heart. No Zeal. Just a spiral wooden ladder fixed to the floor, its spokes twisting upward around the central post like those of the potence in the dovecote. It led up through a hole in the ceiling. Daylight fell dimly from the floor above.

Given what had gone before, the ladder felt too simple.

Circling warily, he looked for signs of another trick. He tested a rung with his foot, then began to climb. Contrary to his expectation, the ladder was just what it seemed.

He emerged into a small antechamber lit only by a narrow window at one end, facing a solid door. Locked. From the window, he could look up the valley of the Shir. He was at the front corner of the house, some way above ground. The only way out was back down the ladder, or through the locked door. He did not think that Wentworth had had time to take her elsewhere and return to the maze.

'Zeal!'

He set his ear to the door. It was too thick to hear whether she replied. But he felt certain that she was behind that door. He tried the lock again, then pounded with his fists. Felt, rather than heard, an answer.

Still alive.

Unless he had imagined that faint vibration of the wood.

He drew a breath. Of course the ladder had been too simple. She had always confounded expectation. And I loved that cussedness, he thought. Still would, if matters weren't so urgent.

He quieted himself and reached for her with his thoughts. Imagined that he felt an answering stillness, a delicate pressure in his mind. Holding him steady.

I know you're there, he told her. Don't fear. Have patience. I will reach you. I'm too close to give up now. But a little help would be useful.

Then he saw an inscription above the door. Hard to read in the dim light.

'I am come out of Egypt, out of the narrow place, into the nothingness. I am no longer where I was, but I have not yet arrived where I am going.'

He thought. Read the inscription again, carefully, fighting disappointment. Could find no secret meaning or instruction in the words.

He searched the little room for a hidden key, a secret panel, a loose floorboard. The walls were plain. No enigmatic images to probe for their secrets. He examined the ceiling. He knelt and studied the lock. It was a beautiful thing, intricately wrought in brass, full of puzzling corners and knobs. And it hid its secrets. It suited her entirely.

He probed it. Pulled. Then hit it.

He settled back on his heels, trying not to give way to terror. The key could be anywhere. It could be of any shape. He pounded on the door again and again imagined a response.

Why make the game quite so hard? he asked her. Surely, if I have followed you this far . . . Tell me what I must do!

He leaned against the wall and stared at the door. His bloodied hand had begun to throb.

I managed to reach the centre, he told himself. What have I learned on the way? What have you been telling me?

His mind flashed back to the passage through the upside down sea. The world is topsy-turvy. But all will nevertheless be well.

I must start there. Believing that you understood my letter and feel the same. That you have therefore arranged for all to be well, so long as I chose to follow you.

But you could not have allowed for the interference of Roger Wentworth when you had the passage made.

He made himself breathe slowly. Tried to slow his heart. He looked up at the inscription again. *'Into the nothingness.'* You as well as I, it seems. But I know where I'm going now. I just don't know how to get there.

He suddenly wondered if she had enough air, and felt his own breathing speed up again.

Or are you bleeding to death, like Wentworth?

He closed his eyes and tried to think. Went back to the moment he had stepped into her place. Deception. All the way. Nothing as it seemed. Sometimes lovely, sometimes terrifying. But always a deception.

Except for that passage. No tricks there, only the need to keep your feet under you. And decide which way was up.

He stared at the door.

Nothing is as it seems.

He stood and searched the wall around the door, inch by inch for the true, hidden door that he suddenly knew must be there. Did not find it. Sat down again.

After a few more moments, he examined the floor again, this time for any sign of a concealed opening. He began to imagine that he must climb out of the window and somehow traverse the outer wall. He opened the window and put out his head. There was no window in the wall where the room must be.

He sat again, still staring at the door.

Nothing is as it seems.

So far you have not knowingly asked me to do anything dangerous, or even very difficult, except for the plunge into darkness. That was the only true test, to follow you through darkness.

What if there is no way in? he suddenly thought. If you never meant for me to reach you after all? Do you mean to stay in nothingness?

No, he told the door. Even at your most contrary, you would never spend such effort to no purpose. From what I have seen so far, your spirit has not been so broken. Something has gone terribly wrong.

He rubbed cold fingertips against his mouth and tried to remember how he had felt while swimming in Paradise.

Nothing is as it seems.

He blinked, arrested in the poised, intense stillness of spirit that accompanies sudden understanding.

And you, my love, never do the obvious.

He stood up and walked to the door. Ignoring the lock, he pushed against the door near the hinges. Felt it shift under his shoulder.

Stop believing in appearances and you walk right in.

She was waiting just behind the door wrapped in one of his old coats. The joy on her face answered any last questions he might have had.

'I'm back,' he said.

87

As instructed, Zeal and John waited on the new bridge, in Lamb's little pavilion for elevated reflection. The sun had just vanished at the western end of the river valley.

'Shepherd's delight,' said Zeal happily, looking at the red-pink sky. 'Too bad he has no sheep left.'

'I expect you'll find some,' said John. 'One way or another.' He was gripping her hand as if to keep her from being snatched away again.

With her free hand, she touched his hair, then the corner of his jaw. Then slid her hand down the solid reality of his sleeve.

'Why?' Zeal demanded, when Rachel once again asked her to cover her eyes. 'Where are you taking us?'

She felt John's hand find hers again. Their fingers locked.

'But we're going together,' his voice said. 'So, you shouldn't care.'

The laughter in his voice made her suddenly suspicious. 'Do you know what's happening?'

'No more than I ever have.'

They had agreed in The Last Resort that, with a lifetime for talking, there was no hurry to answer every question at once. It was enough to know that they both understood the costs of surviving darkness. Then she had shown him the triple portrait and they had wept together for their son. He told her about Tesora's birth while on the run from the plantation, and her mother's death soon afterwards. Later Zeal took him to see their child's tomb next to that of John's uncle. He had slept that night in his place beside her in her new bed. They decided that whether they stayed at Hawkridge or went to the Indies could be resolved at leisure, or at as much leisure as the progress of the war allowed.

'But I won't leave you again,' he told her. 'Not for king nor Parliament.'

Now, three days later, they seemed to walk a very long way after leaving the bridge. When they had turned and Zeal felt soft grass under her feet, she warned Rachel, 'No more wishes! I don't have any left to make.'

Gifford's apology, followed by what many people felt was a severe Divine rebuke, had turned public opinion dramatically back in her favour. She had even had half a dozen shame-faced apologies (though not from Jake Grindley). When they became known, Wentworth's attempts on both her life and John's had further confirmed the rightness of her cause. Meanwhile, the unexpected return of John Nightingale, well liked and much missed, had released a widespread impulse to celebrate.

'I expect we could think of something to wish for,' said John. 'Peace, perhaps. But I agree with you in the broader sense.' He pulled her close enough to put his arm around her waist.

She realized that John, not Rachel was now leading her. 'Can you see when I can't?' she demanded. She did not hear his answer because she was noticing the familiar warmth of his arm and her own sense of absolute ease.

Then she smelled water and rotting weed. And duck nests. She heard the splattering run of a duck landing on the water.

'Please sit now, madam,' said Rachel, guiding her into a chair.

When she removed the scarf, she saw that she sat beside John at the top of the highest fishpond, where Nereus had once pointed out to his dolphin the piglet-sized grazing carp. The muddy spots where the nymphs had once stood had long grown over with grass. She still found their absence odd, as if someone had unexpectedly left the room when you thought to find them there.

Six ducks swam up to the bank beyond their feet and quacked for food. Nothing else seemed to be happening except the slow descent of dusk.

John leaned to her. 'Philip,' he said quietly.

She stiffened.

'There's something you should know.'

'I'm not sure I'm ready yet to learn anything more. I thought we had agreed . . .'

'No, listen!' He shook his head and took her hand again. 'He made it possible for me to return. Whatever else he did, he helped to bring about this night.' He looked at her startled face in the dimming light. 'Truly. I once wrote to him . . . I will tell you more later, about why I did it. But, in short, he wrote back telling me where to find a hidden cache he had left behind on St Kitt's. And giving me names I needed to make my way back to England. You should know he did that.'

After a moment, he gave her his handkerchief to wipe her eyes. Then he whispered, 'I think you should look now.'

Pale shapes glimmered among the trees and bushes, each carrying the hot tiny flower of a lighted candle. They approached slowly, as silently as ghosts. Zeal could see now that they were robed in the ancient fashion. Fifteen figures slowly walking closer, from every side. Upstream from the river, from the left over the river berm, from the right down the slope from the old basse-court. They arrived on their spots almost exactly together with her understanding. The fifteen nymphs once again surrounded the ponds. They raised their candles in greeting. As they did, the notes of a fiddle broke the silence, from somewhere among the trees.

The hair stood up on Zeal's arms. She pressed her hand to her mouth. The fiddle continued to sing alone, a haunting, incautiously pagan tune.

'It can't be!' she gasped. 'Dear God! It can't be!'

John squeezed her other hand. 'Nothing is as it seems.' He

leaned so close that she felt his breath warm in her hair. 'But sometimes you must make a leap of faith.'

During the music, the nymphs made a slow deep, dream-like reverence and, just as slowly, straightened again. They turned and danced gravely in a procession around the banks of the ponds until each had taken another's place. Then they danced on again.

'Who is that playing?' whispered Zeal.

'Who do you know it to be?'

'Has he been hiding at High House?'

'Singing to Sir Richard. And at Gifford's sickbed. But I'll let him tell you about that.'

Four of the nymphs danced up the slope towards the basse-court. Zeal braced herself for their departure and the end of this wonder. Then she saw that they went to meet two other figures, one large and one very small. All six returned to the ponds. As the sound of the fiddle died away, Tesora and her nurse arrived in front of Zeal and John.

John spoke encouragingly to the child in their strange tongue and the little girl replied. Then, prompted and helped along by her nurse, she began to sing.

It was like no music Zeal had ever heard. She was reminded of Philip's description of the musicians beside the lake in the city of gold, panting out their souls. Or of an animal's cry. And yet the shape of music was also clear.

After one verse, the little girl suddenly ran forward and climbed onto John's lap. He whispered into her ear. She hid her face in his neck for a moment. Then she thrust her fist out to Zeal, clutching a necklace of golden leaves.

Meanwhile, her nurse continued to sing, joined by the fiddle, which echoed and tracked after her but never lost her.

Zeal bent and kissed the little hand holding the necklace. Slowly, slowly, she thought. Don't frighten the fish.

Later, she could remember little clearly after that point. Except that there had been a rush of candles and torches towards the ponds. That she had hugged Doctor Bowler until he squeaked. That Tesora had at last agreed to come into her arms. And that thirty people, including John, had each taken a turn at setting Signor Monteverdi free into the Hampshire night by grinding the crank of the Antichrist.

CAERLEON 4/06/04